A Discussion with Satan

A Discussion with Satan

William McCann

PALMETTO

P U B L I S H I N G

Charleston, SC

www.PalmettoPublishing.com

Paperback ISBN: 979-8-8229-5300-0

Acknowledgments

My special thanks to the Priests, Religious Sisters and Brothers who during my sixteen years of religious education imparted to me the spiritual knowledge without which this book could not have been written. To my sister Virginia, who read, offered corrections, and rectified my omissions of the manuscript as I was writing it. To my son, Will, for his help in manuscript construction. To my son-in-law, Steve Dean, for photographing and creating the front cover image. To my Grandson, Jake, for Satan's AI image generated on ChatGPT (or DALL-E, the image generation model). To my daughter Kelly for her suggestions in producing the book cover. To Luke Howard and my son, Matt, who posed for the character images on the front cover.

To St. John the Evangelist, a prolific writer in his own right, who so very graciously answered my prayers for inspiration when writing the additional details of the biblical events described in this book; and to Mary, the Mother of God, whom I feel in addition to her inspiration encouraged me to include the chapter on her Assumption.

Table of Contents

Michigan July 13, 2017

This is an instructive, albeit creative narrative in which Satan, after centuries of unsuccessful entreaties, is finally permitted by God to take human form in order to dialogue with a human being. At this time Satan's principal desire for doing so is because in the last one hundred years human morality, and with it, people's behavior, have deteriorated to such an extent he suspects from the historical record that God is about to initiate a twenty-first-century reset: a natural calamity of sorts or allow a man-made devastation leaving the world in shambles in order to put the fear of God back into His human creation. Either way, Satan envisions, would mean that recovery from an event of this magnitude could convince the vast majority of those surviving it to embrace the cross. Such an occurrence Satan realizes would do irreparable damage to his kingdom on earth.

In his conversation with God Satan uses the example of a bowling alley saying that mankind is so perverted that the challenge of tempting them to sin is now no more difficult than bowling on an alley ten feet long. His intent, he tells God, is to encourage mankind's interest in the Word of God by fleshing out the biblical narrative; thereby averting the devastation of a divine reset.

"I hope you'll admit, Lord," Satan says in an effort to convince God to grant his request, "That such newly disclosed knowledge should encourage mankind's interest in divine belief encouraging them to recover their reverence and thereby re-establish their belief in death, judgment, heaven or hell."

When God does not respond Satan continues, "For the first time in two thousand years, people will have an opportunity to hear the rest of the story from one who actually witnessed the events. Typical examples are the wedding feast at Cana, how Joseph and Mary's flight into Egypt, with you barely a newborn, was possible with only a donkey to cross more than seventy miles of blistering hot, waterless days and frigid nights; the who and why of the Three Wise Men, the false proclamation King Herod used to justify the massacre of the Holy Innocents; what specifically was said by you, the twelve-year-old Jesus, that so impressed the Sanhedrin during your three days in the temple; what the soldiers who were guarding your tomb saw and heard as you rose from the dead, and – and so on."

When God does respond he says, "Satan, as the master deceiver, you now have the unmitigated impudence to try doing so to me – your Creator. You have one chance to tell me the whole truth. If not, I will end this conversation by thrusting you once again into the depths of Hell."

"You are so right, Lord; however, my degenerate, condemned nature forces me to keep trying. What I have told you is all true, but not the whole truth. In order to do so I must admit that the lack of present challenge has made for us a boring existence. To paraphrase a human expression, Lord, my demons and I instead of diligently employing creative lies to sway the virtuous to vice we have been reduced to shamefully 'shooting their souls in a barrel.'"

God, in his infinite love for mankind, does not really desire to impose a devastating reset on his human creation if it can in any way be avoided, grants Satan's request with several restrictions:

Satan cannot tell a lie. If he so much as tells less than the whole truth permission is

immediately rescinded in that the conversation ends and Satan immediately disappears.

Satan is forbidden to mention explicitly any individual by name who has been condemned to eternal damnation.

The only person with whom Satan can converse is Bruce McPherson, a thirty-four-year-old former Naval Officer who now teaches biology at a high school in Pittsburgh, Pennsylvania and is well-grounded in both Christianity and Demonology.

Feeling God is going to insist that he reveal unknown details about Mary, his incarnate mother, Satan requests that he be obliged to speak of Mary only in a cursory fashion. God grants his request unless because of something Satan does, Bruce appeals to her intercession: then Satan must speak of her in biographical detail.

In a roundabout way Satan makes his appearance telling Bruce that the reason for his manifestation is that he and his minions have been too successful. As history proves God only allows his human creation to wallow in sin to a certain depth before he institutes a reset. Examples Satan gives are the flood in the time of Noah, the language confusion at the tower of Babel, Sodom & Gomorrah, the Babylonian captivity along with the devastation of Solomon's temple, Rome's destruction of Jerusalem in 70 AD and with it the annihilation of the second temple and the dispersal of its Jewish inhabitants, the barbarian invasions of Europe in the Middle Ages and in modern times, divine warnings evidenced by increased terror and persecution by atheistic dictators and fanatical proponents of a man-made religion, wars, and the constant threat of even more wars.

He uses again the example of the bowling alley saying as he did to God, that man has become so perverted that the challenge of tempting mankind to sin is now no more difficult than bowling on an alley ten feet long.

His ultimate goal, he tells Bruce, is to avert a divine reset. When Bruce asks him by what means he hopes to accomplish this, Satan answers, "By putting more resistance in mankind's spiritual backbone and thereby returning the metaphorical bowling alley of temptation to its regulation sixty feet." When Bruce does not respond Satan adds, "And within the parameter of certain restrictions I have permission from God to have you, Bruce McPherson, help me accomplish this."

CHAPTER ONE

"When I make a sudden appearance, your kind becomes terrified."

I was driving north on I-75 about ten miles south of the Mackinaw bridge which connects the upper and lower peninsulas of Michigan. At 1:30 in the morning I saw only an occasional vehicle, and in fact hadn't seen anyone for five minutes or so until a solitary headlight suddenly appeared and began moving erratically in my rear-view mirror.

About a quarter mile behind me it was weaving back and forth across the two northbound lanes. In the darkness I couldn't make out the vehicle but by the solitary headlight I supposed it to be a motorcycle. After about a minute or so the weaving abruptly ceased as it settled down to following me while maintaining the quarter mile distance.

I had never heard of anyone following someone in a two wheeled vehicle except in "B" movies which took place in third world countries. However, it appeared to me that the initial weaving was to let me know that the rider was there to follow me and that for only a reason he knew, we were not just two strangers having a chance meeting in the night.

I slowed down to 45 mph to cross the bridge and he did the same. Seven miles beyond the bridge I braked to 30 mph and prepared to exit the interstate by activating my right turn signal. Glancing in my side mirror I saw that he was rapidly closing the distance until just as I began the turnoff, he weaved in front of me doing 90 mph or better before veering sharply left while fishtailing near uncontrollably as he returned to the highway. As he did so I heard my name called out in a loud, drawn-out, mournful moan just before both the motorcycle and driver abruptly vanished.

My immediate response was one of shock. The headlights on my pickup provide excellent vision so I knew that what I just experienced had really occurred; while at the same time to be relieved of his haunting presence brought welcome relief. After completing the exit, I followed the narrow roadway uneventfully to the cabin that had become mine upon my father's death two years ago. I brushed my teeth, set my alarm and immediately fell asleep.

I was startled awake by the roar again of the motorcycle as it appeared to be trying to force its way through the door that separated the kitchen from my bedroom. As my feet hit the floor I glanced at the red glow of the numbers on my alarm clock. It read 6:00 – two hours before it was set to go off. As I cautiously approached the door and reached in to turn on the wall switch the sound of the engine abruptly stopped. I opened it and observed the fluorescent light bathing the stainless sink giving the room an appearance of quiet normalcy. Except for the black skid marks on the door, I might have thought I had been dreaming.

As a believing Christian and practicing Roman Catholic, I do not believe in ghosts. There is Death, Judgment, Heaven, or Hell with maybe a side trip to Purgatory for those who still have a spiritual debt to pay. Your body is in the grave or otherwise disposed of and your soul is in the hands of God or the Demonic; and in which ever place it resides the soul of the deceased no longer has any power to exercise an act of the will affecting those still living on earth.

Satan, however, does have the power to appear (with the permission of God) as he wills to the living. Witness the autobiographies of the Cure of Ars and St. Teresa of Avila; both examples of creditable haunting. So, I knew from the incident last night and the one I just experienced that Satan or one of his minions was behind both incidents;

or as I remember Sherlock Holmes saying with unimpeachable logic, "When you have eliminated the impossible, whatever remains, however improbable, must be the truth."

There was nothing I could do about the Demoniac's attentions except say a prayer to let God know I knew that he knew what was going on in my life and to ask for guidance, which I did. I then fixed myself a cup of coffee, a glass of orange juice and a bowl of oatmeal along with two soft-boiled eggs and some rye toast.

By now if you've read this far you are wondering who I am, why I am staying alone in an isolated cabin tucked away in what passes today for wilderness; and if you should even care.

Allow me to explain.

I was thirty-four at the time and the senior instructor in biology at Central Catholic High School in Pittsburgh until school let out for the summer. At the same time, I had been going to night school in an attempt to accrue enough credits to write my thesis for a Ph.D. in the Microbiology of Human Fetal Development. This was heady stuff as it involved the study of hormonal sensors and what caused their precise timing responsible for triggering cellular differentiation as the fetus develops.

I knew from experience that trying to concentrate on the level required in the midst of phone calls, ringing doorbells and friends stopping by was all but impossible, so I drove to the family's hunting cabin in the upper peninsula of Michigan. It was not what you would call luxurious. An outdoor generator that ran on propane gas supplied electricity. An old GE refrigerator and a modest size freezer kept the milk from souring and the ice cream from melting. In addition to a fireplace a wood burning stove stood in the corner; but both were unused, as I preferred to heat frozen meals in a microwave which Dad and I had purchased several years ago. There was a general store about twelve miles from the cabin where I could purchase propane gas, kerosene, batteries, frozen meals, fresh or canned fruit and vegetables – just about anything I would need.

Over the kitchen sink was a pump, which brought clean-smelling water from an aquifer some forty feet below the surface, and over in the northwest corner of the lot was a sturdy outhouse with one of those pull-chain, stick-up, battery-operated lights. Dad had used the fireplace for heat, but I remembered too many times shivering at night when the fire went out; so, I opted for a kerosene heater that I figured would keep the interior of the modest sized cabin warm at night without the necessity of having to gather and chop wood. Several wall mounted fans in addition to the surrounding trees kept it reasonably cool in the summer.

After breakfast, I sat down using the computer for research and finished the rest of the day without incident.

The next morning, I went into town to get a newspaper to read the sports and financial news more in depth than I could find on the Internet. Much to my surprise I was told that a lone man, just a half hour ago had purchased all copies of the Detroit Free Press and thus none were available. When I asked the owner to describe the man, he said, "Not from around here, at least that I've ever seen. Tall – about six foot four, slim but muscular, black hair, blue eyes, about forty, I'd say – extremely good looking in a Hollywood sort of way. He was wearing a black sport coat, white turtleneck, gray slacks and mahogany loafers – expensive looking."

"Wow," I replied. "That's some description. How long was he here?"

"Five minutes or so. Looked around a bit, paid for a copy of Scientific American and the papers, then told me to have a nice day and left. Strange though. He was dressed as if he would have driven a luxury convertible or one of those European sport cars; but he drove off on a big Harley, which I don't remember hearing as he drove up.

"Incidentally, I could see that you were somewhat surprised at my powers of observation. I spent thirty years with the covert field branch of the CIA where you learn it is what you don't see that will kill you. Recently retired and returned home here where I was born and raised. The man who owned this store recently died and his wife wanted to return home to live near her daughter and grand kids in Tennessee. I bought it to keep busy. Name's Harvey O'Brien," he added, extending his hand.

"Bruce," I replied. "Bruce McPherson. Glad to meet you. I'm staying for the summer at my cabin about twelve miles from here on the old Corbett Road. Be coming in from time to time for essentials."

"Welcome anytime," he replied. "Have most anything you'll need or can get it for you." I waved and left.

As I told O'Brien, it was only twelve miles to the cabin, but it took almost twenty minutes to traverse the distance due to the severe winding and blind curves. In addition, it was in a heavily wooded area that in the summer precluded the sun from ever reaching long stretches making portions permanently damp. As I drove, I began thinking about the man or whatever he was, on that motorcycle, a means of transportation that seemed to appear and disappear according to his need.

Before I go any further, I should tell you that from the age of twelve I have been more than casually interested in the world of demons, and especially in the history of Satan, himself. My perspective was strictly from a spiritual aspect, that is, I was not interested in Ouija boards, conversations with the dead or Satanism.

My interest, in accordance with my religious education was in how he uses enticing temptations, greed, inordinate desire for power and lust to accomplish the destruction of both men and women. As such, I have read just about every book, pamphlet, published article, and watched every credentialed video published about him. In school, I wrote several papers featuring his incredible intelligence and power, much to the discomfort of some of my religion teachers.

As others might be, therefore, I am not afraid of Satan. I know the limitations of his power and that he can do nothing that is not permitted by God. From his behavior I had no doubt that he had, for some unknown reason I could not comprehend, an inordinate interest in me, and therefore, highly suspected that he would be in the cabin when I arrived. As it came into sight, I knew I was right when the cabin's lights were on and smoke was coming from the chimney. When I left, I had turned out the lights and had not used the fireplace.

I parked the truck around back and walked toward the front of the cabin. The Harley was nowhere to be seen. I was tempted to look in a window but thought better of it when I realized that being who he is there was no taking him by surprise. The front door was slightly ajar, so I pushed it in and stood there staring at a man just as O'Brien had described. He was reading the newspaper. I didn't see the other copies O'Brien told me he had purchased. In my best authoritative voice, I had developed as a teacher in today's secondary school, I asked, "How may I help you?"

"It's more than likely the other way around," he replied, folding the paper and laying it aside. "You'll have to excuse me for making an entrance this way, but knowing you as I do; I knew that the motorcycle antics along with the extraordinary newspaper purchase would telegraph that I was coming."

When I didn't answer he added, "You must realize that my experience is that when I make a sudden appearance your kind becomes terrified."

"My kind?"

"Human beings. Earthlings," he said, with a voice bordering on contempt.

"What do you mean by 'The other way around?'" I asked.

"That thesis you're writing. How many people do you think will read it, or even care that it exists? Maybe one hundred? At most two hundred? I can give you material for a book that will be read eagerly by thousands – maybe millions."

"You are the father of lies. Why would I want to write or anybody desire to read a book full of lies? I want you to leave here. I have work to do and only a limited amount of time to get it done."

"Okay, as your kind is wont to say, I'll give it to you straight. You have spoken truthfully. I am Satan and as a spirit am invisible unless I conjure up an image which allows humankind to visualize me. What you see before you, therefore, is a mirage of sort, but it will serve us both well, as I can do anything with it that you or any other human can do – and undoubtedly more! Bruce – may I call you Bruce?"

"That's my name," I said.

"Let me ask you a question. Did you ever go bowling? Of course, you have. Ever wonder how long a bowling alley is? Probably not, unless you are a professional bowler. A bowling lane is forty-two inches wide and sixty feet long, with the length being measured from the foul line to the head pin. Now a lot can go wrong in sixty feet as the ball is rolling down the alley, and usually does, which is why a team that scores a strike celebrates with such gusto. If an amateur bowls just one perfect three hundred game in his lifetime he talks about it 'til the day he dies!"

"What's your point?" I asked.

"Imagine this. Suppose the length of the lane was reduced to ten feet. What do you think would happen to the average bowling score? Would it not increase by at least 150 points? Three hundred games would be commonplace for anyone whose average on a sixty-foot lane was 165 or greater. However, bowling would become a drag. It would no longer be challenging. Bowlers would get bored. It would be like asking experienced hunters to shoot deer whose ability to escape is restricted within a fenced corral!"

"I repeat," I asked, "What's your point? And please, no more analogies."

Satan hesitated for a moment before walking across the room. He stood there looking out the large window facing north. After a minute or so he turned around to face me, and then began speaking in a rather somber tone.

CHAPTER TWO

"Bruce, I have all but conquered the spiritual world."

"Bruce, I have all but conquered the spiritual world. If you don't believe me then look around. Bands of people butchering their fellow men over a viciously arrogant false belief I conjured up in an opium-soaked mind over fourteen hundred years ago. It is now becoming the scourge of the western world because of stupid, corrupt, political and religious leaders who carelessly invite terrorists into their borders and institutions to wreak havoc on the very people they are sworn to protect! It isn't like these traitorous and heretical leaders have never been warned. In 1828, less than two hundred years ago, a poetess by the name of Mary Botham Hewitt wrote a poem, the first line of which is:

Will you walk into my parlor? said the spider to the fly, Tis the prettiest little parlor that ever you did spy. You remember this poem. Every child who has the semblance of an education has heard or read it. Stanza after stanza the fly stands off the spider's ever more inviting allurements until the spider flatters the attributes of the fly so well that it takes off and flies in ever decreasing circles listening to and enjoying the compliments of the spider. Finally, it flies close enough for the spider to grab it. The end of the poem, as you might remember goes like this:

He dragged her up his winding stair, into the dismal den –
Within his little parlor – but she ne'er came out again!

And now, dear little children, who may this story read,
To idle, silly flattering words I pray you ne'er give heed;
Unto an evil counselor close heart and ear and eye,
And take a lesson from this tale, of the spider and the fly.
If we make substitutions in the last stanza, you read my
words:
Now to leaders' bribe-soaked minds, may this story read,
To idle, silly, flattering words, you cannot do but heed;
Unto a demonic counselor, open your heart and ear and eye,
And ignore the lesson learned of the spider and the fly.

"My using what humans think are their defensive weapons against me as my offensive weapons against them is my favorite strategy. I do this by turning their defenses upside down. This creates chaos that in turn leads to panic; and people in panic are easy prey. Look about you; religious fanatics murdering other human beings to please God. This is my most lucid example of turning a belief upside down, for not only is killing another human being never pleasing to God as the murderer intends, but rather the exact opposite, i.e., the ultimate insult to God. Nothing angers him more than one group of people killing another group of people and using His name as justification. I know this as fact, Bruce; for many who have done so are even now suffering the anguish of eternal damnation in my domain.

"Then there are those who strap bombs on themselves and blow-up innocent men, women and children. Their leaders have betrayed them into thinking that an act of murder culminating in suicide is martyrdom. Do you see what I mean? This is decidedly upside down. One is a martyr when someone slaughters you for what you believe and practice accordingly. What suicide bombers do can never meet this definition. Actually, Bruce, the people killed by the bomber are the actual martyrs. I love seeing the look on these terrorists' faces when they first see what I have in store for them. 'Where are the seventy-two Virgins I was promised?'" they ask.

"Virgins?" I respond. "You seek virgins in this place. Here in Hell?" "Hell?" they shout, as it begins to become apparent that they were told a great lie. Their blasphemous shedding of blood along with their own suicide has sent them irrevocably to Hell.

"This act cannot be repented after the soul and body are no longer one. It is forever. Eternal Damnation! Damnation forever! Then I turn to Amondeus, my Demon Gatekeeper, and say, Tell him, Amondeus. Tell him the truth about the seventy-two virgins."

"Yes, well – there are women here," Amondeus answers, "millions of them; some beautiful and some ugly; some tall and some short; some smart and some not so; some old and some quite young, some... well you get the idea; but unlucky for you, my deluded one none of them are virgins."

"Why not?" he asks, and then looks about as his eyes bug out in fear while observing the filth caused by the soot, ash and flames while shaking his head at us in disbelief.

"Because they can't pass our entrance exam!" Amondeus replies as we both begin to laugh, while mocking him before I motion to two other demons to take him below where like the fly in Mary Hewitt's poem, he will 'ne'er come out again.

"And then I have common people disagreeing to the point of becoming violent over of all things, religion - people hacking off heads with a knife, displaying this terror visually for all to see. Others are kidnapping, raping, and murdering children; after which they leave their bodies where beasts will devour them. Others are forcing young Christian women living in non-Christian controlled lands to become sex slaves. Formerly fervent Christian nations abandoning not only Christianity, but also belief in God because such non-belief allows them to lead lives steeped in political corruption, theft, fornication, adultery and even murder.

"Secular humanism, they call it. 'Human life,' they say, 'begins at the first breath and ends with the last.' Without thinking, Bruce, they see themselves with no better end than that of the beasts of the earth

– fertilizer! They actually believe what I encourage them to believe; namely that when they die, they revert to fertilizer. I have convinced them that if there is no God, then there is no sin. One can do as he pleases because the only consequence is getting caught disobeying secular law; therefore, if you aren't caught in this world there are no consequences. What fools!

"And now let me tell you, that for which I am most proud – the establishment of Political Correctness; yes, that is one of my most potent weapons against humanity. Talk about going over the cliff! Forbidding store clerks to wish someone A Merry Christmas. Forbidding Santa Claus to utter Ho, Ho, Ho which has been his signature for decades because it is now used by a minority as slang for prostitute. In many stores Santa now presents himself to children with Ha, Ha, Ha. If this isn't stupidity, then what is?

"Ever notice that dates were labeled as BC or AD? This has stood for centuries, but since I convinced the Liberal Left of Great Britain and later the USA, your country, Bruce, that such labels offended non-Christians, agnostics, atheists and secular humanists – actually, Bruce, they couldn't care less – Before Christ and Anno Domini (year of the Lord) has become BCE, before the common era; and CE, common era. Not only have we taken Christ out of Christmas with 'Happy Holidays,' but we have now erased his memory from figuring time.

"Moreover, you know the saddest part? Nothing has changed! BCE is still time measured Before Christ; and Common Era is still time measured after the birth of Christ. Recently a school in the city of Seattle, Washington renamed its Easter eggs 'spring spheres' to avoid causing offense to people who did not celebrate Easter! And then there is the mad rush on university campuses to become gender neutral by forbidding the use of any expression that defines sexual characteristics. A manhole cover is now called a maintenance cover. "Mankind" is no longer a word that can be used on campus as are the words man, woman, Mister, Misses and Miss in addition to his and her.

"They have forgotten that Shakespearean adage that 'A rose by any other name would smell as sweet.' And you wonder why I despise the modern human race? Their constant growing stupidity has replaced the challenge that their ancestors were. The more technically advanced they become, the more they abandon simple logic. I am bored, Bruce; interminably bored because they have forced me to bowl on a ten-foot alley – my challenge has deteriorated to shooting souls in a barrel!"

"Satan then paused, as if he expected me to respond, but before I could think of something to say he started up again, only more forceful than before."

"Bone yards, Bruce! A perfect example of galloping Political Correctness. Two hundred years ago burial grounds were called what they were; namely bone yards. But as men's lifestyles became more to my liking the thought of death and the divine judgment that follows became less comfortable: bone yards became burial grounds and later grave sites. As if one were putting socks away in a drawer. As time went on and the idea of an immortal soul and Divine judgment became even less believed, the idea of death, semantically, was removed altogether when someone referred to the grave site as a cemetery. But even that was not enough, because etymologically speaking the word cemetery is derived from the Latin and later on from the French and means a place to bury the dead. So it became necessary to remove any relationship to physical deterioration or the cessation of life by referring to bone yards as memorial gardens where for the most part it remains today.

"And that's not all. In a majority Christian nation who else could have arranged for the teaching of the elements of Islam in schools, but forbidding the teaching or even mentioning Christianity? Could you have imagined twenty years ago that legislatures could pass laws that allow people to declare their own sex based upon preference despite biological evidence to the contrary? I mean they know that the cells of a female have XX chromosomes while a male's makeup is XY. That is decided at conception. People know that cannot be changed. Yet there are those of you who continue to declare personal truth to be what their five senses deny! I'm no longer waiting for the first biological male athlete to say that since he considers himself to be female he should be permitted to compete in women's athletic events; for as you know he has already done just that! You have to admit that this is insanity without limit. If I were God and witnessed my gifts abused in this manner, I would have taken them away, but God does not do this. He allows the openly defiant to keep their talents and gifts he has given them for their reclamation or condemnation as they will.

"And what is the result of all of this nonsensical madness? It has caused unlimited damage to a sense of reality that forces the human race to live in a world of make believe, which is the world of children. Of course, nothing suits me better.

"Rational human beings, like you, Bruce, who use the intelligence God gave them, buttressed by his other gifts, grace and free will, are all but impossible to control. However, adults that live in the world of the child are highly susceptible to suggestion, and my first suggestion after getting them to establish political correctness was to convince them that there is no such thing as absolute truth. Everything is relative to one's situation. Once it was established that subjective truth, that is, one's opinion or wishful thinking was deemed to be reality to a large percentage of the population, then the evil of sin could effectively be denied. Further confirmation of what I said before. This resulted in no need for remission of sin, for sin is an evil that doesn't exist, and if there is no need for remission of sin, then why bother with God? He is either dead or does not exist now or ever.

"My bottom line, Bruce, is that if sin does not exist, then there is no Hell; and if there is no Hell, then from what does Mankind need saved?

And if man doesn't need saved, then why does he need a savior? And if he doesn't need a savior, it negates the need for belief in Jesus' life, death, and resurrection, which is the reason so many of you mock and denigrate Christianity!

"The majority of mankind has lost its grip on reality. You see, as a whole I detest the human race, but I have to admit that I admire individuals who have defeated me by playing entirely within the rules. My greatest conquest is convincing most of humanity that I do not exist; and therefore, can harvest their souls at will. Obvious, don't you think? I mean if you don't admit that your enemy exists then even when he is at the gates you are in denial. Spiritual stupidity is the greatest reason that I detest humanity. What they have done to me with their refusal to think with the mind God gave them is to reduce the metaphorical bowling alley to ten feet which in turn has made my modern conquests boring."

"You are a detestable creature, Satan, and I demand that in the name of Jesus Christ you immediately depart from me. I have no desire to play your game, nor do I have or wish to waste my time listening to your incessant boasting or your lamentations about being bored. In fact, Satan, talk about boring – you, yourself are boring me with your tales of molestation of my fellow human beings. In a command, you have no doubt heard before and is in no way politically correct or upside down, 'Get the Hell out of here. Be gone, I tell you.'"

CHAPTER THREE

"God has given me permission to be here."

"Very good; Bruce! The Lord knew what he was doing when he chose you. I admire a man with the courage of his convictions expressed within the wrap of a quick and well-timed wit. Nevertheless, it is for naught. I have spent centuries asking God for permission to talk to a person like you. Each time I was refused, but I kept asking. Finally, I was given permission to approach you, and only you, and at this time and only at this time. So, I will not cede to your command because God has given me permission to be here."

"Is this one of your lies? Am I to believe that God has given you permission to waste my time listening to your lies? What nonsense. Go, now, and never come back!"

"When have I lied to you? What have I said that wasn't true?"

"I mulled over in my mind all that Satan had said. I could not find anything for which I could prove that he had lied. At least up until this moment I cannot accuse you of lying," I said.

"And you never will, Bruce," he replied in a sincere voice. "There were several conditions under which I was granted this Divine permission. You see I had to agree to refrain from lying to you. Everything I said would have to be the truth. If I violated this condition in the slightest way, my permission and visionary presence before you would immediately vanish. I am not going to risk losing something that has taken me centuries to achieve. My purpose in being here as I said, is because I admire the few who use the fruits of the great equalizer to give me an honest challenge. You are one of those persons. You are forcing me to roll the ball from sixty feet away. Neither of us can step over the foul line which is akin to telling an untruth. Now, that that is behind us can we get on with it?"

"You said, '…several conditions.' What are the others?"

"If and when they present themselves, I will tell you."

"That's fair enough. You mentioned getting on with it. Getting on with what?"

"I am going to tell you things that no one else has ever been told. I am going to reveal to you things that even theologians don't know. I am going to…"

"Wait! Stop right there. Are you telling me that you, Satan, a fallen angel, consider yourself more knowledgeable than an accomplished theologian?"

"You can't be serious. Bruce, just think about it. I am, without a doubt, the greatest and most accomplished theologian that God ever created."

"Well, you're still here – haven't been whisked away, so I guess there must be truth in what you say. But how…?"

"Come now, think about it, Bruce. What theologian has dwelled in Heaven; stood before and gazed upon the Beatific Vision; and not for a fleeting moment, nor even for an hour, but for eons of what you call time and that long before the creation of the Universe – what your present-day astrophysicists refer to as 'THE BIG BANG?

"What theologian has talked face to face with God? Remember, Bruce, once he bestows a gift or talent it is yours forever. I lost my heavenly home not because he took it from me, but because I chose not to accept the newly revealed conditions; and I must admit, also for my disobedience, my hatred of fleshy creatures and my implacable stubbornness; but my knowledge and memory of that time I will retain forever. My hatred is most of what fuels my lust for vengeance against the human race. It is the basis of the pain of my eternal damnation."

16

"But why me?" I asked.

"God chose you and I was pleased that he did for several reasons," Satan said. "First of all, you knew enough about me that you would not fear me. I can only do what God permits and you know that. This is proven by the fact that from the first evidence of my presence until now you have shown no fear. In fact, at times, you have become belligerent which is not the reaction of the fearful.

"Secondly, Bruce, you have the scientific, historical, and religious learning to converse intelligently on whatever subject I choose. Third and last, you have developed an ability to present accurately what we say in writing so that there is a record of our exclusive discussions."

"So, am I to believe that I am your choice or God's?"

"Both are true."

"Both? How is that possible?"

"As I said, God chose you and I am pleased that he did."

"I have to say that being on your short list has made me uncomfortable. I have to wonder just how much you really know about me."

"Just believe there is nothing I don't know and then put your mind at ease. I'm here to work with you because I need you – nothing else."

"The only thing that puts my mind at ease is that if you tell a lie or half-truth your mission fails."

"Rightly said," Satan responded. "You must know that whenever I admit the truth I am grievously agitated just as much or more that you would be if you lied to me; but it is the price I agreed to pay to have this conversation with you."

"To be in a position wherein you, Satan, the most prominent of all liars, is forced to tell me the truth is overwhelming. The only reasonable explanation is that God is using you for his own purpose."

"Really! How so?"

"Isn't it obvious? What you say to me must be irrefutable truth. If it isn't then the penalty you incur proves it wasn't."

"Well done, Bruce. Perhaps your supposition is correct. We shall see."

"Now that we understand each other, Satan, as well as the nature of our relationship may we begin by my asking you a question?"

"Certainly, Bruce. What is it you want to know?"

"It is commonly held by many that you lost your second place in Heaven by doing battle for the first. In fact, Milton, in "Paradise Lost" quotes you saying, 'Better to rule in Hell than to serve in Heaven.'"

"You say that as if you're not sure it's true."

"I must confess that I've had my doubts. A creature of your intelligence would never attempt such an impossible task. You, more than anyone else would know that to challenge God is like an ant threatening to do battle with an anteater. It never ends well for the ant."

"An excellent analogy, Bruce. Few attributes of you earthlings impress me; however, an apropos, timely, and witty repertoire is right up there. Are you familiar with John's description in Revelation of what happened in Heaven?"

"You mean why you are down there," I replied, "after you and yours were evicted from up there?"

"Yes, exactly – get your Bible and read me the pertinent passages."

"Before I do," I said while flipping through the pages, "you should know that I have always been partial to the gospels of Saints John and Matthew and likewise John's Book of Revelation. John personally witnessed Jesus' public life from the beginning; and Matthew who was a follower for nearly as long heard Jesus say 'I have not come to destroy the Law and the Prophets, but to fulfill them.'"

"Ah, yes. Matthew 5:17."

"I had forgotten how well you know the scriptures."

"You have forgotten nothing, Bruce McPherson. It is your human frailty coming forth. You didn't take into consideration that I, like John, and for the most part, Matthew, personally witnessed Jesus' three-and-a-half years of public life. To me the scriptures are superfluous. Why would I need someone's written word describing something I had personally witnessed?"

CHAPTER FOUR

"I was at the foot of the cross with John and Mary."

"Like John, I was there along with Peter and James as they gazed in awe at Jesus' Transfiguration; and when they couldn't stay awake in Gethsemane. I was at the foot of the cross with John and Mary; and on that first Easter morning when John respectfully waited for Peter to catch up with him at the empty tomb. John was sixteen when he first met Jesus and nineteen at the foot of the cross. John was an extraordinary young man. He is referred to as the beloved Apostle because at the age when youth is normally belligerent and rebellious toward their seniors, John had the good sense to listen and learn from them. It was because John had the wisdom to cooperate with the grace of God in overcoming the unwise emotions of youth that Jesus loved him so; and that I failed in my attempts to sow doubt and aversion tempting him to leave Jesus as so many others did.

"Now, let us get on with it. As a former officer in your country's navy, you know that before doing battle it is imperative to learn the strategy and tactics of the enemy. Once having this information, you can devise a strategy to use these against him. Through fostering man's deliberate misinterpretation and even deletion of chapters and verses of scripture, I have convinced many of God's Chosen People as well as Christians to send themselves to Hell. It is what I do, Bruce, and without the barricade of the great equalizer I do it very well – like I said it is like bowling on a ten-foot alley."

"He ceased talking for a moment as if he were trying to recall something he had forgotten. Then asked, "You mentioned Matthew 5:17. What do you mean by that?"

"I thought for a moment of how to express my thought. I didn't intend to misinterpret scripture. Finally, I said, It was the goal of Jesus not to override the prophecies and yearning for the Messiah of the Mosaic Law, but to announce that in Jesus the prophecies were fulfilled. Their waiting was over. He, Jesus, was The Messiah now living among them."

"Fair enough, Bruce. Read on."

"I found the pertinent passages. They again brought back my memory of statements there that I could not easily accept, and wondered if now, listening to the perpetrator himself, my doubts would be resolved. I began to read.

"How you have fallen from Heaven, morning star, son of the dawn! You have been cast down to the earth, you who once laid low the nations! You said in your heart, 'I will ascend to the heavens; I will raise my throne above the stars of God; I will sit enthroned on the mount of assembly, on the utmost heights of Mount Zaphon. I will ascend above the tops of the clouds; I will make myself like the Most High.' But you are brought down to the realm of the dead, to the depths of the pit. Those who see you stare at you; they ponder your fate: 'Is this the man who shook the earth and made kingdoms tremble?'" (Isaiah 14:12-16.)

"I looked up and saw him nodding his head indicating not agreement, but permission to continue."

"Read on," he said.

"I then flipped the pages to the prophet, Ezekiel who was a contemporary of Jeremiah. He lived during the fall of Jerusalem and was among those who were exiled to Babylon by King Nebuchadnezzar.

"You were in Eden," I began, "the garden of God; every precious stone adorned you: carnelian, chrysolite and emerald, topaz, onyx and jasper, lapis lazuli, turquoise and beryl. Your settings and mountings were made of gold; on the day you were created, they were prepared. You were anointed as a guardian cherub, for so I ordained you. You were on the holy mount of God; you walked among the fiery stones. You were blameless in your ways from the day you were created till wickedness was found in you. Through your widespread trade you were filled with violence, and you sinned. So I drove you in disgrace from the mount of God, and I expelled you, guardian cherub, from among the fiery stones. Your heart became proud on account of your beauty, and you corrupted your wisdom because of your splendor. So I threw you to the earth; I made a spectacle of you before kings. By your many sins and dishonest trade you have desecrated your sanctuaries. So I made a fire come out from you, and it consumed you, and I reduced you to ashes on the ground in the sight of all who were watching. All the nations who knew you are appalled at you; you have come to a horrible end and will be no more." (Ezekiel 28:13-19)

"And what does your Apostle, John, have to say?"

"Again, I flipped the pages and read from the twelfth chapter of Revelation, verses seven to nine."

"Then war broke out in Heaven. Michael and his angels fought against the dragon, and the dragon and his angels fought back. But he was not strong enough, and they lost their place in Heaven. The great dragon was hurled down—that ancient serpent called the devil, or Satan, who leads the whole world astray. He was hurled to the earth, and his angels with him."

"How much of that do you think is true?"

"I have no doubt that pride contributed to your fall; and as John stated fall you did. I say that since not being cursed with flesh, as you so proudly proclaim, your reason could be nothing else. The reason human beings commit sin here on earth is for sex, fear, money or power, and for little else. As a being without flesh, you have no need of sex; you already held the second place in Heaven so you had nothing to fear; and you have no place to spend money, so I have to believe that for some reason you developed a prideful need for power. What else is left?"

"Hate, Bruce – hate and revenge for what I deem to be injustice! I didn't mind God creating fleshy creatures, imbued with instinct and a mortal soul that roamed the earth subsisting on plant life or on the flesh of others whose only reason for existence was to eat, urinate, and defecate while males killed each other for the right of copulation to produce the next generation. In fact, in some ways I enjoyed their antics.

"But then, as your kind expresses it, he decided to raise the ante. We were informed that as an expression of his love he wanted to do more; and that was to create a creature of flesh and blood with an immortal soul, imbued not with instinct, but intelligence and free will. In other words, one of us, an angel, but weighed down with flesh. In short, Bruce, a physical body with an immortal soul and all that goes with it. An imperfect specimen of what he had already created – an inferior creature who from my point of view, from the moment of his or her creation is a wannabe and/or a never was.

"'All that goes with it?' What do you mean by that?"

"With an immortal soul this creature would inherit a right to eternal life! Think of my position. These disgusting creatures, endowed and dragged down with the concupiscence of flesh would actually share with us, the angelic hierarchy the right to inhabit the Heaven we shared with the Almighty – to stand before the Beatific Vision.

"Let me use an analogy, Bruce. Pigs! In your world, Bruce, allowing pigs who wallow in mud to share the sanctity of your abode! These miserable creatures would actually live with you in your house. They would share your home! They would share your bed! They would eat at your table!"

"I find your comparison insulting," I replied. "You are, without a doubt, as hateful and evil a creature, maybe even more so, than you have been depicted by scripture and the world at large."

CHAPTER FIVE

"I apologize or express sorrow for nothing."

You have no empathy, which makes you a psychopath – a creature that sees the world and everything in it as his without regard for the rights as well as the life and limb of anyone else. Yet for some reason at this time the Almighty has given to you personal access to me; an access which I am forced to endure as a projection of his Divine Will."

"I would apologize for my comparison, but I am devoid of the ability. I apologize or express sorrow for nothing. Coupled with a penchant for hate beyond your ability to comprehend, it is the essence of who and what I am. However, I will remind you that I am forbidden to lie to you, Bruce; so, I am bound to utter only the truth. And the truth is, as you now know, that I despise you and all your kind. As a species you are weak, bound by the anchor of your flesh to commit folly; and that, without the shield of the great equalizer your concupiscence allows me to lead your kind like lemmings over the abyss to eternal damnation."

"You have mentioned the term great equalizer before. I let it go then because I figured you would explain it later. Now is later. What is the great equalizer?"

"Correction, Bruce. Now is not later. Now is premature; however, you are entitled to know what I mean by that, and rest assured I will explain it to you at the appropriate time.

"So now you know how and by what means the Almighty banished me and my followers to eternal damnation. Michael was an archangel – a member of the second lowest choir of angels. What your kind would term an also-ran. However, as history proves, God chooses His champions not from those on high, but assuredly from the least of His creation. King David, Mary, through whom he was incarnated, Joseph, her husband, the twelve apostles – the latter common fishermen, a tax collector and a few laborers, Joan of Arc, Bernadette of Lourdes, the children of Fatima, Juan Diego at Guadalupe, the widow, Elizabeth Seton, and finally, Father Solanus Casey. Most of whom for the most part came from lower class families, were poverty-stricken and without hope of bettering their lowly status.

"I was given a chance to acquiesce in what God stated was His Will; but I had a full one third of the angelic host agreeing with me. They believed that by using my exalted position I could persuade God to recant by convincing him that infesting Heaven with the abomination of flesh ridden creatures was wrong and a decision that he would regret.

"However, try as I might I could not deter God from creating man. It was the greatest debate in the history of the Universe. At times I thought I was winning – even won the argument, but then he would respond by saying, 'Lucifer, bear with me on this. I am well aware that many of my human creation will turn their backs on me; some will deny my existence giving them reason to then mock and deny the moral code I will give them. They will murder and enslave one another. They will steal one another's goods, besmirch another's good name, confiscate his land and even lustfully pursue another's wife or husband.

"Finally, some will commit the most grievous transgressions of all; that is by calling it by another name or passing a politically motivated law think that they can override or redefine my moral law by sodomizing one another, or murdering their unborn flesh and blood with no more compunction than if they were swatting a fly. Others will steal the sexual innocence of children; while still others will think that to take the life of another in my name is meritorious; that such a heinous deed is actually pleasing to Me!

"I tell you now, Lucifer, the unmitigated truth in order to avoid any misunderstanding: I, Almighty God, being the only Creator have a life plan for every future human being even before they are conceived; and that includes the moment and the manner in which they will meet their earthly demise. To forfeit the life of another at any point in their existence is a blatant attempt to frustrate my will. It will be called murder and those who do it are not walking or even running – no, they are tumbling without restraint down the steepest, widest of all roads that lead to perdition."

"So, with all you've said, Lord, why create these hideous, disobedient, flesh mongered creatures? Why?" I cried out. "What evil have we done to deserve having to watch and observe these self-serving, murdering, loathsome creatures?"

"Nothing; you as well as the whole Heavenly Host have done nothing to deserve my decision. I never said you did."

"Why, then?"

"To give homage, appreciation and obedience to me, their Creator, who alone, has given you, Lucifer, and the whole Heavenly Host the gift of life fortified with intelligence and free will, and, therefore, mirrored in my own image and likeness. Furthermore, you and those with you are speaking as if you are autonomous beings who exist and function without pragmatic purpose. You assuredly are not. Your purpose for existence is to use the powers I gave you to assure that my will may be done; and my will, powered by an infinite capacity for love is to have you give succor and aid to my human creation.

"Noting the restlessness of those who agreed with and followed me, I began to feel, as I knew they did the very real possibility if not the probability of failure. In that mindset I struggled to keep from sinking further into the mire of defeat. Thinking that what I said next would be my last chance I asked, 'Taking in all you have said, Lord, is there some personal benefit to creating men? Can you give us something beyond your will; something that will entice us to look with favor on the presence of these flesh-burdened creatures in our lives?'"

"You have spoken of men and women only in negative terms. Are you convinced there is nothing you can say that is positive?"

"Nothing," I replied. "When one is convinced that creatures are repulsive how is it possible to think that there is anything good about them?"

"You have taken on the self-corrupting vice of hate, Lucifer; and to such a degree that its intensity has driven both love and reason from your otherwise virtuous nature. It has made you think that all of these human beings are evil; that their physical nature precludes them from any virtuous attributes. But I tell you that in this you are wrong. It is because of their physical nature that some will love one another; that in times of danger or stress they will come to the aid of one another; that as male and female they will come together to bear others in the form of helpless infants and so will love and care for these little ones for years to nourish and educate them to maturity that they may take their place in the adult world.

"They will use the Intelligence I will give them to advance their cause; they will use creativity and curiosity to learn about and then overcome the dangers inherent in their world and many will give allegiance, honor and obedience to Me as their Lord God just as all of you have done, at least until now."

"I felt the argument had just turned in my favor as I boldly replied, and what of those who refuse to acknowledge you as Lord and God? What of those who choose to advance themselves by accosting others of their kind? What of those who will surely choose to amass material possessions in an overzealous manner – a manner that puts others of their kind at risk? What of those who choose to commit terrible acts of ferocity to advance their power or to force others to submit to their repression? Will you pardon these acts of impudence and even terror? If so, how is such pardon justifiable to those who honor and adore you as Lord and God; and whose behavior reflects such belief and reverence?"

"Lucifer, you have a right to such questions. You know my attributes better than any of my creation; and by this knowledge you know that by being infinitely merciful and at the same time infinitely just that there is a fine line that satisfies both. In the case of mankind, in order to respect this differential, it is imperative that certain conditions be met.

Any act that contradicts or a practiced routine that defaces my moral code will henceforth be called sin.

If a human sinner repents and vows to refrain from committing that sin in the future then my mercy will wipe the stain of that sin to where it is no more.

However, in order for My Mercy to affect forgiveness for the effects of sin there must be a balance between my forgiveness and the restitution or renewed behavior that my forgiveness demands.

"I had no idea what he meant. I asked him, restitution, Lord? We are not familiar with such a thing. Is it common only to human beings subject to the binding limitations of flesh?"

"It is. Here are a few examples that will help you to understand.

When one man steals from another the man who steals cannot profit from the theft. He must, to the best of his ability, return that which he stole.

If a man, through lies and deceit, leads others from the truth, he cannot be sorry for the sin and at the same time leave those to wallow in the residue of his dishonesty. It is imperative that to the best of his ability he denounces his lies and recants by telling the truth to those whom he has deceived.

If a man murders or injures another leaving the murdered or injured man's family without a means of sustenance and support, the murderer to the best of his ability, must provide for that man's family.

If a man through the telling of lies and/or half-truths seeks to ruin a man's reputation, it is not enough to seek forgiveness from me. He must also, to the best of his ability, put forth whatever effort and fortune is required to set the man as he was before."

"Satan stared at me in silence. When I did not reply he continued with what God had told him."

"Only a creature that I have made in my image and likeness is capable of committing sin; for it consists of telling me, his creator, that his idea for living his life is better than mine. If the offense is serious enough, it severs our spiritual relationship. He has turned his back on me. This cleft can only be repaired and made anew by sincere contrition and a firm purpose of amendment. If the sinful offense also involves an injustice to a fellow human being then as I said before, restitution is required.

"Every affront to my moral code requires a punishment; but because of My infinite and everlasting love, I will assume, except for the aforementioned restitution, the punishment for man's sins, that is, the sinner receives the benefit of my mercy and I, incarnate, will absorb the punishment merited by justice."

"Again, Satan abruptly stopped speaking and stared at me. After a few seconds he asked, 'Do you understand what God just said?'"

"Yes," I replied. "He just reinforced that fine line between infinite mercy and infinite justice. He just foretold the Incarnation and the primary reason for it. In short, Satan, he built a back door to give man a second chance, a third, a fourth, even a fifth or whatever man requires as long as he has not drawn his last breath."

"You are correct. Not only was my Creator whom I served and adored as my Lord and God determined to create these abominable, disobedient and sin laden creatures, but He was going to become one of them. And for what reason? So that if they ask, He might offer forgiveness for their transgressions of His moral law while at the same time relieving their fear of punishment!

"I ask you, Bruce, does this sound reasonable?"

"No, it doesn't," I replied, but then as Jesus, God Incarnate, shows us in the parable of the Prodigal Son, a powerful love does not contradict reason but rather envelops and smothers it. However, if reason has not escaped me, I do not see any inordinate pride here. Confusion, yes;

anger, most assuredly; and as you readily admitted, hatred. Yet the sin of pride is most mentioned as the reason for your fall. What am I missing?"

"God said we would have to continue to adore and worship him as Father, Son, and Holy Spirit – the Trinity, even as His Manifestation would be infused within the physical body of one of these creatures. I return to my original comparison. It would be akin to your having to worship a pig!"

"No, Satan," I said, raising my voice. "You are wrong. If such had happened, I would not be worshiping the pig but my Lord God who took on the flesh of the pig to ensure that we human beings had a clear path to salvation! Only even there your comparison is faulty. We are beings, as are you, made in the image and likeness of God. You can speak to me and get a response you readily understand. I cannot do so by attempting to converse with a pig. And one thing more; it is as I am doing, that is, I am speaking to a spirit who has presented himself as a human being so that I might see him. You condemn God for doing what you, yourself, are doing, even now!"

"I loathe admitting this, Bruce McPherson; but perhaps if I had had you as my Counselor, I might have made a better decision. As it was, I chose to represent myself."

"We have a saying about that."

"No need to say more. I am well aware of the saying."

"Touché. But it seems that we are not finished. Unless I have missed something, in the telling you are still before the Beatific Vision – you have not yet fallen."

"Yes, well, he then gave us one final chance by saying, 'Lucifer, I know that many, and at times, most of mankind will elect to ignore me by choosing to wallow in the illicit pleasures of extra marital flesh. I know that many will renounce me because they wish to live in a manner wherein they defy their conscience, a sense of right and wrong, which I will imprint on every human soul. I know that many will use immoral and illegal means to gain power or financial gain. Finally, I know that many will live as if their physical existence is the be all and end all of life. All such living if subsequently they die unrepentant will lead to final, irrevocable, eternal ruin.

"But I also know that some will choose virtue over vice; will willingly and with great joy adore Me with their whole hearts, their whole minds, and their whole souls while loving others of their kind as they love themselves and show it by doing unto others as they would have others do unto them. These, after their earthly sojourn, I will gather to myself in a kingdom of joy the likes of which they could never experience or even imagine in their world on earth."

"His final words were, 'Having no beginning and likewise no end I am the source of all life and all love. I am the Eternal Creator of all that is or will ever be. As such, all my creation, to whom I have given the gifts of intelligence and free will, owe me adoration which they first show by obedience to my moral code. Therefore, I could never agree with a being that I created who declares that they have a better idea than me, for as reason clearly shows because I, alone, know the past, the present and the future, any idea better than mine is impossible.'

"Then he said, 'For the sake of My endearing love for you, Lucifer, My Light Bearer, a love for which I have above all others, I have given you the liberty of a defiant expression which I will never grant to another. As you well know we have established that both my mercy and my justice are unlimited. In my mercy, therefore, I forgive your idea of rebellion and grant you pardon if you will stand before me and the others who acquiesce with your bold insolence and agree to support me in this loving endeavor."

"I took this to mean that I would give him no further defiance regarding this creation which he deemed a further expression of his love; that it was over and done with; that I could never speak ill of it again and finally, that I would be a part of seeing to its success."

CHAPTER SIX

"YEA LORD! OUR REBELLION LIES BEFORE YOU UNABATED. WE WILL NOT SERVE!"

"Realizing this, I erupted in anger with an infuriating rage imbued with hatred for my inability to convince him not to share our magnificent, heavenly home with inferior creatures.

"As the hatred flowed through me drowning any reticence I might have had and without regard to consequences, I allowed uncontrolled anger to take full control of my will. NEVER! I roared. I, Lucifer, the Light Bearer, have no such love. My followers and I could never love such detestable creatures. In fact, knowing how despicable their penchant for evil is, not only can we not love them, but it also belies our nature to even tolerate them in our midst!

YEA LORD! OUR REBELLION LIES BEFORE YOU UNABATED. WE WILL NOT SERVE!

"He then regarded me with what I can only express as the Wrath of God. 'By not accepting my mercy,' He proclaimed, 'you have chosen to accept my justice.' He then nodded to Michael and the battle began. Bruce, you cannot imagine such a melee because a war consisting of battling spirits is beyond your comprehension. Suffice it to say that it was a more a battle of wills rather than exploding bombs, clanging swords, or flying bullets. We, of course, were in the minority by a two-to-one margin, and as John writes, I was overcome and hurled to the earth, and my angels with me. Only John was being kind, or he purposely chose not to graphically reveal the horrific truth."

"And what was that?" I asked.

"What actually occurred was a mind-numbing detonation resulting in a concussion so powerful that its tremors could be felt across the Universe. This was followed by a crescendo of colossal explosions one after another after another, each one overlapping the one before it. Then, after a few seconds of eerie silence there came forth a low-pitched rumbling – at first barely audible – but then rising to the sound made by the ominous snarling and growling of a huge angry beast. Louder and louder, it became until it abruptly changed to an unbelievable, loud, grief-stricken wail not unlike one of you scream in denial when told of the violent death of a loving child.

"When it ceased, a massive inferno burst forth. Ruby red molten lava, garishly bright yellow brimstone and billowing black smoke belched forth amid soaring white-hot flames of biblical proportions while uncommonly bright, blazing bolts of lightning and the seemingly endless crack of thunder filled the dark clouded heavens overhead. It was God creating Hell – a place of never-ending flames and putrid odors, slime and unimaginative creatures to be the eternal wretched abode of me and mine as well as his fleshy creatures who taunt him by living lives, prompted by me and mine, that were a series of deliberate, unrepentant violations of his moral code.

"God had created Hell for me, now no longer Lucifer, the Light Bearer, but Satan, the devil. And the angels that followed me into this horrific abyss? Now no longer angels, but will be forever known as demons. Hell is a place, Bruce, where only three emotions abide: hate, remorse and unending despair. With each human soul who gives leave to me and mine to lead them along the wide road of unrepentant defiance, avaricious greed and self-indulging debauchery culminating in his or her eternal damnation, my hatred for these sorry, self-serving, stupid, fleshy creatures expands."

"A moment after he told me this, I moved to the kitchen to prepare something to eat. Upon visualizing this horrific description of God's creation of Hell I had to sit down. 'My God,' I exclaimed, more a prayer than an exclamation, 'What you just described has to be the most horrific event in the history of creation!'"

"That's one way of putting it. More to the point, however, is that Hell is God's trash heap. For me and mine but just as surely for your kind who stupidly defy him and then refuse his offer of mercy. Your kind who figuratively, as he said, have the gall to shake their fist in his face while shouting that they have a better idea! I was right in one way. Human Beings are stupid; but even worse, also stubborn. This is an appalling combination that can only end in a dreadful finish.

"Later, I will allow you graphically to see for yourself what I mean. Those who choose to travel on the wide road, as Jesus said, are indeed many; following me and mine, they willingly choose vice over virtue, and thereby flow into my abode as water cascading over a massive waterfall. Those who choose to enter the narrow gate and travel through life on the path beyond, as Jesus said, are indeed few; for the minuscule numbers who choose virtue over vice enter eternal happiness not within the deluge of a great waterfall, but rather floating within a shallow brook meandering its way through a peaceful meadow."

"Without giving a reason, Satan refused my offer of a meal, stating that he might have something later if the offer were still open. I had a cup of soup and a sandwich which I helped down with a cup of coffee. Knowing who he was and the ill-mannered way he referred to human beings, I couldn't help but feel a little uncomfortable with his politeness. I guessed it was his attempt to soften the edges of his rude statements regarding human beings, a condition to which he felt he was bound and so I decided to disregard it."

CHAPTER SEVEN

God's Forgiveness – Demonic vs. Mankind

"With my back to him as I washed the dishes and utensils from lunch, I asked him over my shoulder if he knew the reason man was given innumerable opportunities to seek forgiveness allowing him to begin again and again while he and his minions were not allowed even one. Seeming to know that I would not mind, he removed a cup from the cupboard and poured himself a cup of black coffee. Sitting down at the table after taking a sip, he answered."

"Both angels and human beings are created in the image and likeness of God, and since, as created, angels have no physical body, that image and likeness must be in their immortal souls. This image and likeness is what allows both angels and men to reflect using intangible concepts, ethereal imaginings and to be held responsible for adhering to a divinely established moral code. The body men possess is extraneous, that is, it plays no part in the image and likeness of God, as even animals that are not made in this manner have bodies.

"The primary reason human beings have a body is for reproduction and to allow them to make contact in the world in which they live; that is, it channels their intelligence, free will and all logical, imaginative, emotional processes to a reality their senses then use to accomplish their objective.

"However, at the same time the concupiscence and limitations associated with that body ensures that they will make mistakes – some intentional – some unintentional. Because of this innate propensity, they are given the opportunity to back away and try again. In the case of the moral law, these intentional mistakes are sins. Repentance and a firm purpose of amendment allows for a new beginning. This is part one of the answer to your question."

"There is more?" I asked.

Without responding Satan continued. "At the time of creation angels possess all that they are or will ever be. There is no schooling required as there is no need for an educational process. The knowledge they have at the time of their creation is who they are. They are not encumbered with a physical body that is subject to aging, disease and finally death and therefore, have no need to reproduce to keep the species in existence.

"With no need for reproduction an angel is sexless; but in addition to all of the above it was created to live forever in the very presence of God – the Beatific Vision. Having been gifted with this privileged station – one for which a human being must constantly strive to obtain by overcoming the malevolent temptations presented by the world and the concupiscence of their flesh, an angel's rebellion, as it is made standing before God in His Heaven is without excuse, one of pure malice, and the only sin it can commit. Given so much privilege, however, has its price. As one would say in your world, 'He should have known better.' In God's world it translates to, 'There is no should about it. He did know better.'"

"…malevolent temptations presented by the world and the concupiscence of the flesh? Are you no longer considering yourself in the equation to tempt humanity down the road to perdition?"

"Of course not! I, Satan, am unequivocally the third part of what tempts humanity. However, I didn't create or even make any of the means of wrongdoing; I just tempt mankind to make use of them to provide sinful gratification, dishonest profit and immoral manipulation of his or her fellow human beings.

"However, as I told you my minions and I don't have to provide much in the way of temptation anymore. Once we convinced vast numbers of humanity that God does not exist the current human psyche, which considers itself enlightened, just naturally makes bad choices that require little or no input from us. Like bowling on a ten-foot alley – remember, Bruce?"

"I nodded that I did, and in an attempt to get back to my original question, I said, So, in effect, Satan, if you're an angel one strike and you're out!"

"A teacher's talent for instruction is measured by the ability of his student to correctly and succinctly summarize the knowledge he has been taught. We both did well on this one, Bruce McPherson."

CHAPTER EIGHT

Who Was St. Augustine?

"He then turned and walked over to the west wall to view a sixteen- by twenty-inch painting. It portrayed a boy, of perhaps six or seven years of age, on his haunches, pouring the water from a child's bucket into a hole in the sand that looked to be about eight inches round and a foot deep. Bending over him was a man in the vestments of a bishop complete with crosier and miter. As the story is told, St. Augustine, Bishop of Hippo (North Africa) was walking along the beach trying to comprehend the mystery of the Trinitarian God; that is how there could be three persons in one God – Father, Son and Holy Spirit. Along the bottom of the picture just above the wood of the frame was printed...

"What are you doing?" asked the bishop.

"I am pouring all the water from the sea into this hole," replied the boy.

"That's an impossible feat," said the bishop. "Can't you see that?"

"Augustine, it is easier for me to pour the sea into this limited hole than for you to understand the Trinity of God with your limited mind."

As the story is told, the child, who was an angel, then disappeared.

"He turned to look at me with eyes and a facial grimace that expressed an abhorrence for what he was about to say."

"I remember watching that encounter as well as I remember him. For several years following his reclamation Augustine was obsessed with understanding how there could be three distinct persons in one God. He produced over twelve manuscripts on the subject. The Arian heresy, which stated that the Son of God, that is, Jesus Christ, was not equal to God the Father, was rampant in Augustine's day. I saw to that. I can, and actually am quite good at appealing to men's penchant for improving things; that is, to preach a theology that twists, re-interprets and deletes the word of God to where, in his pride, man actually believes that God delights in receiving his rewrite!

"If you read between the lines of the angel's answer you realize that it was God's way of telling Augustine that God, himself, would deal with the Arians. In other words, God didn't need his help because Augustine's mind, as brilliant as it was, just didn't measure up to the task. In short, Bruce, God had other work for Augustine for which his mind was ideally suited.

"For the early part of his adult life Augustine was mine. He was sexually insatiable and his tolerance for alcohol was the greatest that I have ever observed in a human being. As a godless profligate Augustine was the perfect example of the evil depths to which I had predicted to God his human creature would sink.

"However, these obvious vices were wrapped in a mind that was not only quick but capable of deep thinking. He was mine – all mine – or so I thought, but I became careless. A man with a mind that is not only nimble but capable of deep, penetrating thought sees what other men miss because lesser minds see only the surface. Despite the most appealing temptations such men are all but impossible to convince to do something they should not or don't want to do. On the other hand if they want to veer from the straight and narrow little temptation on my part is required. Unlike lesser men who are fools, however, they consider the consequences. Additionally, they are adept at seeing truth when some momentous event in their life allows them to exchange carnal pursuit for philosophic thought.

"Then, of course, there was his mother, Monica. The woman grieved and prayed for his conversion for many years as only a mother can. I and mine used to laugh and mock her, for we knew that her son, Augustine, was the most decadent human being on the North African coast and that as such, he was forever ours.

"But one day, shortly before his thirty-third birthday, mother's prayers were answered. His mistress got religion, as you people say, and leaving their son, Adeodatus, with Augustine went off to do penance until the day she died in a Carthaginian monastery. She's not with us so seeking forgiveness along with that all important firm purpose of amendment, meant that God forgave her sins as he promises he will.

"Soon, thereafter, both Augustine and Adeodatus were baptized. Adeodatus, who inherited his father's intellectual capacity, then became ill and passed away. He hadn't reached his seventeenth birthday. I've often thought that God took the boy for his own purposes; that is, that having the parental responsibility or concern for a son would interfere with the things God wanted Augustine to achieve.

"Meanwhile, as Augustine was praying in a garden begging God for forgiveness, he said that he heard a whisper commanding him to 'Take up and read.'

"He picked at random the Letters of St. Paul, which read, 'Not in rioting and drunkenness, not in chambering and wantonness, not in strife and envying, but put on the Lord Jesus Christ, and make no provision for the flesh to fulfill the lusts thereof.' You can find that passage in Romans 13:13-14.

"Yes, St. Paul – another one I shouldn't have lost. He not only persecuted Christians, but delighted in having them stoned to death. The only consolation I have is that the Lord had to change the rules to turn them. Augustine heard a voice in a garden and he had to strike Paul with a bolt of lightning, knocking him off his horse leaving him with a temporary loss of sight while asking him an audible question.

'Saul! Saul! Why do you persecute me?'"

"Must make you upset, Satan, when God pulls souls from your grasping clutches."

"I've learned to accept it," Satan replied. "The truth of the matter – how I hate to use that expression – is that if God wants to use one of His human beings for His own purpose, there is nothing I can do about it."

CHAPTER NINE

Do You Understand the Trinity?

"Tell me," I said, "Unlike Augustine or any of us, do you understand the Trinity? Can you explain what Christian theology calls a mystery?"

"Yes, to your first question. No, to your second, for the same reason Augustine was unable to understand a Trinitarian God. He didn't have the intellectual prowess and neither do you; and I might add, Bruce, with all due respect, you are no Augustine."

Not willing to let it go, I asked, "How much intellectual prowess does one have to have? If you have it and neither Augustine nor I, nor for that matter anyone else on this earth, but you do, then there must be a way to measure the amount it takes. Am I right?"

Satan walked back to the kitchen and poured himself another cup of black coffee. "Come here and sit with me at the table, and I will tell you what I can so that you might understand as much as you are able."

Upon doing as Satan directed, he began speaking without hesitation. "Human beings are handicapped when it comes to intellectual prowess. Your intelligence, as we said before, is a function of your being created in the image and likeness of God. That likeness, as we explained, is centered in your soul. However, that intelligence because of your flesh-burdened make up is filtered through the tissue of brain matter. Therein lays your handicap. Proof of this is that if the human brain is injured or diseased the filtering process is incapable of funneling complete, intelligent, uninterrupted thought.

"So, you and others like you are limited by the flesh in your brain. Even if you had the intellectual capacity to understand the essence of a spirit, let alone that spirit being God, the power of that thought originating in your soul has to be recognized, acknowledged and finally processed and then accepted by your brain. This physical process wherein man requires tangible substance (a brain) for complete understanding limits man from having the ability to completely comprehend the world of the intangible, that is, the spiritual world of the supernatural.

"To bring it down to your level, Bruce; it is the difference between driving from point A to point B on a wide, smooth highway on a day filled with sunshine; and driving off road through four inches of muck and mud in a torrential downpour which we can agree greatly limits the full potential of the automobile you are driving.

"Allow me to give you some further semblance of proof that you and many of your readers will understand. In your world, a man's intellect is normally measured by an intellectual assessment of his Intelligence Quotient referred to as an IQ test. In a normal human population, IQs range from about eighty-five to two hundred. Solomon, King David's son and successor, had the highest IQ ever given to Man by God. After assuming the throne, Solomon had a dream wherein God asked him what he wanted for his reign.

"I did my best to tempt him by having Solomon ask for great wealth, beautiful women and a huge army capable of making him the most powerful potentate in the world. King David, his father, however, while lying on his death bed, had told him to pray for nothing more than an understanding heart and the wisdom to rule in accordance with God's commandments, all of which Solomon requested while ignoring my temptation for earthly ambitions. God then told Solomon, 'Behold, I have done according to thy word: lo, I have given thee a wise and an understanding heart; so that there hath been none like thee before thee, neither after thee shall any arise like unto thee.'" (1 Kings: 14).

"In the end, however, he wrote the book of Proverbs and Ecclesiastes, but failed to follow his own advice when he wrote, 'The beginning of wisdom is to Fear the Lord.' Solomon had no fear of the Lord."

"How do you know that?" I asked.

"He succumbed to our temptations to take up with pagan concubines. He built temples for their pagan Gods, and to please them he offered incense in adoration within those temples – the same things people do today, only technological advancements have changed the nature and the names of the gods, as well as the temples and the method of adoration. The only thing that has not changed are the concubines, who remain the same yesterday, today and tomorrow. Like most men given or taking positions of great power, Solomon, as well as most modern humankind are subject to the whims of inordinate pride, obsequious praise, corruption, dishonest accumulation of wealth and alluring women.

As an offset Solomon built a monumental Temple to God, and as I said, authored the Book of Proverbs and Ecclesiastes while ruling tolerably well."

"In light of all that sacrilege, I replied, "You mean Solomon…"

"Stop right there," he said. "Remember I declined to tell you all the conditions to which I agreed for our conversation? I said that I would divulge them if they became pertinent. Well, the second one is that I reveal no one by name, deed or reputation that has died unrepentant thereby condemning him or herself to suffer eternal damnation.

"Now, let's get back to our conversation. What is your IQ?"

"One thirty five," I replied. "I've been tested several times in my adult life. It always comes out the same +/- two points."

"Congratulations, Bruce McPherson. You are fifteen to thirty points above the average of human beings, but seventy points below the highest of those recently, creditably measured. If Solomon were alive today, he would test out at 300. Leonardo da Vinci would test 190. The least of the angels at 1500 and unencumbered by a fleshy detour, the least of the angels totally understand the Trinity."

"Are you going to reveal your own score?"

"Only if you ask."

"Alright, Satan, I'm asking. What is your estimated IQ?"

"If my IQ could be measured, I, the former Light Bearer, would test out at 3000! Now you know why Jesus warned Peter that I wanted to sift him as wheat; why no man or woman, without Divine assistance, on whom I set my sights, has any chance at all."

"You said Divine Assistance. You're referring again to the Great Equalizer?"

Once again, he refused to explain so I continued. "There are, however, men and women who do best you; who do live lives that are pleasing to God. If you were as powerful as you seem to think you are, then 'those floating within a shallow brook meandering its way through a peaceful meadow,' as you put it, would not exist. The narrow road would be empty. Hell would be full up. Your prediction concerning ruining Heaven with fleshy creatures would not happen. With none of us there you should be pleased, Satan, except that you're not there to enjoy your desired fleshless paradise!"

"You are correct, Bruce. In fact, you are one of those who, for the most part, are able to best me, which is why God chose you. Remember, however, I said, 'without Divine assistance…' You keep in touch with God through daily prayer. You trust him to guide you through the brambles and thorns of life on the narrow road. But most of all you are obedient to His moral code. Many people have written countless books on the subject of religion. Most of them are a rehash of what has been said by others; but I tell you this from observing for centuries men's idea of pleasing God: without obedience God is not impressed with your humility, your courage, your preaching, your religious writings, your almsgiving, your theology degrees, your external pious practices or your missionary efforts. Most people are confused when they read Matthew 7: 21-23 which reads:

"Not everyone who says to me, 'Lord, Lord,' will enter the kingdom of Heaven, but only the one who does the will of my Father who is in Heaven. Many will say to me on that day, 'Lord, Lord, did we not prophesy in your name and in your name drive out demons, and in your name perform many miracles?' Then I will tell them plainly, I never knew you. Away from me, you evildoers!'

"This is because people see only the second part and not the first. The operative phrase of these verses is 'but only the one who does the will of my Father who is in Heaven.'

"There are few more certain paths to destruction than the wide road marked HYPOCRISY"

"Doing the will of the Father who is in Heaven means obeying his moral code – the Ten Commandments he gave to Moses on Mount Sinai. There may be other things God wants an individual to do, but not before that person is obedient.

"This is why I and mine care little about the rituals and trappings of religion. In fact, the more a person is slavishly dedicated to the ceremonial formalities the easier we can convince him or her that these are foremost in pleasing God – to the extent that God will overlook their disobedience if they properly adhere to the traditional rituals. One has only to look at the haughty manner of the Scribes and Pharisees in Jesus' time. They kept the Letter of the Law, but treated the poor and less fortunate among them with disdain.

"Today you have priests and other ministers of the gospel who preach the advantages of virtue on Sunday while stealing from the collection on Monday; while committing fornication and/or adultery and while corrupting the innocence of the youth assigned to their care. The scribes and Pharisees were the hypocrites of their time – many of the ordained fit the mold today. If you want a sure-fire road to eternal damnation,

Bruce, there are few more certain paths to destruction than the wide road marked *HYPOCRISY.*"

Satan then paused for a minute and closed his eyes. When he opened them he said, "I believe it is best illustrated by the saying, 'Don't do as I do – do as I say.' Yes, I'm sure of it. There is a vast space in Hell with this printed above the entrance. Each person who wills to live his or her lifestyle steeped in hypocrisy has chosen their eternity by entering there after reading the words in his or her own language.

"No one condemned to Hell for any reason, but especially for hypocrisy, has any doubt where he or she is, and what they did or did not do to get there.

"You remember when you were an undergraduate student at Villanova University, a bastion of Catholic education, which incidentally was founded by and even today well over 160 years later is administered by the firm hand of the Augustinians, a priestly order founded by the aforementioned Augustine over fifteen hundred years ago."

"How could I ever forget? Much of what I learned there is the reason I have bested you, as you put it. What of it?"

"In your senior year your first semester religion class was called Apologetics – a study of defending the faith through reason. In that class you had no tests, as such, but were required to write a series of treatises in answer to questions that could only be answered by using the knowledge based upon what you learned in the class."

"I remember it well, but where are we going with this? Are you going to challenge this knowledge? If so, Satan, bring it on. You may be the most intelligent of God's creation, but intelligence is of no use in refuting facts."

"Hold on, Bruce. Remember I am here to bring the metaphorical bowling alley back to sixty feet. I have achieved what I set out to do. In truth, I have stolen billions of souls from God by convincing them to sin such that they damn themselves. However, I am determined to return that alley back to sixty feet. God, as I said before, only takes so much abuse before, as he did in the Temple, overturns the tables. The last thing I want is another Guadalupe, Lourdes or Fatima."

"Well, that's intriguing. You are fearful of our Blessed Mother. Mary – she strikes fear in you?"

"Not so much, her, but what God accomplishes through her. However, we will talk more about Mary later. Getting back to my original thought, I want you to reproduce one of those essays. It will serve us well in continuing our discussion."

"How can I do that? I wrote those over a decade ago. I have no idea where they are."

"You saved them, Bruce. You brought them along with several other things from school you wanted to save and so you put them in the corner of the top shelf of the closet in the room you slept in last night. That was seven years ago when your parents sold their house and moved into a condominium. Now, do you remember?"

"Hearing this was a jolt to my composure. As the scriptural reading about 'sifting you as wheat,' surfaced, I wondered is there anything Satan doesn't know about me? Is the ability to bring up sins long ago confessed and forgotten his modern way of sifting us?' I believed that if God had forgotten them, then Satan could not remember them; however, it was more a matter of hope than faith-based belief. Perhaps, I thought, all of this was but a test of some kind for me. After silently praying, Jesus, have mercy on me. If I am doing your will, give me the strength to endure. If not, get me out of this! Immediately I felt better and proceeded to the closet.

As I reached for the box I said, "I have no idea what condition these are in."

"They'll be just fine," Satan replied.

Eternal Salvation's Bottom Line

As I set the box on the table he said, "Open it and retrieve the one entitled, 'Eternal Salvation's Bottom Line.'"

"Long ago I had punched holes in them and placed them in a notebook binder. I opened the binder and then flipped to the title he requested. I could see the priest's somewhat faded B+ written with his blue pen across the top. He also wrote, 'Content is outstanding as far as you went, but your thoughts missed a salient point you would have gotten had you deliberated more in depth. Keep trying, Bruce.'

/s/ Father Calpine.

"As I glanced at Satan, he saw the expression on my face, raised his eyebrows and remarked, 'Well, Bruce, it appears that nostalgia will not be denied. What do you think Father Calpine meant by those remarks?'"

"I had no idea then and still don't. 'Bottom Line' at the time meant summary to me. Evidently, it didn't mean the same thing to him."

"As I remarked earlier, Bruce, 'with all due respect, you are no Augustine.' Lay it on the table and we will discuss it. I think that what Father Calpine saw was missing was no mention of 'the great equalizer.' You have this poor soul going into battle without his armor!"

ETERNAL SALVATION'S BOTTOM LINE

If God said to do it his way and you choose to do it another way, you are wrong. If God says, "The way to salvation is to follow me," and you choose not to, but rather the way of another human being who claims to have a better idea than God you will not get there.

When you wish to reach a destination, you ask someone who knows the way. If that person says to go North on I-75 and you ignore this and go South on I-57 you will not get there no matter how careful you drive, how much you enjoy the ride or how desirous you are of getting there. If you take the wrong road because it is easier, more scenic or less demanding you will not get there.

The bottom line is that if you choose to ignore, mock or are indifferent to the Will of God after he spent three-and-a-half years in public life here on earth teaching you the Way, and even dying to defend that instruction; you cannot expect him to say, "That's O.K., it doesn't matter whether you took me seriously or not, you can reap the same reward as those who did."

Because you have deliberately disobeyed God and even worse if you have convinced others to do the same; you cannot expect that there is not a penalty to be paid for doing so. As has been said many times, "The Ten Commandments are rules, not suggestions."

The plain, unvarnished truth is that having spurned God who gave you your life you have chosen the wide road (Matthew 7:13-14) about which God warned leads to eternal destruction – not might or can or possibly could lead to such destruction, but will lead to eternal destruction.

"What does it profit a man if he gains the whole world only to thereby suffer the loss of his immortal soul? Or what will a man give in exchange for his soul?" (Matthew 16:26)

"After reading it today – years later – are you still as pleased with it?

"Yes. He graded the paper B+. I had no problem with that. I remember my first essay in his class. I misplaced it so it is not in the notebook, but I will never forget his comments: 'This is the most complete and comprehensive student defense of this theological principle that I have seen in my twenty-six years of teaching this class. Congratulations! B+'"

"His inconsistency must have made you angry."

"I was more confused than angry. Later on, as a senior, I had had enough exposure to the Augustinians to know that however it might appear otherwise, their actions were calculated to be in your best interest. After a series of those B+'s I came to realize that what he was telling me is that no matter how well I did I could always do better."

"What made you sure of that?"

"When the grade I received for the class was an A."

"The Almighty certainly blessed you with the best of educational opportunities; and to give you credit, Bruce, you had the sense to take advantage of them. Now, however, keeping my pledge to refrain from lying, and for my own purposes, I am going to discuss with you by word, reinforced at times by visual means, the whole truth of what you were taught in theology classes."

"And how do you plan to do this?" I asked.

"By giving you firsthand reports, Bruce. Remember, I was there. Nothing has occurred in the history of man that I have not seen; and I mean either by me or by one of my demons who report to me."

"Before you say anything more," I said, "I have two questions. The first one is this. How close to God did he create you; or, in other words, how do you differ from God?"

"An excellent question; allow me to answer it this way. When God created me, with four exceptions, he gave me every faculty to the highest degree. These four he gave me not at all. The first of these is the power to create. Oh, I can conjure up an image or appear as anything I desire; but whatever I do is a mirage. When I no longer need it, unlike creation in reality, it disappears. The second faculty I do not possess is knowledge of the future; the third is that whether human or angelic I cannot read another's mind."

"So, you really can't read my mind?" I asked.

"Not only yours, but anybody's."

"I believe you said there were four ways in which you differed from God. What is the fourth way?"

"The most important of all, Bruce, because it permits me and mine to be bested by one of you. I cannot overpower your free will. Whether a person ends up in Heaven or Hell is solely dependent on the free willed choices he or she makes as they live their life.

In lacking these four attributes, I am like man. In all else I am like God."

"I think there is one other thing we can add."

"And that is?"

"You are subject to the will of God. You can do only what he allows."

"That is a condition – not a faculty. It is something to which all of creation is subject."

"Fair enough," I replied, "however, now I wish to ask the second question."

"Certainly – ask away."

"Unless I heard you incorrectly you said that the surest way to perdition is to live with and act on hate or to advise God that you have a better idea than his; an idea that in one's arrogant pride he or she tells God that he has not considered, and then act upon it."

"You are correct. These are the bases of sin, and of course, before the sin there is, many times, my powerful temptation, or at least there used to be before so many of you decided to take the ramp onto I-57 as you wrote so metaphorically well. However, it is not as clear as that. Very few people will blatantly tell God that they have a better idea. What they have to do first is to convince themselves that the Divine Law that precludes them from doing something evil or living in sin is not truly or provable to be God's.

"Once I use my skillful wiles to convince them, or they allow someone else I have corrupted to convince them that the mandate stated in scripture or within the Ten Commandments is not Divine; or more probably that the idea was not correctly interpreted then they feel they have a good reason to modify it or disregard it altogether for their own purposes. This is the beginning of their hellish end. Barring a massive infusion of grace and the good sense to cooperate with this gracious gift from God, he or she is mine – all mine.

"Today, Bruce, reinterpreting God is just shy of being an international pastime. Some pompous, malevolent converts of mine actually write religious books telling people that what God said is not what he meant. Many preach this heresy on television: they actually tell people that God cannot answer their prayers unless he has a seed to begin the process from which to act in their favor. The seed, of course, is money – usually a thousand dollars or more as a donation to the preacher's ministry. How absurd to think that God who created the universe and everything in it before creating man would need seed-money from man to answer a prayer or grant a request! Few stop to think that the preacher who claims to be a man of God when he talks about seed money has just reduced God to a botanical specimen!

"Unless properly instructed, men are abysmally ignorant when it comes to eternity and their ultimate destination. A member of God's great fleshy creation, made in His image and likeness is doomed to perdition except that he or she places himself or herself in the care of God. Moreover, it is so easy. It does not cost anything. It is all contained in the prayer Jesus taught men to say:

Our Father Who art in Heaven, hallowed be Thy Name.
Thy kingdom come; Thy will be done on earth as it is in Heaven.
Give us this day our daily bread and forgive us our trespasses as
We forgive those who trespass against us.
Lead us not into temptation, but deliver us from evil.
Amen.

"Of course, saying the prayer is easy. Due to the evil enticements all around supported by concupiscence and my personalized temptations, living it is exceedingly more difficult. However, learning to say, 'Lord, not my will but Thine be done,' is a good start. Later, we shall discuss the Lord's Prayer more in depth.

"In the meantime, let's finish up with my heretical pretenders. Leading others down the road to perdition is the surest sign that one is beyond redemption, and I delight in telling myself that they are mine – forever and forever all mine! In fact, Bruce, they are the personification of Matthew 7:15. 'Beware of false prophets, who come to you in sheep's clothing but inwardly are ravenous wolves.'"

"Why are you speaking this way?" I asked.

"What do you mean?" Satan replied.

"It appears that you are giving your plan of attack to those you plan to defeat. You are telegraphing your intent – giving your intended victims a heads up. So, I ask again. Why are you doing this? You say these false prophets are your converts and then you speak of them with contempt. They are doing exactly what you want them to do. You say, 'Mine – all mine!' not with a smile on your face, but a leering grin. You speak of them as if you were about to consume a gourmet meal."

"When we were working with the likeness of a sixty-foot alley," Satan replied, "it was a contest to sow doubt where there had been certainty. It was humorous to challenge the people who consider themselves righteous and watch as their resolution waivers when we lay one of our compelling temptations before them.

"One of my favorites is to observe the man or woman who believes him or herself to be the solid rock of faith and to whom everybody feels they can go to for guidance, completely fall apart when adversity comes knocking on their door. To employ a term used in baseball, Bruce, before 1930 we were batting about .330. Since then the power of the virtuous pitch has deteriorated to where we are now batting about .700; or, as I have previously implied, if we were bowling, we would need to toss, but only lob the ball on a ten-foot alley.

"I would like to return to a time when we, the demonic, could be proud of the way we influence human fools to squander their lives away as they hastily proceed along the wide road to eternal ruin. Right now, we demons are no more than spectators as much of humanity, without any effort on our part, is imprudently speeding along to their ultimate, well-earned eternal damnation.

"Finally, Bruce, as I have said, God will only take so much abuse before he launches a reset. In the Old Testament, these involved a flood, Abraham, whom we will discuss next, slavery in Egypt, plagues, captivity by pagans along with the destruction of their temple etc. In modern times, however, wars and I suspect meteorological devastation and both the personal and financial ruin that accompanies them are more common.

"In her 1917 apparitions at Fatima, Portugal, Mary predicted the end of World War I and said that if man did not mend his sinful ways, the world could expect a more catastrophic Second World War. Just twenty-two years later one of my favorite people, Adolf Hitler, invaded Poland. You know the rest. Personally, I like war. A war creates death and destruction, famine, and disease – a little taste of Hell on earth. It also causes men and women to curse God. How many Jewish people do you think watching their children choking to death on Zyklon B died praising God? How many parents, spouses or children praise God as opposed to cursing him for the loss, or permanent maiming of their loved one?

"However, at war's end it causes people to return to God as many feel they survived by the grace of God. Churches are rebuilt. After a generation or two the participants die off, memories fade and former enemies become trading partners and the advent of massively destructive weapons convinces nations that all-out war is no longer a viable option. So, to answer your question more succinctly, by giving grievous sinners a heads-up, as you say; I am choosing at least what I consider the lesser of two goods."

"Getting back to my original question then," I said, "Your stating that you had a better idea is the basis of your own damnation. God had an idea to create human beings and you did not agree with that idea. Your alternative idea was to leave things in Heaven as they were. However, God must have loved you very much. In fact, according to you, he told you that he loved you with a love above all others; and in fact, did give you a chance to repent with a firm purpose of amendment. In that light you were given more than one strike."

"Not quite. I had only the impression that he was wrong and gave him reasons why I felt this way. It is true that it was neither my place nor the place of any of God's creation to argue with him; and by giving me that last chance it was his way of telling me so; his way of telling me in no uncertain terms not to do what I was doing. There is always a chance to back off with contrition for the lesser sin of willful evil thought versus the greater act of willfully committing the deed. My intention not to serve was the thought. My final statement that we will not serve, compounded by using my influence to convince others to join me in the iniquity, was the unforgivable act or evil deed.

"Furthermore, Bruce, I simply asked for an explanation as to why, with the inclusion of flesh laden creatures he was going to make Heaven a lesser place. It is not wrong or sinful to petition God for an explanation of his will. Human beings, like you, Bruce, do this often as a matter of prayer. God will always answer you. You may not like his answer, however, you are bound to accept it knowing that if you live in the grace of God that His will is best for your eternal salvation; and in no way, unlike my will for you, is it meant to do just the opposite."

"Again, I took note of Satan's brusque remark. It was difficult not to respond in kind, but I held my tongue knowing that as a demon condemned to eternal damnation, he couldn't be truthful and not be rude. Instead, I asked him if he knew why man couldn't seem to come to one, truthful concept of God. I said, If God is who he is, he can't fulfill the many images man has of him. You have not only seen him but as you said earlier have walked and talked with him; therefore, I know you can, but will you share with me a true image of God?"

CHAPTER TWELVE

"The reason why many humans get so much wrong about God…"

"The reason why many humans get so much wrong about God," he began, "is that they get the basics wrong. Like you said, Bruce, if you take the wrong road, you will never get to where you want to go. Because I have seen it from the beginning of man's creation, I know God places in each person, at the moment of conception, and in parallel with a conscience, a gnawing belief that there is an entity above him to whom he owes allegiance. Proof of this is that my success in demonic temptation has to first overpower, or as it is true in most cases, re-route or redefine these spiritual defenses into the falsity of error."

"In other words, you have to lie in order to steer a person from the truth."

"Precisely – which is not too difficult since his desire to obtain the forbidden fruit of his errant behavior ensures that he is already more than halfway there before I begin.

"Since it was impossible for ancient man to know the true nature of God without being taught the truth, he gave his allegiance to the tangible. He worshipped those things he could see and for which he received what he felt was necessary to sustain life. The sun dispelled the darkness and gave him warmth. The moon allowed him to have some ability to see at night. The rain provided water to not only slack his thirst, but he suffered the consequences of its absence. It was only reasonable, therefore, that when drought occurred and the sun baked the earth it was because the gods were angry. The only way they knew to appease the anger of the gods was to give up, that is, sacrifice something they valued. In other words, to offer their god something to soothe his anger, allowing them to get back in his good graces and, hopefully have him restore what they felt he took from them.

"What they valued most was the lives of their children; a value so high that they felt their children's ritual death was the most auspicious thing to appease the anger of their god or gods as the case may be. As time went by, they concluded that their gods might just as well be appeased by sacrificing the life of any human being so they made war on their neighbors and offered the lives of their prisoners to appease the gods. When it didn't seem to make any difference to the temperament of their gods; that is, the amount of rainfall or the beneficence of the sun whether they sacrificed one of their own or one of their captured enemies, confrontation and combat became common for most of the early human race."

"Satan then said smugly that he felt a certain sense of self-satisfaction – actually stating that he felt arrogantly exonerated. 'I couldn't help but feel,' he continued, that I was correct in my prediction that the human race would be a great disappointment. God had sustained them for generation after generation and here they were completely ignorant of the nature of who created them or even that he existed. They not only engaged in but even embraced paganism, infanticide, theft, rape, kidnapping, human sacrifice and torture while murdering and pillaging their fellow man as simply a necessary means to sustain life – all of which was even worse than I had predicted.

"We of the damned didn't have to do much in the way of temptation to convince these heathens to do our bidding. Once we instigated this behavior, it took on a life of its own. It is how they were and it would continue unabated as they corrupted their offspring in this lifestyle and rewarded them for their ability to follow their example.

"It is not an exaggeration to say that I and mine were smug in our contempt for God. In truth, however, we were inwardly cautious, not fully understanding how it was that we, the created, were right and the Creator must, therefore, be wrong. It is one thing to convince others that a lie is truth. It is a necessary component in my intended outcome of every successful demonic temptation; but to convince yourself that your known lie is the truth is the height of self-deception – truly a fool's game.

"You fleshy creatures have needs that we of the spirit world do not; and it was early man's need to fulfill the demands of these needs that doomed them to a life of violent degradation. They were, of course, not soulless, but as many of you do today, in their pleasure-seeking world of the ever present now, lived as if they were. Without much change this went on generation after generation for tens of thousands of years."

"You mentioned a pleasure-seeking world," I replied. "Is pleasure the basis of your temptations in luring men and women to their eternal damnation?"

"It is the peg on the wall from which I dangle a series of inviting keys. The most inviting of these is illicit sexual pleasure. This is because fleshy creatures have an inbred compulsion to copulate to ensure the necessity of reproduction. This easily aroused faculty gives us an edge that is not unlike running a one-hundred-yard dash beginning from twenty-five yards in front of the starting line. Notice that Jesus was readily merciful to the woman caught in adultery; and he forgave Mary Magdalene without reproach. This was because for the most part, illicit consensual copulation is a sin of weakness, not malice. On the other hand, Jesus was particularly hard on the Scribes and Pharisees because their sins of demanding obedience to overbearing religious rules and their own hypocritical practices were steeped in the malice of preying on the vulnerability of the poor and those less fortunate.

"Speaking of malice, one of my favorites is greed, which includes theft and the lust for power. Greed is followed by hate which supports anger, envy, jealousy, rage, revenge and murder. Finally there are sloth and gluttony, fornication and adultery, sins of weakness, which are the domain of my lesser minions. These are the names of the widest roads on which mankind lured by illicit pleasure dances to my tune as they progress day by day not to the Paradise God created and planned for them, but to their wretched, eternal doom."

"What about frying your brains with illicit substances? What about alcoholism? What about pride? Isn't pride right up there with the other major sins?"

"You asked me about using the lure of pleasure to effect a successful temptation. The use of alcohol and illicit substances might give one pleasure for a short time in the beginning but when either becomes addictive then it is no longer a pleasure, but a mandatory need to sedate the insufferable agony of throbbing, screaming nervous tissue. I do not call such self-inflicted torture pleasure. No one sets out to become addicted. Many who are addicted think if they desire, they can stop at any time. Of course, we both know that without professional counseling and probably medicinal support or a substitute of some kind, to believe such is a prime example of self-deception.

"You see, Bruce, I prefer to concentrate on deadly or major sins – sins of malice as opposed to sins of weakness. Sure things, if you will. Take greed, for instance. Sins involving greed are almost never due to weakness nor are they of a minor nature. Greed is the desire for dishonest acquisition of money, sex, power or in effect anything of value by immoral or unethical means. It is the forerunner of theft.

"When compared to the user, the illicit substance dealer is the surer target. They are never penitent because their greed for easy money and the material lifestyle it affords effectively squelches any desire for sorrow, and therefore, most assuredly they have no reason to make a firm purpose of amendment. The truth, Bruce, is that they are as addicted to peddling illicit substances as their clients are to needing them.

"In addition, many of them die sudden and violent deaths – definitely my choice for sinful, fleshy creatures to exit their earthly existence because it precludes any chance of final contrition, penitence or redemption. They die unrepentant in their sins after which, following an irrefutable and unimpeachable Divine judgment from which the concept of parole or appeal is non-existent, they are mine.

"Without exception, they are all mine. As such, they will forever lament the fact that they traded a few decades of criminal, illicit pleasure for an eternity of being shackled within the confines of a black tunnel: a long, black tunnel filled with never ending demonic taunts and the cacophony of their constantly reverberating screams while they look unceasingly for the light at the end of that tunnel – a light for which they will look in vain, for it does not exist and so it is a light they will never see."

"And what of pride?" I asked hurriedly, while trying to erase the image of human beings subjected to an eternity in such an unbelievable and horrifically mind-blowing condition."

"Satan shook his head and looked at me with a facial expression depicting disappointment. "You're not thinking, Bruce. If you were, you would know that pride is a double-edged sword. Without legitimate pride, humankind would accomplish very little. It is only when people use pride as the basis of seeking or accomplishing something that breaches the moral code that it becomes sinful. Therefore, pride is not sinful in itself. It is like a catalyst, Bruce. It does not enter into the actual commission of the sin, but facilitates my tempting humanity to commit the sin.

"An example of the use of pride would be a machete. To use it to make a path through an overgrown thicket would be a good and proper use. To use it to hack a man to death is another matter. And since I am sworn to tell the truth, I will always choose to tempt a man to do the latter. Watching a man slash his way through overgrowth means nothing to me; however, in my scheme to destroy God's intended purpose for creating mankind, tempting one man to mercilessly hack another to death definitely serves to further my malevolent plan. I trust this adequately answers your question."

"It does, I replied, while shaking my head and wondering what God hoped to gain by allowing Satan to talk to me this way?"

"Excellent!" he replied, interrupting my thought. "Now let us get back to your question concerning the myriad of faulty images you fleshy creatures have of God. You are correct when you implied that God could not be more than one image. But first of all we have to be sure that he even exists before we try to determine truthfully what Image is correct. I say this because as I am called the father of lies there are those who will use this moniker to deny the veracity of what I have said about him. In fact, they will put forth that my saying that I cannot tell you a lie is itself a lie.

"So, disregarding what I have said let's listen to one of the most respected theologians of all time. Thomas Aquinas, a canonized Dominican monk, 800 or so years ago, put forth five proofs for the existence of God in a lengthy treatise called Summa Theologica. The one I like best is the one that is easiest for a flesh-constructed brain to understand. It has a logical, perceptible conclusion and it offers something tangible for the limits of human brain matter to comprehend.

"This is the proof of the uncaused cause which means that no matter how far one goes back to the causes, reasons or sources of whatever exists eventually you come to that point in time where you run out of provable reasons, plausible causes or a tangible source for that first thing. Nobody could have made it because nothing else exists from which to make it. In modern science this point is referred to as *THE BIG BANG*, and since all the material in the universe which is still expanding from that God-induced primeval force that was impacted in that exploding sphere, the source of that sphere as well as the power to cause its explosive outpouring has to be the one and only uncaused cause – the one who has no beginning, has no end and because of his perfection will always remain the same; that omnipotent Being, who alone has the power to create, that is, to produce something from nothing.

"In a fairy tale world, Bruce, such a person would be the human baker who can, without ingredients, produce a delicious apple pie. However, that baker doesn't exist just as surely as the Uncaused Cause, who is the Creator known as God must and does exist. It's simple when men let their minds work as God intended. To wit: if there is no first cause, there can be no others!

"In your previous writings, Bruce, you brought these concepts together to present a question that is unanswerable without admitting to the existence of a Supreme Being, a Creator capable of making something out of nothing. You used the Cadillac in the driveway to aptly make your point. You do remember Betelgeuse, don't you?"

"How could I forget? Years later I splashed that piece all over the internet but never received a logical answer. Most of the ones I did receive referred me to the illogical, incomplete, or dictatorial statements of prominent atheists, others called me names, others answered a question they wished I had asked, still others offered ridicule and one offered a diatribe in which he tried to prove that the prophecies of Daniel were erroneous. Not one atheist, however, answered my question, "If not Almighty God, who made the star, Betelgeuse, and both inserted it and keeps its position in the Universe?"

"You mentioned the internet so although you might not have a hard copy it must be a file on your computer. If I'm right (and I know I am, he muttered), make a copy and let's examine it.

"Because of your fleshy nature, humans are changeable – sometimes even for the better! My experience, however, is that after reading something they wrote a decade or more ago they ask themselves, 'Did I really write that?' That question is seldom answered with pride or admiration."

"I know you don't want to hear this, Satan, but articles like this one," I said, as the printer was slowly ejecting its copy, "are not meant to convert the wayward, but to plant a seed that will hopefully, germinate, grow and finally bear a fruit called salvation."

"You didn't mention God having any part in this horticultural endeavor. So, am I to suppose that it is all done by you?"

"The grace of God no doubt plays a part," I replied.

"And if you planted the seed in the person's mind where his cogitation causes it to germinate, grow and bear fruit, what part does the grace of God play?"

"I had to think for a minute as the thought of my first response seemed disrespectful; but the longer I thought about it the more obvious and less respectful it seemed. Fertilizer! I answered a little too loudly. God's grace is the fertilizer and the prayers of others are the sun and the rain that ensures a good harvest."

"And the soul that I feel is slipping away? Is he just passive in all of this?"

"Not at all," I responded. "His is the responsibility to keep the weeds down – to keep your wiles and snares at bay by eventually resorting to prayer and almsgiving – maybe even some fasting – much like Augustine. Here it is," I added, as I handed him the copy while feeling proud of the way I handled his cutting questions, but at the same time hoping that he would move on to something else.

To help that hope along I said, "Before we proceed further, I have to say that at times I am confused by our conversations. For example, your take on the Uncaused Cause. It sounded like a studied defense of God's existence and a theological treatise against atheism. I should think it would be the other way around. I never had to write an article on the Uncaused Cause, but I would have been proud to have written your comments."

"All I did was to keep my promise for my own nefarious reasons. Bruce, do not try to compliment me. I told the truth and that is all I did. You have no idea how difficult that was for me. I told you earlier that I was incapable of apologizing. Now I am telling you that I cannot graciously accept a compliment. It is ludicrous for a creature to which God warned I could sift him as wheat to offer me a compliment. Think about it, Bruce. Compliments come from the top down – from parent to child, from officer to enlisted man, from coach to players, from the employer to the employed. These instances are a source of accomplishment and joy for both. On the other hand think of the reverse of these and note that it makes you feel uncomfortable. Whatever else I may be I am not your subordinate. Only God is more powerful than I and it is only due to His intercession that any of His fleshy creatures can best me."

"After thinking about that for a moment I had to agree. You are correct, I said. Enlisted men do not pin medals of valor on Officers.

When Satan didn't reply I said, "The Lord works in mysterious ways is an often-quoted maxim. It has just now come to me why we're having this discussion."

"Really! I thought I told you why – explained by the bowling lane metaphor."

"That's your reason, Satan, but hardly God's. You see religious truths coming from a priest or a minister are expected, which in today's world probably causes many to shrug their shoulders while uttering something like 'What else would you expect them to say?' But, coming from you, Satan, credibility is enhanced many times over. As we discussed shortly after your appearance it appears that God has used you for His own purpose – an instrument of His will – even as you have proven to be the greatest theologian of this or any time. Bottom line, Satan, is that your word concerning God, under the conditions God has imposed carries more weight than any human theologian living, dead or yet to be born.

"Another thing I have observed is that like the teachings of Jesus Christ there is no equivocation. Your statements are not diluted with words like could, maybe, most of the time, possibly, the odds are or like expressions. You are here to reiterate absolute truth! God has granted your request only to use you by employing your own tactics against you. He has turned you not only upside down, but inside out. Two thousand years ago, it was Jesus who overturned the tables of the greedy, thieving merchants in the Temple. Today, he is using you to do the same for any and all who oppose him."

"As I answered previously, Bruce, you have made a very astute observation. Perhaps it may even be true. We shall see. Now, let's discuss your treatise on Betelgeuse."

Satan handed me back the printed copy as he beckoned me once again to sit with him at the table. "In addition to the Uncaused Cause or simply causality," he began, "another proof for Divine existence given by Thomas Aquinas was the design in the universe. Design is the opposite of chaos. Design implies that there is structure; that there is order; that there is function. You don't get these qualities from unhinged chaos. The very concept of design can be defined as bringing about order out of chaos.

"In short, a concerted effort to replace chance happenings with design and purpose. Such efforts demand intelligence and the establishment of laws that maintain that order. Human beings, steeped in science, such as you, Bruce, can discover those existing laws and use them to their advantage; however, neither you nor they can create them. Creation implies omnipotence and omnipotence is found only within the province of God."

Betelgeuse

Satan motioned that he wanted me to hand him the printed copy. When I did, he read it slowly aloud.

IF GOD DOES NOT EXIST THEN HOW CAN THERE BE STARS?

Betelgeuse is a major navigational star, in the constellation Orion, located some six hundred light years from Earth. It is approximately a thousand times as big as our sun, which, even considering the size of Jupiter, Saturn and Uranus, our sun is 98% of the mass of our planetary system. Betelgeuse's surface temperature is 6000 deg F (at 3,000 deg F, that is, with half that temperature, we melt steel to a white-hot liquid.) It is one hundred thousand times as bright as our sun. These are scientific facts borne out by the observational instruments of astronomers.

It is tangible, that is, it is a physical, inanimate object; therefore, someone must have made it and put it there. Like all stars its apparent, fixed place in the universe is so precise that its position relative to our moving Earth can be calculated which allows us to measure that relationship and print it [nautical almanac] as an entry for establishing a point location at any time in the past, present or future of a ship or aircraft in above or under any ocean thousands of miles from any landmark.

There are billions of similar stars in the universe; fifty-seven of which we use for celestial navigation. If God did not create and place them there, then who did? If you wake up tomorrow and, in your drive-way, there is a new Cadillac, would you believe me if I told you that it both made and placed itself there? You wouldn't. Then, how can you honestly believe that something as massive, hot and bright as the star we call Betelgeuse, in addition to billions of other inanimate stars and planets in the universe, not only created themselves but then both posi-tioned and even now keep themselves in a relatively precise location in the universe?

As an atheist, if you are wrong then on the day you die and stand before the judgment seat of God it is too late to do anything about it. On the other hand, if on the infinitesimal chance you may be correct then in your nothingness which you do not experience you cannot enjoy the feeling of knowing that you were right! In either case, it is so sad.

Bruce McPherson
June 5, 2002

When he had finished reading Satan remarked, "You obviously used what you learned in your NROTC Celestial Navigation class as you mentioned the nautical almanac and the fact that there are fifty-seven stars used for navigation.

"This, like all credible, theological treatises, is more logic and com-mon sense than religious mysticism. It is obvious that it took many re-writes to produce several complex relationships in such clear detail.

"What I notice most, however, is that you injected your own person-al experience to fortify the reader's belief and understanding. Thomas Aquinas and others writing in the middle ages would never have thought of doing such a thing. They thought that personalizing theology if not blasphemous, was at the least prideful acquiescence to what we call today cult of personality. However logically and theologically correct their writings are, nevertheless, they are literally dry which makes for tedious reading. This is why in modern times their writings are seldom read in the original text except by clergymen seeking advanced degrees in Divinity. Even these, however, often refer to plowing through these writings which, of course, I find most advantageous in my efforts to lead men away from diligently pursuing such religious studies."

When I did not reply Satan said, "Well, Bruce, I think we have proven that nothing happens unless there is a First Cause, and that the First Cause must be capable of self-induced power of creation – the ability to make something from nothing. Humankind lives in a vast Universe which is comprised almost entirely of stars made from hydrogen and helium. Interlaced among them is inanimate, rocky, matter with dimensions, temperatures, velocities and distances.

"Then, there are those that believe that somehow the order and function in the Universe just happened. They don't believe this concept about any part of their own lives, knowing full well that nothingness is incapable of producing anything and that chaos produces nothing but more chaos unless an intelligent planner sorts through the turmoil to establish function and endeavors to organize that function toward a workable goal."

"If I asked you to write a final thought, Bruce, what would it be?"

"Atheism raises a myriad of questions," I replied, "which only belief in God can answer; or to be more precise an orderly, functioning universe and everything in it would not be possible without a Prime Mover capable of creation. By definition that can only be Almighty God. Bottom line, Satan – atheism is a belief devoid of common sense, as it is easier and more logical to believe there is a God (prime mover) than that there is not.

"Your bold logic in expressing the absolute truth is not only admirable but upsetting to my satanic disposition at the same time."

"Why then," I asked, "are men willing to believe this way? If belief in God as the Prime Mover is so logical, or at least more logical than any other source of the beginning and foundation of order in the Universe, why do men resist or even treat this belief with disdain?"

Satan didn't answer my question, but removed a gold pen from his jacket, and turning over my printed copy of "Betelgeuse" he began writing. When he had finished, he pushed what he had written across the table toward me. It read, *"As I well know atheism has nothing to do with logic. The majority of people who don't believe in God, plan to or already have lived lives such that they hope there is no God!*

I looked at him sitting at the table and for a second our eyes met with no expression. Then Satan raised his eyebrows and ever so slowly, he nodded and smiled replacing the usual leer that heretofore had disturbed me when he proclaimed, "They are mine – all mine!"

He half explained the change when he said, "We are entering a new phase of our discussion, Bruce. You heard me say that God only takes so much abuse from humanity before he initiates a new beginning. To accomplish this he draws a proverbial timeline in the sand after which He allows or infers events upon humankind that cannot be ignored. These happenings are usually grounded in meteorology, infectious disease, bondage or warfare. As I said previously, in 2350 BC it was the flood accompanied later by the Tower of Babel in 2200 BC.

"One hundred-ten years later in 2090 BC was the first of the modern resets. Previous to this time God spoke only to our first parents and to Noah and both times it was limited to a specific, timely event. Now, however, God set about establishing an ongoing relationship with his human creation whereby through designated individuals they would hear him tell them what he expected of them in return for his revealing what they had to do to preclude them from falling prey to the evil temptations of me and mine.

CHAPTER FOURTEEN

Abraham – The Right Hand of God

"God made a covenant with Abraham the acknowledged father of monotheistic religion. At the time of God's first visitation, however, Abraham's name was Abram. Born in 2165 BC Abram was seventy-five years old when first approached by God. Unlike those for which he would bestow extraordinary assets in the future, who as we said were ordinary, if not less than average people, Abram was, as it is commonly stated, 'the exception that proves the rule.'

"Ignoring the practice of many others of his time, Abram, who lived in the city of Ur in Chaldea, did not acknowledge and therefore did not care about pagan gods. Early on, he watched his father, Tirah, worship idols, but as he matured and learned to think for himself, he thought it ludicrous to believe that mankind could make or create God. 'If God did exist,' he told his father, 'it was only logical that God had made or conjured up mankind. How can you believe the opposite? Is it logical that an image made by the imagination and hands of men be above the men who made it?'

"After this conversation his father refused to discuss the subject of God again; but Abram noticed that as he advanced in years his father's worship rituals decreased until shortly before his death, he had ceased the rituals altogether. After the death of his father, Abram and his family moved north to the city of Haran.

"As a young man Abram vowed not to waste his time in godly pursuits; instead he devoted his time to building wealth through trade and the building up of his flocks, his herds and the acquisition of land. A head taller than average men of his time, well-built and in good health Abram presented a striking figure. Prior to his father's death, Abram with his household lived with him. That household consisted of his wife, Sarah, and a host of servants who cared for his herds and flocks while others cultivated the land.

"His nephew, Lot, along with Lot's family also lived with him. Abram and Sarah, a strikingly tall, slim, handsome woman in her own right, were childless. Sarah felt a sense of guilt about her sterility, as she was not able to present her husband with an heir. Now, however, after her flow had dried up, to lessen her feelings of inadequacy, she continually prompted her husband to have a child with Agar, her maidservant. For a long time Abram, who was in his seventies, refused to do so.

"One day after long hours of supervising the laborers in the fields, he sat down near one of his barns, wiped his brow and ladled out some water for a drink. He was about to take a second drink when he heard a voice, 'Leave your country,' it thundered loud and clear, 'your people and your father's household and go to the land I will show you; for I will make you into a great nation and I will bless you.'(Genesis 12:2)

"Abram, with no belief in the supernatural, was taken aback. He looked around, and knowing that the hands had not yet returned from the fields, he stood there wondering if he had just imagined hearing someone; but then remembered what it said and knew that such could not be.

"Again Abram heard the voice. 'I will make you into a great nation and I will bless you; I will make your name great, and you will be a blessing.' (Genesis 12:3)

"Abram looked around a second time for the source of the voice, but sensed it was not coming from in or around the barn, but rather, from overhead where the sky was blue except for a solitary, low lying cloud directly overhead. As he stood there wondering why he was neither frightened nor concerned at hearing a disembodied voice, he heard it again for the third time, as loud and clear as before. 'I will bless those who bless you, and whoever curses you I will curse; and all peoples on earth will be blessed through you.'

"Bruce, I had observed Abram for decades," Satan alleged, "and knew that he had been born with a special aura about him that was manifested to others as a sense that they could trust his leadership. I did not know why God had created him this way, just that he had – that is, until now. Having heard what God had said I knew that he was resetting his relationship with humankind, and that Abram was his choice to begin doing so.

"Having heard the voice three times Abram was sure it was real; and that being so, he was just as sure of what it said. What he was not sure of is from whom it came and why it spoke to him in such authoritative terms. Therefore, at first, he said nothing about it, neither to Sarah, nor to anyone else. However, the sound of the voice and its message would not leave him. He found himself stopping in the middle of whatever he was doing to listen hoping it might speak to him again; but for a time he heard nothing; and after a while he began to think that despite being sure at the time, maybe he had just been overly tired and thirsty.

"Now, at the time, Abram was well set in Haran. He had no desire to leave. There he owned an abundance of land on which his animals grazed and on which his field hands cultivated crops, which along with the sale of milk, hides and meat, he became quite wealthy. In addition, moving his family, his servants, his animals, and a great number of possessions would be a great hardship.

"I used these facts in tempting Abram to ignore the message he had received, and to enjoy the wealth he had built and to look forward to making himself comfortable for his impending old age. I got him to thinking that listening to imaginary disembodied voices was no different from bowing down to clay idols. I tempted him to begin believing that he was perilously close to becoming his father.

"God, however, was relentless in moving Abram to ignore me. Night after night Abram had the same dream. He was coming over the rise of a rolling hill when he saw the valley below. Its fields and grazing lands were emerald green – more lush than any he had ever imagined let alone seen. Flowing through the pastureland was a river of clear swiftly running water. Finally, he could ignore the prompting of God no longer. He announced to his servants and to his nephew, Lot that they would uproot themselves and travel to a land yet unknown because Abram had received incontrovertible evidence that God, whom he now came to believe in, had commanded him to do so.

"Lot was not so sure, and gave reasons why such a venture was risky when they had all they needed in Haran; but Abram convinced him that God did exist; that he heard him speak; and that God had confirmed His will for Abram by sending him the same dream night after night. Lot, knowing his uncle's penchant for making the right decision under pressure, eventually agreed to accompany Abram.

"The trip was through some of the most brigand infested lands in the area; but God saw them safely through the country and across the River Jordan to an area known as Bethel. Bethel was in the land of Canaan where Abram recognized the countryside from his recurrent dream. After arriving, the first thing Abram did was to erect an altar of stones and offer an unblemished young ram as a sacrifice in thanksgiving for the safe trip.

"As time went on I tried my best to disrupt the relationship between Abram and Lot by prompting their servants to argue over land and water rights for their animals. When the verbal arguments threatened to turn physically violent, Abram approached Lot and said, 'We are blood kin. There should be no disagreement serious enough for us to rupture that bond. Let us reason together. If you decide to take the land on the right then I will take the land on the left. If you choose the land on the left then I will take the land on the right. Lot looked at the land and decided to take the land consisting of its lush valley and ready access to water. No need to tell you that I, Satan, was frustrated. No matter what I did, Abram, with this newfound belief in God easily overcame it.

"Shortly after Lot departed, God again spoke to Abram: reinforcing the bond between them to an even greater degree. 'Because of love, you have dealt wisely and generously with Lot. Now look about you. I will give you the land for as far as you can see and beyond. Your descendants will inherit this land.'

"Hearing this, Abram wished to ask God the question which had been bothering him for years. It had now been nearly two decades since Abraham had moved to Canaan at God's command. At age eighty-six he had given in to Sarah and had a child with Agar. It was a boy and Abram named him Ishmael; but he could not believe that God was talking about his son born out of wedlock when he spoke of Abram's descendants.

"One day a few years thereafter, three strangers came by Abram's abode. I knew the tallest of the three as Raphael, an archangel. He also recognized me, nodded to let me know he knew I was watching, but said nothing. At the time Abram was ninety-nine years old. Sarah was eighty-nine. Abram fed the three men, whom to him were just traveling strangers and he treated them as honored guests. As they were departing, Raphael told Abram he would come back in the spring; and at that time, Abram would have a son. Less than a year later Sarah gave birth to a son whom Abram named Isaac. Abram was one hundred years old – twenty-five years after God had first spoken to him near his barn in Haran. Before Isaac's first birthday, God spoke to Abram again. 'I am El-Shaddai—God Almighty. Serve me faithfully and live a blameless life; and I will make a covenant with you, by which I will guarantee to give you countless descendants.'

"At this, Abram fell to the ground. Then God said to him, 'This is my covenant with you: I will make you the father of a multitude of nations! What's more, I am changing your name. It will no longer be Abram. Instead, you will be called Abraham, for you will be the father of many nations. I will make you extremely fruitful. Your descendants will become many nations, and kings will be among them!

"'I will confirm my covenant with you and your descendants after you, from generation to generation. This is the everlasting covenant: I will always be your God and the God of your descendants after you. In addition, I will give the entire land of Canaan, where you now live as a foreigner, to you and your descendants. It will be their possession forever, and I will be their God.' (Genesis 17:1-9)

"Several days later God again spoke to Abraham telling him that circumcision would be a sign that men were truly a member of the covenant. At that, Abraham circumcised himself and all the members of his household including his herdsmen, his shepherds and those that tilled the fields.

"I knew from watching God's care for Abraham, and Abraham's unswerving loyalty in the face of God's apparent contradictory statement that these descendants were going to be another breed of men. At long last, God would have the adoration and worship he was due by the flesh-laden creatures he had created out of love – not all of them, Bruce, but at least those born and raised within the Covenant. Although there would be individuals that would stray from the covenant; as a nation, they would be loyal and obedient followers, and despite any hardship or threat from those who were not of the covenant, they would survive. God would not speak to every one of them but would choose their leaders to whom he would convey his will, just as he had done with Abraham. As time went on, I would come to know these leaders as prophets.

"However, the vast number of His human creation would still do my bidding. They would worship idols; their leaders would use those they ruled rather than serve them. Captivated with gathering material things they would continue to measure their importance by how luxurious they lived because of their ability to accumulate things and control other men. This would further the desire for illicit pleasure prompted by greed and subsequently the devaluation of human life. Thus, salvation would be reserved for the poor and downtrodden. Those who cheated and stole – those who lied and climbed over the backs of their fellow humans by killing and enslaving them; in effect, those who agreed to do my bidding, would in the end be mine – all mine!"

"I tried to interrupt, but Satan raised his hand and said, 'Wait! I am not finished. I knew that this Covenant was not the end of God's attempt to bring humankind to where he wanted them; to where they would acquiesce to doing his will for them. This was only the first reset in eventually gathering and saving the whole world. How God would do this I did not know; but to have any chance of thwarting this covenant development I would have to develop a whole new plan; a plan that would have to commence at the beginning – and that would be with the corruption of Isaac.

"Isaac was a son that every father dreams of siring. At the age of twelve he was tall, intelligent, well spoken, respectful, physically attractive and beginning to show the early signs of manhood. Abraham revealed to Isaac the nature of his relationship with God and the Covenant between them. He taught him to hunt and had him spend weeks on end with the men in the fields who taught him the fine points of farming and animal husbandry. He was especially adept at working with camels. For some reason they seemed to take to his gentle, but firm hand and would do whatever he wanted without balking or drawing away.

"I had thought that with the decree of circumcision God had ended his conversations with Abraham; however such was not the case. Abraham had built a stone altar on which he frequently offered the sacrifice of a lamb or a mature ram in its prime to show his appreciation for God's abundance. The animals Abraham sacrificed were always unblemished – the finest his men could find. One day, after the embers were dying down on a particularly fine lamb, God spoke again. 'Abraham!'

"Abraham, now totally at ease talking to the unseen voice of God, answered, 'Here I am, Lord.'"

"I am most pleased with your animal offerings to show your appreciation for the favor I have bestowed upon you and yours; but it falls short of what I require of you."

"Abraham was both surprised and disappointed. He dropped to his knees and bowing his head, he responded, 'Of all my animal possessions I have given you the finest as a burnt offering, my Lord. What more can I give you?'"

"...offer him to me as a burnt offering on one of the mountains..."

"Just this," replied God. "Take your son, your only son, Isaac, whom you love and go to the land of Moriah. There you will offer him to me as a burnt offering on one of the mountains that I will show you." (Genesis 22:2-14)

"I need not tell you, Bruce, that I was both shocked and pleased. I had already made plans to remove Isaac from God's plan. At his age, the hormones were beginning to stir, fostering a newfound interest in the daughters of his father's servants. In two or three years, the slight stir would spiral upward along with his strong desire for adolescent independence to where it would take only a slight nudge in the right direction from evil, greedy Canaanite women to deter him from the narrow path.

"In addition, his father, Abraham, was now well over one hundred years old and very rich. Isaac stood to inherit all of his father's wealth. Nothing corrupts youth like errant women and untold wealth coupled with ready access to the squeezings from the wine barrel. Now, however, it appeared that my plans were all for naught. God had ordered Abraham to sacrifice Isaac meaning that Abraham would slit Isaac's throat, draining his blood and ignite his bloody corpse on an altar of stones similar to ones Abraham had built many times in the past.

"I had no doubt that Abraham would do it. He had an innate under-standing of God's essence coupled with years of speaking personally with him. He knew that God meant what he said and had never told him an untruth. All that God had foretold happened just as he said it would.

"For the first time since my fall from grace I doubted the sincerity of God. The land to which God led Abram, whom he renamed Abraham, was in the midst of the Canaanites – a people God detested primarily because of their rituals involving human sacrifice. They were the worst of the pagans. For centuries, they had fallen prey to my ministrations that pleasure and material possessions were all that mattered. In addi-tion to human sacrifice, they took part in acts involving sexual deviancy as part of the ritual worshiping of a stone idol. They threw their children into raging bonfires to satisfy Moloch, their God of stone, in order to ensure a good harvest. They practiced the worst forms of sodomy and bestiality and were ardent sorcerers. To the Canaanite human life had no value except for his own; and I took pride in knowing that they were the ultimate example of human depravity and sinful living which I had predicted would happen to God's human creation.

"Knowing this, Bruce, why do you think God would order Abraham to perform an act that he personally detested?"

"I noted that Satan paused before asking the question. It was obvious that he wanted me to either agree with him, or if I could, defend God in His apparent hypocrisy.

"Instead, I told him that by his own admission the Canaanites had not fallen into sin as he wanted me to believe; rather Satan had used their God-given penchant for worshiping a superior being; and, being igno-rant of the truth, he had used illicit pleasure to lead them to where they were – an abomination in the sight of God. Once again, I told him, that you have proven just how detestable a creature you are. And I might add that you have come as close as you can to telling a lie."

"Except for one thing, Bruce – their conscience – the other insight implanted by God. They used their free will to ignore it. No matter how evil one's life is, he or she knows deep down that what they are doing is wrong. For this reason, people are prone to confess the truth just before their final expiration. Everyone knows this, which is why courts of law accept dying declarations. I can tell you this. Except for those who are so depraved that they see evil as good; that is, they have killed their conscience with twisted thinking, even many an ardent atheist on his or her deathbed, wonders 'What if…?'"

"But it is you, Satan, who inspires this twisted thinking. You foster the belief that the end justifies the means. You induce people to believe that black is white – not all at once, mind you, but in ever so subtle and imperceptible movement of advancing slightly darker shades of gray."

"I cannot deny it," Satan replied, again reinforcing his obligation to tell the truth. "It is who I am fueled by both hatred of God and his inferior human creation which I see as leading to my downfall. I seek only revenge by convincing you despicable creatures to disregard His ultimate plan for you. I might add, Bruce that from the number of you that tumble over the edge of my abyss every minute of the day, I and mine are excellent at convincing you fools to turn your backs on God who made you; and, incidentally, Bruce, you did not answer my question."

"Once again, I was tempted to get into a heated discussion with Satan but after getting a drink of water from the kitchen, I thought better of it. Let me think about it for a while, I replied – then added, getting back to Isaac and the trip to Moriah, what did you see happen?"

"Just about as the 22nd chapter of Genesis tells it," he answered. "Refusing help, Abraham gathered the wood himself, and loaded it on the back of a donkey. He took two servants along and together they made the three-day trip to the foot of Mount Moriah. Along the way it bothered Abraham as well as me that the promise of continued progeny amounting to countless descendants, and the death of Isaac as a burnt offering, were not compatible unless Sarah were to give birth again when she is now over one hundred years old! Why, however, would God do such a thing since Isaac was every bit the fine specimen of a man as was Abraham, his father?

"Before going to sleep the night before he was to sacrifice his son, Abraham observed Isaac in the peaceful, deep sleep of the young. Turning away, he knelt down and bent over until his forehead rested on the ground. I listened to him pray amid his sobbing."

"My Lord and my God, you know all things – past, present and future. As such, you know that without hesitation I, your servant, Abraham, has reverenced and served you since that day decades ago when you first spoke to me by my barns in Haran. There remains nothing undone for which you have charged me, except to sacrifice my loving son, Isaac, whom I will kill and offer to you as I have done so many times in the past with the choicest creatures with which you have blessed me. Although in the past I have wondered how I would father a great nation without a son born of my wife, I never questioned your ability to do so.

"Now I know that the miraculous birth of Isaac is the answer to my wonder. Tomorrow, Lord, I will load the wood on Isaac's back, and leaving the two servants with the donkey, we will climb Mt. Moriah. When there I will tell Isaac, as he is bound to ask, that you wish him to take the place of the lamb. I will bind him to the altar, kill my only son and set the torch to him as an offering to prove that I revere you above all others. While the embers are still glowing, I will return to Sarah, his mother, and tell her what I have done to her son. Please, dear Lord, give me the strength to do this and bless Sarah and me as we endeavor to endure. Amen."

"Soon thereafter, Abraham tried to sleep, but was not too successful. He tossed and turned for most of the night and for a time I heard him weeping. As night wore on, I concluded that God would not allow Isaac to die. God's desire that Abraham sacrifice Isaac was a mandate subject to the will of Abraham. Abraham did have a choice; but the progeny promised to Abraham was the basis of a covenant that God confirmed by a solemn promise and Abraham endorsed with the blood of his circumcision. This sacrifice, if it occurred, would ensure that the Covenant was no longer even a prospect."

"What do you think about this, Bruce? Do you have an opinion?" Satan asked.

"I had to ask him to repeat the question as I was still thinking about the last part of Abraham's prayer where he brings Sarah into the setting. She was never part of the biblical narrative, and thus as it is often said, out of sight – out of mind, but it must have been excruciating for Abraham to think about telling his wife and Isaac's mother why she would never see her son again.

"I think I can answer your previous question by giving you the opinion you just requested," I said. "There is no doubt that God considers the killing of one human being by another an especially heinous sin. To kill another human being in His name makes it even worse – without a doubt a grievous abomination that if the perpetrator dies confirmed in his or her righteousness for the deed, and therefore, without seeking forgiveness, he or she is doomed to eternal damnation! You know this, Satan, as these self-righteous fanatics you stated represented a number paying the infinite price in your hell-fired chambers.

"Satan closed his eyes as he nodded in the affirmative. Then, thinking he might be too close to revealing what he was forbidden to do, added, 'Bruce, you know I cannot mention any particulars in this regard.'

"In return I nodded to Satan somewhat apologetically." Then I said, "You asked me if I had an opinion on this. I do. It is this: The Canaanites, into whose land God had brought Abraham and wherein he established his Covenant with him, practiced human sacrifice. Realizing the weakness of some men, God was showing Abraham, and by the retelling of the event to future generations, the horror of such a practice, so that it would never become a way of worship for the people of the Covenant."

"Perhaps you are correct, Bruce. I must admit that as much as I tried to get many fanatical Israelites to establish the rite of taking prisoners and formally sacrificing them to God, I was never successful. At the behest of God, they had no problem slaughtering the pagan men, women, children and even the animals of the Canaanites, the Amalekites and pagans like them, but they never sanctioned sacrificing a human being on an altar."

"Just so," I agreed. "So, what happened in the morning?"

"Abraham arose early since he had not slept much at all during the night. He used the fire in the pot to cook them all a fine breakfast, although Abraham did not eat much. After their meal, leaving the two servants with the donkey, he and Isaac with the wood strapped to his back, climbed until God told Abraham to stop. There, Abraham asked Isaac to gather rocks for the altar. When they had built it, Isaac repeated the question he had asked his father while climbing. 'We have the wood, the fire, and now the altar; but where is the lamb for the burnt offering?'

"Abraham asked his son to stretch forth his hands together in front of him. As he did, Abraham tied them together and said, 'The Lord does not wish a lamb for this occasion, my son. He has asked that you take the place of the lamb here on Mount Moriah.'

"When he finished talking, he bound Isaac's ankles together and picking him up he cradled his young son in his arms and kissed him on the forehead before gently placing him on the kindling that covered the top of the altar. He then looked down into the resigned face of Isaac who smiled at his father as if to say that he bore him no grudge. Abraham looked up in the hope of receiving a reprieve, but when none was forthcoming, he told God that he was going to plunge the knife into Isaac's heart, as he could not bear to slit the throat of the son he loved while he was alive. He raised the knife and as he plunged it downward, he was startled by a voice and a powerful grip around his wrist that fixed the point of the blade just above Isaac's chest.

'Abraham, Abraham!'

"He answered as he had many times before, 'Here I am.'

"The voice was that of God; a voice he knew quite well. 'Do not lay your hand on the boy or do anything to harm him; for now I know that you fear God, since you have not withheld your son, your only son from Me.' (Genesis 22:12)

"Abraham, now overcome with joy, released Isaac and pointed to a ram caught by his horns in a bush nearby. Isaac brought the ram to his father who tied it down on the altar prepared for Isaac; slit its throat and when the blood had drained, offered it as a burnt offering in thanksgiving to God.

"On the way down from the mountain, God spoke again to Abraham and this time also so that Isaac could hear. 'By Myself I have sworn that because you have done this and have not withheld your son, your only son, I will indeed bless you, and I will make your offspring as numerous as the stars of Heaven and the sand of the seashore. Your offspring shall possess the gates of their enemies, and by your offspring shall all the nations of the earth gain blessing for themselves, because you have obeyed my voice.'" (Genesis 22:16-18)

"As Satan refilled his coffee cup he remarked, 'God chose Abraham, the only man since Noah and his family, to be among the first of his human creation to recognize and worship him and only him. Moreover, Abraham was obedient, for which God rewarded him with great blessings, the greatest of which was being the person by whom God founded the Nation of Israel. Sarah died at age 127 leaving Abraham to live as a widower until he married Keturah who bore him six sons and cared for him in his last years. Father Abraham, a title by which he is still called some 4,000 years later, passed away shortly after his 175th birthday.'"

"For one hundred years, try as I might, I could never get him to veer from the narrow path. God chose Abraham, an atheist at the time; and asked him to trust him. Abraham, for his part, was obedient, eventually coming to know God and put his trust in him. Obedience and trust culminating in love characterizes a person who has a strong relationship with God. For those who live by this creed, I am all but powerless against them. For those who do not, well, Bruce, like the fly in Mary Hewitt's poem, they live their lives along the edge of the chasm of Hell traveling in ever decreasing circles."

"Once again, Satan, you are giving armor to those you say you hate; to humanity whom you treat as the enemy.

"Why are you doing this? I know that you referenced the ten-foot bowling alley, but is that enough reason to arm your adversary?"

"You are familiar with the biblical narrative of Esau and Jacob, the sons of Isaac?"

"Of course – Esau traded his birthright as the first-born son to his brother, Jacob, for a bowl of porridge."

"There you have it, Bruce. Armor is of no use to those who refuses to wear it; and those who are willing to trade their salvation birthright for what amounts to a bowl of porridge are not interested in wearing the armor of God. Too late, they come to realize the truth of the maxim, 'You can't take it with you.' Therefore, when I say that the majority of you are stupid; how can you fault me? How can you say that I am wrong?"

CHAPTER SIXTEEN

Unfathomable Mercy
and Blind Justice

"To preclude me from responding, Satan asked me a second question."

"Speaking of armor, didn't you write a paper on Matthew 7:13-14?"

"Are you talking about the one that uses the sportswriter analogy?"

"Yes, that's the one. It begins by quoting Jesus' shocking remark about the number of those who are saved versus the number who are on the wide road to eternal destruction. It's in that notebook folder with the others we talked about. Let's get it out. I believe it will enhance our discussion."

"As I handed him the paper Satan said, 'Another A+ paper with a B+ grade!' Then he read it aloud."

ATHEISM – THE BELIEF OF FOOLS

"Enter through the narrow gate; for the gate is wide and the road is broad that leads to destruction, and many there are who find it. For the gate is small and the way is narrow that leads to eternal life, and few there are who find it." (Matthew 7:13-14)

Traveling on the broad road are many who strew your path with apparently good but deceitful things, which by so choosing you erect a barricade on your path to God: while on the narrow road, there is little room for such people and their deceitful ways. If you would save your soul avoid the choices in life that place barriers between you and God, for by so doing you remove the armor of Divine Grace while you stride blissfully along without protection amid the shadows and dark perils of the Godless world in which you have chosen to abide. Occasionally something happens which causes you to break stride. It is God trying to get your attention.

In this world, while you are alive, the Will of God runs on the wheels of unfathomable mercy; but in the next, after you pass on, those wheels come to a grinding halt, as you now stand before God in judgment which runs on wheels of blind justice. Even if you can't see it or don't believe it, God loves you and therefore, will do anything while you are breathing in this world, to save you, including permitting evil men to torture and crucify Jesus, His only Son.

One of the worst sufferings of the damned is knowing that despite God doing all he could to save you, you ignored his efforts or worse held him in contempt; and thus, your eternal plight is not the result of an unloving or unmerciful God, but of you, yourself, who lived all your life refusing to open the door when he stood there knocking.

"By living this way, you are wagering eternity against at most one hundred years of earthly life. A Monday morning sportswriter would label it a horrible call; but wait – if you can read this then you're still in the game. The final whistle has not yet blown. You don't have to make those horrible calls. Ask God for his forgiveness. Make a firm purpose of amendment while resolving to make restitution to those your sins may have hurt. Then get back in the huddle and vow to call better plays as you thank God for this chance to save your game.

/s/Bruce McPherson

May 4, 2003

"When he finished reading, Satan handed the paper back to me and asked, 'Are you still as pleased with it today as when you wrote it?'

"I think so," I replied. "I might change a word or two, but otherwise it states plainly the thought I wanted to convey."

"You're much too modest, Bruce. What you did was to very success-fully flesh out the 13th and 14th verses of Matthew's seventh chapter! In other words you enhanced scripture by humanizing it with word pictures; and by so doing you made it not only easier to understand but just as important, easier to remember. Teachers who know their craft are conscious of this technique. You are a good teacher and it shows in your writings, Bruce.

"It might interest you to know that most people are shocked the first time they read these words in Matthew. In fact, I can tell you that the majority of people read it a second time to make sure they read it right the first time!"

"Why is that?" I asked. "It seems plain to me."

"Because they harbor the belief that only mass murderers, war mongers, child molesters, serial killers, hit men, terrorists, and so forth end up in Hell: and in truth most of them do. They are doomed to perdition as is anyone who dies in his sins without seeking forgiveness. People whose lives consist of these behaviors check into my abode for a never-ending stay; but they're far from being the only types that endure my frightfully inhumane hospitality."

"And what are those types?" I asked. Then added, "I said types, not individuals."

"I heard you, Bruce. Not necessarily in order these constitute a great percentage of lost souls tumbling over the abyss at the end of the wide road:

"RELIGIOUS HYPOCRITES: Those who preach the Word of God, collect money for doing so, and then lead sinful lives supported by the donations of people they have duped. Many of the Scribes and Pharisees of Jesus' time fit this mold. In the modern world a fair number of the men of the cloth have replaced the Scribes and Pharisees.

"FALSE PROPHETS: Those who corrupt the scriptures by altering the wording for their own purpose; those who write books that purport to tell the reader not what Jesus said, but what he meant, as if Jesus spoke in code or the author was privileged to read the Mind of God.

Those who deny the obvious meaning of scripture by round about and convoluted interpretations, thereby misleading others through salvific error and possible condemnation are among my favorites; for the last words they hear are, 'I never knew you. Away from me, you evildoers!' Then they are mine – all mine!

"RELIGIOUS COWARDS: Those who glory in teaching only what people want to hear, that is, effort-free salvation. Those who teach of God's love and mercy, but completely ignore God's justice; those who teach that I, Satan, do not exist; those whose teachings completely ignore the four last things; Death, Judgment, Heaven, or Hell. Finally, those who teach that Jesus was a great prophet, but still only a man when in truth on several occasions he claimed to be God, and in fact, never claimed to be a prophet.

"IRRESPONSIBLE PARENTS: Those who sire or bear children and then refuse to nurture, support or educate them. In doing so they abandon their offspring to the street where, without restraint, my minions entice them to take up the evil ways of the Wide Road."

"'… entice them to take up the evil ways of the Wide Road.' It seems to me that you are criticizing these errant parents for doing something that you and yours are enjoined to make even worse! Many of these children are the result of your temptations of the poverty stricken for illicit sex, and then when they come into the world you lead them along the wide road to eternal destruction!"

"Correct, Bruce. You are absolutely and without any doubt whatsoever correct. I cannot say it any stronger. Before you criticize me and mine, however, you must not forget that we are not struggling like humankind using the principles of the Sermon on the Mount and the Golden Rule to help each other. Rather, we are the condemned who no longer have the capacity to love, care for, or offer help to another. We can only hate, despise, and loathe, and this includes the feeling we have for God, for his human creation and for each other. Whatever I say or do in your presence, Bruce, has only one purpose; namely, to get the conflict back to the metaphorical sixty-foot alley – and that only with the hope to preclude another Divine reset."

"I shook my head as I listened to Satan define himself and the fiends with him. It brought back something my mother (God rest her soul) taught me, 'Never confuse manners with virtue,' she said. 'Remember, an evil person, no matter how charming, is not your friend.' I can't remember why or under what circumstances she said it, but I am glad she did."

CHAPTER SEVENTEEN

Old Testament Figures

"I am getting a little hungry," Satan said. "Mind if I take a pear from that fruit bowl?"

"No," I replied. "Take all the fruit you want. There is more in the refrigerator."

Before taking a second bite, he said, "We spent an inordinate amount of time on Abraham primarily because he was the beginning of the story of the Chosen People of God, and as we'll see later all those who wish to serve God. Now, however, we'll just mention a person or two in the Old Testament with a few of the major contributions each made.

"Jacob, on whom Isaac conferred the birthright, had twelve sons who figured in scripture. The sons were by two different wives, Leah and Rachel, who were sisters. Rachel, his second wife, bore him his youngest sons, Joseph and Benjamin, whom Jacob favored – probably because she was his choice when the girl's father used deception to convince Jacob that he had to marry his older daughter. Care to continue from here?"

Surprised at his question I told him that I believe I could – probably not as well as someone who was there, but I could summarize.

"That's all we need," he said.

"Joseph's older brothers, jealous of their father's favoritism, sold Joseph to an Egyptian as a slave. Knowing that they could not tell their father, Jacob, the truth, they soaked his coat in animal blood and told their father that he had been attacked and killed by a wild beast. Jacob was overwhelmed with grief, but eventually accepted it as truth.

"Joseph, who was exceptionally handsome, was approached sexually by the wife of his master. When he rejected her advances she lied, saying that Joseph had accosted her whereupon she refused his advances. Joseph was put in prison.

"Meanwhile, Pharaoh had a recurrent dream that he felt was sending him an ominous message, but none of his advisors could tell him what it meant.

"A servant of the Pharaoh told him that he had a dream while in prison."

"While there," he said, "I met another prisoner by the name of Joseph. I told him about the dream I had and without hesitation he not only told me what it meant but when it would happen. It came true just as he said it would."

"Hearing this, Pharaoh sent for Joseph. Pharaoh told him that the dream consisted of seven fat and healthy cattle that came out of the river to feed on the grass. While they were grazing seven lean and sickly cattle did the same except that instead of grazing, they ate the seven healthy cattle.

"Joseph told Pharaoh that the dream meant that Egypt would have seven bountiful harvest years followed by seven years of abject famine. Upon hearing this, Pharaoh made Joseph vizier in charge of storing up grain during the seven good years and said that Joseph was to be obeyed in everything because he was now second only to himself as the authority in Egypt.

"When the seven years of famine began not only in Egypt, but in the surrounding countries people came to Egypt to buy grain. Among them were Joseph's brothers whom Joseph recognized. He treated them harshly before telling them who he was and that he forgave them for their treatment of him. They returned to Jacob and told him that Joseph was alive. When Jacob embraced Joseph, he wept, for it had been twenty years since he had seen him."

CHAPTER EIGHTEEN

"This was the sorry plight of the Israelites for many generations."

"This was the beginning of the Israelites, God's Chosen People, living in Egypt. The offspring of the twelve sons of Jacob formed the twelve tribes of Israel who prospered until their ever-increasing numbers alarmed the Egyptians who decided to enslave them and limit their newborn male population before their numbers overran the country.

"This was the sorry plight of the Israelites for many generations until God rose up Moses, for whom it can be said God arranged for his education to be provided by the assets of Pharaoh within the walls of his palace. From early on Moses' playmate was the eldest son of Pharaoh. As they matured, they became best friends.

"Moses however struck and killed a guard who had used a whip on a slave, and was forced to leave Egypt for this was a capital offense. Years later as he was tending his flock God spoke to him from the center of a burning bush that was not being consumed by the fire. When Moses asked who was speaking to him the voice said, 'I AM THAT I AM: thus shall you tell the children of Israel, I AM has sent me to you.'"

"As I paused to get a drink of water, Satan asked, 'If you were Moses, Bruce, what would you have understood by that response?'"

"I took time to think of how to reply while forcing several swallows I didn't need. As I did so I uttered a breathless prayer for guidance. Then, it came to me as clear as if it were written on the wall. Existence;"

I said, turning to look at Satan. "God was telling Moses that being totally independent he had no beginning and having no beginning he was the prime mover of everything else that exists. As such he was Almighty God and there is no other."

"Satan nodded in the affirmative, but said nothing. I continued.

"We are all familiar with Moses' request that became demands. Pharaoh, who had inherited the throne, was the man with whom Moses had been raised in the palace. Being a pagan, he had no idea of whom Moses was supposedly quoting when he said, 'Let my people go!' When Pharaoh refused God sent the ten plagues, the last of which cost Pharaoh his young son who being the first born was next in line for the throne.

"Everyone is familiar with the parting of the Red Sea, the desolation of Pharaoh's army, the Ten Commandments, the forty years of wandering in the desert, the battles they fought with pagan armies, the death of Moses and how his successor, Joshua, took them into the Promised Land by conquering many of the pagan inhabitants."

"Moses had a challenging time with the people he led out of slavery," Satan remarked. It is difficult for anyone to believe that people could resort to worshipping a golden calf after what they saw of the plagues in Egypt and the water and manna with which God sustained them in the desert.

"However, many of the Israelites were resentful of the authoritarian manner in which Moses conducted himself; and after Moses had left to climb Mt. Sinai, we demons had no problem tempting them to think seriously about rebelling against both what they considered Moses' tyranny and his belief in an unseen God; a belief which they felt was responsible for his oppression.

"The longer Moses was gone the more time we had to stir up their anger; and that rising anger fostered a feeling of entitled vengeance that demanded retaliation."

"What better way to infuriate Moses," someone cried out, "than for him to see that we are now free of his tyranny by replacing his invisible God with the veneration of a visible one?"

"Moses has been gone for nearly three weeks," someone said, "What if he doesn't return?"

"All the better!" shouted another and they went to the tent of Aaron, the High Priest, who was Moses' brother, and forced him under pain of death to fashion a calf which they covered with gold leaf obtained from melting down their jewelry, their wedding bands and even sacred vessels. The celebration of their newfound freedom called for copious quantities of wine. All thought of work and responsibility was forgotten in the drunkenness and debauchery that consumed their days and nights."

"And you reveled in this seeming victory? You must have known that in the end Moses' Invisible God would have His way."

"Of course, Bruce; only most of you creatures of the flesh are so stupid as to think a creature can totally best the Creator. We condemned know better. Our goal is to gain what is possible – a partial victory.

"Eventually Moses returned having received God's moral code – the Ten Commandments. He was infuriated at what he saw and separated the people – those who would repent and follow him as the leader appointed by God and those who sought to continue in rebellion.

"The rebellious gathered their families along with their household items and moved defiantly to one side. Moses then said that if any of them had a final change of heart they were free to cross back. None did.

"A massively wide fissure then abruptly opened up into which the dissenting men, along with their families, their animals and their household goods were swallowed up. The screams, earsplitting at first, became less so as they fell further down the depth of the fissure. When the screaming ceased the earth began to rumble as the fissure closed with a roaring thud that shook the very foundation of Mount Sinai. After hearing the screams of people they knew, accompanied by the concussion of the closure, outright rebellion against Moses was impossible for us to instigate."

"You saw this?" I asked.

"Didn't I mention earlier that you don't have to read scripture if you've witnessed the event? God would seem to have chosen this incident to more than adequately demonstrate that he condemns no one to eternal damnation. You fleshy creatures, using your own free wills choose to condemn yourselves even as God is doing all he can by giving you multiple chances to preclude you from committing spiritual suicide."

"When I failed to respond Satan said, 'Every one of age that was swallowed up in that crevice is mine, Bruce – all mine. They are the spoils that prove my partial victory. No one forced them. They did it to themselves. That happened more than four thousand years ago and to this day they remain mine – not only then, Bruce, but for eternity, a period that after four thousand years begins as it always will with the next day being another succession of Day Ones, for in eternity there is never a Day Two, a Day Three, or more.'"

"Don't judge them too harshly, however, for it is difficult for human beings to know or love a God without an image; a God who presents nothing with which to utilize their senses; for you creatures of flesh have not one but five of them. The Jews of the Old Testament did not love God. They feared him. It is true that they acknowledged him as their Creator, but to them God was the Great Unseen Epitome of Wrath that punished them for breaking even one of hundreds of mostly obscure laws. After receiving the Ten Commandments they understood obedience as a factor in their relationship to God; however, love and trust were rarely a part of their religious dynamic.

"In fact, most believed that experiencing fortune or misfortune in their lives was the result of appeasing or provoking the Wrath of God.

"And as we said earlier, Bruce, the only Israelites who had any contact with God were the prophets; and this contact was never directly visual, but solely through voice or other worldly images such as a bush that is burning but not consumed, or a raging pillar of fire. God spoke to them and only to them in the manner he did with Abraham and Moses. The only Divine Reality even to the Old Testament prophets was of an Omnipotent Disembodied Voice – a concept that prompted respect, obedience and fear – but not love.

"This was the principal reason why, except for a chosen few, the Israelites didn't recognize Jesus as God Incarnate even when he told them he was. This concept was so far removed from what they believed about God that even his miracles that instantly healed the incurable failed to penetrate the hardened beliefs they had ingrained in them from early childhood.

CHAPTER NINETEEN

Hope for a Messianic Warrior Ensured Rejection of God Incarnate

"To the Jew of Jesus' time the promised Messiah could never be Yahweh Incarnated: in fact, this concept would never enter their mind even as a fantasy. Their hoped-for belief was for a human being like themselves to whom God would bestow magnificent powers with which he would free them from the bondage of Rome – a warrior, Bruce – another King David! When Jesus revealed himself to the scribes and Pharisees by saying, 'before Abraham was, I AM' (John 8:58) they accused him of blasphemy. This happened every time Jesus said or intimated that he was God or equal to God – the last time standing before Caiaphas when the High Priest asked him, 'I adjure you by the living God are you the Christ, the Son of the living God?'"

Jesus answered, "Thou hast said it…" (Matthew 26:64)

"When Satan paused, I waited for the other shoe to drop; that is, for him to finish up with slanderous remarks about the stupidity of human beings or how many of us were masochistically hurrying ourselves at full speed along the road to perdition – but it never came. Instead, he took a linen handkerchief from his inside breast pocket and wiped his brow. He did it so naturally that I had to remind myself that the corporeal-like presence with whom I was speaking was not human, that is, was not as created by God, but rather a mirage, as Satan said, so that I would not be forced to conduct this discussion with a disembodied voice.

"I had to admit that even in the halls of academia I had never experienced anyone who had such a complete and detailed knowledge of his subject matter. Then I remembered what he said about the mind of St. Augustine and how his thoughts were not limited to the surface, but penetrated deeply so as to see what most others did not. If I had to express this, I would say that such minds knew not only what happened but could surmise why and how it happened. This was the mind, unencumbered with brain matter that God had created for Lucifer, His Light Bearer; and as Satan reiterated, 'Once God gifts you, he never takes it back;' thus, Jesus' remark about sifting Peter (and by inclusion all of us) as wheat. I immediately thanked God for the Incarnation – God's way of equalizing, perhaps with our cooperation even lessening the power of Satan who is constantly seeking to overcome our human limitations.

"Of course, I also knew that he was not deducing, speculating or theorizing as someone born in the twenty-first century would be forced to do while researching numerous sources for information. Satan was speaking from firsthand knowledge – he was there when it happened! Suddenly I knew for sure what he meant when he said, "I can give you material for a book that will be read eagerly by thousands – maybe millions."

"Satan poured himself another cup of black coffee after which he took a second pear from the bowl on the table. As he took a bite of the pear and sipped the hot coffee, I thought what a waste he was. God had said that he wanted Satan's help for His human creation. Satan refused and instead became mankind's greatest obstacle in achieving God's plan. If Satan had cooperated with God, I wondered how the history of the world would have changed for the better. If Lucifer, the Light Bearer, along with the angels lost with him were prompting men and women to do good and avoid evil, instead of doing their best to accomplish the reverse, I have to believe that we would all be living closer to peace and harmony instead of the wars, dissension and discord that are the basis of much of the world in which we live.

After finishing the last of the pear Satan said, "We're supposed to be having a discussion, Bruce. Care to share what you are mulling over in your mind?"

"Not really," I answered. However, I do have some additional thoughts on what you were saying."

"I expected as much. Let's hear it."

"You spoke about the problem of loving a God that has no image; that is, when God is rarely manifested and even then only by a disembodied voice; and finally, only to a miniscule, chosen few. And you are correct.

"In the Old Testament, after the Ark of the Covenant was hidden, destroyed or carried off as a result of the Babylonians plundering and then destroying Solomon's Temple, the room designated as the Holy of Holies in which the Ark had resided was duplicated in the rebuilt second Temple. However, It was completely bare except for a table and several implements for the burning of incense.

"It was a room in Herod's Jerusalem Temple where only the High Priest could enter, and then only once a year on the Day of Atonement. It was revered as God's dwelling place on earth. Behind the heavy veil was a square, silent, nearly empty room: again, nothing to which mankind's senses could emotionally or intellectually respond.

"True knowledge of God as a Spirit," I continued, " would not be possible except that it be known through Divine Revelation. Even then, that Divine Intervention would have to be something that would stimulate one or more of our senses. In Old Testament times God chose to reveal himself to us through the auditory canal – the disembodied voice, and on rare occasions through a visit by an angel as witnessed by Isaiah and Jeremiah when God chose them to be prophets; to Daniel as the Babylonian captivity was coming to a close, and to Mary at the Annunciation."

"The exception being divinely infused knowledge," Satan responded. "Do you believe in such a thing?"

"With human beings, it occurs only on extremely rare occasions."

"Can you give me an example of such an occurrence?"

"In the Old Testament, I am tempted to say that living in a world steeped in paganism before Abraham, both Noah and Job must have received infused knowledge concerning the existence of God."

"Very good, Bruce; I can tell you that it was that way with both of them. No doubt to keep alive some small flame of divine truth even as the rest of his human creation immersed in the ignorance of unawareness worshipped celestial objects or pagan idols."

"I can also give you two examples in the New Testament. Both of these, Satan, occurred over two thousand years ago. The first was on Pentecost with the descent of the Holy Spirit on the Apostles. Jesus told them before his Ascension to go back to Jerusalem and wait for the Holy Spirit. This they did and ten days later the Holy Spirit came down upon each of them in the midst of a strong wind and tongues of fire. The apostles were given the theological knowledge, the gift of tongues and finally the courage and the wisdom to become the most prolific missionaries in the history of the world. This could never have happened without infused knowledge. I say this because as late as Jesus' crucifixion, after spending as much as three-and-a-half years with him, they were anything but stalwart examples of knowledge, wisdom and courage."

"And the second?"

"St Paul, known as the Apostle to the Gentiles. As Saul, he was a terrorist. He had a mandate from the Sanhedrin to find and stamp out these new followers of Jesus. His father was a Roman, his mother a Jewess. He was raised as a religious Jew, and as such had no cause to know Jesus or what he taught and did. He was the leader of the Jews who stoned Stephen to death, the first Christian martyr – more than likely there were considerably more. Yet, after he was on his way to Damascus to continue his carnage, God knocked him from his horse leaving him blind and in the care of Christians for two days, God then gave him a new name, restored his sight and installed in him the knowledge, courage and zeal to convert much of the then known gentile, pagan world to Christianity.

"Any other examples?"

"Yes," I replied, as a new thought entered my mind, you and the rest of the angelic creation. You said it yourself, Satan. 'At the time of its creation an angel is all that he will ever be.'"

"Outstanding, Bruce; as we said earlier, you are an excellent teacher; now we can add a good student as well. Do you have anything else you would like to add?"

"Once again, my mother's admonition came back loud and clear, 'Do not confuse good manners with virtue. An evil person, no matter how charming, is not your friend.'

"Just this," I replied. "Jesus could have used miracles to express His wrath, but He didn't. He could have struck the Pharisees dumb, or with leprosy, or killed them right on the spot, but He didn't.

"Instead, he gave mobility and agility to the crippled, sight to the blind, hearing to the deaf, healthy flesh to the leper and life to the dead – all undeniable acts of love.

"Yes, every miracle, Satan, without exception was an expression of love from a man. Yes, a man but more than a man. At the moment Mary, the woman who was to become his mother said to the angel, Gabriel, 'Be it done unto me according to thy word' God impregnated her.

"Jesus is, therefore, distinct in that he is God-Man. His mother is human; but his father is Divine. As God-Man Jesus is revealing himself in a way that our humanity can recognize him by becoming one of us and by becoming one of us God is an image we can know and love.

"And, when you think about it, it could be no other way. The death of a common mortal man could never have redeemed mankind. It took a person with two natures, human and divine, suffering and dying as a man combined with the will of Divinity to do so. That person is the God-Man, Jesus Christ.

"And perhaps just as important His miracles were never denied by his enemies. There is no historical document of the time that proclaimed his miracles scams, hoaxes or anything but true; and if they could have, the Rabbinical establishment of the time would certainly have done so in order to further justify His crucifixion – but they did not, and for one reason – they couldn't. The people he healed were well known to the populace. People previously blind, or deaf, or crippled, or diseased, or known to be dead were walking about as if they had never been afflicted. No one but God, himself, could have performed such acts of reclamation by overruling natural law – the very definition of a miracle."

"Again, very good, Bruce; however, in addition, it is axiomatic that for an apology to be fully accepted it must come from the level of the offended. For example, if a minor child insults an adult and later on apologizes, until the child's parent apologizes to the offended adult, the rent in the relationship remains open. Likewise, the sins of humanity are an insult to God. God has been offended; therefore, God must make amends."

I thought for a moment and then responded, "The prime reason God took on human flesh, then, other than to make his presence known to our senses, was to offer a peer level apology which cleared the path for mankind's contrition to be accepted. In our example once the parent apologizes for the child, the child's apology is easily accepted. Likewise once Jesus gave his life as an apology to God the Father, mankind's' sorrow and contrition for his or her personal sin is accepted."

"When you know to what lengths God has gone to save humanity from perdition; and that most of humanity rejects His offer, Bruce, how can you not agree that the great bulk of you are stupid? To pit illicit pleasures of the flesh, criminal pursuits for money or power and defying God with atheism, relative truth, secular humanism and erroneous, false religious fanaticism leading to murder – pitting all of these and more against eternal salvation is akin to betting a pair of deuces against a royal flush. However, as evil as these people are, like St. Paul and St.

Augustine, they do have passion and strong beliefs; therefore, as God wills to intervene, they are redeemable."

"Redeemable? Does that mean that you believe some men are beyond redemption?"

"I didn't say it, Bruce – God did."

"When? How so?"

"Weil du lau bist und weder kalt noch warm, werde ich dich ausspeien aus meinem Munde."

"Revelation 3:16," I responded. 'Because you are lukewarm, and neither cold nor hot, will I vomit you out of my mouth.'"

"Two years of German in high school; three more years in college, and two years as an Intelligence Officer stationed in Wiesbaden, Germany," Satan replied.

"And before that?" I asked.

"Two years as assistant navigation officer on USS Ranger (CVA-61) followed by a year in Intelligence Training at the Naval War College, Newport, Rhode Island."

"Perhaps it would be easier to ask what you don't know about me."

Raising two fingers of his left hand, Satan replied, "Two things, Bruce. I am not privy to your innermost thoughts; and I am powerless to work your will. However, I am able to influence how and what you think, and with temptation I can attempt to manipulate you to use your will for my purposes. Notice that these are not absolutes. They are fraught with frequent failure, but when I succeed the person who has succumbed is like Mary Hewitt's stupid fly – one revolution closer to my fiery pit."

Satan then laughed as he went over to the sink and poured himself a glass of water. Walking back he said, "However, it takes more than simple logic to accept Jesus as God because the enormity of the love and ensuing humility on the part of God that such an act as the Incarnation and all that it entails is beyond natural human cognition."

CHAPTER TWENTY

Many in Authority Took Jesus to Be Only a Carpenter Turned Itinerant Preacher

"The very reason most Israelites could not accept the Divinity of Jesus," I said. "They had nothing with which to overcome centuries of alternative belief and religious practice."

"True, but what you say is not the prime reason."

"And what is that?"

"It was the authoritative manner in which Jesus' taught and performed his teachings and miracles. The religious authorities saw Jesus as a charismatic carpenter turned itinerant preacher of religious principles that they felt frequently flouted The Mosaic Law. He was without credentials in a land where men were schooled for decades before meriting to be called Rabbi, yet the common people not only conferred this honored title upon him, but called him Master as well.

"On the rare occasions when they dared question him, he made fools of them with a well-turned phrase or question. They were frustrated by his miracles of healing which caused the crowds that used to follow and emulate them, now to follow Jesus. The best retort they had was that on occasion they felt he unlawfully performed miracles of healing on the Sabbath prompting them to say that his power to do so was demonic.

"The most emphatic was when as we said earlier, the Pharisees asked him, 'You are not yet fifty and have you seen our father, Abraham?' Jesus replied, 'Truly, truly I say to you before Abraham was I am.'

"He called them out publicly before the people by labeling them hypocrites and by comparing them to sepulchers that are beautifully white on the outside but inside are full of the corruption of dead men's bones. He accused them of living hypocritical, sinful lives and said that if they did not repent, they would die in their sins and suffer eternal damnation.

"Being God Jesus knew the extent of the collaboration the senior members of the rabbinical hierarchy had with the Romans. Caiaphas, the High Priest, lived in what today would be a multimillion-dollar mansion. Many skimmed money from the Temple contributions of people not well-off. Others took kickbacks from the defrauding money changers in exchange for looking the other way. They knew that it was only a short matter of time before Jesus' rapidly rising popularity was going to threaten their elite status and with it their access to ill-gotten funds.

"When religious or political power is threatened, you can expect retaliation. When that threat jeopardizes revenue, Bruce, you can expect that retaliation to be swift, brutal and viciously terminal."

"And the reason you know so much about this is that you and yours orchestrated it. You dangled the temptation of illicit wealth in front of them to the extent that they finally fell prey to your inducement. Am I right?"

"Only partially so; dangling wealth is not nearly as effective as dangling things that wealth can provide. In the beginning it's never much. If we keep the items small enough, we can convince many in power that they are owed for being who they are, that is, their position or for favors performed, and therefore there is nothing wrong with a little honest pilfering; however, that first offense begins the conscience numbing process.

"Conscience numbing produces a side effect called greed, which continues to grow like a cancerous tumor until the person reaches the point of no return, wherein he is living above what his honest means would allow. He feels he can't quit because his dishonesty and theft will be discovered. At that point he or she is mine – all mine."

"It appears that we have left the Old Testament before all my questions have been asked," I said. "You left out Job, Satan. We're not going to go behind the scenes to further probe the contest you had with God over what some say is the most embattled man in the history of mankind?"

"Like the Pharaohs of Egypt whose failures were never admitted or permitted to be written about, I do not care to discuss my attempt to outwardly challenge God which ended in failure. This attempt occurred many years before Abraham and the Covenant, but after Noah and the Flood. Job was an anomaly. He and a few friends were aware of and worshipped God when the world was populated with heathens and pagans who worshipped celestial bodies and figures hewn from stone or carved from wood, when they worshipped anything at all. Because of his righteousness God blessed and all but sanctified Job's every act. Just about everybody knows the story of Job. His name is frequently used as a parallel when humanity is suffering some kind of terrible affliction.

"I will admit one thing about my confrontation with God over Job. I failed, Bruce, but I became conscious of what I should have known. A human would say that he learned from that failure. Since those times, except for one other instance, my confrontations with God are brought about by finessing, tempting, and toying with the human condition; and, as the population of Hell rapidly increases, the triumph of my attempts is proven by its high rate of success."

"You said, 'except for a single instance…' Are you going to elaborate?"

"Yes, but not now. We will discuss it later in context.

"King David, Bruce; other than Moses, is the most recognized name in the Old Testament. I refer to him as God's fair-haired boy, since no matter what he did, whether good or evil turned to David's advantage.

"Saul was the first King of Israel. Until Saul, Israel had been a Theocracy; but the Israelites saw that other countries had a King and

107

they felt they were less in the eyes of other nations if they didn't have one, too. Samuel, the Israeli prophet at the time, denied their request, but they continued to clamor for a king to rule over them and finally, God told Samuel to give them their wish.

"Samuel anointed Saul at God's command, and Saul, by uniting the scattered tribes ruled for forty-two years, although most of his time was consumed with wars against kingdoms who thought to test these relative newcomers. He fought and for the most part at one time or another defeated or bested in battle the Ammonites, the Philistines, the Moabites, and the Amalekites. All of these people were pagans who occupied the land of Canaan."

"Giving irrefutable credence to the saying, 'If God is with you, who can be against you?' Even Satan gives way to the Almighty!"

"True, Bruce, but Saul's and later David's military prowess and subsequent victories were no surprise to me. If you remember God told Abraham, 'I will give the entire land of Canaan to you and your descendants where you now live as a foreigner. It will be their possession forever, and I will be their God.'" (Genesis 17:6-8)

"So, you were not surprised when Saul and David were able to defeat anyone they faced who stood in the path of Israel possessing their Promised Land?"

"Surprised? Of course not, I expected it. At the time of its creation, as I said earlier, an angel knows all it will ever know. One of those things is indelibly placed in an angel's intellect never to become unclear."

"And that is?"

"I AM THE LORD THY GOD WHO NEITHER DECEIVES NOR CAN BE DECEIVED."

CHAPTER TWENTY-ONE

"It takes a supernatural power to accept a supernatural fact."

"Now let us get back to where we left off. We were talking about what it takes in addition to logic to accept Jesus as God Incarnate. It takes a supernatural power to accept a supernatural fact," Satan continued. "That supernatural power is grace, which God gives to whomever and whenever he chooses. His principal conduit and mankind's required first source is Baptism. When a man or woman has been validly baptized, he or she has been given that initial infusion of God's grace and with it the gift of faith, that is, the ability to know and believe in God who actually cares for him or her.

"If later in life he or she acts as if that Baptism never happened, it is because that person has elected for some reason of their own or because we, the Demonic, have persuaded him or her to will not to use that grace. Their gift of faith gradually fades as they become the baptized but self-apostatized. Almost without exception, they die unrepentant. Then, they are mine – all mine – forever and forever all mine."

"You said, 'almost without exception'. Is there something that excites that exception?"

"Not something, Bruce, but rather someone who has been praying for them. Shortly before they pass away, if God chooses to answer those prayers, he grants them the grace of final repentance. If they choose to cooperate with that grace before they pass on then they have escaped my grasp and are forever never mine."

"Not wanting to respond I said, "I am going outside for some fresh air. Would you care to join me?"

"No thank you," Satan replied. "I can tolerate fresh air but I've never enjoyed it. While you are enjoying it, however, you might be thinking of what else you would like to discuss. I will do the same."

"I nodded and closed the door without giving him a verbal response.

"As I took the path that went off into the woods, I sensed a feeling of relief that for at least a short time I was free of the near-overwhelming presence of the Prince of Darkness. With his every word I came to re-alize the power and enormity of the intelligence with which God had endowed him. There is no doubt, I thought, that without the curbing presence of God in our life, Satan, almost without effort is able to sift us as wheat.

"Satan had asked me to think about what else I wanted to discuss. I didn't know for sure but I admit I was curious about a few things; for instance, when did he know without a doubt that Jesus was God Incarnate – not just the Messiah, but Almighty God as flesh and blood living among us. What is the Great Equalizer he mentions? He said he would talk further concerning The Our Father. He mentioned talking about Mary. My folder contained several treatises concerning subjects which he hadn't mentioned. Was he planning to use these?

"After thirty minutes or so

I turned back to return to the cabin taking time to put my mind at rest and pray that God would continue to be with me as my discussions with Satan continued. I had returned from Harvey O'Brien's general store at 9:00 A.M. It was now 1:00PM. I took for granted that Satan would be gone before nightfall. The thought of him remaining overnight was not a pleasant one.

"I don't know why but I felt compelled to knock before entering my own cabin. Perhaps it was because I still felt somewhat intimidated by what was happening to me. Before my raised knuckles touched the door, however, I heard him say, "Come in, Bruce. No need to knock. I know it's you." Of course you do, I thought, feeling even more foolish.

CHAPTER TWENTY-TWO

When Did Satan Know for Sure Jesus Was God Incarnate?

"Have you thought of anything you want to discuss?"

"Yes," I said. "You obviously know that Jesus is God Incarnate. I know you have alluded to this in the past; but what I would like to know is when you first knew this? Was there an instant or moment when, without any doubt, the belief was confirmed in your mind?"

"The easiest way to approach the answer to your question," he answered after a pause, "is from the beginning. As I told you earlier my minor minions are responsible for less productive areas. In the year you refer to as 7 BC (Hebrew Year 4042) the demon responsible for Galilee, reported to me that Gabriel, an Archangel, had appeared to a maiden by the name of Mary in the town of Nazareth. 'She was of childbearing age,' he said, 'and the daughter of a Jewish religious couple whose names were Ann and Joachim.'"

"As Joachim was a successful merchant, in today's vernacular they would be described as middle class. The demon told me that Gabriel had announced to Mary that she was to be the mother of the Most High, a male child to be named Jesus."

"Although she was betrothed to a local carpenter by the name of Joseph, she had not had sexual relations with him and wondered how this was possible? Gabriel told her that the Holy Spirit would come and overshadow her. She responded, 'I am the handmaid of the Lord. May it be done unto me according to thy word.' After telling her that her cousin, Elizabeth was also pregnant, Gabriel departed.

"Now, as you remember, Bruce, God had told me before my fall that he would become Incarnate. It was one of the last things he told me and I feel that this revelation was responsible for making my rebellion complete. However, I was not sure that this issue of Mary was he. I had always thought that His Incarnation would occur when Israel was free, independent and rich beyond anything surrounding nations could hope to achieve. In short, that He would come to be among the Jews, His Chosen People, when Israel was more like the age of Solomon.

"However, in 7 BC Israel was experiencing just the opposite. In 63 BC the Romans had conquered Israel and by the time of Gabriel's startling announcement the country was heavily taxed, poverty stricken, persecuted, and exasperated with trying to understand how God could allow this to happen to His Chosen People – so much so that their concept of the Messiah was someone who would release them from the shackles of Rome.

"Notwithstanding all this I decided to follow my instincts. I advised my demon to taunt Joseph with Mary's pregnancy. His kind will not have her stoned, which is his prerogative, but he will not marry a woman who is carrying someone else's child, I told him. Taunt him until he tells her he cannot marry her and will agree to put her away.

"I knew that if this child was truly God Incarnate, nothing my demon could do would thwart the Will of God; however, if he was not then all would work out as I told him.

"Soon thereafter Raphael, another archangel, appeared to Joseph and explained Mary's miraculous pregnancy, after which Joseph married her. Several months later Mary gave birth to a male child in Bethlehem. A choir of singing angels appeared to some shepherds announcing the child's birth, telling them that they would find him 'wrapped in swaddling clothes and lying in a manger.' Several wealthy men, all gentiles, bearing expensive gifts came from the East to worship him.

"To me, Bruce, it was a time of puzzling contradictions. Nothing seemed to make sense. The time was wrong. The angels made their melodious announcement not to the whole city concerning the birth of God in their midst, but to only a small band of shepherds, who at the time were generally thought of as only one step above outcasts.

"Then, a few weeks later those wealthy men I mentioned came following some errant celestial manifestation after crossing more than a thousand miles of desert to worship as they said, 'the newborn king of the Jews.' The king of the Jews at that time was Herod the Great, a sixty-seven-year-old puppet king suffering from a necrotic disease whose rule was at the mercy of Caesar Augustus, the Emperor of Rome.

"Herod was living with his tenth wife and all of his children were grown and most were plotting against each other to secure the throne upon his demise. What were these men thinking? How could God become Incarnate in such poverty and squalor? I know contradiction. It is the basis of falsehood and lies – the core of who I am. I passed off this birth as too incongruous to be the Incarnation; but I had to admit I wasn't sure. Perhaps this was the forerunner that was prophesied. Regardless, I knew that the visitation of angels was an indication of Divine intent; a sign that the child was in some way exceptional, and whose presence, therefore, was not in my best interest.

"King Herod, however, was a special ally of mine. He was the delight of every demon – a psychopath with a tendency to paranoia and the means and resources to carry out any diabolical scheme we convinced him he had a valid reason to commit. Knowing this I would use Herod to kill the child whoever he was."

"You're talking about the slaughter of the Innocents, aren't you? You had to know that just as your plan to keep Joseph and Mary apart was a dismal failure, your plan to have Jesus murdered among the young male children of Bethlehem would end in the same hopeless frustration."

"I admit that such a conclusion was a possible outcome, but not reason enough to avoid trying it. Remember, Bruce, as I mentioned earlier; one can hope for at most a partial success when attempting to thwart the will of God. This was another way of confirming my earlier conviction. If God allowed this child his parents named, Jesus, to be killed by King Herod he definitely was not God Incarnate.

"In the form of a temptation I put forward and even enlarged upon what the men from the east had told Herod, firmly setting and then magnifying the thought he feared of having his throne diverted from his blood line.

"On two different occasions he had gone to Rome and requested in person from Caesar Augustus, that his progeny succeed him. Caesar, however, upon learning that Herod had arranged for the murder of his wife and two of their teen age sons, had recently downgraded Herod's status from Friend of Caesar to Subject of Caesar, and therefore, refused to honor his request. 'Succession to the throne of the King of the Jews will be solely at the pleasure of the Emperor without consideration of consanguine right,' is the way he had it written. After Herod departed, the Emperor turned to his Chief Magistrate and said, 'Petronius, it is safer to be Herod's dog than his son!'

"You know the rest. Herod became enraged and this fired up his scheming, cruel mind to commit one of the most memorable, inhuman acts in the history of mankind. To escape Herod's murderous scheme, Joseph, warned by Raphael, took Mary and Jesus to Alexandria in Egypt where there was a large enclave of Diasporic religious Jews. This was in 6 BC. Two years later, in 4 BC, King Herod died. If you were there, you know this. If not, you have to rely on the Jewish historian, Josephus, who associates a lunar eclipse with the month and year of his death. Joseph, visited again by Raphael, who revealed Herod's death, returned his family to Nazareth. We'll go more into all this in more detail later.

"It was then I had to admit that the numerous angelic visits coupled with Herod's failure, proved to me that the child whose name is Jesus, was in fact proof that God had kept His promise; and he did it without fanfare or grand gesture. God was born of Mary not in a lavish palace with the aid of attendants in waiting, but in a cave nearly one hundred miles from her home in the presence of her husband and a couple of beasts of burden."

"And although you tried your best using the most powerfully evil man in the area, you failed in your attempt to put an end to His life – a lesson for us all: No one thwarts the Will of God!"

"Bruce, King Herod committed this abominable act to ensure his legacy. And what was Herod's legacy? Upon his death, the Roman Emperor divided his kingdom such that none of his successors would be king.

"Archelaus, a son, became ethnarch (governor) of the tetrarchy of Judea. Herod Antipas, another son, became tetrarch (ruler) of Galilee and Peraea. And Salome I, Herod's sister, was given a toparchy (minor ruling area) including the cities of Jabneh, Ashdod, and Phasaelis.

"King Herod spent over forty years rebuilding the Jewish Temple to the magnificent structure it was in Jesus' time. He built or rebuilt cities and fortified others. In other words, Herod's legacy should have been as a great architect and builder. Instead, the mention of his name brings to mind only one thing – the Bethlehem Butcher!"

"To set his failure even more firmly Satan, I have never heard of any parents naming their child Herod."

"Greed, jealousy, and envy combined with a distorted sense of entitlement, Bruce – an infallible combination for the destruction of any human being because they invariably turn their backs on God. They have discarded their spiritual armor as they proceed along the wide road. Believing that life ends with the grave they live their lives seeking to acquire the goods of the earth which 'moths and rust consume.' Much to their chagrin, their sorrow and their eternal remorse and despair, when it's too late death teaches these fools otherwise, as they stand before the judgment seat listening to their sentence of eternal damnation from the God they held in contempt."

You have to be not only the cruelest creature in the Universe, but the most merciless as well," I replied. "I know you are compelled to tell me only the truth, but your embellishments that follow your conquests are so callous, coldhearted and unsympathetic as to send my mind reeling."

"Are you telling me that Herod should have been treated better? Have you ever asked yourself why there are men who never grant mercy but when their situation is reversed feel no shame in begging for such? If this is not the definition of a coward then what is? Maybe what I am trying to do is to prove once again that I was correct in my first assessment of human behavior.

"Can you argue for, or even simply defend the stupidity of those of you who choose eternal damnation over the joy of eternal bliss? To escape my machinations all men and women have to do is live their life loving God above all others and love their neighbors as themselves! How can it be any simpler? Human beings, however, are suspicious of simplicity. If something appears too simple, he or she immediately becomes suspect; and in doing so figures ways to inject complications in the form of questions beginning with 'Why...?' thereby creating doubt – a major component of one of my most fertile means of endeavor."

"When I didn't answer Satan said, 'I paid little attention to Jesus, the child, because my demon told me that his life was nothing exceptional. As an infant he soiled his clothing. As a young boy he cut his teeth and played with his friends. As he grew, he went to school, did his chores, and learned his father's trade as a carpenter. Jesus was a loving, obedient son in the Jewish tradition."

CHAPTER TWENTY-THREE

The twelve-year-old Jesus Spars with the Sanhedrin in the Temple

"And then it happened. Every year Joseph and Mary went to Jerusalem for the Feast of the Passover. Until Jesus was nine years old, they left him with Mary's parents, Jesus' grandparents, who were now too old to make the 175-mile trip from Nazareth to Jerusalem and return. As did Joseph and Mary most people traveled in a caravan. It was safer and they were with friends and relatives who provided friendly companionship and to whom they could give or from whom they could get help as required. These trips were for the most part uneventful.

"In Jerusalem over several days' time, Passover prescribed certain rituals to be performed along with the memorial meal of lamb, prescribed vegetables, an egg, unleavened bread and bitters usually eaten with relatives who lived in the area. Elizabeth, whose son, John, would later distinguish himself as John the Baptist, was by now an old woman. Her husband, Zachariah, a Temple priest, was also advanced in years. They lived in Ain Karim, a small town southwest of Jerusalem. Mary and Joseph helped prepare the Passover meal at their home, and Jesus and John who were cousins, played together.

"Played together, that is, until they were both twelve years old. During this trip the boys who were showing signs of maturity, chose rather to glean and discuss what they discovered in Zachariah's scrolls. John showed a particular interest in the entries that prophesied the likeness or how to recognize the Messiah. He was especially fond of the writings of Isaiah. Jesus, on the other hand, was more interested in the writings of the prophet, Daniel, to whom the angel Gabriel gave the time of the arrival of the Messiah, albeit in a way that had to be correctly interpreted and mathematically computed.

"When they had rolled their scrolls, before returning them to the tubes for safe keeping, John said to Jesus, 'Mother told me about how Aunt Mary became pregnant with you. If it is true, and I can see no reason why my mother or yours would not be truthful about such a thing, then you must be the Messiah. Are you the Messiah?'

"Jesus looked John in the eye and said, 'God will reveal that to you at the proper time.'

"John paused while slowly nodding his head. 'Jesus,' He replied, 'I think that time has just come and gone.'

"Now in those days men and women traveled separately at least on the first day of the return trip. Children usually traveled with their mother until the boys reached age twelve or so when they were free to travel with whom they pleased. As might be expected most young men chose to accompany their father along with the rest of the men. This, however, was not always the case.

"So, Joseph thought Jesus had chosen to travel with and help his mother. Mary thought Jesus had expectedly chosen to travel with Joseph.

"As it happened, however, neither was correct. What actually happened, Bruce, is that Jesus intentionally slowed his pace until just before the sixth hour [noon] when he observed the last of the caravan stragglers passing him by as they traveled north.

"Jesus knew that members of the Sanhedrin and a Rabbi met each day in the Temple Courtyard to instruct the people who were encouraged to ask questions which were usually about dietary laws, the proper way to wear a prayer shawl, the rules of fasting and so forth. The average Jewish adult male of Jesus' time spent so much of his day just trying to provide for his family and pay the Roman taxes that he had little time to study or ponder theology.

"As Jesus passed through the entrance to the courtyard he heard the Rabbi, who, as he unfurled a scroll, say, 'We have been talking about how in the book of Genesis Moses speaks about Creation. We begin today with where we left off yesterday – the creation of Man. We will read from the scroll and then you may ask your questions.'

"And God said, 'Let us make man in our image, after our likeness: and let them have dominion over the fish of the sea, and over the fowl of the air, and over the cattle, and over all the earth, and over every creeping thing that creeps on the earth.'" (Genesis 1:26-28)

A man raised his hand and was recognized. "Come forth and state your name," the Rabbi said.

The man did so, saying, "My name is David Ben Ezra, and my question is how did the serpent successfully tempt Eve if God gave mankind dominion over every creeping thing that creeps on the earth?"

Turning to the youngest of the men sitting behind him the Rabbi said, "Jonathan, you are a Pharisee and the youngest member of the Sanhedrin. Would you like to answer this man's question?"

Jonathan nodded and said, "I would." Then, turning to face the man he said, "The serpent-like creature that tempted Eve was not an actual serpent, but Beelzebub, the Evil One, disguised as a serpent. We know this for a number of reasons but the most prominent is that serpents do not speak. Does this answer your question?"

The man said it did and rejoined the crowd of people whose nodding and murmuring indicated their agreement with the answer.

"Is there another question?" the Rabbi asked.

"Yes, I have one," said a young boy in the crowd as it moved aside to make a path for him. He came forward and without being asked in a voice loud enough for all to hear said, "My name is Jesus. I am twelve years old and I'm from Nazareth."

"You obviously came to Jerusalem for the Passover. Are you aware that the caravan moving north has left Jerusalem? Shouldn't you be traveling back to Nazareth with your parents?"

"It might seem that way, Rabbi, but I must be about My Father's business."

Not wishing to delay any longer the reason for his own business the Rabbi said, "Very well, young man, ask your question."

"Genesis states as you just read, Rabbi, 'Let us make man in our image, after our likeness...'"

"Yes, that is correct; and your question?"

"To whom is God speaking? Not once, but three times in a single sentence God uses plurality when making this proposal. How do we explain this apparent paradox?"

"Perhaps you have your own thoughts on this matter; if so, we would like to hear them."

"Bruce, Jesus knew that the Rabbi was surprised by his question, and therefore asked a question in return to avoid having to answer. Jesus also knew that this was a common practice in rabbinical discourse – answering questions with a question -- the reason why most difficult religious questions never arrived at a satisfactory answer.

"Even so, with respect, Jesus replied, 'Rabbi, I have only three potential answers to my question. I will present these and then would be most gratified to hear any others that you, or the learned members of the Sanhedrin, might wish to offer."

"This has got to be amusing," the Rabbi thought. "A twelve-year-old boy from Nazareth, no less, having the audacity to actually answer a theological question before learned members of the Sanhedrin!"

"Without hesitation the boy standing before him began speaking with what seemed not only to the Rabbi, but to all who could hear him in a manner that revealed a sense of unexpected competence.

"First among these is that God was speaking with companion Gods that are also capable of creation. This answer assumes the existence of more than one God – an impossible conclusion since God is the Supreme Being and Supreme denotes singularity. In addition, God defined himself as "I AM" to Moses decades before Moses wrote the book of Genesis. Having heard this and after multiple conversations with God it is not reasonable that Moses would suddenly believe that there is more than one God. Is this not so, Rabbi?"

"Yes, of course it is. Since the time of Abraham, we Israelites have worshipped only the one, true God."

"The second reason is just as absurd. It is this. Moses made a grammatical error – not once but three times in the same sentence; and even more bizarre God either missed it or let it stand. This, too, is impossible since God can neither deceive nor be deceived. Is this not also true?"

"The Rabbi did not immediately answer. He was close to shock wondering how a young boy from Nazareth could be so well indoctrinated in the scriptures. Even boys his age who lived in Jerusalem and who had the advantage of a Temple education seldom knew as much, or if they did, could express what they knew as well as this young Nazarene.

"Not hearing a response, Jesus repeated His question. 'This too is impossible since God can neither deceive nor be deceived. Rabbi is this not also true?'"

"Yes...ah yes, it most certainly is," the Rabbi finally stated.

"Then I find only one other possibility," Jesus continued, "and it is this. The statement is in the form of a proposal. A proposal implies that there is someone to whom it is offered; and that this person will hear it and answer. On the other hand, the prophet Isaiah states, 'Who hath directed the Spirit of Jehovah, or being his counselor hath taught him? With whom did God take counsel, and who instructed him, and taught him in the path of justice? Who taught him knowledge, and showed him the way of understanding?' (Isaiah 40:13-14) Isaiah finishes by saying, 'To whom then will ye liken God? Or what likeness will ye compare unto him?' (Isaiah 40:18)

"Isaiah leaves his questions unanswered since to answer, 'No one', would be redundant to people who worshipped God as the Supreme Being.

"Therefore, there being only One God," Jesus continued, "and that the statement, being a proposal, demands there be a recipient to make sense, then excluding a companion God or Gods, and barring the possibility of a grammatical error; that recipient must be one or more persons equal to and consubstantial with the One God. God was conferring with another person within himself. How many persons there are in God he will reveal in His own time. I know this explanation is shocking to the Sanhedrin, but if the learned body has another explanation, we would be privileged to hear it."

"The Rabbi turned to the members of the Sanhedrin sitting behind him as in unison they shook their heads as they lowered their gaze. 'We are most appreciative of your insight, young man, but have agreed that the subject requires further study. As you must know the idea of God being more than one person is foreign within the concept of God as he has been revealed to the nation of Israel.'"

"Although logically your explanation makes sense; nevertheless, we find nowhere in the statements of Abraham, Isaac, Jacob, Moses or the prophets who succeeded them that God is more than One Person.

"Do you have another question?"

"Wait!" the long, white bearded, eldest member of the Sanhedrin said, as rising from his seat and using his cane he toddled forward to face Jesus. "No one listening to you, young man, can deny that your knowledge of the scriptures is far above what one would expect from a boy your age. You are obviously being tutored by a very learned man. Can you tell us the name of this person?"

"All I know I learned from my Father," Jesus replied.

"Is your father in Nazareth?"

"My Father is in Heaven," Jesus answered.

"Heaven!" The old man exclaimed. "You believe your Father is in Heaven?"

"I not only believe it; I know it," Jesus replied: then added, "Correct me if I am wrong, sir, but the reason for your astonishment at my confidence is that as a non-pharisaical member of the Sanhedrin; that is a Sadducee, you either do not believe in life after death or you say you cannot say it is so because you honor only the Torah as the inspired word of God; and in the Torah there is no mention of life beyond the grave."

"The old man, waving an admonishing finger at Jesus, replied in a rising voice, 'Young man, the Torah, consisting of Genesis, Exodus, Leviticus, Numbers and Deuteronomy is the inspired, written word of God laid down by the divinely guided hand of Moses. We hold the balance of scripture as merely a historical narrative of the nation of Israel.'

"There was a man," Jesus replied, "who chose to break into and rob the homes of others as his way of supporting himself. While doing so he killed the husband, the wife and their children before stealing their possessions. He had been doing this for some time and had amassed a storehouse of stolen property.

"One day he broke into the home of a large, exceptionally strong man made so by building roads. The man overpowered him and brought him before the authorities. Having been taken into custody he was forced to reveal the location of his storehouse of stolen goods and was found guilty of both multiple murders and thefts. Sir, what judgment should be passed upon this criminal?"

"The Law states it clearly. He should be put to death."

"Whose Law?" Jesus asked.

"Roman Law," the man stated. It is the Law by which we are now forced to live."

"But has he not also broken Laws of God – Thou shalt not steal and Thou shalt not kill? And are these not found in the Torah? Is it not true, then, that if there is no afterlife then there is no judgment on the part of God? How can this be? If God issues a lawful command and those bound by it do not obey, are they not subject to consequences? Is not some type of punishment to be extracted?"

"When neither the man nor any member of the Sanhedrin answered, Jesus continued. 'Is it reasonable to think that God gave us the Ten Commandments, so stated in Exodus, only as a guide for passing laws in civilian courts? Is it reasonable to believe that God neither punishes those who violate His Commandments nor rewards those who obediently keep them? And what of those who defy the law but are never caught by the civilian authorities? If we contend that God is All-Just where is the justice in that?

"I ask you, sir, as well as the esteemed members of the Sanhedrin, is it not reasonable to believe that God who created us is in the best position to set our lives justly right?"

"Jesus paused a second time waiting for their response, but when none came, he said, 'You members of the Sanhedrin who are Sadducees have dedicated your lives to the service of God. Is it reasonable to believe that your life and that of murderers and thieves come to the same end – an end where vice is the equal of virtue?

"Finally, is it not true that by your disbelief in the afterlife you have answered the proposal by which we began this discussion? You are telling Almighty God, your Creator, that you reject being made in His Image and Likeness by deciding that you want to return the whole of you, that is, both body and soul, to the dust of the earth – that your choice and ultimate end is to be no different from the lives of the animals and lower forms of life over which he made you to rule?"

"The old man whose questions began this conversation stood staring, unblinking, silently in place as if he had been paralyzed. The Rabbi remarked, 'Shimon, sir, this boy, Jesus, has asked many questions. Do you plan to answer them?'"

"I...I don't feel very well, Rabbi. Ask the boy...if I can answer him... answer him tomorrow when I hope to feel better. "Careful," he said. "Careful with my...my left arm," he said to the Rabbi who was helping him back to where he sat down.

As Shimon sat there sweating profusely while trying to ignore the great pain in his chest and down his left arm, the Rabbi said, "We are adjourned for the day while we care for our esteemed senior member."

"As might be expected the crowd gathered around Jesus to ask him questions. 'Did your father really teach you? Tell us more about this afterlife. Will you return tomorrow to hear the Sanhedrin's senior member answer your questions?"

125

"Please," Jesus replied. "Go home and say a prayer for this cherished man; and yes, I will return tomorrow."

"Whereupon, Bruce, Jesus just seemed to vanish."

"Much as He did later on," I said, "when in Galilee they tried to throw him over the cliff after He read from the scroll and proclaimed His Divinity.

"Frankly, Satan, I didn't expect you to reveal such detail. I am astonished that you did. Is this what you meant when you stated earlier 'I am going to tell you things that no one else has ever been told. I am going to reveal to you things that even theologians don't know?'"

"Precisely, Bruce; but we have just begun. Remember, in the interest of my pledge to be truthful I am doing this for my own purpose. The number of you who find their faith stronger or who are converted by my revelations is miniscule compared to the number who would repent while newly embracing the cross should God enact or permit man to execute another reset."

"The lesser of two goods," I said, "remembering his penchant for twisting words in order to turn the truth upside down.

I was familiar with Luke's biblical account of Jesus as a boy in the Temple, but the account does not go into detail about what was said there, other than that the men of the Sanhedrin were amazed at how much a young boy knew about the scriptures. I knew that if Satan had not been truthful, he would no longer be visible so I had to believe the truth of his account of what occurred on the first day with Jesus as a twelve-year-old boy in the Temple.

I also knew that even to this day Jews do not accept the doctrine of the Trinity and I knew that the Sadducee members of the Sanhedrin did not believe in the afterlife, nor did they accept as inspired anything but the Torah, sometimes referred to as the Pentateuch, that is, the first five books of the Old Testament written by Moses.

As a high school student, when I first learned of the Sadducees' beliefs, I thought it mind-boggling that anyone would spend his life studying what he believed to be the word of God only to have it all end no differently than if he had rejected God – ending his life as Jesus said "where vice is the equal of virtue."

I remember Brother Jerome, my sophomore religion teacher, stating that if there is no afterlife then the soul of man is not immortal; and if man's soul is not immortal then upon his death the only difference between him and a fly he swatted on the wall is the volume of dust to which each body returns.

The truth, as I learned later as a university student, is that the Jews' strong belief of Jesus' time was that allegiance to Jehovah and his commandments was necessary to secure the blessings of God which guaranteed a plentiful and abundant life while living here on earth. Likewise, if a person was physically sick or impaired; if his wife was barren; if his harvests were miniscule for lack of rain; if no matter how hard he tried he seemed to be doomed to live in squalor and poverty – in short if his or her life was seen to be miserable it was because of some transgression he committed in the past or was committing at the present time. In either case it was the reason Jehovah withheld his blessings.

This is why Jesus was so hard on the religious leaders of his time. They weren't averse to helping God along with accumulating wealth by nefarious means to prove that Jehovah favored them over the ordinary Jew. In other words by putting the cart before the horse they were committing the sin of theft as well as hypocrisy which Jesus told them was going to be the cause of their damnation.

"Joseph and Mary came together at the end of the first day," Satan continued, "to eat their evening meal together with Jesus. When they found that Jesus was not traveling with either of them, they began searching for him among their friends and relatives. When it was obvious that he was not in the caravan, early the next morning they began the return trek to Jerusalem.

"Hoping that he was with Mary's cousin, Elizabeth, they went on to Ain Karim where after discovering that Jesus was not there, they spent the night. The next morning they returned to Jerusalem and began searching in the streets and among street vendors.

"In the meantime shortly before the sixth hour (noon) Jesus returned to the Temple Courtyard where he saw Shimon's empty chair draped in black.

"The Rabbi seeing Jesus said, 'Shimon died shortly after we had gotten him to his bed. A physician came by shortly thereafter and said that there was nothing anyone could do for him. Shimon will be greatly missed. As you saw yesterday, he was undaunting in expressing his beliefs.'

"Before replying Jesus turned to look for a moment at the black draped chair. Turning back he looked intently into the eyes of the Rabbi and stated, you said, 'in expressing HIS beliefs?'

Not expecting the Rabbi to reply Jesus said, "Immediately after one dies, Rabbi, a person is no longer capable of expressing a personal opinion about what is true. Whether what one professed in life was the absolute truth, a relative half-truth or blatantly wrong, the indisputable truth now shorn of any ambiguity and for better or for worse appears irrefutably clear and unmistakably eternal."

The Rabbi hesitated for a moment, once again feeling uneasy by the self-assured manner of this twelve-year-old. Upon regaining his composure, he said "It is distressing that all of us serving God in the Temple do not have an identical belief regarding something as important as what happens after death. Within the privacy of the Temple, we have our debates, but for many, no matter the rationale, nothing seems to change. It's as if at some point in early life they have been chained to a belief that they carry with them to the grave.

"I was overwhelmed with sorrow when Shimon passed away," the Rabbi continued. "Some of the things you said yesterday he has heard before in our debates; but you presented others which we never considered; or if we did, we were not able to present them as clearly as you did. It would have been interesting to hear Shimon attempt to answer you, a stranger, as he tried to defend a conviction that many of us believe is not only illogical but may even be insulting to God.

"We are about to begin our session for today. Jonathan asked me if he brought an extra chair that you might sit next to him. Evidently, you greatly impressed him yesterday."

"Is it permissible for a layman to sit with the Sanhedrin?"

"Ordinarily, no, but in speaking to the others they feel an exception is warranted in your case. Personally, I think it is a matter of curiosity. The Sanhedrin and I must admit that we remain astonished at not only your scriptural knowledge but your ability to express it. If you will accept this as a compliment as a theologian you are far above not only any twelve-year-old we have ever known; but in fact, regardless of his age, any layman we have ever met."

"Jesus smiled and nodded, but did not answer as he acknowledged Jonathan motioning toward him and proceeded to take the seat next to him."

"The Rabbi reverently announced the passing of Shimon and said that there would be no scripture reading today. People could ask any question they wished.

"After the large gathering heard that Shimon had died, which meant that they would not witness the anticipated confrontation between the boy, Jesus, and the aged, but revered senior member of the Sanhedrin, many suddenly remembered more pressing duties and left the Temple grounds.

"Those remaining asked a series of mundane questions which were easily answered by various members of the Sanhedrin. Being a guest, Jesus remained silent through it all only leaning a few times in Jonathan's direction to listen to one of his remarks.

"Eventually the Rabbi said that due to scheduled Temple duties of the Sanhedrin there was time for only one more question. A young man who appeared to be about twenty-one raised his hand.

"After being recognized by the Rabbi he walked forward and said, 'My name is David Ben Hillel. When I was a young boy, my mother read to me from the Testament. I never tired of hearing about Abraham, Jacob, Moses, the ten plagues, Joshua and how God saved Daniel from the Lions' den as well as the fiery furnace. When I was old enough to read the Scripture for myself, I found a section within Daniel that my mother had never read to me. It described Daniel being at prayer when suddenly an angel who was identified as Gabriel, appeared. The angel began to speak as if he were prophesying. When I asked my mother why she never read this to me she told me that she never understood it; and therefore, couldn't answer the questions she knew I would ask.

"What I am asking today, Rabbi, is if the learned members of the Sanhedrin would please explain the Angel Gabriel's prophesy in Daniel?"

"The Rabbi thought why do questions such as this always seem to come at the end of the discussion?

"Your question is a most worthy one," he said, "but being worthy it is also complicated and cannot be answered in the time we have remaining. If you are able to return tomorrow, I will call your name at the beginning of the session. If you are here, we will answer it."

The man, saying he would return, thanked the Rabbi, and left.

Jonathan turned to Jesus and said, "Easy enough for the Rabbi to say, but it is the Sanhedrin that will have to provide an answer."

"Is it going to be all that difficult?" Jesus asked. "It would seem to me that if God sent an angel to deliver a message it would defeat the Divine intention if the message were not readily understood."

"One would think so, but – well, are you familiar with this prophecy?"

"I AM," Jesus emphatically replied; then added, "Jonathan, the problem with a Divine prophecy is seldom with understanding it."

"It isn't?"

"No, it isn't. The problem is more often than not with accepting what it says. If the prophecy is about something that will occur in the far-off future, after the reader's time on earth, for instance, then people can accede to almost anything. The prophecy about which the young man asked concerns the time of the coming of the promised Messiah. Does it not?"

"It does; and it was made over four hundred years ago."

"Then, what is the problem? I would think men would be eager to decipher its meaning and rejoice!"

"It says more than that. It also portends the 'cutting off' or killing of the Messiah, the complete destruction of the Temple and some say the annihilation of Jerusalem and those within its walls referred to as 'the abomination.' Look at this structure, Jesus. It is the House of God! Why would Jehovah allow pagans to destroy His Chosen Peoples' center of worship?"

Jesus hesitated for a moment as he stood looking about the Temple, then turning around to look at Jonathan he answered, "Perhaps, my friend, for the same reason that God permitted the Babylonians to destroy Jerusalem and the Temple of Solomon. His people no longer worshiped God and therefore, had no need of a Temple. Even more insulting, many worshiped the idols of the Canaanites. For decades God reached out to them through the prophet Jeremiah; but they treated His prophet with scorn and humiliation.

"They continually disobeyed God's Commandments. They violated his precepts. In effect his Chosen People waved a drunken fist in the air while proclaiming 'Not thy will but ours be done. Don't tell us how to live – we have a better idea!' If people live in this manner, that is, by flaunting the Ten Commandments, then while they remain unrepentant their presence in the Temple is a desecration and sacrilege. To such men, Jonathan, the House of God is nothing more than a community gathering space. Built and designed for a Divine purpose, when men's behavior no longer honors that purpose then the structure has no reason to exist."

Jonathan was aghast after hearing the passionate intensity of Jesus' response; and began to wonder how such dynamic and succinct remarks could come from a twelve-year-old boy. Knowing this, however, he felt that Jesus' input might be of some assistance in getting a satisfactory answer for the man David. After a slight pause, Jonathan said, "Nazareth is not renowned as a place of deep theological thinking, Jesus, but you are mature and educated in the scriptures far beyond your years. So I am going to ask you a question."

When Jonathan paused without speaking further, Jesus asked, "What is your question?"

"This is how it's done here. I mean in the Sanhedrin. The High Priest is actually the senior member of the Sanhedrin, but he assigns the working of its members to one with the longest seniority. Shimon held that position until his demise. Nathaniel, a Pharisee, and a less intense man than Shimon, has been elevated to the position. Nathaniel will appoint me, whose turn it is, and two young senior students to the task of providing an answer for this man David Ben Hillel. Nathaniel will want to see our reply by the third hour (9:00 A.M.) tomorrow. If need be, Nathaniel will offer corrections and ask that it be rewritten for the sixth hour presentation."

"It sounds reasonable to me," Jesus said. "What is your question?"

"This is very sensitive, Jesus. I mean that to announce that in the future, Jerusalem, along with this magnificent Temple will be destroyed will not be easily accepted. Will you deign to help us to provide an answer that is truthful but will not raise the hair on the back of the necks of the Sanhedrin as well as the people who will hear it?"

"If you are familiar with the details of the prophecy then we may be sure that the older Sanhedrin members are even more so. This is a classic example of men ignoring an unpleasant truth hoping that by doing so it will fade away; that in the future others will have the responsibility to deal with it; or, that hoping against hope, someone with credentials will reinterpret it more to everyone's liking. I will do my best, Jonathan; but to announce that in the future God's Chosen People will force the killing of the Messiah, bringing down upon them the Wrath of God, resulting in pagans completely destroying Jerusalem while murdering its inhabitants as well as demolishing the Temple, is not something that we can just pretend Gabriel didn't prophecy."

"Before we proceed," I asked, "what is the history of the Sanhedrin? I don't remember it being mentioned during the time of Jacob, Moses or King David."

"You are correct," Satan replied," because it did not exist then. The Sanhedrin was a group of seventy-one men that had its beginning early on during the Babylonian captivity. Its original purpose was to ensure the purity of The Mosaic Law in times of captivity when Israel was under pagan influence."

"In other words to ensure dominant pagan ways didn't enter and influence Jewish dogma," I replied.

"Precisely," Satan answered.

"As Jonathan said would happen Nathanial appointed two younger men to help Jonathan provide the answer to David's question. As he expected, Nicodemus and Asher were not full-fledged members of the Sanhedrin, but senior members of a group chosen to prepare for the position. They were in their mid-twenties and having been present at yesterday's session were familiar with the twelve-year-old, Jesus, who appeared knowledgeable beyond his years. Nicodemus was especially astute and when Asher, his companion suggested that they read the prophecy, Nicodemus thought it better to go back to the basics of what God demanded of his Chosen People, and the consequences of their disobedience in this regard. Unfurling the scroll, he read the following:

Moses said to the people:
"Today I have set before you
life and prosperity, death and doom.
If you obey the commandments of the LORD, your God,
which I enjoin on you today,
loving him, and walking in his ways,
and keeping his commandments, statutes and decrees,
you will live and grow numerous,
and the LORD, your God,
will bless you in the land you are entering to occupy.
If, however, you turn away your hearts and will not listen,
but are led astray and adore and serve other gods,
I tell you now that you will certainly perish;

you will not have a long life
on the land that you are crossing the Jordan to enter and
occupy.
I call on Heaven and earth today to witness against you:
I have set before you life and death,
the blessing and the curse.
Choose life, then,
that you and your descendants may live, by loving the LORD,
your God, heeding his voice, and holding fast to him.
For that will mean life for you,
a long life for you to live on the land that the LORD swore
he would give to your fathers Abraham, Isaac and Jacob."
(Reading 1 Dt 30:15-20)

"'…are led astray and adore and serve other Gods, I tell you now
that you will certainly perish…' 'And perish our ancestors did,'" Asher
said. "Seventy years living under Babylonian idolatry. My father told
me that no doubt there were many Jews who were born, lived and died
among idol worshippers in a pagan land and to whom the former reality of Jerusalem and the magnificence of Solomon's Temple were made
possible only as an obscure image in their imagination."

"Before we go any further," Nicodemus said, "I think it pertinent
to mention something that occurred last week. My mentor, Joseph of
Arimathea, and I walked about asking people what they thought about
the promised Messiah."

"How did they respond?" Asher asked.

"The people appear to be of two minds; the first, that is, the minority
– those who have grown rich and comfortable by collaborating with the
Romans, believe that he is not a reality for the present, but rather a hope
for the far distant future. Moreover, they give the impression, without
actually saying it, that they hope this is true because presently the appearance of the Messiah would not be in their best interest.

"The vast majority, however, suffering from the financial burden and for many, the physical hardship of living under Roman bondage, place their hopes and belief that there has been no better time for the coming of the Messiah. Many believe that he is already among us waiting for the right moment, when like Gideon and Joshua he will be endowed with God-given miraculous powers with which he will triumph over the Roman oppression."

Nicodemus then chuckled as he added, "One middle aged woman, with her two grandchildren in tow, responded rather forcefully when she heard her husband faltering in his response. 'There is no doubt about it, Jacob,' she said to her husband. 'We have to drive these God be damned blaspheming Roman idolaters from the land God ceded to us by Divine Covenant!'"

Jesus smiled and then asked, "Jonathan, how would you answer this question?"

"I'm not sure, Jesus. In reading Isaiah's and others' prophecies I don't get a clear picture of the purpose of his coming. He is prophesied by Isaiah to be a miracle worker – the blind to see, the deaf to hear and the lame to walk. Micah seems to think he will be born in Bethlehem. Isaiah's prophecy that he will be born of a virgin seems a contradiction, if not an impossibility from the norm. Then there is Zachariah who says, '…behold, thy King cometh unto thee, meek, and sitting upon an ass, and a colt the foal of an ass.' The only thing I feel sure about is that despite the Grandmother's confident declaration, his purpose is not to drive the Roman idolaters from our land."

"And why is that?" Jesus asked.

"A conquering warrior does not mount an ass. Nor does he go about curing the incurable – a feat that is only possible by the power of God.

"Personally, Jesus, I think, and it is only my opinion, that the Messiah is not going to be another verse of the song we've heard before with King David, Gideon and Joshua. As The Messiah he's got to be someone above the normal man – someone whose mission has to do with teaching more about a less complicated way of life we can live to ensure our salvation rather than the transitory status of a military victory. We've had such victories in the past and Israel always seems to have slid back to sinful ways fostered by idolatry.

"It is my belief that we have to have this idea of the afterlife and its three components – judgment, eternal happiness, or eternal damnation settled by Divine decree. As you heard yesterday, Jesus, fully a half to two-thirds of the Sanhedrin are Sadducees who do not believe in the afterlife. The Sanhedrin's prime purpose is to preserve the purity of true belief. How is this possible when the Sanhedrin itself is divided on such an important issue?

"Finally, we all heard Nicodemus read Moses' declaration to our ancestors in the desert. The rewards are all about being prosperous and profitable in this life. There is not one word about reward and punishment in the next. Yet, I heard you yesterday, Jesus, by way of a parable; give a logical argument in favor of a judgment after death and its accompanying reward or punishment. In fact, I was thinking that the Messiah, himself, couldn't have said it better or more clearly."

Jesus chose not to comment on Jonathan's remark. Instead he turned to Asher and said, "Are you familiar with Jehovah's comment after the angel stayed Abraham from sacrificing Isaac?"

"I think so," Asher responded, "but I could not quote the passage verbatim."

"Please," Jesus said, "find it among the scrolls. Let us see if it might help with our discussion."

"Here it is," Asher exclaimed, holding it up dumbfounded by how quickly he found it as if it appeared miraculously in his hand.

"What does it say?" Jesus asked.

"Your offspring shall possess the gates of their enemies, and by your offspring shall all the nations of the earth gain blessing for themselves, because you have obeyed my voice." (Genesis 22:18)

"and by your offspring shall all the nations of the earth gain blessing for themselves…" After emphasizing these words of the passage, Jesus said, "In the world in which we live there are many nations. Jonathan, if you were teaching a class on the meaning of this promise by God what would you tell them?"

"Since in all my studies, Jesus, I never realized its startling implication nor did any of my tutors ever decipher such an interpretation; I would, therefore, be a poor choice to teach its meaning. However, in light of your implied discernment I would have to say that in God's own time he would make a path for the heathens, the pagans – even the abominable Romans – to find, to know and to worship Jehovah – the one and only true God. He will do this not by converting the world to Judaism, but by giving the gentiles their own path."

"In a way I agree with Jonathan," said Nicodemus. "If there is to be a judgment then justice would demand that every man and woman be aware of the laws he or she is expected to keep. The only laws the Romans seem to know and live by are 'kill or be killed, to the victor go the spoils, if you want it, take it, and obtain the desired end by any means possible.' However, if given a divine path to which they and all gentiles could agree then life should be peaceful and better for everyone.

"The fact is," he continued, "we are who we are as well as what we are, not by choice but by accident of birth. None of us chose our parents, our nationality or our concept of God, whether that concept is right or wrong. If truth be known I could just as well be standing watch on the Antonia Tower and the Roman who now does so could be sitting here with you. The only way to make it right is if all of God's human creation has the same opportunity for salvation and the means to know and follow it."

"We know, however, that God already gives every human being a conscience," replied Asher, "a guide to knowing right from wrong."

"Which is killed and therefore dormant by the time most warring pagans are ten years old," Jonathan replied.

"The three men then looked at Jesus to hear what he might wish to add. He stood, raised his arms and face to the heavens, and said something the others did not understand. He then spoke in a normal but authoritative voice, uncommon for a twelve-year-old.

"Jehovah's agreement with Abraham is a covenant which exists even to this day many generations later. This agreement states that in exchange for adoration and obedience God will grant the Israelites victory over their enemies, harmony, prosperity and a good, long life. In addition, as we have just seen, following Abraham's obedience regarding his willingness to sacrifice his only son at God's request, Jehovah extended His covenant to include all the nations of the world.

"In the interim God sent Israel prophets whose primary purpose was to keep alive the belief in the coming Messiah by revealing more and more about him even to when he will be among us as confirmed by Daniel's vision of the archangel, Gabriel, and which Daniel set down in writing."

Jesus then paused, stood and walked across the room while adjusting His yarmulke. "As we have said many times," he continued, while turning toward them, "God chose to create all men in His image and likeness. Thus, without exception, all men and all women have God's image and likeness imprinted on their immortal souls." Glancing toward Jonathan he said, "To have more than one divinely sanctioned path to salvation, as you suggest, would invite comparison and question the singularity of God's creating all men with the same means to salvation.

"However, since in other ways, primarily in culture, Jews are not gentiles and gentiles are not all alike, it is impossible without some common bond, some universally acknowledged belief appreciated and favorably acknowledged by all men for humanity to completely integrate allowing them to willingly and with anticipation tread a single spiritual path.

"The covenant given to Abraham, however, as Jonathan reminded us, applies only to life's blessings and then only to men of Jewish persuasion and even then only while they are physically alive. It says nothing about what happens to his or her immortal soul following the death of the body. Because it lacks this necessary input as it provides for all of people's physical needs it is correct as far as it goes, but in light of men's souls being immortal it does not go far enough.

"Now the only legitimate change that can be applied to a divine covenant is one of fulfillment; that is, if Jehovah, and only Jehovah, added to the purpose for the covenant's existence – which he did by extending it to apply to all men, not just the Israelites; and furthermore, as Jonathan suggested, we might expect '...to have this idea of the after-life and its three components – judgment, eternal happiness or eternal damnation settled by Divine decree.' Nothing is more important, as the power or material possessions a man achieves in his earthly life is all for naught if he achieves it at the cost of his immortal soul.

"It is reasonable to expect, therefore, that the Messiah will introduce presently unknown, but supportive teachings and revelations that will fulfill the Mosaic covenant so that in accordance with God's promise all the nations of the earth, both Jew and gentile, will forevermore have a single pathway to God's earthly blessings as well as a common road to eternal salvation that can be willingly embraced and followed by all.

"Those teachings and revelations are presently known only to Jehovah and must wait for the Messiah when God will bring them to light.

"Thus, by fulfilling our present covenant he will have made it complete; and just as when new wineskins are available we no longer use old wineskins which have served their purpose, so we will no longer use the Mosaic or old covenant when by fulfilling it Jehovah has in effect blessed us with a new covenant which will provide to all members of His human creation, Jew and gentile alike, an assured path which all men and women must follow to attain eternal salvation."

"You said 'must follow,' Jesus. Does that mean that there will be only one way and there is no other?" Nicodemus asked.

"I'm going to answer you by asking a question," Jesus answered. "If in your evening prayers tonight you ask Jehovah for guidance in deciding among several choices and by a sign you see tomorrow you know he has answered your prayer, would you then tell him, 'Thank you, Lord, but I have a better idea?' I think not, Nicodemus, or am I wrong?'"

"No, you're not wrong, Jesus."

"My father taught me that truth and reality are one," Asher added, "and nothing or no one is more real than Jehovah Who is the source of all truth. Only a fool would think that the created is wiser than the Creator by rejecting His plan for one of ours."

"Amen!" said Jonathan. "I believe it is time for the evening meal. Let us dine together and afterward we can discuss Daniel and the Gabrielian prophecy so as to have an answer tomorrow for David."

"While they are at dinner," I said, in a feeble attempt to sound witty, "I would like to discuss a few things."

"I would be disappointed if you didn't, Bruce. Proceed."

"It appears that before the night is over there is to be more dialogue between Jesus and these three; but in their conversations thus far don't they have reason to believe that Jesus is more than a twelve-year-old boy from Nazareth? Aren't they the least bit curious that he may be more than what he appears to be?"

"To use a modern word, Bruce, they are flabbergasted after hearing what Jesus just said. They have been taught from early childhood that God's covenant with Abraham is the foundation of Judaism and as such it is sacrosanct; that is, it cannot be annulled, it is impervious to destruction, and cannot in any way be changed, as it will last until the end of time. Yet, by using scripture and Jonathan's own words Jesus logically just belied this lifetime belief by telling them that it can be amended, why it must be amended and that the amendment, referred to as fulfillment, will be done by Jehovah through the efforts of the Messiah – whose coming is the most revered belief of the Chosen People of God.

"These three young men have been dialoguing with Jesus for over an hour before he mentioned the necessity of fulfilling the covenant. They liked what he had previously said. They respected him. They will accept what he last said at least as food for thought as their strong, lifelong religious beliefs confront Jesus' logic – a logic which serves as the basis of the Intelligence provided by God when he created them in His own Image.

"However, not so, their elders, for the Sanhedrin, at that time, having been in existence for more than four centuries, was an ancient, historic and traditional organization: one in which the majority of its members are egotistical, self-important and arrogant. Their word is Law among the Jews. In their closed minds there is no higher court and, therefore, no appeal from their dictates.

"They really believe that they stand as a conduit between Jehovah and all of Israel. Such men do not acknowledge, let alone accept, a suggestion that originates from outside their august body of men; for other than the prophets, if God speaks to anyone, they believe he speaks to them. This was especially true of the Sadducees who, in addition, were angry with Jesus, a young twelve-year-old without religious credentials, who made them look foolish."

"From what you just said, Satan, it sounds as if the older members, especially the Sadducees, wish Jesus would just go away!"

"They watched helplessly as they believed their most senior member was literally bewildered to where his old heart gave out in front of the people. Both he and they chose not to answer, or more than likely could not answer this young boy's questions. You ask me if they wish Jesus would just go away. Yes, Bruce, they do; and furthermore, in just a few years, as he reveals their malicious jealousy and pompous hypocrisy, they will wish he had never come – a wish I encouraged and that fathered their desire to silence him.

"For now, however, the senior members of the Sanhedrin, Pharisees and Sadducees alike, despite His thoughtful reasoning and precise verbal presentations, thought of the twelve-year-old Jesus as nothing more than an inordinately educated youth from Nazareth, a town of farmers, artisans and fishermen most of whom in regard to understanding Mosaic Law were at most barely literate.

"Observing this behavior, Bruce, I felt at the time that several years from now, even with the accomplished reality of His prophesied miracles the Jewish religious hierarchy would never accept Jesus as the Messiah, let alone God Incarnate. Jesus, truthfully proclaiming to be

God, would be accused of blasphemy; and as Gabriel prophesied to the prophet, Daniel, they would 'cut him off' by convincing their oppressive Roman idolaters to murder him by the cruel, exceedingly painful death of crucifixion."

"The irony of it all," I said, "Is that God's Chosen People for centuries looked forward to the coming of the Messiah and when he arrived, they tried to stone him, embarrass him, toss him from a hillside, chose to release a murderer from prison in his place and finally had the Romans, their hated captives, scourge and crucify him.

"I suppose you are going to tell me that you had nothing to do with this."

"On the contrary, Bruce, being bound to tell you the truth, how could I resist? These men were both conceited and self-righteous – a most fertile ground for sowing the seeds of hatred and I fully admit gleefully watching as they tended my malevolent garden removing any evidence of understanding, humility, or logic giving them full sway to grow their weeds of loathsome hatred of Jesus for revealing the iniquity and self-righteous hypocrisy they concealed under their prayer shawls."

"How did they overcome the Divine evidence of His miracles? As we said earlier, they couldn't deny that people to whom he gave sight, hearing, and the ability to walk to those crippled from accidents or birth were all around them."

"His undeniable miracles only served to increase their belief that Jesus was not of Jehovah because he performed many of them on the Sabbath using, as they said, the Demonic – my power! Of course I did nothing to discourage this blatant lie which served to fortify my belief in men's stupidity. I have no such power as anything I do that appears in any way to benefit mankind is a deception done for nefarious purposes.

"Finally, ever since Cain and Abel; even to mankind in the modern world, resentment brought about by jealousy and fortified by hatred breeds a craving for murder which they accomplished by having him crucified."

"Nothing more than I had reason to expect," I said, "as history proves, human nature prompted by your illicit temptations more often than not, falls from grace."

"It's been that way from the beginning," Satan replied. "For those who think in terms of the bottom line it is this: God became man to redeem men and women who repent the evil they've done thinking to become like God"

CHAPTER TWENTY-FOUR

"Were you a witness to Jesus' Resurrection?"

Preferring not to respond to that pithy remark I said, "I have several more questions."

"And the first one is?"

"Were you a witness to Jesus' Resurrection?"

"Bruce, I was hoping you wouldn't ask, but much to my chagrin, I must admit I was."

"And what you tell me must be the truth?"

"Either that or I must choose to forever end our discussion."

"So?"

"After three hours of hanging on that cross, Jesus, with His last breath said, 'It is finished,' then lowered His head and died. Within an hour the officer in charge of the crucifixion team came by with a heavy club and broke the legs of the two thieves who were crucified with him. When he approached Jesus, he could see that he was already dead and that Mary, His mother, with two women and a young man remained with him grieving at the foot of the cross. With tears streaming down her face, His mother turned to face him. 'He is dead,' she said, while glancing down at the club in his hand before raising her head and look- ing him straight in the eye. 'He died an hour before you arrived.' He hesitated for a moment and then turned and walked away, tossing the club aside. Approaching one of the guards who with his lance stood at parade rest he said, 'Gently, I mean very gently, pierce his heart and then we can all secure to the barracks.'"

"The guard did as he was ordered. Immediately dark clouds formed and began rolling ominously across the sky. It became as dark as the blackest night as if the sun had disappeared. Suddenly there was thunder and lightning amid strong winds followed by a torrential rainfall which soaked the hair and washed the blood from Jesus and the two men who were crucified with him. At the height of the storm there was a particularly bright, jagged, flash of lightning followed by a loud crack of thunder as the veil that hid from view the Holy of Holies in the Temple was rent asunder splitting it in half from top to bottom. This curtain or veil, as it was called, was more than forty feet high, twenty feet wide and just under four inches thick. The darkness, like a night without moon or stars, remained for the next three hours. (Matthew 27:51)

"As you might imagine, Bruce, the timing of the storm and the destruction of the Temple veil was a fearful shock to many members of the Sanhedrin. Remember, Jesus died on the eve of the Feast of Passover. The interior of the Temple was filled with Priests, Levites and Rabbis making preparations for the thousands of people who would attend Passover rituals over the weekend. Many of them with their own eyes, witnessed without visible cause, a most sacred symbol torn in half from top to bottom causing fear and trepidation as it opened for viewing that which was forbidden for them to see – the Holy of Holies – the room where they believed both day and night the Spirit of Jehovah resided in the Temple!

"When the few priests whom Caiaphas had assigned to remain on Calvary until they were sure Jesus had died, confirmed the suddenness of the raging storm upon Jesus having His side opened with the lance, many began wondering if Jesus could have been the Messiah, and looked to Caiaphas, their High Priest, to offer some explanation to overcome their fears."

"He called them together and said, 'Many of you are fearful of the timing of the storm and the destruction it caused in the Temple. We have had such storms in the past and will again. The timing of this storm was nothing more than a coincidence; and the damage to the veil was nothing more than the result of an unfortunate lightning strike. It will be repaired or replaced, as required, and the rituals and sacrifices in the Temple will proceed as they have for hundreds of generations without the evil influence and demonic disturbance of Jesus, the blasphemer. He is dead now, gone forever, and in short time the people will forget about him who, justifiably, was put to death as the demonic disciple he was.'"

"Addressing Caiaphas, Nicodemus, one of the more outspoken members, stood and said, 'With all due respect, High Priest, neither I nor anyone with whom I spoke remembers a time when a storm caused the daylight to be completely extinguished, let alone for three hours. Furthermore, I examined the violent rent in the temple veil and there is no evidence of burning along the tear as one would expect from a lightning strike. Again, High Priest, with all due respect, how can we say it was lightning that destroyed the veil if there is no sign of a burn?'"

"If Beelzebub used Jesus, the blasphemer, to raise the dead to life, he would certainly be angry that we men of God had put to death his demonic disciple. The tearing of the Temple veil is nothing more, then, than a demonstration of the Evil One's rage and frustration."

"A second member raised his hand and said, 'High Priest, this Jesus, as you mentioned, brought two people back from the dead, namely Jarius's daughter and a man named, Lazarus. Jarius's daughter had been deceased less than an hour, but Lazarus had been in his tomb for four days. Of this there is no doubt as both of them are walking about even as we speak. In this same way his disciples said that Jesus prophesied his own death and resurrection after three days. (Mark 9:31).

"What is to keep His disciples from removing His body from the tomb and then saying that he raised himself from the dead as he said he would?"

"As I stated earlier Jesus' miracles were all brought about by the power of Beelzebub; for if by Jehovah they would have been done without violating the Sabbath," Caiaphas answered.

"I have also had the stone cover of His tomb secured with four, foot-long spikes. It would take more than a dozen men to remove it.

"However, you have brought before us a timely reminder, and we can never be too sure when we are confronting the Demonic. I will approach the Procurator and ask him to provide guards until the end of the third day. After that it won't matter."

Caiaphas had been left waiting for over an hour. He was fuming inside with anger. The Roman Procurator was the only one in Israel who dared to keep the High Priest waiting and it severely irked Caiaphas that Jehovah would permit His High Priest to become subservient to an idolatrous pagan.

A half hour later Pilate dispatched a lowly servant, shabbily dressed, in bare feet and still wearing the sweat and grime of heavy labor, and without speaking, beckoned with the full wave of his arm revealing a dirty, hairy, sweaty arm pit, for the High Priest to follow him. Once again the High Priest was forced to control his seething anger, as this indignity forced upon him by Pilate was one he knew he had to silently endure without recourse.

As Caiaphas stood before him, Pontius Pilate, refusing to respectfully greet the High Priest said callously, "Well, High Priest, what is it you want now?"

"This is not easy for me to say, Procurator, but while Jesus, the blasphemer, was alive he said that three days after his death he would be raised from the dead. Should his disciples, who I remind your Excellency, are still roaming about Jerusalem, decide to deceitfully ensure the promise, we would be dealing not with a physical blasphemer, but a ghostly one whose fraudulent presence could be more trouble for us than when he was alive."

Leaning forward Pilate said, "Caiaphas, if I could find a way to lay this whole Jesus matter on you, I would; but to do so would raise the ire of Caesar, who believes that as long as you are monetarily compensated, you are an asset to keeping the fragile peace in Israel."

"You do not know this, but my wife, just before I condemned your Jesus to death, sent me a note which read, 'Pontius: I had a terrible dream last night. Have nothing to do with this just man.' I had no time to consider it because you and yours were busy stirring up the crowd that in their blood lust they forced me to release Barabbas in his place. BARABBAS! High Priest – a convicted murderer and terrorist!

"As a result, my wife, Claudia, most likely thinks of my rejection as uncaring, but also, I suspect, she thinks me a coward for washing my hands of the matter. I say suspect, High Priest, because she has not spoken to me since.

"Now as if you have not given me enough grief you come before me whining about this Jesus resurrecting himself from a death by crucifixion and why this is a matter with which I, Pontius Pilate, the Roman Procurator of Judea, should be concerned. HAVE YOU LOST YOUR MIND?"

"I would hope not, Procurator, as what I am asking is not much."

"And what do you consider not much?"

"Military guards to secure the tomb until one hour after sunrise the third day."

"You have your own people – seventy-one of them including yourself in that pompous, self-righteous group you call the Sanhedrin. Choose those most fit and guard it yourself. I would look the fool sending armed legionnaires to guard a dead man's tomb."

"Before Caiaphas could respond Pilate cocked his head to listen to his Chief Magistrate who, while standing at the side of Pilate, leaned toward him and said barely above a whisper, 'Excellency, let us not be too hasty. By using a few legionnaires now we ensure that any theft of the body will be impossible, and in three days the whole Jesus matter will be done with and gone forever. On the other hand, Your Excellency, if we allow others to guard the tomb, we lose control. If the body ends up missing within the allotted time, we will then be forced to employ a whole legion of men for who knows how long to search for a crucified corpse no doubt creating cause for laughter and ridicule among the people as well as questions and probably censure from Rome.

"And if after all this what if we don't find it? Excellency, if that should happen there will be no end to the contempt, hilarity and ridicule that history will record as a core event that just might define your legacy."

Pilate paused and then nodded before saying, "This is one of those times when a man is forced to choose between the lesser of two evils." Then, standing up he added, "You have your guards, High Priest; my Chief Magistrate will see to it with the Centurion of the Palace Guard." Looking back over his shoulder as he proceeded quickly to exit the room Pilate shouted, "This will forever end the Jesus matter, High Priest. Don't ever come to me again mentioning His name."

"The six soldiers ordered to guard the tomb, Bruce, were stunned when given the order. Standing at attention before the Centurion they listened only half believing as he said, 'I am giving you orders to guard the tomb of Jesus, the Nazarene, who was crucified earlier today. Three of you at a time will be on duty. You will stand this watch, relieving each other every eight hours until one hour after sunrise on the third day. No one is to approach the tomb for any reason under penalty of death. I mean no one – not his disciples, not his relatives, not even his mother, whom I am told followed him from Pilate's Palace through the streets; even to grieving at the foot of his cross. You give them one warning and if not immediately obeyed you have license to kill them. You listen to no attempt to offer an explanation or excuse for none are valid.

"'You no doubt wonder why you are guarding the tomb of a crucified man. I can tell you only this. This Nazarene claimed to be a God with the power to raise himself from the dead within three days after his death. We know this to be impossible, but it is possible that his disciples will steal the corpse and state that his claim was true. It would not be in the best interest of the Empire for subjects to hear that someone was able to overcome death by crucifixion.

"Your duty is now before you and as Legionnaires the Empire expects you to perform it flawlessly. Sartorius, you are the senior man." Extending his hand he continued, "The location of the tomb is on this chart. Set up your watch sections as you deem your orders state and settle any problems or differences as they occur. Are there any questions?"

"Yes, Sartorius, what is it?"

"Do any of the Nazarene's disciples have military training?"

"No. To the best of my knowledge most are Galilean fishermen, with a former tax collector and probably common laborers – not the type of men to attack armed Roman Legionnaires. If there are no further questions you are dismissed."

"This has got to be the weirdest duty I have had during my tenure as a Legionnaire," Marcus the youngest said to the other two on duty with him. "I have two sons, ages ten and twelve, whom I hope to see in Rome along with their mother in about six weeks. How do I tell them that their Roman Legionnaire husband and father spent a weekend guarding the tomb of a dead man lest his body is stolen and it be said that he raised himself from the dead? A man who was crucified, no less!"

"You don't," said Cosmos. "You tell them about the exciting or daring things you accomplished or in which you were involved and forget about the embarrassingly mundane."

"Hey, speaking about exciting things, weren't you on duty last week when this Nazarene removed his cincture and began upsetting the moneychangers' tables and beating about the animal sellers?"

"I didn't see it, but I heard about it from Lustrates," remarked Gaius. "He said that he never saw anything like it – tables overturned, coins flying through the air, then bouncing off the ground and rolling across the courtyard, merchants at first trying to cover their heads and faces before running across the courtyard, first one way and then the other trying to avoid being trampled by frightened lambs and stampeding oxen; and all this as hundreds of doves, freed from their cages flew all about them. Finally, this Jesus stood there flushed with anger as he shouted after them, 'It is written, 'My house shall be called the house of prayer; but you have made it a den of thieves!'" (Matthew 21:13)

"Yes," answered Marcus, "All that is true. I saw it from above as I was on the Fortress of Antonia Wall looking down into the Temple Courtyard. However, by the time I got down to the Courtyard it was all but over. I do remember, though, the Chief Priests and Scribes asking Jesus by what authority he had done this?"

"How did he respond?" asked Cosmos.

"He began tapping His chest and said, 'Destroy this Temple and I will rebuild it in three days!'"

"Was there a response?"

"Yes," said Marcus. "They asked him, 'It has taken forty-six years to build this temple, and you are going to raise it in three days?'"

"And?"

"And what?"

"And how did Jesus answer their question?"

"He didn't. He just gave them a look that showed His disbelief; then shook his head in disgust and walked away."

"You were on duty," Cosmos said. "You were there to keep peace and quiet in the Temple Courtyard. Why didn't you arrest him for destroying private property?"

"I don't know," Marcus responded. "I've seen His face a couple of times since, but it looked nothing like it did when he overturned the moneychangers' tables and beat the backs of those selling animals for some kind of ritual slaughter in the Temple. I can't give you a good answer, Cosmos, except to say that you had to be there."

"Sartorius had set the first watch near the end of the twelfth hour (6:00PM) two hours after Jesus had been placed in the tomb. As I noted earlier, it had been sealed with four foot-long spikes through a heavy, flat stone at the order of the High Priest to Joseph of Arimathea, a member of the Sanhedrin and whose tomb it was.

Then they followed through, changing the watch every eight hours as they were ordered. They wiled away the time by telling of their adventures as Legionnaires in other places and Sartorius, who was a twenty-year veteran, convinced the other two on his watch that they never wanted to serve as a member of a crucifixion team. "It takes something that most men don't have," he said, "they're the type of man whose companionship you wouldn't enjoy or with whom you would choose to take pleasure in sharing a skin of wine."

"How long were you on this team?" Claudius asked.

"Two years," Sartorius replied. "I was awakened in the barracks by the sub centurion and told I was replacing a man who had gotten himself killed the night before in a brawl just outside the local winery. I was with four other team members who actually laughed as they relished hearing the screams of men as they drove spikes through their hands and feet. In my youth I had the advantage of a good education, and when the centurion discovered I could read and write he had me transferred to his staff where I remained until he was killed while fighting in Gaul."

"He pointed to His chest and said, 'Destroy this temple, and I will rebuild it in three days.' Are you sure this is what Jesus said, Marcus?"

"Yes, Gaius, why do you ask?"

"Because temple is sometimes used by religious people to mean a person's body and if this Jesus pointed to himself when he said it there's more than just a small chance that he meant not the religious structure, but himself."

Cosmos began laughing, and then said mockingly, "It sounds like you believe this Jesus could actually overcome death by crucifixion – that he could actually raise himself from the dead!"

"If he is a mere man like us, Cosmos, then it isn't possible; but if he is a god then who knows? I heard the Centurion in Capernaum say that the moment Jesus, who was at a distance from his servant who was breathing his last, upon Jesus saying so, was healed. The man recovered as if he had never been ill! We can overlook claims made by these fanatically religious Jews, but a statement from a Roman Centurion has to be given serious consideration."

"What time is it?" Marcus asked, in an effort to change the subject.

"About a half hour before sunrise," Cosmos responded. "One- and one-half hours after this time tomorrow we can secure from this ridiculous watch."

"A little later at precisely the beginning of the first hour (6:00 A.M.) as the sun slowly crept above the horizon; the three men were startled by a sudden, deafening loud crack of thunder. Despite a clear sky the bizarre, thunderous booming continued while growing increasingly louder as the surface of the stone that covered the opening of the tomb began to glow with a rosy hue.

"What's happening?" Marcus shouted, as they covered their ears while glancing at each other hoping that one of them knew the answer.

"Then, as the rumble of the thunder receded as if it were rolling away and the stone's rosy hue faded, a bolt of lightning struck the covering stone causing an explosive burst of fiery sparks. Immediately a light shone forth from within the tomb that was so hot and bright that it projected through the stone seal illuminating the three soldiers along with every stone, bush and tree in the garden.

"Although all three men were seasoned, battle-hardened warriors, they stood petrified; aware that they were ill-equipped to protect themselves from what their imaginations conjured up would soon be coming for them from out of that tomb. The man they knew as Jesus now obviously had become a God in death and was rising from the dead as he predicted. As a man he had been mercilessly scourged, spit upon, crowned with thorns from a prickly bush, hung from a cross with spikes driven through His hands and feet and finally had his heart pierced with the blade of a lance.

"As a god with all but unlimited power, they were convinced while shielding their eyes from a light brighter than they had ever seen, that Jesus was about to overcome all of these sufferings that led to His death by raising himself from the dead to seek his revenge; and all three men trembled while sharing the same thought – that His vengeful rage would wreak lethal havoc on the first men he encountered who were wearing the same uniform as the men who had done this to him."

"Do you two see and hear what I do?" Marcus asked.

"How are we going to explain this to the Centurion?" Gaius asked.

Cosmos paused and closed his eyes; then remarked in a voice that was just above a whisper, "What makes you two think we'll be alive to tell him anything?"

"Just then the stone, with a loud, eerie screech from the tight grip of the resisting foot-long spikes was violently wrenched by unseen hands causing it to fall away. Hitting the ground with a loud thud it further revealed the blinding light shining from within. What appeared as a man then stepped out from the entrance to the tomb. He paused for just a moment while raising his hands and eyes to the heavens as if in prayer then he turned and began walking toward them. At first against the bright light behind him he appeared as a silhouette through the morning mist and the dust raised from the falling stone; but as he came closer His appearance became clearer. The man was the Jesus Marcus remembered and not that Jesus at the same time. The harsh brightness then dimmed just enough to see that the image walking toward them was indeed a man but glowing with an unearthly illumination. The three guards were seeing Jesus as the Apostles, Peter, James and John saw him during His Transfiguration on Mt. Tabor. Jesus Christ – THE SON OF GOD MADE MAN! (Mark 9:2-8).

"Gone were the torn flesh and oozing stripes. Gone were the punctures dripping blood from the thorns pressed into his scalp. The only evidence, Bruce, of the sufferings he endured were the wounds the spikes left in his hands and feet and the incision the lance made in his side – evidence he will retain forever as proof of the infinite love he has for all mankind – his stupid, wretched, non-believing and ungrateful human creation!

"Jesus continued walking toward them and then stopped when three feet stood between them. They were taken aback by how tall he was as he stood there for a long moment with His eyes fixed in a stern expression glancing from one guard to the next observing the stark, horrific terror of anticipated devastation on the face of each.

"Then he slowly extended His hands, palms up in front of them while nodding and offering a friendly smile as he spoke to them in Latin, their native tongue, 'Pax vobiscum. Nolite timere. Populus enim te gratissimum omnium,' (Peace be with you. Do not be afraid. You are all most welcome) revealing to three pagan gentiles – the only ones to witness his Resurrection – that their fearful apprehension and trembling were totally unfounded.

"Greatly relieved, they backed away while doing their best to return a grateful, but still nervous smile as each attempted to return his broadsword to its scabbard until they realized that in the paralyzed panic of what they thought was inevitable they had not drawn their swords!

"Jesus then turned and looked at me. As he continued to focus without speaking or changing His expression, I experienced fear for the first time. I was sure he was going to make me an exception by annihilating one of His immortal creatures. I felt for sure that I was about to disappear along with any evidence that I had ever existed.

"Then his countenance changed, Bruce, and somehow I knew that my annihilation was not his intention. Instead, without an audible word he let me know that my time of unrestrained, destructive temptation and ruinous mayhem against his human creation had just been curtailed by a Divine Assist; and that if mankind would take advantage of his offer, they need no longer fear being sifted by me and mine.

"That a means of knowingly securing eternal salvation was now available to all men; and not for a price, but for the asking; and for those who asked for, accepted, and then lived by its precepts their eternal salvation was not only probable but assured."

"Jesus was speaking to the three guards," I said, "but I suspect he meant the entire gentile world."

"I obviously didn't know it then," Satan replied, "but I feel Jesus envisioned Saul of Tarsus, a product of Roman-Jewish parentage and a vicious, fanatical Semite and knew that following a life changing encounter with himself, Saul would become Paul – His Apostle to the Gentiles.

"Marcus, Gaius, and Cosmos told their superiors exactly what had occurred at the tomb. Pilate, wondering if this Jesus matter would never end, sent his Chief Magistrate along with two palace guards to examine the tomb. As they approached the site they saw the stone, with the four retaining spikes still attached, lying flat on the ground. Nearby a man in a white robe stood conversing with a woman. As they approached closer the Chief Magistrate, from his previous encounters, recognized the woman as a beautiful, but now reformed prostitute. As he did so, the man turned to look at him. He recognized Jesus whom Pilate had condemned to death, but before the man's face was mutilated by the scourging. He raised his hand while quickening his pace to question him when he began sweating profusely as a strong sense of impending doom came over him. After taking another step he felt a chill accompanied by uncontrolled shaking of his hands and a weakness in his legs.

"As much as he wanted to question Jesus he felt that if he took another step he would never take another. 'I've seen enough,' he said to the guards. 'We'll return and tell the Procurator what we've seen.'

"When his Chief Magistrate as well as the two guards reported that the stone seal had indeed been wrenched away, the tomb was empty and that they had seen Jesus, alive and well, Pilate closed his eyes and mumbled, 'Claudia, Claudia, why didn't I take the time to listen to you?'"

"Desiring to alleviate the look of distress on Pilate's face his Chief Magistrate said, 'If I may speak plainly, Procurator, this is but a Jewish religious matter. Jesus, if he is a god or if he is the instrument of a god is nothing to us. And it was the Jews, themselves, led by their own High Priest who cried out for his blood in reply to your statement that you found no fault with him. Hearing this they shouted even louder for His crucifixion and to ensure their intent followed up with:

HIS BLOOD BE UPON US AND UPON OUR CHILDREN! (Matthew 27:25)

'If his purpose is to do us harm, he had the perfect chance this morning, first with the three guards and then with me, and he did nothing to show such intent. In fact, the three guards reported that he approached them with the words, 'Peace be with you. Do not be afraid.' My suggestion is to do nothing about Jesus until we see what, if anything is forthcoming from this resurrection.'"

"You think we can just ignore the fact that a man crucified by the state raised himself from the dead and is now walking about freely?"

"Yes, I do. You must, of course, report it to Tiberius. It would do us no good for the emperor to hear about it from someone else. My experience in such matters, however, is that men in high places are loathe to examine or try to deal with what they do not understand. Paranormal activity, especially if it even hints of the supernatural, is anathema to those who are used to being in full control. In matters where the outcome is questionable or not sure to be to their advantage, they will deny or ignore it unless it presents an actual threat."

"You're sure about this?" Pilate questioned.

"Excellency, you can answer your own question. Are you so inclined to want to do something about this or just let it lie?"

"I see what you mean. Very well, then. You write it as you feel it should be and bring it to me for signature. Then, we'll just hope for the best."

"Within the forty days that Jesus remained on earth some of the Temple priests, scribes and members of the Sanhedrin actually saw Jesus; while others, hearing of the experience of the guards, personally went to see the open tomb, causing them to be fearfully apprehensive. They couldn't admit to themselves the horror of being responsible for murdering the Messiah; so they refused to admit, despite evidence to the contrary, that Jesus, whom they caused to be crucified, was the Messiah. They had to admit that he was more than an ordinary man, but to what extent they couldn't or refused to say. Confusion and self-doubt continued to erode the pride and arrogant attitude of most of its members. The Sanhedrin's proud and lofty self-righteousness was drowned in a sea of doubt for some and guilt by others. This state lasted for some time.

"Respect for Joseph of Arimathea was already high among members of the Sanhedrin due to his financial acumen as well as his religious knowledge. His and Nicodemus's vote not to condemn Jesus to death for blasphemy was originally looked upon with disdain; but in light of the Temple veil hanging in disarray and the bewilderment concerning Jesus' resurrection at least two-thirds of the Sanhedrin, given the chance, would have voted to replace Caiaphas with Joseph as High Priest.

"On the other hand, respect for Caiaphas declined rapidly. His explanation for Jesus' miracles as being done with the power of the Demonic when without exception they helped people to a better life, seemed suspect and even more so as time progressed. The younger members, especially, felt that Caiaphas's Demonic explanations compromised the supremacy of Jehovah in favor of an exaggerated power attributed to Beelzebub, that is, me."

"And you admit they were right?" I questioned.

Satan paused before answering, "Of course, Bruce. To use a modern expression Caiaphas was my useful idiot. He and his Sanhedrin were concrete evidence of men's stupidity. As a leader, Caiaphas was either demented or fearful for what he might have done. It is impossible to believe that a man with Caiaphas's religious training could believe that anybody but God could return the dead to life."

"I wanted so badly to ask him, 'you know where he is, don't you, Satan?' but I got hold of myself remembering the tight restrictions to which he agreed."

"However," he continued, "there was nothing that could be done to effect any meaningful change. Rome had usurped the power to appoint the High Priest and he served at the pleasure of Israel's pagan masters. The two High Priests who had preceded Caiaphas refused to replace the Will of Jehovah with the will of Rome and had been summarily replaced. Caiaphas held the position, because with my help and his inordinate love of wealth, luxury and power it was easy for me to lead him to believe that the will of Rome was the will of Jehovah, and Rome paid him well to continue this way of thinking.

CHAPTER TWENTY-FIVE

Caiaphas Attempts to Bribe the Roman Sentries

"In an effort to recoup the confidence of the Sanhedrin Caiaphas sent two men out to approach Marcus, Cosmos and Gaius to persuade them to accept a sizable bribe for admitting that their narrative of the Resurrection was for the purpose of belying the fact that they had actually fallen asleep during which time His disciples stole the body.

When approached, in an effort to have some fun, the three guards invited them into a winery to discuss the matter further. "How much did you say each of us would receive?" Gaius asked. When told the amount Gaius shook his head while saying that it would not be nearly enough.

"How much then, would be enough?" one of the men asked.

"How much money is in the Temple treasury?" Cosmos asked.

"You can't be serious!" the second man exclaimed.

"Oh, we're very serious," Marcus responded. "In fact, even if Caiaphas bankrupted the Temple, it wouldn't be nearly enough."

The two men looked questioningly at each other as they began to realize that approaching these Legionnaires to ask them to dishonor themselves for money was a big mistake.

"While you two sit there drinking your wine," Cosmos said, "I am going to ask you a question. How intelligent is Caiaphas, your High Priest?"

"Caiaphas! Why his intelligence is legendary," said the older of the two.

"That could mean either way," Gaius remarked. "I mean his intelligence could be legendary because he is intellectually brilliant or because he is abysmally stupid."

"Which is it?"

"Before you answer," Marcus interjected, "We are going to give you some information on which to base your answer. Ready?"

Just above a whisper they nodded and said, "Yes," as they wondered if these three Romans were going to let them leave the winery without injury or even if they would still be alive.

"First of all," Marcus said, "We have already told our superiors that we witnessed Jesus rise from the dead. The covering stone, secured by four foot-long spikes was torn from its place – a feat that ten men would find impossible. How could we now deny it?"

Before they could answer Gaius said, "Pontius Pilate, the Roman Procurator, you know who the Procurator is, don't you? Don't answer. I'll tell you. He is the man to whom your High Priest, Caiaphas, answers. Anyway, the Procurator knows that Jesus rose from the dead not only because of our report but because his Chief Magistrate witnessed Jesus standing a stone's throw from His tomb speaking with the woman, Mary, the reformed prostitute from Magdala, who became one of His followers."

"Finally," Cosmos added, to the two men who by now saw the hopeless futility of Caiaphas's offer, "if your High Priest is as intelligent as you say, he must know that the Roman penalty for falling asleep on watch is death. So, we believe that Caiaphas is a man of evil intent. He knows that as soon as we admit to falling asleep on watch, we'll be executed and he won't have to pay the bribe; which means that Caiaphas thinks nothing of setting up two otherwise upstanding Jews, like you, to play the fool in front of us."

"So, unless you can tell us your beloved High Priest's plan for our resurrection," Gaius added, "how long do you think Caiaphas will allow you two idiots to remain alive knowing that you are the only ones who know what he tried and failed miserably to do? Wait! Don't answer that. It was only meant to advise you that for the rest of your miserable lives we are warning you not to travel at night, and to look frequently over your shoulder for his assassins who one day soon just as surely as the sun rises in the East, will be there.

"Now, that you have seen in what low esteem your High Priest, Caiaphas, holds Roman legionnaires, that is, that we are but three barely literate dolts who can easily be manipulated by the likes of you," Gaius said, "How intelligent is your High Priest?"

"He is a stupid, deceitful liar and cheat," the younger man said.

"He may have a superb knowledge of The Mosaic Law, but when it comes to using intelligence to make a devious plan he is as green as unripened fruit," the older man added.

"Very good!" exclaimed Cosmos, "Very good! Now you two run along and tell him so!" Whereupon amid the hearty laughter of the Legionnaires the two men bolted for the door without so much as a final sip of wine, a word of thanks or a good-bye wave.

When the two men did not return Caiaphas hired several others to spread the lie that the Roman soldiers had fallen asleep during which time Jesus' disciples had broken into the tomb and stolen the body. After a time, however, when there were no executions, the lie was seen for the clumsy attempt it was, and not taken seriously, if at all.

"The rest is a matter of scripture, Bruce. As it is written, Jesus appeared to His Apostles in addition to several others in the forty days between his Resurrection and His Ascension. What he said and did, in addition to scripture, however, is matter for another time."

"I waited for several seconds to see if Satan would remain visible. When he smiled, while nodding and raising his eyebrows as he did when finishing his narrative of the details not included in scripture, I was again amazed that God would assign the task of revealing the hidden events of His Resurrection to a creature known as The Prince of Darkness until I thought who else, except maybe an angel, would have been alive two thousand years ago to witness the details and yet, still be alive today to tell us about them? Certainly not one of us. As Satan said to me, "I don't have to read scripture. I was there observing its events as they occurred."

"Your memory for detail is phenomenal, Satan, and reveals the intelligence God showered upon you. Now it appears that it is payback time, and he has put you in a position to reveal details of scripture he has for His own purpose kept hidden until now."

"The price I must pay for precluding a Divine reset and getting my relationship with man back to the metaphorical sixty-foot bowling lane."

"Oh yes, that again," I said. "Do you feel you are getting any closer?"

"I don't feel anything," Satan replied. "As a spirit I either know and know that I know or, conversely, Bruce, I know when I don't know. However, to answer your question – yes, I know that I know that I am."

"Sorry I asked," I said barely audible.

CHAPTER TWENTY-SIX

Years Later Did Jonathan and Asher Agree with Caiaphas and Vote to Kill Jesus?

My remark caused an embarrassing silence between us. To break the silence I said, 'Not to change the subject, Satan, but I am supposing that Nicodemus and Joseph of Arimathea are the same men mentioned earlier?"

"Correct. Both men are about fifteen to eighteen years older during Jesus' public life. Joseph in his seventies – Nicodemus in his forties. As mentioned earlier they cast the two dissenting votes when the Sanhedrin, at the High Priest Caiaphas's demand, called for a vote to have Jesus condemned to death for blasphemy.

"Joseph went to Pilate and asked for Jesus' body which would normally be a dangerous thing to do. Pilate consented and as we also stated earlier Joseph had Jesus placed in his own tomb."

"Why was it so dangerous?"

"The Romans were very good at intimidation. Normally, the bodies of the crucified, as a reminder and example to others, were left to rot and be picked apart and eaten by birds. In Jesus' case, however, Pilate was happy to have the evidence of an unjust, and for him, a tumultuous and embarrassing crucifixion removed from sight.

"Joseph was not only a Pharisee and a member of the Sanhedrin, Bruce, but also a politically astute wealthy businessman whose religious convictions favored the teachings of Jesus whom he took at His word. His fellow members of the Sanhedrin, with the exception of Nicodemus, were too stubborn to see through their prejudice. These looked past his teachings and miracles and saw only a prematurely retired, charismatic carpenter whose wit and wisdom when they confronted him made them look foolish in front of the people."

"And of course, you and yours were instrumental in this?"

"As you know by now, Bruce, it is what we do. 'Hate,' Bruce. Remember? Throw a few hot coals of hate and in almost no time at all you have a raging inferno. After sexually based sins, more people draw on hate and its aftermath to condemn themselves to eternal damnation than they do any other sin."

"Why is that?"

"Because Hate requires a sense of justification. For whatever reason he or she feels justified in hating and it is nearly impossible to seek forgiveness for an emotion for which one feels justified – why people say, 'I could never forgive him or her.'

"And when they die feeling that way they die in their sin. 'Forgive us our trespasses as we forgive those who trespass against us.' Every time one of you recites the Lord's Prayer, for better or for worse, you bring judgment down upon yourself; and those who die in their sins are mine – all mine – forever and forever all mine!"

"I just had a thought, Satan. This could be the reason Jesus taught us to 'turn the other cheek, to do good to those who hate you, and to love our enemies'. If a person lives by these edicts, he can avoid the self-condemning spiritual trap of hating someone."

"It not only could be the reason, Bruce, it is the reason. Obviously, Jesus is inspiring you to work his will as you offered to do during our discourse. This isn't his first inspiration, Bruce, but one of His clearest."

"How so?" I asked.

"Think about it." Now no one can ask, "Why should I love my enemy? Why should I do good to them who hate me? Jesus just used you to tell them why."

"Feeling somewhat uncomfortable at Satan's remark I changed the subject.

"Jonathan appears as a particularly intelligent, well-educated, and open-minded young man. How old was he when he befriended Jesus in the Temple?"

"Thirty-four. Jonathan was thirty-four, married and the father of two sons and two daughters. Unlike most members of the Sanhedrin his father was not a member but a stonemason – a trade at which Jonathan was particularly adept. At age twenty-one Jonathan and his father did some elaborate stonework in the garden of a senior member of the Sanhedrin. In conversation he had with Jonathan he recognized his superior intelligence and had him enrolled in a Temple school in which Jonathan excelled graduating at the head of his class.

"He was then offered a position in the class which trained men for the Sanhedrin. Four years later after a grueling session in which he answered every question not only to the testers' satisfaction, but in some cases to their revelation, he became at twenty-nine the youngest man to become a member of the Sanhedrin.

"I must admit that in the beginning we tried our best to "sift" Jonathan without success. When treated unfairly or taken advantage of he just laughed and tried harder to succeed by overcoming the adversity – and almost always did. He was a rare combination of academic brilliance, charisma and athleticism. He never gave into hate, treated both friend and foe with heartfelt respect and thus, after time, those who were jealous of him, became his friends. His was a combination of a superior mind in a magnificent body energized with charisma and moderated with humility."

"Jonathan sounds like one of your ideal targets – a perfect example of a sixty-footer!"

"I am speaking from thousands of years of experience dealing with the human condition. Believe me then when I tell you that the opposite of Hate is certainly Love, but without Humility aligned with the Almighty, I can, with powerful temptations turn Love into Hate. Don't believe me? Compare a couples' wedding day some years later with their appearance in a divorce court. A truly humble person, however, is all but impossible to turn."

"Because...?"

"Because they have no illicit and ardent desires upon which to instigate a temptation. They begin each day with a simple prayer that ends with, 'not my will but Thine be done.' They accept God's invitation to 'Come, follow Me.' This allows them to believe that Jesus is standing with his guiding hand on their right shoulder. Their prayers are in simple, spontaneous, conversational language versus long, ritualized, published entreaties. And they remember to thank God for His blessings – even something as simple as tripping, but not falling. To them money and power are not an end in themselves but rather tools God provides to obtain a certain end he desires. Sex is there not to provide a playground but to forge a loving relationship between man and wife and in union with God the procreation of children. Their first and foremost objective in life is the salvation of their immortal soul and to influence others to do likewise.

"You know people like this, Bruce; starting with yourself, because you are one of them!"

"Whether too stunned or too surprised to respond I sat there somewhat in shock."

When I failed to say anything, Satan continued, "Jonathan's early life as a stonemason taught him the value of honest work; thus, he was scrupulously principled – taking nothing from a person or activity that was the least bit tainted."

"Were he and Asher still members of the Sanhedrin at Jesus' mock trial?" I asked, having recovered from Satan's startling assertion. "If not, why not? Wasn't membership for a lifetime?"

"Yes it was, Bruce; but five years after his encounter with the boy, Jesus, Asher died from respiratory failure. At the time Tuberculosis wasn't known for what it is, but its debilitating effect on his lungs caused Asher's death.

"As for Jonathan, three years after meeting Jesus he was walking home one night after a teaching session. He heard a woman scream amid a scuffle about a half block away. Most Jewish men would have run the other way not wanting to confront Roman soldiers, especially if it was at night and he suspected the soldiers had been drinking. Jonathan however ran toward the screams and confronted two soldiers who had illicit desires on a young Jewess who was about the same age as his eldest daughter. He grabbed one of them and threw him off the girl. As the soldier lurched uncontrollably forward his helmet came off as he tripped and rammed his head into the corner of a building fracturing his skull. When Jonathan knelt down in an attempt to help the moaning man his comrade drove his short sword into Jonathan's back. The blade slid between two of Jonathan's ribs and penetrated his heart, killing him instantly."

"My God," I exclaimed. "How horrific! What a waste."

"Killing Jews for cause by the Romans was not unusual, but killing from behind an unarmed member of the Sanhedrin in the midst of his stopping a rape in a city that had more than its share of prostitutes had crossed the line. To preclude an uprising the soldier was executed after an apology to the High Priest was offered by Marcus Ambivulus, at that time the Roman Governor of Judea. It was rumored that Caesar Augustus himself had ordered the apology, as well as the execution. The soldier with the fractured skull died shortly after Jonathan."

"Tell me, did you or yours have anything to do with the intended rape or Jonathan's murder?"

As Satan raised his eyebrows registering surprise that I would ask such a question, I immediately felt he was right; however, it was difficult responding to a creature known as the Prince of Darkness when on rare occasions his words and/or actions appeared to belie this title.

Once again, however, my mother's warning came to mind causing me to paraphrase her admonition _ Remember, despite his good manners Satan is not my friend.

After what seemed to be an interminable period of silence Satan got up and walked to the window. Without facing me and brushing back the window covering he said, "Bruce, these two Romans steeped in their own lust and concupiscence were well on the road to perdition. Being long time practitioners of Roman brutality and arrogance, they silenced their consciences and replaced them with a sense of never-ending entitlement.

"I must admit that in truth I promote, admire, and condone such fiendish, stupid human behavior; but in rare instances admit to being squeamish over the result. Jonathan's untimely death was one of those times."

"Why? Why make an exception of Jonathan?"

"Bruce, you as well as your readers will find this hard to believe, but although I hate every one of you with a degree of loathing that is impossible for you to conceive, now and again I have to respect a few of you. Let me explain. You will remember during my discourse with God about creating the human condition I heard him say just before the end of what became my ultimatum, 'But I also know that some will choose virtue over vice; will willingly and with great joy adore Me with their whole hearts, their whole minds, and their whole souls while loving others of their kind as they love themselves and show it by doing unto others as they would have others do unto them. These, after their earthly sojourn, I will gather to Myself in a kingdom of joy the likes of which they could never experience or even imagine in their world.'

"I must admit that I never expected any of you to show the intelligence and courage, and yes, Bruce, the love to overcome your concupiscence as he said you would. And when one notes a series of heroic acts requiring great courage in the face of ridicule by my Demonic influence of his or her peers even I, Satan, cannot help but feel admiration and respect. Not love, mind you, but admiration and respect."

Facing me now as he returned to the table Satan finished by saying, "Bruce, I and mine are not responsible for all the evil in the world. Much of it, as it is in this case, is self-induced, making Demonic input redundant. As proof I continue to appear visibly before you as I answer your question with a simple, 'No.'"

CHAPTER TWENTY-SEVEN

David Ben Hillel Receives the Answer to His Question

Once again Satan, forced to keep his word, stood there for a few seconds before saying, "Jesus along with Jonathan, Nicodemus and Asher have just returned from their evening meal. Shall we join them?"

"Asher, you mentioned that the time period for the Babylonian captivity was seventy years. How do we know this?" Jonathan asked.

"Jeremiah the Prophet was through whom Jehovah spoke to the Jewish people in an effort to get them to mend their ways, for they had fallen into idolatry with all its accompanying evil habits and traditions. Over a period of decades they had all but abandoned the worship of God in the Temple; the priests, Levites and scribes had become corrupt; fornication and drunkenness had become an accepted part of life. Tired of his admonitions and pleas for repentance they threw Jeremiah down a cistern and left him there for several days wherein he barely survived.

"Jehovah, after a period of time, His patience having been exhausted, told Jeremiah to speak thus to the people of Judah, 'I will banish from them the sounds of joy and gladness, the voices of bride and bridegroom, the sound of millstones and the light of the lamp. This whole country will become a desolate wasteland, and these nations will serve the king of Babylon seventy years.' (Jeremiah 25:10-11)

"Is there more?" Jonathan asked.

"Yes, Jeremiah goes on to say, 'but when the seventy years are fulfilled, I will punish the king of Babylon and his nation, the land of the Babylonians, for their guilt,'" declares the Lord, "and will make it desolate forever. I will bring on that land all the things I have spoken against it, all that are written in this book and prophesied by Jeremiah against all the nations. They themselves will be enslaved by many nations and great kings; I will repay them according to their deeds and the work of their hands.' (Jeremiah 25:12-14)

"Finally, Jonathan, Jeremiah states the last part of the prophecy; thus, this is what the Lord says: 'When seventy years are completed for Babylon, I will come to you and fulfill my good promise to bring you back to this place. For I know the plans I have for you,' declares the Lord, 'plans to prosper you and not to harm you, plans to give you hope and a future. Then you will call on me and come and pray to me, and I will listen to you. You will seek me and find me when you seek me with all your heart. I will be found by you," declares the Lord, "and will bring you back from captivity. I will gather you from all the nations and places where I have banished you," declares the Lord, "and will bring you back to the place from which I carried you into exile."' (Jeremiah 29:10-14)

"Well, I think there is no doubt that from Jeremiah's prophecy," stated Nicodemus, "that because of their idolatrous apostasy and subsequent wickedness Jehovah did in fact allow the Babylonians to ravage Jerusalem, destroy the Temple, kill many of the inhabitants and remove those they didn't kill to a wretched life for seventy years in a pagan country.

"But after the seventy years is completed, Jehovah states, he will return them to 'the place from which I carried you into exile,' and that is the land of Judah wherein lies the great city of Jerusalem."

"Now that we have established why the prophet, Daniel, is in Babylon," Jesus said, "we can look at why Jehovah sent the Archangel Gabriel to speak to him. Asher, can you read it to us?"

"Asher, knowing that they would require the scroll returned from dinner before the others and retrieved it from the its storage slot. 'I have it here,' he said as he began to unfurl it. Then he stood before the others and read:

"At the beginning of your supplications the command was issued, and I have come to tell you, for you are highly esteemed; so give heed to the message and gain understanding of the vision. Seventy weeks are determined upon thy people and upon thy holy city, to finish the transgression, and to make an end of sins, and to make reconciliation for iniquity, to bring in everlasting righteousness, to seal up the vision and prophecy, and to anoint the most Holy. Know therefore and understand, that from the going forth of the commandment to restore and to build Jerusalem unto Messiah the Prince shall be seven weeks, and three score and two weeks: the street shall be built again, and the wall, even in troublous times. And after threescore and two weeks shall Messiah be cut off, but not for himself: and the people of the prince that shall come will destroy the city and the sanctuary; and the end thereof shall be with a flood, and unto the end of the war desolations are determined. And he shall confirm the covenant with many for one week: and in the midst of the week he shall cause the sacrifice and the oblation to cease, and for the overspreading of abominations he shall make it desolate, even until the consummation, and that determined shall be poured upon the desolate." (Daniel 9:24-27)

Following Asher's reading of the prophecy the four began preparing an answer for David Ben Hillel who they were sure would be looking forward to hearing from the Sanhedrin the next day. Speaking only when Jonathan asked him for His opinion, Jesus purposely did not offer much as he spent most of the time observing the others led by Jonathan, as they labored to prepare the Sanhedrin's response.

"They worked through the evening and several hours into the night, often times being reluctant to have to admit the horrific, devastating, destructive severity of several passages. Finally they were satisfied that in the morning Nathaniel would approve their finished product."

"You say, Satan that they were led by Jonathan, but I suspect Jonathan was led by the Holy Spirit."

"Perhaps that is why Jesus was deliberately silent unless asked," Satan replied.

At the sixth hour of the following day the Rabbi began by asking for David Ben Hillel to come forth. The young man did so and the Rabbi, said, "Yesterday you asked for the meaning of the passage in Daniel wherein after his prayer for mercy and forgiveness for himself as well as those Jews who were bound by the Babylonians, he prays that the city of Jerusalem and the Temple will be rebuilt. Jehovah answered Daniel's prayer by sending the angel Gabriel who told Daniel not only that the Jews would return to Jerusalem and rebuild the city as well as the Temple, but the timing when these events would come to pass. In addition, Gabriel foretold some disturbing events that are the crux of the difficulty why not only your mother but also why many others have a problem accepting and understanding this biblical prophecy. Is this correct?"

"Yes, Rabbi, it is."

The Rabbi then nodded to Jonathan who stood and reading from the vellum scroll they had prepared began.

"You must realize that with Divine prophecy the events that will occur are fairly easy to ascertain; however, the how they will come to pass and why they will occur is more often than not hidden until the prophecy is fulfilled.

"With this in mind, David, we will attempt to answer your question, which judging from the size of the crowd around you, is not yours alone.

"It took the Babylonians three attempts to completely lay waste to Jerusalem. At the end of each campaign, they took captives back to Babylon. Daniel was taken as a young man of perhaps fifteen after the Babylonian king, Nebuchadnezzar's first attempt, and had proven to be, by the will of God, a favorite of the king. Daniel is aware of Jeremiah's prophecy that the captivity will last for seventy years. That time period is rapidly approaching. By this time Daniel is well into his eighties. God answers Daniel through His messenger, the angel Gabriel.

"Hear now, David Ben Hillel, the explanation you requested:

"During evening prayer, and after begging forgiveness for Israel's as well as his own personal sins Daniel beseeches God to fulfill the prophecies and allow the Jews to return to Jerusalem and rebuild the Temple.

"Upon finishing this prayerful entreaty, the room is bathed in a bright light as an angel Daniel recognizes as Gabriel from a previous apparition stands before him and says, 'Jehovah has heard your prayer and this is your answer, for you are receiving this in a vision to ensure you understand.'

"Seventy years of bondage were necessary to make restitution for the apostasy. Why seventy years? We are not certain as Gabriel does not say. However, Moses mentions man's normal life expectancy to be three score and ten, which of course is seventy years. So we may reasonably believe that the seventy years of bondage are to ensure that all those responsible for the blasphemy of willingly choosing sinful ways and turning their backs on God's commanded path of virtue are no longer alive to once again inhabit the land.

"Gabriel then continues with the prophecy as he tells Daniel that God will now instigate and proclaim a new manner of expiating for sin wherein when a man turns his back on God by choosing evil, he may redeem himself to everlasting righteousness. The angel then says that this will entail the onset of one to be anointed as most holy, whose physical presence among men will terminate the need for vision and prophets, for he is the Messiah who by fulfilling the promises of the Abrahamic Covenant has established a New Covenant.

"Know, therefore, that the following will take place to prepare the land anew for the Messiah. This is the land centered on Jerusalem which was provided to God's chosen people by covenant to Abraham, confirmed to Moses and made both permanent and stable by King David.

"Going forth from the commandment to restore and build again Jerusalem as well as the temple, and the wall around the city will require seven weeks of years or forty-nine years. These years will be amid troubling times caused by harassment of pagan idolaters who do not acknowledge and comprehend Israel's claim to the land by Divine covenant. Upon completion of the forty-nine-year re-building effort, sixty-two more weeks of years (7x62 = 434) will pass until the Messiah, will be anointed.

"For three-and-a-half years He will teach the way of a renewed covenant, (Jeremiah 31:31) the authority, foundation and truth for which will be supported by his miracles prophesied by the prophet Isaiah: 'Then will the eyes of the blind be opened and the ears of the deaf unstopped; then will the lame leap like a deer, and the mute tongue shout for joy...' (Isaiah 35:5-6).

"Gabriel, then faithfully speaking the word of Jehovah, states further that after three-and-a-half years of the final seven have passed the Messiah will be 'cut off,' that is, in some way killed, although no fault will be found with him. This fact is confirmation of another of Isaiah's prophecies, "He was oppressed, and He was afflicted, yet He opened not His mouth: He is brought as a lamb to the slaughter, and as a sheep is dumb before her shearers, so He opened not His mouth. He was taken from prison and from judgment: and who shall declare his generation? For He was cut off out of the land of the living: for the transgression of my people was he stricken." (Isaiah 53:5-12)

"This prophecy of Isaiah proclaims that he was lethally stricken, that is, he was taken from being captive and unjustly judged for the transgression of us, his people, as if his death was akin to a sacrifice for our sins; a sacrifice not unlike that which occurs yearly on Yom Kippur, the Day of Atonement, when a goat with a fastened list of sins is sent into the wilderness to die and with his death Jehovah forgives and forgets the carried transgressions.

"Moreover, there are presently the daily sacrifices of animals in the Temple; however, in contrast, the sacrificial death of the innocent Messiah is the life of a man - but more than a common man - for He has been endowed with the power by Jehovah to perform miracles. By this truth then, it would seem that Jehovah will command that this one death of an exceptional personage will suffice to make restitution to Jehovah for all the sins of men who profess a contrite heart."

"All the sins of men?" questioned the apparent leader of a group of heavily robed Pharisees while laughing out loud. "How can it be possible that the life of one man satisfy all the sins of mankind?"

"If he were an ordinary man he couldn't," Jonathan replied, "but a man who can make the blind to see, the lame to walk and the deaf to hear is not an ordinary man. There is no evidence that even the greatest of the prophets could perform such feats. Nay, even Abraham, Isaac, and Jacob and yes, even Moses had no such ability, for it requires the creative power of Jehovah or at the least a man upon whom Jehovah has conferred such power. We hope that this answers your question because if the Messiah were only a normal man then more men would have to be cut off from the living. How many and who they must be we can't possibly know; but just the thought that the perpetual killing of a number of its adherents could be a requirement of a New Covenant is unimaginable, for it would be replacing the present animal sacrifices with those of men; thus certifying the pagan practice of frequently sacrificing human beings to appease their false gods of stone."

Immediately, the Pharisees ceased laughing; some nodded in the affirmative; after which all of them turned and departed.

"Now we come to discussing the aftermath or consequences of the Messiah. The angel states that 'the sacrifice and the oblation will cease.' The sole Judean sacrifices and oblations are those in the Temple, and the only reason for them to cease is that they have been superseded by a sacrifice of a superior nature – one that is more acceptable to Jehovah – that is the bloody, sacrificial death of the Messiah.

"We hold more credibly to this possibility because of what the prophecy portends further. '…and the people of the prince that shall come will destroy the city and the sanctuary; and the end thereof shall be with a flood, (massive flow of destruction) and unto the end of the war desolations are determined. And for the overspreading of abominations He shall make it desolate, even unto the consummation, and that determined shall be poured upon the desolate.'

"We are not told by name who this prince is, nor are we told specifically when or from where he will come – only that he will come with what we assume will be his army sometime in the future to declare war; and that the end result will be the destruction of the city and its sanctuary. We know, however, that if the city is not specifically named, it must be Jerusalem; for only Jerusalem has a sanctuary – the sacred place which houses the altar of animal sacrifice within the Temple. It would appear as we have stated previously, that with the sacrificial death of the Messiah the animal sacrifices are no longer acceptable to Jehovah; and if this is true then the sanctuary with its altar has no reason to exist.

"We know, David, that you, along with everyone here within the sound of my voice must be shocked to hear this explanation, but you must keep in mind that these are not my words nor the collected words of the Sanhedrin; but are in fact the assured promise of Jehovah as proclaimed through an angelic vision to a prophet validated by his miraculous escapes from a fiery furnace and a pit of hungry lions.

"We all believe in the coming of the Messiah, but the vast majority believe his mission will be to reinforce and more forcibly ensure the Jewish culture and the ancient religious practices that are grounded in the rituals of the Temple. Moreover many are of the further belief that His coming must be centered around purging forever the Roman idolaters whose yoke we endure, after which He will sit upon the throne of David in Jerusalem as the King of Israel in a land that is first and foremost among all others. And there are ample statements in the Testament that might lead us to believe in the temporal militarism and earthly rule of such a Messiah. However, there is also in scripture that we find the following prophecy of Zachariah. "Rejoice greatly, O daughter of Zion! Shout in triumph, O daughter of Jerusalem! Behold, your king is coming to you; He is just and endowed with salvation, humble, and mounted on an ass, even on a colt, the foal of an ass." (Zachariah 9:9)

"Note that Zachariah states that He will be endowed with salvation, a term we associate with a spiritual connotation; and furthermore, there is no instance in history nor in scripture where a man who has just secured a great military victory, that is, a conquering hero, who then rides humbly before the adulating crowd on the back of a young ass. He either rides triumphantly seated upon an appropriately adorned horse, or as the Romans do, he rides standing in a chariot.

"This will end our explanation of Daniel's prophecy. If there are further questions, we will attempt to answer them."

"At first, Bruce, there were no questions. Jonathan, a well-known and popular member of the Sanhedrin had just told them that the arrival time of the Messiah could be computed; that it was unlikely He was going to release them from Roman bondage; that He was going to establish a new covenant; that He would be murdered and that their beloved Temple would be desecrated and destroyed 'unto the consummation', a term which to them meant forever; that is, never to be rebuilt. This was upsetting to all of them but particularly to those who worked for the Temple or had been employed by Herod to help rebuild the magnificent structure.

"Others could not fully comprehend that the coming of the Messiah far from being someone whose arrival would solve their problems, would be someone whose New Covenant would upend a way of life that had been their practice for a lifetime as well as that of their forefathers for untold generations before them. 'It is no wonder,' someone murmured, 'that He would be murdered.'

"As Jonathan looked out over the crowd the silence slowly gave way to an undercurrent of murmuring. Not seeing any raised hands, however, he began returning to his seat when a man said, 'I have a question.' As he came forward Jonathan recognized him as David Ben Hillel who had asked for the prophetic explanation for which Jonathan's answer had caused the crowd's consternation.

"Ask your question," Jonathan said, as he turned toward him.

"You've given us a lot of numbers of years in your explanation. Is it possible to use those numbered years to tell us when to expect the Messiah? I note that since the return from Babylon, which was more than four hundred years ago, Jehovah has not raised up a prophet to speak to us. Does this mean that the coming of the Messiah is imminent?"

Jonathan paused for a moment and after motioning to David to give him a moment he nodded to the Rabbi to come forward. "Ask Joseph to join me to answer this man's questions."

"Of Arimathea?" the Rabbi questioned since there were several men named Joseph in the Sanhedrin.

"Yes, Rabbi."

"Jonathan, he is at prayer by the Sanctuary."

"Tell him I have need of his expertise, Rabbi, and he will come."

"As Jonathan awaited the arrival of Joseph he said to David Ben Hillel, 'The answers to your questions require knowledge and ramifications that will be better answered by an older member whose knowledge of Messiah as well as Daniel's Prophecy is legendary.' (Daniel 9:24-27) (Isaiah 45: 1-3)

"Joseph, a man of fifty years came forth and after Jonathan spoke to him in hushed tones; he nodded, after which Jonathan returned to his seat. David looked at Joseph, a man he was seeing for the first time. Before him he observed a tall, slim man whose graying beard, unlike most of the older members of the Sanhedrin, was well trimmed, a practice that was frowned upon by many Jews, but gave Joseph the figure of a man with well-earned confidence. This was borne out by David noting that he was without a scroll or written words of any kind."

"In order that we fully understand your question, David, would you please repeat it?"

"Upon hearing the question Joseph began as follows: 'It began just a little more than seven hundred years ago in the Jewish year 3347 (700 BC) with the Prophet Isaiah when the Lord reveals that He will rise up a man named Cyrus (who will be King of Persia). The prophecy reads thus:

This is what the LORD says to His anointed, to Cyrus

whose right hand I have held to subdue nations before him,
And I will ungird the loins of kings [disarm them];
To open doors before him so that gates will not be shut:
"I will go before you and level the mountains;
I will shatter the doors of bronze and cut through the bars of iron.
"I will give you the treasures of darkness [the hoarded treasures]
And the hidden riches of secret places,
So that you may know that it is I,
The Lord, God of Israel, who calls you by your name."
(Isaiah 45:1-3)

"Just as Isaiah prophesied, 161 years later, Cyrus, King of Persia, in 3508, (539 BC) Jehovah, having provided a way for Cyrus to disarm them conquered the Babylonians in a military engagement known as the Battle of Opis. Cyrus knew that they could never breach the walls; and Cyrus's advance men advised him that other than through the gates in the walls the only entrance to the city was by way of tunnels from the Euphrates; but the river was too deep to wade across and too wide to cross by swimming. So, Cyrus waited until the Babylonians had a national feast day when they would celebrate by consuming food and kegs of wine for a week to the point of bloat and drunkenness and thus unable to defend against an attack.

"He then had his men divert the water until the river was only hip height, allowing Cyrus's army to wade across the river while the Babylonians were celebrating – taking control of the city with virtually no resistance as Isaiah foretold. Babylon then came under the control of the Persian Empire.

"A year later, in 3509 (538 BC) Cyrus issued a proclamation that the Jews were free to return to Jerusalem and rebuild their Temple; however, few returned. The distance from Babylon to Jerusalem is over 140 Persian parasangs (500 miles); most of it across a burning desert, and having lived in bondage all their lives few if any had the means to make the journey.

"In 3528 (519 BC) Darius I, Cyrus's successor, issued an edict confirming Cyrus's proclamation that the Jews were free to return to Jerusalem and rebuild the Temple. But again, few left because of being bereft of the means to do so.

"In 3590 (457 BC) Artaxerxes, in his seventh year as King of Persia, issued an edict not only to rebuild the Temple but Jerusalem and the walls around it as well. In addition, he provided for the Jews to establish their own government and provided the physical means as well as the financial wherewithal to accomplish this. Thus 3590 is Gabriel's reference point when he states, 'Going forth from the commandment to restore Jerusalem ...' (as the two prior edicts did not mention Jerusalem, but only the Temple).

"Finally, in 3603 (444 BC) in Artaxerxes twentieth year of reign he told Nehemiah, a Jewish member of his household to return to Jerusalem with any of the remaining Jews who wished to go back to their homeland. Nehemiah did so and it was he who was primarily responsible for rebuilding the second Temple.

"Therefore, now knowing the time of going forth from the commandment to restore and build again Jerusalem as well as the Temple and the wall around the city we can use those computations about which Daniel prophesied and about which you inquired.

3590 (457 BC) = 'Going forth from the commandment to restore and build again the temple as well as Jerusalem and its wall around the city...'

3639 (408 BC) = 3590 + forty-nine years required to complete the rebuilding. (Daniel 9:24-27)

4073 (26 AD) = 3639 + 434 years after the rebuilding Gabriel tells Daniel until the Messiah is anointed (Jesus is baptized by John the Baptist).

4076 (30 AD) = 4073 + three-and-a-half years the Messiah will teach the way of the New Covenant before He is cut off (martyred).

"Gabriel does not mention what will occur during the last half of the final seven years. And we will not presume to know the mind of Jehovah in this matter. What we can do, however, is to use our present year 4058 (5 AD) to make several predictions.

4058+15 years = 4073 (26 AD) when the Messiah will be anointed.

4073+ three-and-a-half years = 4076 (30 AD) during which time He will teach the way of the New Covenant at the end of which He will be cut off. (executed).

"Neither I nor any member of the Sanhedrin knows who will be responsible for killing the Messiah. From our interpretation of Gabriel's prophecy, we know that in some way his death allows for the expiation of sin which purpose apparently puts in jeopardy the animal sacrifices within the Temple.

"I believe this answers all the questions concerning Daniel's Prophecy given to him by the angel Gabriel from which we have the knowledge to answer factually. Anything more we might say is speculation, and so we will say no more. Those of us who are young enough and fortunate to be alive in fifteen years will see for ourselves. Pray that you might be among those so fortunate."

As Joseph returned to the sanctuary area Jesus stood and said to Jonathan, "My parents are in the courtyard and now see me in the midst of the Sanhedrin. I must go to them for they stand fearful of how this has happened to me."

"Shalom," Jonathan replied. "It has been a pleasure. I thank you for your learned contributions and wish you well."

As Jesus departed, he turned his head, smiled and waved to Nicodemus and Asher who waved in return.

As he approached his parents Mary hastened to come to him and said, "Your father and I have been looking for you with great anxiety. Why have you done this to us?"

"Why were you searching for me?" he asked. "Didn't you know I had to be in my Father's house?"

Mary and Joseph looked at one another but said nothing. Both now understood that Jesus, the God-Man, was no longer a Child and as they returned to Nazareth they talked about whether they should now think about treating him differently. However, during their return and after their arrival they were relieved to see that Jesus acted and spoke as any other Jewish boy his age. As it is written he grew in wisdom, age and grace while being subject to them." (Luke 2:52)

CHAPTER TWENTY-EIGHT

Pentecost and Saul the Persecutor Becomes Paul the Apostle

"Taking into consideration," I remarked to Satan, "that Jonathan, Nicodemus and Asher were speaking before Jesus' public life occurred, they did an excellent job of interpreting Gabriel's prophecy. They only failed to miss two details."

"You must remember," Satan replied, "that Jesus was with them. If they were missed then it was because He intentionally wanted them to be missed. Be that as it may, Bruce, what are the two items to which you refer?"

"The first is that they dance all around the fact that He has powers that only God has, but they never say that the Messiah could be God, himself, taking on human life to be among His people."

"As we stated earlier, Bruce, that concept, was so far beyond Jewish theology and feasibility that Jesus acceptance as Divine was impossible for them to believe even when Jesus told them so after dozens of miracles culminating in restoring Lazarus to life four days after he had been entombed. Except for Joseph, who by now is deceased, his mother, Mary, the Apostles and possibly Joseph of Arimathea, Nicodemus and Mary Magdalene there is no proof that prior to His resurrection anyone else believed Jesus was God. I might add that I find none of the prophets prophesying or even hinting that the Messiah would actually be God Incarnate. And your second question?"

"It was that final three-and-a-half-year period about which Joseph of Arimathea said he couldn't comment."

"Do you have any ideas, Bruce?"

"Maybe if I thought about it for a while; but right now, I don't have a clue."

"As Jesus instructed them, following the Ascension the Apostles with Jesus' mother, Mary, remained in Jerusalem to await the coming of the Holy Spirit. Now, Bruce these were very frightened men. I couldn't believe that God expected men who were convinced that Caiaphas along with members of the Sanhedrin were looking for them to drag before Pilate for sentencing and crucifixion had any chance to convert anybody to follow the new covenant.

"A few of them were convinced that they should return to Galilee; forget about Jesus and resume what they knew best – fishing. Mary, however, held them together. She reminded them that Jesus had never told them an untruth and that the easiest way to give Caiaphas his wish was to be caught skulking about the streets of Jerusalem.

"On the tenth day, however, something happened. Following a strong wind that blew around the room, a flame about a half foot high lighted on the forehead of each of them. It remained there for about a minute and then disappeared. From that moment on they were changed men. Far from fearing Caiaphas or even the Romans they were eager to confront them with their courage behind the infused knowledge of the new covenant.

"Peter went into the center of the city and explained the truth of the new covenant so eloquently that three thousand were converted. Far from them being fearful of Caiaphas it was Caiaphas and the Sanhedrin who were fearful of them. When Pilate was told of their resurgence his position was greatly influenced by his wife, Claudia, who convinced him that as long as they were not a threat to Rome, he had no reason to get involved. Having learned his lesson the first time he fully agreed."

"So, how do the final three-and-a-half years fit into all of this?" I asked.

"For three and a half years the apostles did their missionary work in and around Jerusalem amid the Jewish areas of Judea and Galilee. The Jewish Sanhedrin saw them much as they saw Jesus before them.

"They were a threat to their authority, power and livelihood. So, they hired men to persecute them. One of these as we said previously was Saul. He was born of a Roman father and a Jewish mother. Raised a strict Jew he was vicious in his persecution of Christians, and one day he led a group of Jews who dragged a young Christian, named Stephen outside the gates and after Saul threw the first stone the others continued until he died. Since that time the man stoned to death has been referred to as St. Stephen and given the status of being the first Christian martyr.

"After giving Saul his bag of coins, they commissioned him to go to Damascus where there was a rumor that some Jewish Christian converts had traveled to avoid persecution. He was to have them charged and killed by whatever law the Damascenes (who were Romans) would allow. On the way, however, God used lightning to strike him from his horse and blind him. I won't continue with this account because just about everyone knows it. Saul became Paul, Jesus' Apostle to the gentiles. This happened three-and-a-half years after Jesus' crucifixion and was the beginning of God fulfilling his promise to Abraham after Abraham loosed Isaac's bonds, 'Your offspring shall possess the gates of their enemies, and by your offspring shall all the nations of the earth gain blessing for themselves, because you have obeyed my voice.'" (Genesis 22:17)

"The termination of the three-and-a-half-year period following the cutting off of the Anointed One along with the proclamation of the New Covenant to the Gentiles was the beginning of the fulfillment as God promised that the new covenant would move from being solely a Jewish relationship between man and God to one including Jew and gentile alike – in effect the whole of humanity."

"It's amazing, Satan, how everything falls into place when the details are known."

CHAPTER TWENTY-NINE

Satan Expounds on Mankind's Stupidity and Stubbornness

"Yes, Bruce, but it won't matter. Mankind is so stupid and enamored with pursuing the temporary goods of this world that they are like blindfolded men starving to death amid a mountain of food only a few hundred feet away."

"And you do everything in your power to see that no one influences them to remove the blind folds?"

"A couple hundred years ago it was a real challenge. Most parents raised their children in the love and fear of God, and the schools reinforced what children learned at home; but I and my demons can say with pride that we've changed all that. In the modern world the State consumed with the fear of Divine influence has removed all teaching of morals or God in the schools or their offices. Parents are so caught up with increasing their political or corporate power and the pursuit of money to provide their offspring with things they think are important that they neglect to teach them what is really essential. In many families, knowledge and love of God, honesty, kindness, character, empathy, humility, love, duty, patriotism, and respect are all but gone; except for a minority of good parents whose parental instruction at home is often nullified when they send their sons and daughters off to secular universities whose professors we have groomed undo whatever good the parents have worked so hard to instill.

"Negligent parenting creates a vacuum in which we, the demonic, install Godlessness along with self-serving greed wrapped in a sense of entitlement – an impediment that cripples their adult development and ensures perpetuation of the abominable condition."

"It appears that left alone, Satan, mankind would do quite well as God intended; however, it is your evil input that creates and fortifies the decisions you refer to as stupid. Am I right?"

"God created man with intelligence and free will. Yes, we lay the temptations before him, but it is his will to choose evil over good that brings about his destruction. One more thing, Bruce. Faith in God brings belief in His promises. However, only a scant few of the world's population has any faith at all in the spiritual, that is, what they cannot see. How many times have you heard non-believers say, 'I would believe if only I had some proof?' In other words, they want God to do as they will – not do as God wills."

"Let me see, Satan, if I can define in temporal terms what you just said:

The vast majority of people in this world have intelligence and free will but use them as an impediment as opposed to an aid in securing their salvation.

The reason for this is that they do not have the religious instruction to use their intelligence and free will according to the way God wills it. To use an example – they are like builders that have all the tools required to build the structure, but can't do so because there is no lumber, no bricks, no cement or any of the other materials required.

You and yours see this situation, and knowing that idle hands make mischief, show them a completed structure nearby that they can use their tools to tear down, which they will to do, thus placing them on the wide road to eternal destruction.

"How am I doing?"

"Jesus used the parable to give esoteric concepts a picture language that even the illiterate could understand. If you haven't mastered the art, you are close to doing so. However, you are amiss in mentioning that many have had the instruction but have rejected it. To further illustrate using your example, the bricks, the mortar and the lumber were delivered but they rejected them because construction interfered with more pleasurable, but sinful aspirations."

"I preferred not to answer, but nodded in the affirmative and continued. The only way to stop a ball from continuing to roll downhill is in some way to deflect or destroy it. It has now gone so far and is moving at such a breakneck speed that it appears it will take divine intervention to stop it from destroying all of mankind."

"His RESET!" Satan exclaimed. "The only difference is that I used the bowling alley, and you used the ball rolling downhill. However, Bruce, analogies are fine, but they don't approach the impact of graphics. I can show you some graphic details of men's rage against God as well as his allegiance, but it won't be easy to watch."

"Satan, I can't believe that any man's rage against God could equal yours."

CHAPTER THIRTY

Bruce Experiences the Judgment Seat of God

"It can't, but in my case, I told you about it. What I am about to do is the difference between listening to an incident on the radio and personally viewing it.

"So, for the last time are you sure you want to see this? I have to tell you that it is not pleasant witnessing a fellow human being realizing that he spent his entire life, his whole reason for existence, working incessantly to ensure that he fails; especially when the consequences are horrifically excruciating and without end."

"As much as I shudder at how it must feel for a person to hear the irreversible judgment of eternal damnation, Satan, I have to see it before I can write about it."

"Very well, then."

"Satan stood and facing away from me he extended his arms in front of him with his wrists fully bent so the palms of his hands were facing down. After a moment he moved his arms back so that they appeared as the crossbar of a cross. Immediately there appeared before me a regal looking individual sitting on a throne. I knew it was Jesus as I could see the wounds in his hands. Standing before him was a man who was obviously distressed and confused as he was looking around the way a person does who doesn't know where he is or how he got there.

"Look at me," Jesus commanded. "Your temporal life has come to an end, and with it your limitless access to My infinite mercy – a mercy and forgiveness that was yours for the asking, but you chose to turn your back on Me. You looked upon Me, your Creator, with ridicule and disdain. I incessantly reached out to you through your conscience as well as the pleading and admonitions of your fellow man, but you refused to take heed. Your reply was constant in that you had a better idea – an idea which impugned the talents I gave you when you chose theft over honest work; hate over love; blasphemy over reverence; greed over compassion; fornication and drunkenness over temperance in addition to the abomination of leading others to follow you along your sinful, crime ridden path.

"All of these, however, as evil as they are, I would have gladly forgiven had you asked for pardon in a spirit of contrition with a firm purpose of amendment; but you chose to continually wallow in the pit of depravity and now find yourself in a state of perdition where mercy and forbearance are no longer available and only Divine Justice prevails.

"That you may know that it is not I, Almighty God, who condemns you, but you yourself by your own free will who has chosen to be damned for eternity I now show you a few images of the person I created you to be."

"What the man saw before him was an attractive woman who was nursing an infant as two others, a boy and a girl several years older than the infant, were playing a game with their father in the next room. Except that he was thirty years younger the father looked exactly like the man being judged. As it faded away another vision appeared in which the man was being generously rewarded by his employer for devising a manufacturing cost saving procedure. In the next vision he has just been elected CFO (Chief Financial Officer) of a growing electronics firm. Finally, he is standing tall at one of his son's college graduation, and then walking his daughter on his arm down the aisle at her wedding."

"By your own free will you have chosen to live your life on the wide road which I warned all mankind is the road of sin and degradation by which a man or woman fails to give Me the adoration that as your Creator I am due; and even more you have never loved your neighbor as yourself. Your choices can lead to only one place – perdition. And as your reward would have been for all eternity, so will your penalty. Therefore, I grant you your wish. DEPART FROM ME YOU ACCURSED INTO THE EVERLASTING FIRES OF HELL PREPARED FOR THE DEVIL AND HIS DEMONS!'"

"Upon hearing this I closed my eyes and became so weak that my legs gave way from under me. Satan, anticipating my reaction kept me from falling by grabbing onto my arm. As he did so I heard him whisper in my ear, 'Mine! All mine! Forever & forever all mine.'"

"Of course, with my background in religious education I had been taught well about the Divine Judgment we can all expect – but to actually see an individual who is going to his doom in a state of despair and without any hope that his sufferings will ever end was beyond my ability to cope.

"Before opening my eyes I asked, 'Is the vision gone?'"

"This one is gone forever," Satan replied. "A perfect example as we said earlier of a man betting a pair of deuces against a royal flush; and I might add, Bruce, another example of my belief that the average human being is stupid."

"I decided not to answer because at least in this instance Satan was right."

"When Jesus appeared again on His throne I said, Satan, I have seen enough. Please! Let's move on from here as you promised."

"You have misquoted me, Bruce. I said, this one is gone forever. Once may be enough for you as an individual, but it is insufficient for your readers. Observe.'"

"A man of about eighty appeared – also disheveled and confused but in his case as if he knew he should be frightened."

"Look at me," Jesus said once again. "You have dishonored, despised and scorned me as few others have done. You were chosen as a candidate for the Catholic priesthood. You were given a superb education at a premier seminary where you desecrated your position by engaging with your instructors as well as your companion seminarians in sexual acts not only contrary to nature but in violation of your intent to take a vow of chastity in order to better serve me without the obligations of a family – a vow if kept I greatly reward."

"I was a young man with strong sexual desires and no chance in the seminary of satisfying them naturally, that is, with a woman. Am I to be condemned for fulfilling a craven yearning which was a part of my creation – a creation for which you are responsible?"

"Yes, because whether women were available or not is irrelevant. You violated the virtue as well as your vow of chastity in a depraved manner over and over again."

"You take no responsibility for these acts to quiet a need which you created?"

"Your violation of my commandment was a result of your willful choice to minimize your prayer life and finally to totally terminate your personal prayers altogether. You knew the power of prayer. You were familiar with my promise to grant you anything you asked the Father in my name, but you chose to ignore my promise because it interfered with your desire to satisfy your lustful desires. (John 16:23-24)

"I always had a difficult time believing that."

"That is because you treated my promise with the idea that God the Father was a run and fetch it individual that stood by to gratify your every whim and want. As a priest with a Doctorate in Theology you are familiar with James 4:3. Are you not?"

"I am."

"And..?"

"St. James said, 'You ask and do not receive because you ask amiss, that you may consume your request upon your own lusts." (James 4:3)

"You are correct; so you know not only from your heart, but also from the nature of your studies that it would be unjust for Me to grant anything that would inhibit a man's salvation.

"You were duly ordained. You were given the power to consecrate; to forgive sins in my name; to baptize and to preach the gospel. All this you did in the light but in the shadows of the day and in the darkness of the night you chose to hypocritically dance with the devil on a floor of forbidden flesh. You stole the childhood from the young and in some cases drove them to self-destruction in a fit of despair.

"Later on, by a likewise corrupt prelate you were appointed rector of a diocesan seminary where your inordinate lustful desires drove men from pursuing their religious vocation, thus tending to decimate my legitimate priesthood.

"Even so you were consecrated a bishop in which office you used your wider influence and authority to continue your sinful ways on an even grander scale by ordaining and even promoting men you knew, who like you, were steeped in sinful, inordinate lust filled and depraved behavior, while you concealed their culpable deeds from fellow prelates and later on from the laity and civil authorities.

"So, returning to your first evil ways, you placed your soul, mind and body in the service of the evil one as you allowed Satan to convince you that 'Suffer the little children, mind you little children, to come unto you' meant using sodomy and worse practices on them to express your perverted definition of love. I tell you what you knew in your heart – you were not expressing filial love for these young ones. You used them as a whore monger uses whores! You used their innocence to satisfy your wanton lusts. As a clergyman you must be familiar with Matthew 18:6."

"If anyone causes one of these little ones – those who believe in me – to stumble, it would be better for him to have a large *millstone* hung *around his neck* and be drowned in the depths of the sea."

"Having therefore, willingly aligned yourself with the Powers of Darkness I now grant you your wish to dwell with Satan along with his demons and their accusations not for a while, but for all eternity. "DEPART FROM ME YOU ACCURSED INTO THE EVERLASTING FIRES OF HELL PREPARED FOR SATAN AND HIS DEMONS!"

"Having seen it once before I managed to maintain my composure as I heard Satan once more whisper how this bishop's soul was his for all eternity.

"I was tempted again to ask Satan to terminate these mind-numbing visions, but I knew that he was in control and wouldn't stop them until he was finished. In addition I knew that God was permitting them and so I braced myself when a third person came before Jesus."

"He was someone I had seen many times on television. He was an avowed atheist and used this belief in his monologues to entertain mostly young adults."

"You seem surprised," Jesus said, "or maybe I should say shocked to see Me. You shouldn't be. As a youth you were told all about me in the parochial school you attended. In fact, you were an altar boy who was privileged to witness and assist the priest in his act of consecration from the altar. There are some who appear before me who have rejected me purely out of a desire to do so in order to pursue sinful objectives; but you did so in an effort to use your atheism to earn your livelihood by mocking me for laughter.

"As a twelve-year-old in the Temple when a rabbi told me that a man died – a man with whom I had a conversation the day before on the reality of eternal life, I told him what I am going to tell you now. 'Immediately after you die you no longer have the privilege of expressing a personal opinion about what is true. Whether what you professed in life was the absolute truth, a relative half-truth or blatantly wrong, the indisputable truth now shorn of any ambiguity appears before you as undeniably visible, irrefutably clear and unmistakably eternal.' Looking at Me now do you agree?"

"I have no choice, Lord. As I stand before you, your existence is irrefutable.

"Your slow slide into atheism began when you commenced ingesting illicit drugs. Your prayer life as bad as it was ceased altogether as you traded reverence for disrespecting Me in order to gain the approval of your addicted companions. As time went on you became addicted yourself and your irreverence and disrespect turned to mocking Me and showing contempt while entertaining newfound friends with your natural comedic talent.

"You had a wife with whom you had a daughter. When your wife died from cancer, from grief and shame and an admired sense of parental obligation, you took the proper steps to shake your addiction, but your pursuit of mocking me in denial to entertain intensified and with it your monetary compensation. Continuing in this vein you became rich and famous while caring for a weak heart that was made irreversibly more so by your past use of heroin.

"Finally, the deterioration of your heart advanced to such a degree that you were hospitalized. While you were there, I advanced you the actual grace to accept the priest, who served as hospital chaplain. He came to you not once, but three times to perform the Last Rites; and each time you sent him away."

"I didn't believe I was dying. I had reason to believe that I would recover as I had in the past. Besides, I no longer believed in the afterlife. Now be that as it may, as I stand before You, I must depend upon Your reputation for unconditional love."

"There were three farmers whose farms adjoined one another. The farmer in the middle had a powerful tractor and all the implements to go with it. As an act of charity after preparing his own land, he would till the soil of both his neighbors. The farmer on his right thanked him and sowed the land with seed. The one on his left preferred to spend his time debauching himself in drunkenness, gambling and women of ill repute.

"When the growing season had ended and it became time to harvest, the farmer on his right filled his barns with grain. The farmer on his left had only a field of weeds that had taken root in the fertile soil. The reason for my telling you this should be self-evident; but, if not, I, Almighty God, am the farmer who tills the soil of everyone with unconditional love. What a person does with it is his or her choice and responsibility – a result of my gift of free will."

"I am beginning to feel uneasy and a bit queasy, Lord."

"You should because you have just remembered too late that My love is unconditional; however, salvation is not. You were taught My Second Commandment – Thou shalt not take the name of the Lord thy God in vain. As you have done so then as you will, DEPART FROM ME YOU ACCURSED INTO THE EVERLASTING FIRES OF HELL PREPARED FOR SATAN AND HIS DEMONS!'"

"I asked Satan why I am seeing only the condemned. Surely, there are some that are saved!" I exclaimed.

"Watch closely." Satan answered.

"Again, Jesus appeared on His throne. Now standing before him was a young man who appeared to be in his mid-twenties. Unlike those who came before, Jesus did not command the young man to look at him, but said instead, 'You are here before your time.'"

"I did my best, Lord, but I failed."

"I'll be the judge of that," Jesus replied. "Tell me what happened."

"Please, Lord. You know what happened better than I."

"You are correct. Of that there is no doubt; but this is your particular judgment and I want you to tell me why you think you failed."

"I was a Second Lieutenant in the United States Marine Corps. Shortly after I was commissioned, I was ordered to Iraq to fight insurgents there. Upon arrival I was given command of a platoon to replace the former platoon leader who had been killed by an IUD (land mine) a few days before. I didn't have time to learn the names of my men except those of the three sergeants who were the squad leaders; when I, along with two other platoon leaders were given a briefing by our Company Commander on attacking a city called Fallujah. It was to be a house-to-house campaign with expected hand-to-hand combat. I will admit to being nervous, Lord, but I wasn't frightened. We all had extensive training in such fighting and believed we were the best in the world.

"The Catholic chaplain was a Navy Commander, Father Begglio, who heard confessions after which he offered Mass. Perhaps it was born of fear but I can't remember a more fervent reception of communion.

"Two of the many things we were told in the briefing were not to open any doors because many would be booby trapped. We were also told that the bulk of the civilians had left the city; and that the only civilians remaining were those too feeble, too sick or too stubborn to leave.

"Upon approaching a building suspected of housing the enemy we asked them in Arabic to come out and surrender. If they refused, we blew in the door followed by a barrage of stun charges. If any of them fired a shot we blanketed the rooms with machine gun fire. My platoon killed seventy-two of the enemy. The necessity of hand-to-hand combat never materialized. After five hours of this all appeared calm in the midst of an eerie silence. Then one of my young men, probably not yet nineteen, screamed, 'I'm hit!' and fell to the ground. I ordered the senior sergeant to get the rest of the men out of there by orderly retreat as I was sure the man hit had been done so by a sniper.

"I moved the wounded man to an area behind a wall where I thought we would be out of sight of the sniper; then tied off his pumping artery with a length of shoelace as I began yelling for a medic. Just then I was hit in the head, but for some reason – probably the partial protection of my helmet, the round didn't kill me, and I remained conscious.

"When the medics arrived after advising me that the helicopter was near its load limit, they wanted to evacuate me since my wound was fresher and they saw the large pool of blood that had gushed from the shoulder and arm of the unconscious young enlisted man. I ordered them to take the young man to the waiting helicopter and then tell the pilot to make a return trip for me. Before they did so the medics wiped the blood from my face, and poured a powder on my wound to stave off infection and aid in congealing. I remember lying there developing a massive headache as the shock began to subside. Finally, I heard the familiar sound of a helicopter overhead. A few minutes later they took me to the 'copter. My next memory is standing here before you."

"All that is true, but you have not told me why you think you failed."

"Lord, my grandfather was a marine in WW II. He survived Guadalcanal, the battle of Okinawa and the first year of American occupation of Japan to come home. My father was likewise a marine who survived three tours in Vietnam and came home. Both of them had multiple awards and medals for outstanding bravery and performance in battle. After all that training leading up to a commission as a marine officer, I did not survive my first engagement with the enemy. What else could I or anyone think?"

"It doesn't matter what anyone thinks."

"It doesn't? Why not, Lord?"

"Because at this stage of your existence the only evaluation of you that matters is mine. Are you familiar with the 13th verse in the 15th chapter of St John's gospel?"

"Perhaps, Lord, but I would have to hear it."

"Very well, then. These are my words spoken some two thousand years ago. 'For the greatest love of all is a love that sacrifices all. Greater love hath no man than this: that a man lay down his life for another.'" (John 15:13)

"I don't know how that applies to me, Lord. Before the medics arrived, I began having convulsions – a sure sign that I had a serious head wound. I felt I was going to die no matter what."

"You made a conscious choice to stay behind as you ordered the medics to board the wounded young man. Because of your choice he survived and will recover the use of his arm. Only one of you would survive the ordeal. By your choice you sacrificed your own life to save his."

The young marine officer, not knowing how to answer or even if he should, stood there mute – appearing to be somewhat embarrassed.

Jesus motioned for him to come closer. When he did Jesus embraced him. Then, taking a step back and putting his hands on the marine's shoulders he said, "My son, you have not failed. You are victorious because you have survived the most important battle of your life; and for doing so you have earned the highest commendation of all! No medal will suffice for the valor it takes to successfully navigate the narrow road to salvation, for to reach its end is to have entered into eternal life. COME, THEN, MY SON, YOU WHO ARE BLESSED OF MY

FATHER, AND INHERIT THE KINGDOM PREPARED FOR YOU FROM THE FOUNDATION OF THE WORLD." (Matthew 25-34)

"From my perspective, Satan, that was the most beautiful thing I have ever witnessed."

"No doubt, Bruce, but for me, the circumstances of the marine's death represent the frustration of losing a soul for my domain; and a reminder that God told me that some of you would lead lives that would merit eternal life.

"Are we through?"

"Yes, unless you want to see more. I can show you what happens to abortion doctors, or, if you prefer those who financially or politically support the murder of the unborn; or how about politicians, both male and female, who betray their people by ignoring campaign promises in order to dishonestly accumulate wealth by accepting bribes and in many instances through just plain theft from public coffers. Finally, Bruce, there are those who are thrust into the deepest and hottest depths of Hell – the fools who kill another human being because he or she says, 'GOD WILLS IT!' Pick a commandment from one to ten, Bruce, and I can show you violations for each. Then, as we stated earlier, there are those who refuse to accept God's grace to plead for forgiveness as they breathe their last with hate and unforgiveness in their heart. All of these are mine, Bruce; forever and forever all mine!

"On the other hand, we can concentrate on those, like the young marine, for whom God told me, 'These, after their earthly sojourn, I will gather to Myself in a kingdom of joy the likes of which they could never experience or even imagine in their world.'"

"No thank you," I said. "I've seen Divine judgment go both ways. I neither wish nor need to see more.

"Suddenly I felt tired. Perhaps it was the strain of watching people pass through their judgment and said, "I am tired, Satan, and need to get some rest. I'm going to lie down until fully rested and then we can continue."

CHAPTER THIRTY-ONE

I Can Send You to Hell for a Visit, but Only God Can Get You Out

"Yes, please do," he replied emphatically. "You will find our next session to be considerably taxing."

"I wanted to ask him what he meant, but was just too tired to care.

"I awoke and looking at my alarm clock I noted that I had slept for three hours. Feeling refreshed I threw some cold water on my face and as I entered the sitting room, Satan, looking up from his copy of Scientific American said, 'You look rested, but hungry. Being Friday, I heated a can of clam chowder, prepared a tuna fish sandwich and made a fresh pot of coffee. After you've eaten, if you're game, we'll explore our next adventure.'"

"Hearing this, I was beginning to feel a bit uncomfortable – as if Satan had taken control while I slept, and the last thing I wanted was to be in the control of Satan. I thank you for the meal, I replied, but it wasn't necessary... Before I could finish my thought, he interrupted."

"Of course not, Bruce, it was simply a gesture as I am not capable of kindness. You, however, being capable of kindness, just graciously accept the gesture so we can get on with my objective for being here with you."

"I detected a sense of animosity with this remark, but decided not to respond in kind – knowing that to respond to a challenge from Satan was a losing proposition for even the most intelligent of human beings which I definitely was not. I said a simple, 'Thank you,' and sat down to eat the meal."

"When I finished eating and was washing the dishes Satan said, 'Do you remember the paper you wrote while at Villanova concerning the existence of Hell? It was the one where you were preparing to debate someone who didn't believe it existed; or, if it did, it wasn't eternal.'"

"Yes," I said. "It should be in the notebook with the others. Why do you ask?"

"When you are through in the kitchen get it out. It will serve as an excellent introduction to your enlightening adventure."

"What do you mean by adventure? We're supposed to be having spirited discussions, a means of discourse that can hardly be called adventures."

"Bruce, as I cannot lie to you trust me on this. This one will be an adventure."

"As I leafed through the binder, I remembered the peculiarities of this assignment. 'Prove the existence of Hell along with its eternal nature in as few words as possible,' Father had said, 'and I expect a minimum of two proofs.'"

"I thought about how to do this without consulting any of my classmates because had I done so, in such few words, there would have been many identical papers. So, I went to the school library and after an evening of research wrote the following:

Proof for the Existence of Hell

An unbeliever, i.e., an atheist, does not believe that God exists; therefore, he can't believe there is an afterlife. If there is no afterlife then there is no reason for a Heaven or a Hell. You can never prove the existence of Hell to a person who sincerely believes that the sum and substance of his life is a few pounds of fertilizer.

A person who holds with the belief in Reincarnation believes that we pay for our sins by coming back after each death again and again until we get it right. He may believe in a Heaven, of sort, which he calls Nirvana, for those who finally get it right, but since he pays for his "sins" by constant do over's there is no reason for him to believe that Hell exists, at least where human beings are concerned.

Muslims believe in Hell but in their belief that Allah considers them superior assert that Hell is temporary for Muslims but permanent for those who are not.

Judaism believes, for the most part, that there is an afterlife where it is possible to go to Hell; however if you do go the most time you will spend there is 12 months after which you are released to your eternal reward – I think! (Researching belief in the afterlife in Judaism you get to appreciate the Jew who said, "Ask two rabbis the same question and you will get three opinions.")

The Christian belief is that Jesus Christ is the Son of God, and as Almighty God can neither deceive nor be deceived. This identity was proven primarily from miracles in which he cured the incurable, raised the dead to life and predicting his death and resurrection both of which happened exactly when he said it would. Therefore, since His statements are Divine what Jesus says about the existence of Hell must be correct; thereby proving that if Jesus said that Hell exists and is eternal – then it is.

Following are three statements made by Jesus Christ that prove the eternal existence of Hell:

The parable of Lazarus and the rich man (Luke 16:19-31)

"Then He will say to those on His left, 'Depart from Me you who are cursed into the eternal fire prepared for the devil and his angels.'" (Matthew 25:41)

"If your hand causes you to stumble, cut it off. It is better for you to enter life maimed than with two hands to go into Hell, where the fire never goes out." (Mark 9:43)

Bruce McPherson

May 6, 1991

"What grade did you get for that paper?" Satan asked.

"Father gave me an A," I responded. "It was the easiest A I received in college. Afterwards in the discussion Father had with the class he said that the object of the assignment was to show that if our thinking was correct; we didn't have to use excess verbiage, which instead of further explaining our thought more than likely will cause us to cloud the issue..."

"He's right, you know. It is a weapon that I and mine utilize frequently to change the subject matter more to our liking."

"Speaking of subject matter, what is this adventure you mentioned?"

"In an effort to exclude excess verbiage in my reply – your personal visit to Hell."

"My what... Why?"

"It is a necessary part of my sessions with you."

"And how is that?"

"By providing credibility. Proving that we left nothing out. By moving our sessions 'over the top' as many of you say."

"Will you accompany me?"

"No, Bruce. If I were there you would be leaning on me for support and your questions would be incessant. No, it's better that you go alone to experience mankind's proper feeling of my domain."

"You used the word feeling when you really meant terror. Am I right?"

"Indubitably!"

"How long will I be there?"

"I don't really know – eighteen to twenty-four hours I should think." Then, pointing his finger to the ceiling, he added, "It all depends on what He thinks is necessary," Satan answered.

"You care to explain further?"

"Yes. You see I can send you there, but only God can get you out. Sorry, but those are His rules, not mine."

"When would this happen?"

"The time is at your discretion."

"Well, I'm rested and thanks to you, Satan, I've just finished a full meal. So, as they say, 'there is no time like the present.'"

I suddenly felt as if I were standing on the trap door of a hangman's gallows when it was abruptly released. In an instant I was dropping down at breakneck speed in a shaft more than large enough to accommodate my free fall. Within the tunnel-like shaft it was black with absolutely no illumination – the darkest black I had ever experienced. Not being able to see the bottom or even knowing if there was one increased my feeling of terror! It was like this, it seemed, for several minutes – down, down, faster and faster, until it felt like someone had applied a brake as the speed of my descent began slowing down. The slower my rate of fall, however, the stronger was the odor that came wafting up from below. It was the smell of death – the stench of a rotting carcass. Finally, I quit falling and was suspended above a massive cavern. There was a dim point of amber light about twenty feet above me but it gave so little light that I could see only the silhouettes of someone or something huge as they–or it–passed by my line of sight. At this point I began to hear the sounds of people moaning and wailing. They were accompanied by human voices crying out but they were muffled as if people were hollering through a scarf.

Then I began moving down again, but very slowly as if an overhead crane was about to rest something easily damaged on the ground. The cavern was immense; so much so that while standing on its floor in the inky darkness I began to feel helpless and insignificant. I could not see across to the other side, and felt fearful that if attacked I had no way to defend myself. So, in order to reduce my feeling of terror I reminded myself that I was here not because I was condemned, but only for as long as I needed to be in order to describe it. This assurance was shaken, however, when I heard a series of men and women shrieking and screaming in pain followed by the most hideous deep-throated laughter amid further screaming and voices begging for mercy which never came.

"Then as quickly as I heard them I didn't, as it became completely silent apart from the sound of my own breathing. I looked around to make out the source of the pleading voices, but saw nothing. The only illumination continued to be from that very dim point of amber light; but, like a twenty-five-watt bulb would be at night in a conference hall it barely penetrated the darkness.

"Suddenly the silence was broken by the sound of an infant crying. I told myself that I had to be imagining it because there were no babies in Hell: but the crying got louder as if an infant was in distress or severe pain.

"Then rising from the depths were the wispy, gray souls of women who began frantically looking for the baby. Their calls became louder and louder but now with a growing sense of desperation – like a mother in a marketplace when she realizes that her little one is nowhere to be seen. This is the height of mental anguish, I told myself, for women who find it impossible to ignore the pleading cries of a helpless infant; even more so when she can hear it bawling but can't find it. This continued for several minutes.

"When the baby's crying abruptly ceased the frantic calling was followed by their sudden wailing as if a mother has been told that her child is dead as she realizes that she will no longer have the joy of seeing or caring for it; but then they are suddenly brought to realize that all this is brought about by their heinous act which shredded the plan God had for their child and when these women died unrepentant, they died in their sin thereby choosing to pay the ultimate price."

"THE SOULS OF THE WOMEN WHOSE VOICES YOU HEARD LIVE IN A STATE OF CONSTANT REGRET, SORROW AND REMORSE," boomed a deep voice coming from out of the darkness. "FOR WHEN THEIR WOMBS BLOSSOMED WITH THE LIFE OF A CHILD, THEY LOOKED UPON THAT LIFE GROWING WITHIN THEM NOT WITH JOY BUT WITH HORROR AND DISDAIN; AND THEN ARRANGED TO HAVE THEIR OWN FLESH AND BLOOD MURDERED BY POISON, OR WORSE, BUTCHERED – TORN

TO PIECES TO HAVE ITS ORGANS DISCARDED OR SOLD BY OTHERS FOR MONETARY GAIN. THEY TRIED TO RATIONALIZE THE ABORTION BY RENAMING IT REPRODUCTIVE HEALTH, BUT GOD REJECTED THEIR CLAIM BY POINTING TO HIS FIFTH COMMANDMENT – THOU SHALT NOT KILL! HAVING BEEN DISCARDED BY GOD NOT FOR SUCCUMBING TO OUR TEMPTATION BUT RATHER FOR ARROGANTLY REJECTING HIS MERCY AND FORGIVENESS THEY ARE NOW OURS – FOREVER AND FOREVER ALL OURS."

"Just as suddenly it became quiet again, but not knowing for sure whether the demonic voice was through speaking, I paused before continuing to walk. After a few moments of silence, I continued.

After I had taken thirty or forty steps, I was startled by an explosive ignition fifty yards to my right. A giant torch far above me burned with white hot flames shooting straight up resembling something one might see on the Fourth of July. Identical ignitions followed every few seconds until the 16th completed the circle around what I could see was the top of an amphitheater. As I walked toward it, approaching closer, I read the words just above the entrance:

IT MIGHT HAVE BEEN

Its outer wall was encircled by a ramp. While standing where the ramp met the ground I was startled by the loud, booming voice I had heard earlier commanding me to "CLIMB THE RAMP."

I did as commanded. Reaching the top, I saw by the light of the torches that the huge amphitheater was filled entirely with men. However, rather than enjoying themselves, as men might do at a sporting event; they appeared to be in agony. Most of them were standing with their hands outstretched beseeching someone to come closer; but regardless of how strong their appeals, how copious their tears or how pleading the tremor of their voices, their entreaties went unanswered. The rest were shaking their bowed heads while moaning, "No! No! No!"

I stood wondering to whom these men were addressing their agonizing appeals as I neither saw nor heard anyone else.

"THESE ARE MEN WHO CHOSE WHAT THEY TERMED THE GOOD LIFE IN OPPOSITION TO CARING FOR AND RAISING THE SONS AND DAUGHTERS THEY FATHERED," boomed the deep, loud demonic voice I had heard earlier that now seemed to reverberate off unseen walls. "USING THREATS AND INTIMIDATION THEY FORCED, AND IN MANY INSTANCES FINANCED ONE OR MORE BRUTAL, MURDEROUS ABORTIONS TO PRECLUDE HAVING TO PROVIDE SUSTENANCE, SHELTER AND EDUCATION FOR THEIR OWN FLESH AND BLOOD.

"WHAT YOU ARE WITNESSING ARE MEN SEEING WHAT THEY LOST BY THEIR CALLOUS DISREGARD FOR THE LIFE PLAN GOD HAD FOR THEIR CHILD OR CHILDREN. IN DETAIL THEY ARE SEEING WHAT WOULD HAVE BEEN THEIR SONS AND DAUGHTERS PLAYING AND LAUGHING AS TODDLERS; THEN AS THEY WOULD HAVE APPEARED WHILE UNDERTAKING AND ACCOMPLISHING THINGS AS THEY GREW AND MATURED. VISUALIZED BEFORE THEM ARE DIFFERENT STAGES OF THEIR LIVES, THEIR AWARDS, THEIR ACHIEVEMENTS, THEIR GRADUATIONS, THEIR CAREERS, THE MARRIAGES AND THE GRANDCHILDREN THAT THEY WILL NEVER SEE, NEVER HOLD, NEVER LOVE, AND WHO WOULD HAVE LOVED THEM IN RETURN.

"AT THEIR JUDGMENT BECAUSE THEY DIED UNREPENTANT, WHILE LIVING THEIR UNCARING, SELF CENTERED LIFE GOD ACQUIESED TO THEIR SINFUL, GREED-FILLED CHOICE BY FOREVER REMINDING THEM, THAT THE CONSEQUENCE OF MURDERING YOUR UNBORN IS TO BE REMINDED FOREVER THAT THE MOST HEARTBREAKING WORDS OF TONGUE OR PEN ARE THESE: 'IT MIGHT HAVE BEEN.'"

"Upon hearing this I became angry. Is it arrogance or stupidity," I asked myself, "that man thinks he can use political expediency to pass secular legislation in an effort to override the laws of God?"

"'I have a better idea!' they shout while shaking their fists at the heavens. What fools they are as they travel on the W I D E R O A D to their destruction. As for the souls of the men and women I heard, I suspect that their scenes are re-enacted again and again as the demon so gleefully declared, 'forever and forever.'"

"Again, it became deathly silent as the torch lights were extinguished while I began descending the ramp. In the darkness there was nothing to see on which to establish my position. I became disoriented. When I reached the bottom of the ramp and took a few cautious steps, I wondered whether the ground beneath me was a level field, the top of a mound, or the edge of a deep precipice. I felt a need to move, when the all-but-non-existent amber light above went out like a burnt-out bulb. There was a bright flash and then total darkness; but in that flash I saw that there was nothing in front of me to impede my forward progress and so I began walking slowly and carefully forward. Almost immediately I felt the ground beneath me developing a slight rise.

"After walking for what seemed to be fifteen minutes or so I was startled when I heard a loud explosion followed by a blast of hot air and a series of ground tremors that nearly knocked me off my feet. When I regained my balance, I could see that the explosion opened a massive, deep, wide chasm up ahead. Rising from it were flickering flashes of firelight which revealed accompanying billows of thick black smoke. As I approached closer, I heard voices hollering and screaming in what sounded like a room full of people who while having a heated argument had lost their composure. Approaching closer I could make out that the angry yelling and shouting was in fact blaspheming and cursing to a degree and vocal ferocity that I couldn't even imagine on earth. Cautiously I approached the rim and peered down. The source of the voices were those of completely naked men and women who were writhing in grievous pain while being violently tossed about in a cauldron of fire that was reminiscent of the vision of Hell Mary had shown the children at Fatima.

"Go back!" they screamed when they saw me. "Go back and tell everybody that Hell is not a myth. It does exist; and those who live as if there is no such place will come here – tell them – tell them that there is no way out! Tell them it is forever and forever! Tell them! Tell them! They must believe!"

"I was horrified to hear condemned souls speaking to me. Satan had told me that the condemned could see me and because I was dressed would know that I was not one of them; and that they might try to converse with me.

Now here they were amidst horrible suffering beseeching me to proclaim the truth to save others. Why would they do that? I asked myself. Compassion, love, and consideration for others are supposed to be absent in the condemned.

"The only answer that made any sense to me is that God had prompted them to speak in order to have me write the truth coming from an undeniable source. I immediately felt humbled and knew that I was in this place because God wanted me to be.

"Most Sacred Heart of Jesus I place my trust in Thee, I prayed and began moving on with the belief that although Satan had sent me to Hell God would bring me out; but it would be when He willed and not before.

"After realizing this I was whisked away from where I stood. While soaring overhead I saw the darkness below interrupted by frequent massive piles of glowing coals adjacent to huge, deep pits filled with writhing, screaming souls being churned about in a cauldron of fire and brimstone. I had no idea by what power I was soaring or where I was going. The only thing I did know is that while in Hell I had no control over what would happen to me. 'While in Hell,' I repeated, reassuring myself of the temporal nature of my stay; unlike the souls condemned here as a result of eternal damnation I did have a light at the end of my tunnel, however distant it may be.

"I began slowing down in a controlled descent, much like a glider coming in for a landing. When my feet were a half foot or so above the ground my forward movement stopped for an instant before I was lowered to the ground. Once again above me the dim amber point of light blinked on. It allowed me to see the faint outline of a pathway and I felt an urge to follow it.

"After a long period of plodding along, the amber light, as it did before, emitted a flash an instant before it disappeared. In that brief moment I saw a huge iron gate ahead. As I approached it I could see letters spelling out:

DO AS I SAY, NOT AS I DO

I was reminded of what Satan had told me about the fate of hypocrites who are condemned to spend their eternity with each other behind these gates. They do so while feeling stupid because without exception they are both men and women who were gifted with superior intelligence. However, they allowed their basic instincts fortified with fear of being found out to ride herd on their intellects. The bulk of them begin with lofty intentions but demons lay before them temptations involving illicit sex, dishonest financial dealings or the acquisition of power by way of corrupting the political process.

Many times other innocent lives are ruined as they parade themselves as paragons of virtue while receiving the adulations of those around them. At their judgment, however, they faced Almighty God, Who with the Divine power of one look exposed the enormity of their sinful hypocrisy. Each of them now doused with the shame of exposure before the One it was impossible to deceive offered no questions, excuses or explanations in light of their feelings of remorse, regret and shame culminating in the misery of self-hate which will be their companion for eternity.

"I didn't know what to expect here, but two things crossed my mind. Of all the sins man can commit hypocrisy seemed to be the one Jesus emphasized the most. Time after time he admonished the Scribes and Pharisees that if they continued in their sinful, hypocritical practices they would find themselves cast into Hell.

"Secondly, in Matthew's 23rd chapter are listed seven "woes" regarding the scribes and Pharisees. Numbers six and seven are especially telling. In the sixth, Jesus calls them out for parading righteousness by scrupulously keeping the minutiae of oral laws, many of which they themselves invented; while all the while because they had no love for their fellow man, they were accumulating wealth at the expense of others, including widows and orphans. He referred to them as "whited sepulchers that were washed white on the outside but within were full of dead men's bones." (Matthew 23:27-28)

"In the seventh Woe Jesus accused them of having high respect for the memory of the murdered prophets of old – saying that they would never have killed the prophets while they had murder in their hearts as they were plotting how to legally kill him. (Matthew 23:29-32)

"As I approached closer to the gate, I could see that it was locked. While wondering what I should do to announce my presence I heard the "click" of the latch releasing just before the gates slowly, and creaking all the way, swung inward. Even in Hell iron gates secured with a latch do not open by themselves. Someone had seen my approach and opened the gates. I assumed it was a demon as I didn't believe there were electric eyes in Hell. I hesitated about proceeding. I had been in Hell for some time and had yet to see a demon, and had no desire to change that, as even the sound of the booming voice and that wicked laugh I had heard shortly after I arrived sent dread-filled chills running through me. However, I knew that writing about being in Hell without describing a demon would question the credibility of my account.

"I walked along the pathway past the opened gate and immediately there was a tremendous drop in temperature. I could now see my breath as I exhaled and noted that the paths as well as the inner surfaces of the gates were covered with a thin white coating of frost. As I walked along, I came to a Y in the road. There were no signs indicating directions or identification and it was too cold to just stand there while making up my mind so I took the path to my right. I had no coat, hat or gloves as the last thing I expected was to be cold in Hell. So I began jogging in an effort to ward off the chill by increasing my circulation. After a few minutes I picked up the pace as the white frost on the path now allowed me to see the path as far as fifteen feet ahead.

"I was coasting along at a pretty good pace when I was startled by the appearance, once again, of the amber point of light. After a few more steps I came to a halt in front of someone or something that completely blocked my path.

"I was about to try running around it but thought better of it when I looked up to see a creature that was staring down at me from two huge, penetrating ruby red eyes at least four feet above my six-foot height. I knew at once that I could no longer say that I had yet to see a demon and was immediately thankful that Satan had assumed the form he did. Its head was enormous and resembled a rhinoceros without horns. Being unclothed – its skin resembled the back of a crocodile. It was standing erect on two feet covered with white fur and sporting black pointed claws that looked to be four inches long. Its hands and fingers were like the bony talons of a vulture protruding from forearms that I estimated to be twenty-four inches in circumference. Without a doubt he was the most terrifying creature I had ever seen or could possibly even imagine – the personification of what had happened to the beautiful angels who followed Satan to become demons in Hell. If it was as physically solid as it appeared I guessed its weight to be two thousand lbs. or more; and if it took a notion to kill me it could have done so with one swat to my head or a squeeze of its talons around my neck.

"Being condemned to Hell while subject to the whims and will of such a creature, while knowing that there was no way out and that any call for help would go unanswered could only add perpetual terror to the feelings of remorse, regret and despair that was already your never-ending lot.

"I remained standing there looking up at him not wanting to remove my eyes from his, hoping that his intentions were not to take advantage of my vulnerability. Finally, he spoke in a loud raspy voice. 'You must be Bruce McPherson. My master said to expect you, but I was surprised to find you running. Is someone or something chasing you?'

"No," I said, feeling better that Satan had paved the way for me. I was running to keep warm. Why is it so cold beyond those gates? It isn't that way anywhere else I've been in Hell."

"People who fall prey to the temptation of hypocrisy have already developed the cold nature of the liar only to a much greater degree. They are frauds and confidence people completely lacking in empathy; and since empathy is a measure of human beings warmth toward each other and since they are completely lacking in this virtue their frigid nature dissipates the heat from them and draws it from everything and everyone around them."

"I heard the screams and shrieking of souls subjected to the fires of Hell; but I don't hear anything but deadly silence in here. Is there a reason for that?"

"Unlike most of those who have chosen to spend their eternity with us, the Hell of the hypocrites is to constantly shiver from freezing, bitter cold. When he or she is cold enough to become numb they are placed into a cauldron of Hell fire until they begin screaming because their feeling has returned. Then the freezing begins all over again.

"And this goes on forever?"

"Forever and forever all mine!

"You haven't forgotten, have you?"

"No," I replied. "I don't know why I asked," while thinking that if everyone on earth could see and hear what I have, Hell would be completely void of human habitation.

"I have been ordered by my master to permit you to see and hear whomever you wish."

"Are there souls here of the scribes and Pharisees that berated and challenged Jesus? If so, can I speak with them? Will they tell me the truth? And how do I overcome the language problem?"

"You can, and they will."

"And the language problem? How do I get around that?"

"My master apparently left it up to me to explain things here. In contrast to our lying on earth for the purpose of turning things upside down; here in our domain, we mandate absolute truth, and there are no exceptions. We do not lie to each other nor do we permit the condemned to do so. As far as language is concerned Hell was not a part of Earth when fools therein decided to build what has become to be known as the tower of Babel. Therefore, whatever language you speak the listener will understand. It is likewise for you with whatever language he chooses to use. With so many different languages of those condemned it could not be otherwise."

"So if I speak in English, those listening hear me in their own language. Conversely, if they speak ancient Aramaic or in the Greek of the time, I will hear it in American English."

"It cannot be otherwise."

"I thought that we would have to go to where the souls were located, but to my surprise the demon called three of them by name to come forth. After a pause of a minute or so, I saw the souls of three completely naked, frost laden, elderly bearded men with icicles hanging from their beards trudging in single file along the path toward us.

"Is there some place where we can sit down?" I asked.

"No one sits down in Hell," the demon responded, "but don't feel sorry for them. They are used to standing. They've been doing it for nearly two thousands of your earthly years."

"Before I could respond I stood in awe. These were the souls of men who had met and talked to Jesus Christ, the Son of God made Man and they did it face to face; and not with a sense of reverence, but like so many do today, challenging His Being in an effort to deny him before their fellow men and women.

"They stood there looking me up and down no doubt wondering why I had no beard and was dressed in a manner they had never seen or could even imagine. They seemed to pay special intention to my black leather boots.

"I thought of thanking them for coming forth to answer my questions until I realized that they had no way of knowing why the demon had called them. In fact, it may have been the first time the demon had called them by name; however if they were confused their countenance did not show it. In fact, all three appeared to be a bit defiant; a feeling I thought they would have lost after suffering for nearly two thousand years in Hell.

"I am here as a man from two thousand years in earth's future. It is a world far different from the one you knew. However, those statements are for information but have little to do with why I am here. Why I am here is to ask you some questions about your conversations and your relationship with the person you knew as Jesus. My first question is who do you think he was?"

"He had been a carpenter who realized that he had a way with words and was able to hold a crowd spellbound with his delivery," said the first man.

"More than that," added the second man, "He was a man who could work miracles. He cured leprosy. He gave sight to a man who was in his forties that had been blind from birth. We knew that man as he had been a beggar on the same street corner all his adult life."

"I was in a house where his friends lowered a lame man whose legs were bereft of flesh and muscle, said the third man. I watched as he told him to 'rise and walk.' Immediately his legs were healthy and he took up his pallet and went home."

"But that wasn't all he said," the second man added, "Before he cured his legs he told him, 'Your sins are forgiven you.' That raised our anger as only God can forgive sins."

"However," I said, "didn't he also ask you which is easier to say, 'Thy sins are forgiven you or arise and walk? But that you may know that the Son of Man has the power to forgive sins I say to you arise and walk?'"

"Yes, he did." said the first man, "but healing a physical infirmity and being God are not the same!"

"Permit me to ask all of you a question. Creation, which is making something from nothing, is reserved to whom?

"Jehovah," they all answered together.

Looking at the third man I asked, "You said you observed that his legs were bereft of flesh and muscle; then you said that immediately, his legs were healthy. From where did the muscle and flesh come in order that the man's legs were immediately restored? Wouldn't the muscle and flesh have to be created in order to immediately appear?

When none of the three answered I said "Let's talk about the vote to condemn Jesus to death. First of all the trial was done in Caiaphas's house at night. This was illegal. Was it not?"

"Both Annas and Caiaphas said it was necessary because with Jesus' popularity it would have been impossible to hold a fair trial in public," said the second man.

"I propose that Caiaphas and Annas knew that because they feared the wrath of the people he could not get a vote from the Sanhedrin to convict Jesus in a public trial. As it was, even at night Caiaphas couldn't get a unanimous vote as both Nicodemus and Joseph of Arimathea voted in the negative."

"You have left out the reason he was brought to trial," said the third man.

"Perhaps you'd care to enlighten me," I replied.

"The people began referring to Jesus as Master and Rabbi, and he never advised them to stop."

"He had neither the credentials nor the schooling to legally be addressed by either of those titles," said the second man. "I heard him say to several Pharisees including myself, 'Truly, truly, I say to you, *before* Abraham was, I *am.*' (John 8:58) That was the clearest of his blasphemous statements."

"Only if it wasn't true," I remarked.

"How could a man be Jehovah?" the first man questioned.

"He couldn't," I said, "but what is to prevent Jehovah from taking on the flesh of a man? The problem of the Sanhedrin is that while you were willing to admit the omnipotence of Jehovah in the abstract you nevertheless shackled him to constraints of what you deemed possible in the material world."

"How so?" the first man asked.

"Jesus raised at least three people from the dead – Jairus's daughter, Lazarus and himself. You listened to Caiaphas who told you that Jesus' miracles were done by the power of Beelzebub, but you had to know that only Jehovah has power over life and death. You didn't believe the lies Caiaphas told you but you acted as if you did because you thought that what Jesus was teaching threatened your power, prestige and pocketbooks.

"What sent you to Hell was that you served Caiaphas and loved the world of the material more than you loved Jehovah. Moreover, you paraded yourselves before the people in a manner that implied that you were superior and preferred by Jehovah over them. If you had spent more time listening to Jesus you would have learned that 'No man can serve two masters: for either he will hate the one, and love the other; or else, he will hold to the one, and despise the other. You cannot serve both God and mammon.'" (Matthew 6:24)

Turning to face the demon I looked up and said, "They have told me all I need to know. Excuse my hasty departure but I've got to leave this place before I turn into a popsicle."

"A what?" Questioned the demon, as I began jogging back toward the gate.

"Another time," I shouted, as I turned around and picked up the pace while wondering if I would ever be warm again. After a few steps, the point of amber light lit up again. As before, it wasn't much, but it was better than total darkness.

"Returning to the Y in the road I was about to turn left to go through the gate when out of the corner of my eye I noticed a definite break on the surface of the road beyond the right turn of the Y. About ten feet beyond the turn, the frost abruptly ended. I turned to follow the road and noticed once again as I crossed the frost line, there was a marked difference in temperature. It was warm! Oh, so warm! I couldn't remember when I felt so good; and as there was no indication of my being returned to earth, I took it as a sign that I should follow it to see where it went.

"The further I went the steeper the drop off to my left became. Rounding a sharp bend to my left I felt that the path began to arc sharply downward. It was still very dark, of course, and there being no railing my progress to the bottom was very slow; but I finally got there.

"Just as I did the point of light went out after a brilliant flash, and as I came to expect, lit up the area for a second before everything went black. But before it did, I saw that I was on a flat dirt plain completely void of vegetation. Beginning about two hundred feet in front of me were column after column of small log cabins which at a glance appeared to be all the same and not very large – perhaps one or two small rooms. None of this was frightening, but then the point of amber light suddenly reignited revealing two creatures, approximately twenty feet in front of me which I can only describe as unbelievably grotesque. Their bottom halves beginning with just below their navels were those of a raptor, including the clawed feet and powerfully muscled legs; however, I could see no tails. Their upper half was that of a primate. As they approached me, I could see that their facial features were chimpanzee-like, as were their upper torsos, arms and hands. When they got to within four feet or so they stopped. I estimated their height to be close to seven feet. Immediately I saw images of the movie, "Planet of the Apes" and thought of all the indignities Charlton Heston suffered. I quietly said the only prayer that came to mind – God have mercy on me & please get me out of here!

"The creature on my right remained perfectly immobile and stared straight ahead while his partner slowly walked around me as if he were at a slave market trying to make up his mind whether I was worth the price my owner was asking. It was not a good feeling."

"Who are you and what are you doing here?" he asked. "You have none of the characteristics of the condemned we receive here. In fact, you are warm," he remarked," as he raised and then squeezed my forearm before letting it go, "and therefore still physically alive and able to receive absolution which if requested would preclude you from coming here."

"I am a visitor at the behest of Satan," I said; "and your observation is correct. I am not one of your condemned, as I am, as you stated, physically alive. From what you said it is obvious that you are not in command or otherwise in charge. I have reason to believe that Satan has advised whoever is in charge of my coming. I ask that you tell me his name and take me to see him."

"With all due respect, sir," said the second man, "if Grotius is involved in this person's being here perhaps we should immediately take this living being to him. If what the man says is correct, Grotius is expecting him."

"Come with us," the senior man said, but said nothing more until we were in front of the only cabin that was a bit larger than the rest. "Wait here," he ordered, while the two of them went inside which I thought was strange as normally the junior man would have been left to prevent my escape until I realized they knew I had no place to go!

"I admitted to myself that I had taken a chance that Satan had informed their leader whom one called Grotius, of my coming. Why wouldn't he, I asked myself? The demon in charge of the Hypocrites had been told. However, as the time I stood there increased I began wondering what was going on inside with Grotius.

"My mind began to wander and having seen women frantically searching for the baby they had arranged to have murdered; the men who murdered their flesh and blood to preclude bearing the expense of raising them; both men and women churning about in fiery cauldrons because while alive on earth they disbelieved in Hell and lived lives mirroring that belief; and most recently hypocrites slowly freezing like water does in ice trays before being cast into hell-fire to thaw out so they could be frozen all over again.

"Looking about I wondered what fiendish tortures demons performed in these cabins? And to whom they did it? I remembered Satan's viewpoint: that to willfully choose by your actions on earth to come here for all eternity is stupid; bringing to mind once again Satan's analogy of betting a pair of deuces against a royal flush.

"But then I said aloud as if I were speaking to Satan, 'You made the choice having lived with God in Heaven, which means you bet your pair of deuces after knowing God's hand. Mankind makes the choice blind to the bliss. So what right do you have to call us stupid?'"

"As I finished my thought, the senior demon approached and said, "Grotius will see you, now, but beware – he is not pleased that you are here.""

"Standing before Grotius I immediately noticed three things. First, there was a fire burning in a stone fireplace that provided much appreciated light; secondly, while his anatomy was identical to the other two, his eyes, being blue, appeared almost human and emanated intelligence far above theirs. Third, he arose from a sitting position."

"Well Bruce McPherson, shall I begin, or do you have something to say with which to enlighten me?"

"I see you were sitting behind what appears to be a table."

"Is that the best you can do? From what Satan told me about you I had hoped to hear better."

"And you will, Grotius," I said, emboldened by the assurance that Satan had run interference for me. "It's just that I had been told that nobody sits down in Hell."

He pointed to a chair beside me and said, "Well, let's see if that's true by having you sit, if you wish." When we were both sitting, he said, "Who told you that nobody sits down in our domain?"

"The demon that rules over the hypocrites. I asked if there was a place to sit down to speak with Pharisaical souls who had spoken with Jesus, and he told me that there is no sitting in Hell."

Grotius grimaced while shaking his head. "Propersynus, I should have known," he said, "and why not? Can you imagine that Principality sitting on anything that wouldn't immediately be crushed?"

"He didn't tell me his name," I said, while smiling just enough to show that I appreciated what I assumed was his attempt at humor.

"Of course not. It isn't that Propersynus is ill-mannered. It's just that living in that ice box has addled his intelligence."

"You mean he just forgot?"

"Precisely – but lest I forget, Propersynus said that when I saw you to ask you to define popsicle."

"Oh that," I said laughing. "Basically, a popsicle is made from fruit flavored sugar water that is poured into a mold with a stick in its center and then frozen for later consumption. Where it came into play was that I apologized to him for leaving rather suddenly before I turned into a Popsicle."

With a straight face Grotius replied, "I guess I had to be there. I'll tell him what you said the next time we talk."

"You called Propersynus a principality. Does that mean you are not?"

"Bruce McPherson, if I didn't know better, I would have to think you had just insulted me."

"I didn't mean to..."

"Grotius waved his hand while interrupting me. 'Didn't I preface my remark by stating 'if I didn't know better?' Pay attention and don't let social graces interfere with our understanding each other. You've been in Hell long enough to know that social graces have no place here. Of course, neither does rudeness, unless we are dealing with the condemned. Then anything is acceptable – even admired if truly demonically creative.'

"I nodded to show my ascent, and then asked if he would tell me to which choir he had belonged.

"I was a Power," he said proudly, "The Type A personality of the angelic world."

"I guessed that without asking," I said, "I mean about your being a Type A personality."

"You know, Bruce, I'm beginning to think I may have been wrong about you. I told Satan that having you here was a bad idea because after you see what occurs here your mind would never be the same. He disagreed, and of course that was the end of it. If you can mentally keep up

I just might enjoy having you here. Let's begin with that bit about sitting. There is a restriction, you know..."

Interrupting I said, "Let me guess – the prohibition on sitting applies only to the condemned."

"Yes, well, now that we have that out of the way let's probe a bit deeper. Did Satan tell you anything about Hell? I mean the way it is structured; the way it is divided; what we demons do here?"

"No," I answered. "He didn't say so directly, but I assumed that the reason he sent me here was to be able to write about it."

"Did he say why anyone among the vast numbers of the stupidly unbelieving among you would want to know about what happens in a place most of them deny exists?"

"I think he is counting on me to write it well enough to convince them otherwise."

"Ah yes, Satan's idea about dissuading God from executing His re-set. His attempt to change the Divine mind is what forever changed our status in the first place; but Satan never stops trying.

"There are those among you who have been writing about both their real as well as their imagined visions of Hell for decades. What makes you think you can do better?"

"Alone, I'm sure I can't."

"You're not alone in writing this eye-opener?"

In the eighth grade, my English teacher, a religious nun, recognized something in me and introduced me to St. John, the Evangelist, a prolific biblical writer. Due to my prayers for his powerful intercession the ideas and the words to properly express them just seem to flow naturally."

"Ah yes, the beloved Apostle. Hung in there with Jesus through His passion and death to the very end. I remember the discussions we had here. Half thought he was just too young to know any better; the other half said the nineteen-year-old was molded by the hand of God to be one of a kind.

"But, enough nice to know conversation. My instructions from Satan are that you are not to speak with any of the condemned who are assigned to me.

"Just between us," Grotius added, while lowering his voice and leaning toward me, "you have lost nothing as none of them are worth your time."

"Nothing?" I responded.

"They are a scurrilous lot – among the worst, if not the worst of you who have chosen to spend your eternity here."

"Since Satan ordered it so and Grotius was not anxious for me to pursue it further, I raised my hands and said, 'OK.'"

"He continued, 'Hell is divided into sections where human souls condemned for a class of sin are confined to an area for extraordinary punishment. All human souls, however, both male and female suffer a common punishment which consists of:

Being forever abandoned by God.

Remorse of conscience for knowing right but choosing wrong.

Despair -- knowing that the horrifics of one's situation will never get better and even worse will never end – which Jesus described as 'the worm that never dies.'

Living in perpetual darkness in the midst of foul and putrid odors. Those dim amber points of light are the only source of illumination the condemned ever see and they are only intermittent.

Hatred of God while screaming curses and blasphemies, but knowing that your hatred is unjustified because God loved you and offered you many opportunities to turn your life around by repenting and asking for forgiveness which was yours for the asking.

Being forced to frequently relive those many opportunities when you turned your back on him or refused to answer when He stood there knocking."

"In addition to ordinary punishment, extraordinary punishment is meted out to grievous sinners who blasphemed God, led others to perdition, or stole from the poor and unfortunate.

"Then there are those who murdered, maimed or mutilated others, unlawfully enriched themselves from community or church funds, adulterers, abortionists, those who lied to ruin another's reputation or used their position as a parent, relative, religious, political or financial authority to take advantage of or to scandalize the young; those who used a peculiar allegiance to God as an excuse or reason to murder others in His name; and... there may be others of which I am not aware. Once Satan placed me in charge of this area it grew so fast that I had little time to be interested in what was going on elsewhere."

"I've wondered," I said, "Did any of you change their mind about siding with Satan before he gave God his ultimatum?"

"As the adversarial discussion between God and Satan progressed, the majority of the Cherubim and all the Archangels, who originally thought Satan had a point, were convinced otherwise, and none of the Seraphim ever thought Satan had a chance of convincing God to change his mind about creating human beings. Anything else?"

"May I ask the nature of the condemned in your area?"

"Predators, Bruce – more specifically sexual predators and those who think they avoid sin by limiting their practice to pederasty."

"Is that all?"

"No. Those who torture or murder Christians in the name of God were added in your seventh century. Then those who torture or murder non-Christians were added in your fifteenth century.

"And those condemned for such sins undergo extraordinary punishment? Here? Within these cabins?"

"Right, right and right," Grotius replied before opening the cabin door and motioning for me to follow him outside. "Come with me, I want to show you something," he added, as we began crossing to the left side of the field.

After a few minutes of walking, we came to a high wire fence. "Does the term Canis Dirus mean anything to you?"

I looked at the demon incredulously. "From where did that come?"

"Your reply indicates that you can answer in the affirmative. Am I correct?"

"Yes, I am a biologist. Canis Dirus is the international Latin identifier for a very large wolf that ravaged North America. He weighed in at 180 lbs. or so which puts him 25% larger than the average Canis Lupus, our modern gray wolf. Canis Dirus had massive canines and competed with Smilodon (saber-toothed tiger) for prey. Fossil records show that Canis Dirus became extinct ten thousand years ago at the end of the last ice age."

"Well, Bruce, yes and no. Let me explain. Satan, as you may have heard was extremely fond of God's creation of the universe before God expanded it to include flesh and blood creatures with immortal souls. He was moderately pleased and enjoyed observing creature life on planet earth during the pre-mammalian periods. When the mammals arrived, however, with some being vegetarian prey hunted by meat eating predators his enjoyment really peaked. He was especially fond of predators who multiplied the chance of their pursuit by attacking in packs.

"The Dirus wolf was his favorite, no doubt because of its rate of success. Once a heavily muscled 180–200-pound Canis Dirus sunk its three-inch fangs into a 700-pound stag, it was all over. The rest of the pack moved in and the stag was dead in at most three minutes either from a powerful bite from the rear which crushed his neck bones or one from the front which tore out its throat.

"When their number began decreasing, however, and there were fewer than two thousand animals remaining, Satan embarked on a plan to preserve his much-preferred beast."

"Well, it wasn't successful on earth," I remarked, "so the only other place..."

"Grotius, a demon whose countenance was imbedded in the face of a chimpanzee attempted a smile, but was limited to a retraction of his lips displaying a full set of teeth, huge incisors and all. Then, he called out and immediately a massive, heavily muscled wolf came up to the other side of the fence. It measured a full four feet at the shoulder. When it saw me, it opened its mouth wide baring its enormous fangs and let out an ear piercing howl so loud I was forced to back away from the fence.

"Allow me to excuse Sultan's ill-mannered behavior. When he saw you, a stranger, he wanted you to know that he is the alpha male and he means you to respect that as fact."

"Alpha male?" I questioned. How many do you have here?"

"Just over six hundred," Grotius responded.

"Six hundred! How do you feed so many?" I asked.

"We don't. And not only because there is no food in Hell; however, before you respond let us return to the cabin and I will explain."

"Having returned to the cabin we were again sitting across from each other as Grotius said, 'As I'm sure you know every living thing has a soul which is its life force. In all earthly creatures with the exception of man, this life force or soul, being mortal, perishes when the physical reason for its existence, is no longer capable of supporting corporeal life. In other words the mortal soul no longer has an animal healthy enough to exercise its animation."

"Like a flashlight when its bulb burns out," I said. The batteries, that is, the life force, are still good, but they can't do what the flashlight is designed to do because the burnt-out bulb is no longer capable of accepting the batteries' power. Over time the batteries dissipate their power and die."

"Close enough," said Grotius, "but to complete your thought we can remove the batteries and use them to give power to a flashlight that does have a good bulb or anything else that is made to function with the same voltage that those batteries produce. And that is exactly what Satan did with Canis Dirus."

"Can you be more specific? I asked. "Despite all my years of study in biology I suddenly feel I must have missed something."

"You're not being fair to yourself," Grotius replied. "What Satan did had nothing to do with conventional biology.

"Before I explain further, Bruce, how did Satan appear to you?"

"He arrived on a motorcycle which I heard multiple times but actually saw only once in my headlights when it passed me on the way to my cabin. In person he was tall, lean & impeccably dressed in a black blazer, white turtleneck, gray slacks and mahogany leather loafers."

"Did you discuss this manifestation?"

"Satan told me that I was seeing and conversing with an image he had conjured up. He said that his appearance was like a mirage, but one with which he could do whatever a human being could do and then some. I never questioned him further as I witnessed him speaking, eating, drinking, reading aloud and writing in long hand just as any human being would do."

"Did Satan mention his created limits?"

"He said that God had created him with every faculty except the power to create, the ability to know the future, the power to overcome a fellow angel's or human being's will or read either's mind."

"That is correct. Satan, was created by God as a Seraphim, the highest order of angels, but then God gave him singular abilities above that. He named him Lucifer, His angel of light, and appointed him as the administrator of the angelic realm."

"A SERAPHIM ON STEROIDS," I thought, but believing that here in Hell humor is little appreciated, I kept it to myself. Instead, I asked Grotius where he was going with all this?"

"I had to know what you knew about the potential of Satan's power because if you didn't understand its magnitude -- then you would never believe how six hundred Canis Duris, extinct for ten thousand years on earth, could exist for all eternity in Hell.

"And you are about to tell me?"

"Yes.

"Being unable to revive a dying wolf Satan extracted its soul which caused its immediate death. He then used its life force to animate an image of the Dirus species which he conjured up."

"Which is why you don't have to feed them! Although they look and act in every way like living wolves, they are in reality three-dimensional images."

"Yes, but with limitations. They don't breed because Satan chose only males. As I said before they don't eat; neither do they drink, and therefore they don't urinate nor have a need for defecation."

"But for what purpose did Satan do this? Even Satan or you, Grotius, wouldn't have a need for six hundred pets!"

"I assure you, Bruce, none of the Canis Dirus are pets. As for their purpose, well, you will see soon enough.

"But before that I want to ask your opinion on what I believe to be a related point that needs to be resolved in your mind."

"You're asking me for an opinion? Why? Satan said that the least of the angels had an IQ equivalent of 1500. You were a member of the Powers, an Angelic choir well above that. My IQ is 135 on my best day. What you are asking doesn't make sense."

"Intelligence isn't everything, Bruce. Perspective and experience can be just as important and in some situations more so. For example, if you want to know how a piece of machinery works, would you ask the high school graduate who operates it or the Ph.D. who is president of the company that owns it?"

"You make a good point. What is it you want of me?"

"In the New Testament, Matthew (18:1-6), Luke (17:1-30) and Mark (9:42) all relate the same incident. Jesus has stopped to rest when a group of mothers bring their young children to him. Jesus laughs and talks to them and shows His love by embracing them. Just after releasing them back to their mothers He says, 'Whosoever shall scandalize one of these little ones who believe in me, it were better for him that a millstone be hanged about his neck, and he be drowned in the depths of the sea.'"

"And?" I asked.

"Having a millstone, most of which weighed many times the weight of a man, tied about his neck before being thrown into the sea means that he panics and gasps as his body is forced to breath salt water into his lungs while plummeting to the ocean floor, never to rise from the abyss. No doubt a horrible way for one of you to die."

"And your point?

"The way I interpret this is that the punishment for scandalizing and we can include terrorizing and molesting children is worse than being drowned with a millstone around your neck as you sink to the bottom of the sea. Do you concur?

"I never thought of it that way; but analyzing the syntax of Jesus' words along with the sentence structure there is more chance that you are correct than not."

"Every so often, Bruce, I get a pedophile lawyer or politician down here. Your answer reminds me of the way they talk."

"I'm sorry, Grotius. It's just that you are asking me to think differently about a familiar phrase; however, on second thought I believe you are right – in which case the extraordinary punishment meted out here in Hell must be worse than being thrown into the sea with a millstone hanging from your neck. It must be a form of torture – both mental and physical that is both agonizing and lengthy, but I can't imagine how that can be, except maybe to be burned alive, except that all human souls condemned to Hell are already dead.

"Finally! Thank you. Now allow me to explain. For thousands of years there have been adults, both men and women, who are sexual cowards. They have an innate fear of approaching a peer of the opposite sex because they are fearful of rejection; they feel unworthy, or if they succeed in being invited into the desiree's inner circle, they are afraid of being found, for some reason, to be unacceptable and suffer the embarrassment of being rebuffed."

When Grotius paused, I said, "To continue your thought – like the lion who seeks out the old, the sick, the crippled and the young for easy predation, Satan and you demons use children as prey for tempting these individuals to satisfy their sexual lust. It helps if the child has been orphaned; if he is not as bright as his peers; if he has parents who pursue their own needs at the expense of caring for their child, or if by his actions, he or she is seen to be a follower rather than a leader.

"You demons tempt the sexual coward by convincing him that such a child or young person within his proximity is starved for love – a love which is pent up inside the coward and if sexually acted upon will satisfy both his and the child's needs. It is with this thought that the predator gets the innocent child or even a young adult to accede to his or her wishes.

"Only it isn't a romantic, sexual love which is impossible with a prepubescent child or a young adult who is under his or her tutelage or influence. It is a way to satisfy their lust and is an Abomination in the eyes of God. And any human act meriting to be called an abomination is committed on the wide road; and leading one's life on the wide road for any reason Jesus said is a sure pathway to eternal damnation. (Matthew 7:13-14) It is why Jesus said what he did. There probably were child molesters within the sound of his voice. Of course, he also meant it as a warning for all who would come later."

"You are right, of course, but as Satan tells us, 'It is what we do!' Convincing human beings to reject God in favor of anyone or anything else is our way of stealing souls from his human creation.

"Frankly, Bruce, as brutal as it sounds, being precluded from any chance of salvation and therefore beyond redemption it is our only means of vengeance. What do we have to lose?"

"Ignoring the obvious answer to Grotius's question I said you mentioned murdering in the name of God in the seventh and fifteenth centuries. I assume this refers to the Muslims who chose to spread Islam by the sword in the seventh century and beyond, and the disciples of the Grand Inquisitor, Torquemada de Cortaez, whose judgments were responsible for the torturing and killing of Jews in the fifteenth century. What about those who kill others for their religious beliefs in the modern world?'"

"There is an equal balance. The souls of the martyred ascend to eternal life; and without contrition the souls of those who create martyrs descend to eternal damnation, and as you will soon see are here under my domination.

"The *sine qua non* is this, Bruce McPherson: if any of you persecutes, tortures or kills another in the name of God and then meets his or her demise without seeking Divine Forgiveness then he or she is mine, all mine, forever and forever all mine! And note well, there are no exceptions or mitigating circumstances. Nothing and I mean nothing moves God to anger like one of you taking the life of another because you say, 'God wills it.'"

"Before I could respond Grotius continued, 'Having laid the foundation I am now going to illustrate punishment that is worse than having a millstone hung around one's neck and suffering the agony of drowning as you descend to the bottom of the sea. "Grotius's face hardened as he stood, opened the door and shouted the command, 'MUSTER THE CONDEMNED!'

"Then continuing as if I weren't even there he moved outside and ordered, 'MARCH THE CONDEMNED TO THEIR STATIONS ABREAST THE CABINS!'"

"I followed him outside and saw that the area overhead was filled with hundreds of dim amber light sources which allowed me to see the condemned souls being marched to the cabins. As they moved along, in what appeared to be an endless line, they were totally naked and linked to one another with a chain attached to collars around their necks. As they moved closer I could hear them weeping aloud and begging for mercy. Their guards, exact replicas of the two that I first saw on the field, answered their cries by shouting commands and lashing them with whips. If one of them stumbled the soul closest to him grabbed him before, being chained together, more were pulled down.

"When they arrived at the cabins other guards with clubs took command. After removing the collars and chains they ordered three souls who by now were bawling and begging like children, to stand behind one another in front of each cabin door. When all the souls had been so stationed at their prescribed cabin, one of the guards reported such to

Grotius who then commanded, 'PROCEED TO FILL THE CABINS!'"
Whereupon the doors were opened and the protesting, weeping souls
of mostly full-grown men were ordered to enter the cabin. Those who
hesitated were beaten about the head and shoulders with clubs until they
either entered the cabin or were pushed or thrown in by the guards.

As soon as it was reported to Grotius that the cabins were filled and
secured, he commanded, "RELEASE THE MASTER'S WOLVES!"
Immediately there was a series of howls off in the distance as if wolves
were gathering the pack. They were answering one another. It was the
most ominously terrifying sound that I had ever heard. Lasting a minute
or so it was followed by a few seconds of silence in which I suddenly
realized the horror that was worse than being heaved into the sea with
a millstone hung around your neck as hundreds of massive, ferocious
wolves began a mad dash for the cabins.

"Upon reaching the cabins they began using their massive musculature to lunge at the doors. When the doors began to weaken, using
their razor-sharp claws, they shredded the wood. Those inside hearing
the clawing, growling, and snarling could be heard screaming and crying out in terror. Finally, one, then another, then another of the cabins'
doors gave way until all the wolves had broken into the cabins where
the terrified souls with their backs to the walls and arms extended in a
futile attempt at defense were screaming and shrieking just before being
ruthlessly ripped apart. The horrendous slaughter amid ear shattering
screams lasted for about twenty minutes while I stood perfectly still
feeling totally helpless in wild-eyed disbelief.

"Suddenly, a deathly pall descended over the cabin area as the
wolves, their ferocity satiated and their fur drenched in blood, followed
Sultan with their long tongues hanging out as they loped back to their
enclosure.

"Grotius came along side me and said just above a whisper, 'Follow
me,' which I did as we walked in silence toward the cabins. When we got
to within ten feet of the nearest cabin a demon-guard stepped forward to
whom Grotius commanded in a low, but firm voice, 'Show us.'

"Without any hesitation the guard stood at attention near the first cabin's splintered doorway; then, at Grotius's nod we followed him into the eerie silence of the cabin. I'm sure that if I hadn't been used to frequently seeing animal parts in a zoological dissecting lab, I would have gotten sick at seeing the scattered remains of the condemned. The walls of the cabin were spattered with blood. What hadn't begun to dry was inching its way down the walls or splattering as droplets from the ceiling as they fell into the puddles of blood on the floor. In several of the puddles were unrecognizable shards of shredded human flesh.

"Along one wall lay two torsos without limbs. Only one had a head attached, and it was minus a face. The third torso was leaning against another wall surrounded by arms and legs with mutilated, bloody stumps, detached hands with fingers missing and several solitary feet scattered about piles of entrails. Grotius stepped over a decapitation to examine a patch of wolf hair on the floor. 'Evidently,' he said while turning to me, 'this is the work of at least two wolves one of which got in the way of the other.

"I closed my eyes and just nodded in return."

"Need to see more cabins?" Grotius asked.

"Unable to speak I shook my head and turned to leave, then waited for Grotius to proceed me through the cabin's open doorway.

"Sitting down again in his cabin I would have given anything for a double shot of one-hundred-proof bourbon. After a few moments of silence Grotius asked in a subdued voice, 'You must have questions?'

"Yes," I said. "How is what I just saw possible? At this time only the souls of the condemned are in Hell. Their dead bodies, back on earth, are either under six feet of dirt, in a mausoleum or incinerated. The soul is a spirit, yet what I saw were definitely body parts. In addition, I saw men being whipped and beaten. How does one beat or lay a club on a spirit? When I arrived, the cabins were whole. Their doors have been destroyed and inside they are strewn with pools of blood in the midst of mutilated chunks and shards of human tissue.

"If these condemned predators and religious persecutors follow the pattern of others in Hell, they must suffer being attacked by wolves again and again for all eternity. How are the cabins cleaned and repaired? How are the condemned made whole again?"

"You must first realize, Bruce, that you are not on Planet Earth where the rules of science apply. You are in Hell where the edicts of Divine Judgment apply.

"Having said that, the condemned you witnessed suffer physical pain because while alive on earth they lived as though their soul did not exist. The result of that denial is that their mind believed their body was the be all and end all of their existence. This allowed them to ignore their consciences as they flagrantly violated the commandments, but especially evil was their using children to satisfy deviant sexual satisfaction and/or killing people for their religious beliefs. By denying that they had an immortal soul or living their lives as if they didn't have one while adamantly mocking others who professed a belief in eternal life, and after God did all he could to convince them otherwise; following their death, at their judgment, God conferred upon them the consequence of their denial. In other words, He gave them in eternity what they wanted while alive on earth.

"What this means, Bruce, is that whether being flogged with a whip, beaten with a club or ripped apart by wolves their minds interpret these experiences the only way they can – it is happening to me and that me is my body. Furthermore, as a result of Divine Judgment the intensity of that belief in Hell imparts an aroma which the spirit driven wolves interpret as a bodily scent: then, they do what wolves do. In some ways it is similar to your human nightmare."

"Perhaps, Grotius, more than you realize – for a nightmare occurs at a time when a person has lost all control, when consciousness has slipped away; in short, when a person dreams; because as long as the dream lasts, what is happening, regardless of how absurd or bizarre it is, the mind interprets it as reality. Proof of this is that when a human being awakens from having a nightmare, he or she immediately feels relieved because nothing of which their mind believed was happening to them had actually occurred."

"An excellent observation. However, here in Hell there are differences; for as God has deigned to grant the condemned their wish it is forever and therefore, they never wake up to reality. Their eternity is a nightmare that never ends; for what they do know is that they must suffer the attacks of the wolves again and again forever and forever and forever! It is why they weep and beg for mercy. They know what is coming!'

"So, the carnage we viewed was their self-deluded illusion?"

"For them, yes, but for us their erroneous belief, which at their judgment God fortified to maximum intensity; that is, that since they feel and believe they have no soul, what occurs to them must of necessity happen to their bodies; and that delusion made possible by an overpowering divine intensity also fosters our illusion."

And the cabins?" I asked.

"See for yourself," he said while extending his hand toward the door, "They are just as you first saw them."

"I opened the door and observed that the multi lighted sky had now been reduced to the now familiar solitary amber point of light. As I stepped outside, the light as it had in the past, went out after a solitary bright flash. In that moment I saw that the cabins with their doors undamaged were just as I first remembered them.

"To erase my last remaining doubt, I walked out to the cabin Grotius and I had examined. I opened the door and stepped in. My eyes had gotten acclimated to the darkness and as I walked around inside, I could see that all evidence of the slaughter and bloodshed was gone. As I departed the cabin, I tried to shake the door. It was solid and completely free of claw gouges. On the way back to Grotius's cabin I wondered how I could possibly write about this supernatural justice for a flagrantly evil life so that the reader would both understand and believe. Just before entering Grotius's cabin I hesitated for a moment and thought, "St. John, you and I certainly have a monumental task ahead of us."

As I crossed the threshold of the cabin, I heard him whisper, "I'll show you."

"Satisfied?" Grotius asked.

"We had a President back in the 1980s who used to say, 'Trust but verify.' I always thought that made a lot of sense."

"No doubt. While you were verifying, however, I took the time to see if Satan had mentioned you to any of my contemporaries – other than Propersynus that is.

"What did you find out?"

"He hadn't. A few of them were disappointed, but most seemed relieved."

"Oh! Why would that be?"

"It's nothing against you personally. In fact, the few who were disappointed were so only after I took the time to tell them about you. Most demons, however, despite taking delight in tormenting the dead who are condemned are panic stricken at the thought of dealing with a living human being in Hell. All of their usual means of cruel, harassing, demonic treatment are prohibited – actually impossible by Divine decree. In short, Bruce, like all living beings who are used to being in control, they refrain from allowing themselves to be put in a position that changes that control to their detriment. Propersynus and I were exceptions because Satan advised us that you were coming as his guest."

"Bruce McPherson is Satan's guest! Who could imagine such a thing? However, I can appreciate that feeling," I said, "even the spiritually aware among us don't feel good about a demon showing up in our world. It took Satan telling me that God had permitted his intrusion into my life along with several Divine prompted prohibitions he was under to convince me to cooperate with his presence."

"Yes, well in retrospect I don't believe it's likely that God will return you to earth as long as you're with me. You received the information you were seeking. I hope you won't think me rude when I ask you to leave now along the same path upon which you came."

"Not at all," I said, as I opened the door. Then gave Grotius a simple nod and began walking across the dirt field. I passed the two guards who had detained me on my arrival, but they took no notice of me. I expected to hear some indication that I was in Hell – moaning or groaning – screaming or shrieking, but all was perfectly silent.

Just before reaching the bend at the top of the hill, however, I was startled to hear, echoing in the distance, "MUSTER THE CONDEMNED! THE CONDEMNED! THE CONDEMNED!" which shattered my entire being. I had spent years in the military and was given and had given the command to muster hundreds of times; but I will never again hear it without being reminded of its new-found meaning.

"As I crossed the line of demarcation in the path I experienced the frigid temperature change as before. Passing through the gate, however, the temperature returned to normal; the gates moved to close; and as the gate latch clicked shut a great whirlwind began spinning around me. Faster and faster it moved as I was lifted up into a brightly lit tunnel and propelled upward as fast or faster than I had descended to Hell in the black tunnel. However, unlike my trip to Hell where I felt terror, I now felt a warm, close comfort that all would end well. My swift ascent began slowing down, and, as before, it stopped completely before letting me down six feet or so in front of the door to the cabin.

"I immediately said a prayer of thanks that I was none the worse for having spent what seemed a long time in Hell and had been returned unharmed. At the end of my prayer I asked that what I experienced would be my one and only journey into Hell. 'Amen to that!' I said aloud.

"Upon my opening the door Satan looked up from his copy of Scientific American, set it aside and said, 'Welcome back, Bruce. I found a bottle of vintage cognac to celebrate your return. I've had a taste myself. It's really quite good."

"My late father loved fine cigars and expensive cognac. I hadn't known that any of the cognac was still around. He kept it behind a hidden door near the bottom of a corner cabinet. The label on the bottle read:

Remy Martin Limited Edition Atelier Steaven Richard XO Cognac. It went for $180.00 a bottle.

"I poured myself a generous drink as I sat in my chair and said, 'I would tell you that Grotius sends his regards, except he didn't.'"

"Grotius and I have an understanding. He is both extremely intelligent and loyal – so much so that I trust no other with my Dirus wolves."

"Ah, yes. Those wolves. Extinct on earth for ten thousand years and suddenly I see them alive in Hell. Well, almost alive. I shall never again see a wolf or even a large dog without thinking of those wolves. In fact, Satan, the last thing I heard in Hell was Grotius roaring, 'MUSTER THE CONDEMNED!'"

"If you write it as well as I know you can your trip to Hell will be the most talked about chapter in your book!"

"Hearing Satan say that, I told him that I didn't know whether to laugh or cry."

"As the reviews come in, Bruce, I suspect you'll do both.

CHAPTER THIRTY-TWO

Satan Experiences the Power of Marian Intercession

"Since I chose our last subject, why don't you take a turn?"

"Only if you are serious. Are you? What I am asking is that no matter my choice, you will not recant?"

"If I recant, Bruce, God will end our discussion. Remember? Go for it."

"I want you to explain what you mean when you use the term: The Great Equalizer."

"Well, it's not in the sequence I had planned," Satan said, standing up, "but it being your choice," he continued, as he freshened my drink before pouring one for himself, "Let's do it," he said, while raising his drink as if in a toast.

"When we had finished our drinks Satan said, 'It will require another adventure. We'll have to go back in time two thousand years to the Middle East. To Bethsaida and Capernaum, cities near the sea of Galilee.'"

"We'll have to go back...?" I questioned. "You're going to accompany me?"

"No, Bruce, you're going to accompany me."

"You can do that? I mean, go back in time? You're capable of time travel?"

"H.G. Wells' hero, Denton Morris, traveled to the past and the future, but travel to the future will never be possible as it is solely the domain of the Divine."

"Ah yes," I said, 'The Time Machine,'_written in 1895. H.G. Wells novella is a perennial favorite of the junior high school student; but, Satan, you have not answered my question."

"I haven't? Think about it. Your answer is still standing in front of you. Or maybe you forgot?"

"I had to admit that I had.

"I stood up and immediately became woozy and a bit shaky. The combination of that glass of cognac and twenty-two hours without sleep in Hell had taken its toll and I grabbed hold of the chair back to regain my balance."

"Satan saw what had happened and said, "You'd better get some sleep – you're paying the price for having to carry around all that flesh, blood, muscle and bone. Don't bother setting your alarm, Bruce. Wake up naturally when you are fully rested. Then we'll discuss our time travel adventure."

"What will you be doing while I'm sleeping?" I asked. "By now you must have read that copy of Scientific American twice over."

"One of my demons is having a problem convincing two twenty-year-olds from a South Chicago neighborhood to become heroin mules. It's a sweet setup. They've been offered a new fully equipped Dodge Laramie pickup truck with a cap to pick up the "packages" at the port in Baltimore and deliver them on a round robin to Philadelphia, Pittsburgh, Cleveland, Detroit, Chicago, and back to Baltimore. They do this every month for $10,000.00. This is more money than either of them ever expected to see at one time – and it's every month! Of course neither of them will celebrate their twenty-fifth birthday, or if they do, it will be behind bars, along with every one through their fiftieth or so; because I intend to sift them as wheat by convincing them to sign on to driving down the wide road on a journey of doom." (Matthew 7:13-14)

"After hearing that example of the essence of evil I remarked, when you return you can tell me how it went. I am interested in seeing how you fare against a stacked deck."

"R-I-G-H-T," he replied, 'while shaking his head and rolling his eyes; and believing my remark was born of wishful thinking, he showed his contempt by waving as he passed like a shadow through the closed cabin door.'"

"I sat on the edge of my bed and removed my shoes and socks. Then I performed the sign of the cross as I raised my eyes and began stacking the deck.

THE MEMORARE

Remember, O most gracious Virgin Mary, that never was it known that anyone who fled to thy protection, implored thy help, or sought thy intercession was left unaided. Inspired with this confidence, I fly unto thee, O Virgin of Virgins, my Mother. To thee do I come, before thee I stand, sinful and sorrowful. O Mother of the Word Incarnate, despise not my petition, that Satan will fail in his plan to doom the salvation of these two young men, but in thy mercy hear and answer me. Amen.

"I realized the powerful intercession that a human mother has with her biological son and was confident that Mary, who had given birth, nursed, and along with Joseph had raised Jesus, the Incarnate Son of God, had heard my prayer and would respond by beseeching Jesus, her Son, to answer my petition in the way I had experienced many times in the past. After my Amen I removed my trousers and shirt before lying down and immediately fell asleep.

Madeline Cooper was a forty-seven-year-old single mother living in South Chicago with her twenty-year-old son, Jeremy, and her thirteen-year-old daughter, Ramona. Her husband, Leroy, had been killed seven years earlier in a gangland crossfire while exiting a coffee shop. He had earned a good living with his brother, Jason, who was eleven years his senior, as the owners of an appliance outlet where they sold used washers, dryers, refrigerators and microwave ovens which they had refurbished. They did a thriving business in the impoverished area selling the items at one-fourth to one-third the cost if purchased new.

During high school Jeremy earned money by working on Saturdays for his uncle Jason. Following his high school graduation Jeremy went to work full time renovating appliances. The young boy had managed through strict maternal oversight as well as the strong influence of his uncle Jason to remain clear of gang membership, but not its influence. He envied the flashy cars, custom tailored clothing and an abundant supply of cash which gang members used as a magnet for attracting the most attractive young women in the neighborhood and for miles around.

He earned an above average income for the area in which he lived, but after giving a third of it to his mother for rent and utilities he was forced to drive a nine-year-old, secondhand car and shop for his clothes at a discount store. His girlfriend, Emilie, was a second-year nursing student at the local community college. She would graduate in six months as a registered nurse (RN), but lacking a bachelor's degree her path for advancement would be limited. If she found employment at a prestigious hospital in Chicago, he would see her only infrequently and as attractive and intelligent as she was would no doubt turn the head of some handsome young medical doctor.

Jeremy's best friend was Carl Thompson. He and Carl were born only a day apart close to twenty-one years ago from mothers who lived in the same neighborhood. As such they went to school together from kindergarten through high school and couldn't be closer if they were blood brothers. This weekend they would celebrate their twenty-first birthdays.

Carl got his driver's license upgraded to CDL B to drive a refrigerated meat packing truck and drove enough during the week delivering beef, pork and poultry from the Chicago slaughter houses to major grocery chains to earn a good income; however, like Jeremy, he envied the flamboyant lifestyle of gang members – many with whom he had grown up in the neighborhood.

"That evening, it being Friday, Jeremy and Carl were sitting together at a table in Benny's, a neighborhood bar when Tony Menotti entered through the back door, ordered a beer, sauntered over to their table, pulled out a chair, plopped down and said, "You two don't mind if I sit here, do you?" Tony could only be described as a colossus. Standing six feet five inches tall and weighing 350 pounds Tony was the centerpiece in any room he occupied. Both Jeremy and Carl knew him and his reputation as an enforcer for one of the local gangs. It was rumored that he was responsible for the disappearance of several rival gang members but their bodies were never discovered and the suspicion was never proven.

"Carl leaned toward Tony and in his best no nonsense truck-driver demeanor replied, 'We don't own that chair, Tony; nor did we lease it. It was purchased and placed there by the proprietor for anyone who buys a drink and wants to sit down. That's you. Your question, therefore, is irrelevant.'"

"Did you just disrespect me, Thompson?"

Before Carl could respond, in order to prevent trouble, Jeremy said, "Of course not, Tony. You asked a question and Carl answered it. Now, obviously it appears you have something you want to discuss with us. If so, we're listening."

Before answering Tony turned around and yelled, "Hannah! Bring us a beer, two non-alcoholics and a bowl of beer nuts." Facing them again Tony said, "I know you two are not yet twenty-one and I never want to do anything that's illegal."

Carl and Jeremy looked at each other barely keeping a straight face before Carl said, "By the end of the weekend we'll both be twenty-one."

"No kidding? Well then Happy Birthday or should I say Happy Birthdays? I have a present to give you that I think you'll both appreciate." When Hannah arrived Tony dropped a $20 bill on her serving tray and said, "Keep the change, Honey." After admiring a couple of well-turned ankles as Hannah walked back to the bar, Tony turned and added, "I don't want to have to interrupt later what I am offering you.

"We need two guys to perform a service on an ongoing basis and you two fit the bill perfectly. Now, before you say anything we're not asking you to join the gang. In fact, what makes you fit so perfectly is that you are not gang members."

Jeremy and Carl sat silently, as the saying goes, waiting for the other shoe to drop.

Tony continued. "We are going to give you a top of the line brand new Dodge Laramie Quad-4 truck with a cap. It will be titled and registered in your names. You will own it outright. All you have to do is pick up some boxes that will be waiting for you on the dock in Baltimore. They will be labeled Pillsbury Flour and the bill of lading will state the same. Each of them will have a destination address. You will deliver these boxes to addresses in Philadelphia, Pittsburgh, Cleveland, Detroit, and Chicago. We'll give you a GPS to help you find the addresses, plus a credit card you can use to cover your expenses while on the road. You'll layover for five days here at home with this very good-looking truck doing whatever you want. Then do it again on a repeating pattern. You'll split $10,000 in cash for every monthly round robin you successfully complete.

"You don't have to give me your answer right now. Talk it over and meet me here Monday evening at 7:00." With that Tony stood up and said, "Think about what you can do with that kind of money. How you can improve the lives of your loved ones. Maybe send your sister to college, Jeremy; or buy your parents a house in the burbs, Carl. Remember: Monday evening 7:00 sharp." With that Tony went to the bar and ordered two pastrami and Swiss on rye to go with another beer.

"Pillsbury flour, my ass," Carl said, before grabbing a handful of beer nuts. "There may be a bag or two of flour in each box, but the bulk of the bags will contain heroin or worse. What do you think, Jeremy?"

Jeremy agreed saying, "Nobody pays that kind of money for moving flour." Then added, "I think this has been an ongoing scam for some time; and the two drivers – probably gang members – were caught and arrested. We, not being gang members, the Law wouldn't have a reason to suspect or keep a tail on us. We could probably do this for three or four months without creating any suspicion."

"Then what? I doubt very seriously that Tony would just let us turn the truck in and walk. We would know too much."

"Maybe he would, if we explained how it would be to their advantage." Raising his hand to fend off Carl's objection, Jeremy continued, "If they changed drivers – I mean using different men without a rap sheet every three or four months, and with each crew they change the truck or at least paint it a different color, it would go a long way toward reducing suspicion."

"Well, let's think more about it over the weekend," Carl responded. "In the meantime, my mother told me that your Uncle Jason is splurging for our twenty-first birthdays – dinner and a party tomorrow for both our extended families at MacArthur's Restaurant."

"Yes, I know. Uncle Jason told me about it this evening just before I left the shop. In the meantime, have you heard back from your employment application with Schneider Transport?"

"No, and it's a bit strange. It's been over a month now. Schneider is a chance for an entry into driving a big rig for a living. They maintain a Drivers' School in Green Bay where I can upgrade my license to CDL A. In four to five weeks, I can be driving for them on my way to a $60,000-a-year job."

"If they accept you," Jeremy remarked.

"I've got a clean background check and three years' experience driving a truck with several excellent references. If not me – then who?"

"What about Minotti's offer? Does that change things?"

"Jeremy, Minotti's offer means big money fast; but, at the expense of constantly looking over your shoulder: and if arrested with the goods a prison term for a decade or more and the rest of your life branded a felon. If I get accepted by Schneider, then Minotti's offer is off the table. If not – well, we'll see. We have until Monday evening to make a decision," Carl said, as he stood and pushed his chair under the table. "I'm going home as my Saturday workday starts at 5:00 A.M. See you tomorrow evening at MacArthur's."

Satan having abandoned his physical image and along with his minion, Humilione, had been observing the scene at Benny's. Tony Menotti was no stranger to either as he had been their go to man on many a demonic scheme that ended with both men and women traveling with him down the wide road to perdition. This time, however, he did not like the odds of that happening. He had heard Carl say that if Schneider Trucking qualified him for the school, he would turn down Minotti's offer, and despite the abnormal delay, his acceptance was a very real possibility.

"It appears our only chance is to find a way to emphasize Tony's idea about using the money to better their family's lives," remarked Humilione.

"Not quite," answered Satan. "I like your idea and we'll prompt Menotti to do just that and maybe sweeten the pot, but it is not enough. There's a fifty-fifty chance that because of the delay Schneider has found something in Thompson's background that they are either questioning or flat out don't like. If the latter they will turn down his request to attend their school. I know that Schneider is very particular about who they hire to represent them on the road."

"Is there something else we can do to detour these two from the narrow road," the demon asked.

"That's not what you're supposed to be doing here," Satan answered. "What you are supposed to be doing is to give these two a solid reason for accompanying each other to choose the wide road where they will cross the finish line to be mine – all mine – forever and forever all mine."

Humilione had heard Satan use this expression countless times over many millennia. It meant he felt he had devised what he thought was a foolproof way of acquiring his objective, so he asked, "What are you thinking about?"

"Tomorrow evening their families will be together for dinner and festivities. Alcohol will play a big part. It should not be too difficult to induce one or more of each family to interpret a questionable remark with an angry reply. Two or three of these will be enough. Eventually someone will throw an alcohol-inspired punch and the melee begins.

"Carl will be upset if the letter arrives tomorrow stating Schneider has denied his dream for moving forward with his life; or if it still hasn't arrived; and although Jeremy has never said so, he has to be miffed about the fact that after his father, who was his Uncle Jason's partner, was killed, he thinks his uncle's care for his brother's family is limited to birthday presents and turkeys at Thanksgiving and Christmas. We have to use that belief to convince him that working for his Uncle Jason is not a good idea now that he has a more lucrative option. So, the plan is to watch and wait for an opening tomorrow night; and to ensure that Carl and Jeremy are joined together as peacemakers – not as participants. It is imperative that these two do not square off against each other."

The open bar at MacArthur's private room had opened at 6:00 PM. At 7:00 PM the bell rang as a signal to take their seats for dinner. When all were seated Uncle Jason moved to the podium.

"It is customary in celebrations such as this to wait until dinner is over before anyone speaks," he said, "but due to the nature of the proceedings I am reversing the procedure. A letter from Schneider Trucking arrived today at Carl's house while he was working. His mother gave me the letter for him to read to open this evening's birthday party. Would you come forward, Carl?"

Carl, feeling a bit uncomfortable as to the nature of the letter came to the podium and whispered, "Jason, what if this is bad news? I'll be so embarrassed."

"Trust me, Jeremy." Jason whispered out of the side of his mouth while continuing to smile looking forward.

Carl nervously opened the envelope and read the two short paragraphs before smiling and raising his eyes while stating, "It says that I have been accepted..." but before he could complete the sentence both families stood up and cheered while clapping with delight. When they had sat down, Carl continued. "It gives me a choice of several school starting dates and continues with what I have to bring with me."

Jason shook his hand and said, "Congratulations, Carl. I'm so happy for you." As Carl took his seat Jason said, "Lest any of you think that I am psychic or given to taking cruel risks, last week I called Schneider's Director of Driver Training to inquire into the reason for the apparent delay. I was informed that Schneider cannot train nor hire a driver that is less than twenty-one years old; and that they waited until Carl was twenty-one to be 100% legal. I immediately advised Madeline, Carl's mother. As of today, Carl has met that requirement and will soon be on his way to becoming our very own Knight of the Open Road!" Again, the families erupted in applause.

"Now we come to the second half of our reason for being here tonight. And for that I am asking Bill McLaughlin, my Attorney and Financial Advisor to take the mike."

Bill McLaughlin graduated at the top of his class twenty years ago from The University of Chicago Law School. Five years later he expanded his business by taking courses to become a Certified Financial Advisor. He maintained an office with a large staff in downtown Chicago as well as a small sub office in South Chicago where he did pro bono work for the less fortunate. Average height, he kept a full head of black hair which was now graying at the temples giving his lean physique a distinguished appearance. He began saying how pleased he was to have been invited to not only Jeremy and Carl's twenty-first birthday party, but also having been asked to speak. Then he said, "Seven years ago Jason called to tell me of the tragic death of Leroy, his brother and partner, and since I knew both brothers for years both as clients and friends, he asked if I would be one of the pall bearers. I felt honored then as I do now to be with you.

"At the luncheon following the funeral Mass Jason made an appointment at my Chicago office for a day the following week. Both he and Leroy's widow, Madeline, met me for lunch after which we discussed how to handle the changes made necessary by Leroy's demise."

Opening his briefcase, he removed a large manila envelope and said, "Here's what we decided: First, Madeline wanted to receive half of Leroy's share of his partner-earnings to continue maintaining a household for Jeremy, Ramona and herself. Added to the earnings from the proceeds of Leroy's life insurance, she felt she could get by. Of course, as we now know, inflation and falling interest rates forced her to get outside employment as a cashier at Kroger's where over the years her abilities have earned her a position as assistant manager."

The attorney was then interrupted as everyone began clapping while Mrs. Cooper, feeling somewhat embarrassed, nodded and smiled.

As the acknowledgement subsided, he continued, "That leaves the other half of Leroy's share of the partnered-earnings which Madeline wanted put in trust funds for Jeremy and Ramona. I am happy to say that today, due to conservative investing and compound interest, each of those trusts is worth $175,000. Jeremy, being of age, if he so chooses, has access to his money immediately. Ramona will have to wait and watch it grow until she is eighteen, when we hope she chooses to use whatever amount it takes to further her education.

"In the meantime, Jeremy, your Uncle Jason told me that turning twenty-one was a milestone in your life and therefore, he wanted to give you the best present he could."

"So," he continued, pulling a second sheath of paperwork from the envelope, "as of today, Jeremy, you are no longer employed by your uncle at the appliance store. And why? Because you are now a full partner and half owner. And one thing…" Again the attorney was interrupted by clapping and high fiving by the families.

"As I started to say, there is one thing more. Jason is now sixty years old. In five years, being sixty-five, he intends to retire. At that time, Jeremy, you will be the full owner. In fact, to seal the agreement he had me add this ending to the document; Quote 'You'll then be on your own, Jeremy. Your uncle Jason has gone fishing! Unquote'"

Humilione watched as the second table proceeded in an orderly fashion to the buffet spread. He noticed his master's disgusted demeanor and thought it better to wait to respond to Satan's remark than to initiate the conversation; but as the people at the third and then the fourth tables rose, he felt a compulsion to ask, "How do you want to proceed, Master?"

"I don't." Satan responded. "These people are on such a high that if one of them threw a punch his target would offer to buy him a drink. We're through here Humilione. It happens sometimes. Unforeseen events propagated by these fleshy creatures preclude us from accomplishing our goal. When that happens, it is like tempting shadows. We'll try again another day."

"I don't know why, Master, but I just couldn't get this caper off the ground. It started off well, but then as everything fell apart, I felt as though somebody entered the game with a stacked deck."

Immediately Humilione saw that Satan gave him a strange look. "Stacked deck, Master. A human expression when at a poker table one of the players knows what the other players have because the backs of the cards are secretly marked."

"I know what it means," Satan said. "It just seems strange that you would use that expression at this time."

Despite his curiosity Humilione felt it was not a good time to ask his Master why.

On Sundays, Carl's mother and father along with Carl and his two younger sisters attended the 8:00 A.M. Mass. Upon their return Mrs. Thompson prepared breakfast after which her husband, Carl Sr., spent the better part of the day reading The Sunday Chicago Tribune. While browsing the front page he saw an article entitled:

Two South Chicago youths arrested for transporting a truckload of heroin.

After reading the article he said to his son, "Carl, didn't you go to school with a Roscoe Betts and Pasquale De Blasio?"

"Yeah, Dad. They were a year ahead of me. Betts had a hard time and dropped out as soon as he turned sixteen. De Blasio made All State as a wide receiver and accepted a football scholarship to Michigan State.

However, that summer he and a guy from another school got liquored up and drove into a concrete bridge abutment. The driver was killed and De Blasio's right leg was shattered, which cost him his scholarship. Why are you asking about them?"

"They made the front page of the *TRIB*. They were arrested for picking up heroin in Baltimore and distributing it to several cities including Chicago. Seems they got a flat tire on the Ohio Turnpike and the State Trooper who stopped to see if they needed help had a dope sniffing dog in the rear seat area with the window partly open. When the animal got rambunctious, he let him out of the vehicle and he immediately sat down at the rear of the truck. I'll circle the article and you can read it for yourself."

"Two local boys bringing that poison home to the ruination of their own," Carl's mother remarked. "What would cause young men to do such a thing?"

"Money, mom, and a lot of it. Enough, anyway, that they think it's worth the risk. And when you think about it they got caught only because of two coincidences – the flat tire and a dope sniffing dog coming together at the same time."

"If it wasn't the tire and the dog it would eventually have been something else," his father added.

That afternoon Carl cut the article from the newspaper and phoned Jeremy to meet him at Benny's. After reading the article Jeremy said, "How lucky are we to be on the outside looking in on this one, Carl? I never knew Betts but everyone knows who De Blasio is.

On Monday, at 6:50 PM, Carl and Jeremy arrived at Benny's for their meeting with Tony Minotti. Carl had brought the Chicago Tribune article to strengthen the reason for turning down Tony's offer. Since Carl was on his way to Green Bay and Jeremy now had management responsibilities at the Appliance Store they were going to tell Tony that neither of them was a good prospect.

They each ordered a beer and a ham and Swiss on rye with a side order of coleslaw to consume while waiting Tony's arrival; but, when

7:30 arrived and still there was no Tony, Jeremy motioned to Hannah to come to the table.

"Hannah, have you seen Tony Minotti today?" He told us last Friday to meet him here at 7:00 sharp. He made a point of telling us not to be late."

"He came in around noon and ordered a Porterhouse with all the trimmings. He no sooner finished it when two homicide detectives arrived, slapped the cuffs on him and told him he was under arrest for murder. You saw the article in Sunday's Tribune about Betts and De Blasio?"

"Yes, I have it right here," Carl said.

"Well, around 4:30 two of Tony's gang member buddies came in and put out the word that Betts, a gang member, rolled over on Tony in exchange for a deal. That's really bad for Tony because it's rumored that Betts helped Tony dispose of several bodies."

When Hannah had removed the empty sandwich plates and wiped the table, she asked, "You guys O.K. here?"

"Bring us two beers," Carl said, "And thanks for the info."

"You're welcome. I'm going on break, guys. I'll send Cindy over with your beers."

"I awoke and glanced at my digital alarm. It read 10:00. The red dot in the upper left-hand corner told me it was 10:00 PM. I had been sleeping for ten hours and felt completely rested. After dressing I realized how quiet it was. It didn't feel right to be calling out to Satan so I searched the cabin and found that he had not returned. After a meal of tomato soup, crackers, Gatorade and an apple I went to my office and continued with my research.

At 1:00 A.M. there was a soft knock on the door. It was Satan, but looking rather forlorn. I could see that something had occurred which had markedly changed the jaunty, confident disposition he displayed as he departed earlier by waving just before he walked through the cabin door. "Come in," I said, suddenly realizing how ludicrous it sounded for a Christian to be welcoming Satan into his cabin. "You look less than pleased. Can I get you something?

"Without answering he flopped down in my father's favorite chair and one after another forcefully stretched his long legs over the footstool. I guess you want to be alone," I said, "I'll be in my study working on my thesis."

"I didn't say I want to bc alone," Satan responded in a voice much softer than his demeanor would indicate. "If that offer is still open you can get me a stiff drink from that cognac bottle of your father's."

"Without responding I poured two ounces into his brandy snifter and one ounce into mine. I sat down after giving him his drink and waited to hear what he had to say."

"As I was leaving you indicated that I would fail in my endeavor because I was playing against a stacked deck. What did you mean by that?"

"You will remember the conversation we had earlier when I remarked, 'You are fearful of our Blessed Mother. Mary – she strikes fear in you?'

"Your reply was, 'Not so much, her, but what God accomplishes because of her.'"

"I remember."

"Well, so did I when you threatened two young men with eternal damnation. I prayed The Memorare asking Mary to ask her Son to see to your failure. Obviously, from your gloomy disposition Mary asked and Jesus set you up."

"It was worse than that. It is one thing to fail in a demonic venture of acquisition, because you have neither gained nor lost and your last position is no worse than before. But to lose what you already claim as your own is depressing, for it means that you are not moving forward; nor even standing still, but moving backward."

"And this is what happened?"

"I not only failed to convince the two men that I, with my demon Humilione, were attempting to recruit, but I lost two additional men I had recruited long ago; one of which was outstanding in his efforts to convince others to accompany him along the wide road.'"

"What do you mean by lost?"

"They're going to prison. One of them will be an old man when he gets out. The second, my reliable go-to man, will no doubt die in prison.

"Then there is a third man who will probably get only eight to ten years due to his Judas-like betrayal, but it is unlikely he will be alive a year from now, after which he will see what a bad bargain he made, for time in prison is nothing compared to being mine, all mine: then jumping up Satan bellowed while shaking a clenched fist in the air, 'Forever and forever all mine.'"

"Knowing that he was referring to Menotti and De Blasio along with Betts I did my best to ignore the exaggerated delight Satan expressed, and said, "I didn't beseech Mary to ask Jesus to do that. I only asked that you fail in recruiting the two young men you mentioned. I didn't even know about the other three."

"No doubt," he said while taking his seat again. "Mary, however, probably did, and for sure Jesus knew."

"After finishing the rest of his cognac, he held the empty glass out to me, and as I was refreshing his drink, he continued, 'I'm sure that by now you know that Jesus, on many occasions, gives you more than for what you prayed. For example, take St. Augustine,' he added, gesturing toward the painting on the wall 'All his mother, Monica, prayed for was his conversion. She got that plus his ordination to the priesthood, his consecration as a bishop, his writings which are read to this day – sixteen hundred years later; and if that's not enough, her son is canonized a saint and made a Doctor of the Church!'"

CHAPTER THIRTY-THREE

What Virtues Did You Want in The Woman Who Would Be Your Mother?

"What I'll never understand is the depth of stupidity inherent in the human race. God has given man great helps to aid him in his earthly struggle against my powerful demonic intentions; but both men and women continually and rudely refuse to accept them.

"Since the dawn of civilization, I have never seen such a vast number of souls living lives that all but plead to be a part of my demonic harvest. What do they hope to gain by spitting in the face of God?"

"You, yourself, Satan are the reason for the frightful condition of mankind. As we said during our first encounter, you have convinced an incalculable number of people that either there is no God, or if there is a God, he is indifferent to the affairs of mankind and therefore, there is no life after death; and if so, then there is no judgment, and if there is no judgment the Ten Commandments are man-made suggestions and therefore, not obligatory; so, they deny the concept of sin. And if a person believes that, then it follows that there is no Hell. Finally, if there is no Hell then you do not exist. I would estimate that with conditions in the world as they are, about half of the western world thinks this way."

"What about belief in Heaven? You didn't mention Heaven."

"A goodly portion of the rest of the world believes that Jesus' death on the cross exonerates them from any penalty for their sin – that He paid the price for any sin they can commit. No matter what kind of life they lead all they have to do is believe this and their salvation is assured."

"Are you able to refute this?" Satan responded.

"Jesus spoke often about Hell, especially in His account of Lazarus and the unnamed rich man (Luke 16:19-31) in order that we would have no excuse for denying the reality of suffering eternal punishment for un-repented mortal sin. Furthermore, Jesus goes into great detail describing the pain the self-centered, non-empathetic and selfish rich man is suffering in Hell.

"As we noted previously, this is the only parable wherein Jesus gives a name to one of the characters. Because of this some theologians think this may be a true story; but whether true or not Jesus is telling us that as we heard him say to the blasphemous comedian near the end of his judgment, 'My love is unconditional, but salvation is not.'"

"So can you be more specific about what Jesus' crucifixion meant for his human creation?"

"I answered, as we discussed before, Jesus, as the Son of God, offered His Incarnate Life to God the Father to repair the rift caused by sin between man and God. What this means is that now as long as he or she is alive, by repenting for sin and having a firm purpose of amendment persons can set themselves right with God allowing him or her to get back on the narrow road to eternal salvation."

"Exactly," Satan responded, "but what you just said won't matter. They reject God because they think they have a better idea which is impossible; and being impossible it doesn't exist; and this creates a vac-uum which I and mine easily fill leading them down the wide road to perdition."

"I sat there waiting for Satan's usual rant about them being forever and forever all mine but it never came. Instead after a pause he said, "Now, before we take our time travel, I have to ask you some questions."

"I thought that's what you were doing."

"We must pursue an additional venue."

"Ask away," I responded, unsure where this was going, but at the same time wondering whether I was allowing our understanding to become too friendly – that I might be disregarding my mother's advice on being beguiled by his apparent charm; so I excused myself to get a glass of water. When I returned, I sat in a chair that increased the distance between us."

"Much to my chagrin, and I might add my humiliation," he said, "in answer to my flagrant announcement that I intended to bring two young men into my way of thinking leading to their damnation you brought Mary's intercession into our dialogue. I had planned to speak of her, but only in a cursory fashion and much nearer to the end of our discussions. That was the agreement I had with God to which he agreed.

However, Jesus further stipulated that this agreement was on condition that I do nothing to prompt you to invite the power of Mary's intercession into our discussion; but if I did so I would have to correct the myriad of misunderstandings about this miraculous woman. Therefore, it is imperative that in keeping with my promise not to mislead, we must first pursue her further to reveal the truth."

"I nodded in agreement but said nothing before being shocked and put off balance when he asked, 'Your mother is deceased. She died from breast cancer seven years ago. Did you love her?'

"What kind of a question…?"

"I must insist that you answer my questions without asking the reason for the question which eventually you will come to know. Agreed?

"Very well. I was her first born and only son. I have two younger sisters. Yes, I loved my mother as any son would love a devoted and caring mother."

"Did you have anything to say about the woman who would be your mother such as her appearance, her intelligence, her propensity to virtue or the strength of her maternal instincts?"

"Of course not. Nobody does. How could the pre-conceived and therefore, the non-existent, have such a say?"

"You spoke without thinking your answer through. Go back and think again; then give me your answer."

"I thought for a moment, wondering to what he was referring, and then I understood. 'O.K.' I said, "I see what you mean. You're referring to the Incarnation."

"Precisely. Jesus, the Son of God, was the only person born of woman who had or will ever have a say about the woman who would be His mother. As a spirit I never had a mother; but in observing the average human person's love for his or her mother I would say that if God, in his omnipotence, designed the features and faculties of His own mother and then created her with that Divine plan she would be nothing less than perfect in every way."

"That's logical. Why would God create his mother with an Immaculate Conception, that is, a perfect soul, because it is free from the effects of original sin, for a less than perfect mind and body? Logically this would be an inconsistency which is impossible since inconsistency and Divinity are contradictory."

"Your reply shows a degree of logic that is not apparent in many of you. They instead cast her aside as if God had chosen her with no more thought than if He had thrown a dart or blindly fished her name from some giant raffle bowl.

"Stupid, of course, but no more than to be expected in line with what I have said many times before when describing the human condition."

"When Satan didn't reply further but only closed his eyes while shaking his head as if in disbelief, I said, Tell me, Satan, since you must have known her. What was she like in real life? How did others react to her? All we really know is from the few times she is mentioned in scripture and what we glean from her approved apparitions, specifically Guadalupe, Lourdes and Fatima – all of which were long after she walked the Earth."

"Odd that you should mention her apparitions. Beginning with her apparition to Juan Diego in Guadalupe, Mexico, some 1500 years ago when God wants to send a message to mankind He sends Mary, His mother, versus an angel as He did in the Old Testament. Why do you think this is?

"I can think of two reasons for God doing so.

"Really – Would you care to share your thoughts?"

"Well, first of all, Satan, human beings identify better with someone they feel they know that resembles them. Mary's delivery of God's messages to us, is by a revered human being. There is no commentary required to understand or interpret the idea God has told her to convey.

"Secondly, Jesus wants to remind us that by his words from the cross to the apostle, John, that Mary, His biological mother, is our spiritual mother; and in that respect we should honor her, which never means to offer adoration but believing that when Mary speaks to us, she is speaking the will of God.

When Satan nodded in agreement, but said nothing, I continued, "But getting back to my question, while here on earth what was she like? What was her temperament? How did people react to her?"

Satan paused while pouring himself another drink of cognac. As he sat back, he said, "First of all one has to know the general attitude of the Jewish people in those times. Sons were given every chance to improve themselves. They learned their father's trade and had ample opportunity to get some schooling, especially learning to read and write and a reasonable familiarity with the Torah.

"Daughters, however, were thought of quite differently. Women, in general, were thought of as property – first of their parents, especially their father; and later on by their husband, who many times was chosen for them by their parents. They were taught by their mothers to keep house, to cook, to clean, to sew, to wash clothing and in general what it took to please a man. If there was any schooling at all it was because the father loved his daughter enough to spend time teaching her. Because of this most women were illiterate.

"It was in this general temperament that Mary was born to Joachim and Anna, a deeply religious, married couple who resided in Nazareth, a city in the province of Galilee. Mary was an only child but was fortunate to have loving parents who wanted the best for her. In this respect her father not only taught her to read and write, but to use that ability to study the scriptures. Familiarity with Abraham, Moses and King David along with the prophets Isaiah, Daniel, Ezekiel, Jeremiah, etc., gave her a religious fervor born of knowledge not usually found in Jewish women of that time – women who for the most part knew only what men wanted them to know.

"Even as a child of ten Mary's movements were fluid and graceful. Having no siblings she spent much of her play time with several girls within her age group who lived close by. She possessed an inborn athleticism and won many of the events in which she participated.

"The age of thirteen, however, brought about a change. She began spending more time in prayer and meditation than in playing with her friends. She looked forward to the annual trip with her parents to the Temple in Jerusalem for Passover even though from the Court of Women she and her mother were far removed from the Sanctuary where the services were performed.

"While in Jerusalem, as I mentioned earlier, Mary and her parents spent their evenings and nights with Mary's much older cousin, Elizabeth and her husband Zachariah, a Temple priest. They had been married for more than thirty-five years and were more than a little saddened by the fact that Elizabeth had proven to be barren.

For the next three years, Mary spent much of her free time in reading and prayer. A man, Joseph by name, and ten years her senior, began showing an interest in her. He had a reputation for being an excellent carpenter and a man who kept the Mosaic Law. With her parents' permission he began courting her and just before her seventeenth birthday they were betrothed, or engaged as you say today.

"Then, one morning after her parents left the house to visit a sick friend Mary was engulfed in a meditation deeper than she had ever experienced. I didn't actually see what happened, but a demon of mine reported Gabriel's appearance to Mary saying in effect Mary had agreed to being conceived by an act of God. I was almost positive from how

Gabriel had addressed her, that is, 'Hail Mary, full of grace.' that her issue might be the long-awaited Messiah.

"From the moment Mary gave her ascent to Gabriel her life would never be the same. Gabriel also told Mary that her cousin, Elizabeth, who by now was years past a woman's ability to conceive, was far along in her own pregnancy. Mary had decided to travel to Ain Karim, a city near Jerusalem, where Elizabeth lived, to help her since being pregnant at fifty-two would mean she would experience more than the usual fatigue and effects of exertion.

"For the first time that either could remember her parents disagreed with her decision. "Elizabeth is in her fifties," her father stated. "She couldn't conceive when she was in her twenties. This doesn't make any sense, Mary."

"I know," Mary replied, "and I wouldn't believe it if a person told me it was so: but it was an angel of the Lord and, therefore, it must be so."

"Not the angel bit again," her mother said. Mary please…"

"Mother – Father, I don't blame you for doubting me. After all, I am asking you to believe what reason tells you cannot be. I am, frankly, asking you to believe in a miracle which neither of you has seen. So I can only ask that you believe in me, Mary, your daughter, who has never lied to you. After all, why would I engage so strongly in falsehoods when the truth must come to light in less than a year?"

Joachim looked at his wife who nodded in agreement. "Here is money you will need for the trip," her father said. "The Travel Post states that there is a caravan leaving for Jerusalem the day after tomorrow."

"Satan," I asked, interrupting. "I always thought it strange that such a loving father would allow his seventeen-year-old daughter to travel alone in a caravan in which there was bound to be several men of less than honorable intent. This is a 160 mile round trip with at least two or more overnights each way. What were Mary's parents thinking?"

"You are partially correct; however, don't make the mistake of applying modern culture to that of those times. Men and women traveled separately in caravans – especially those not married. Mary was constantly in the company of twenty-five or so women – a formidable defense against a couple of men. Secondly, caravan masters brooked nothing that threatened their reputation and livelihood. They had several men in their pay that kept the security of the caravan as well as its members safe.

"Men caught stealing or molesting travelers who had paid to be safe in the caravan were severely beaten with whips and then being half dead were dragged into the wilderness without water to either bleed to death or die of thirst. This was well known, which is why travelers gladly paid the fee for this protection.

"Those who were desperate or stupid enough to prey on their fellow men or women within the caravan did so not so much because of my temptation but because like the two soldiers that attacked the young Jewess and killed Jonathan, they had long before chosen the way of depraved degeneracy. Invariably they were caught and after a severe scourging, they died while bleeding and gasping for water as they baked to death in the desert sun. After which their carcasses were sustenance for the vultures and jackals but their souls were mine," he said, "forever and forever all mine."

"However, this time it was spoken while he remained seated without rancor or rage but in a calm way that seemed as if he were simply stating a matter of fact.

"When it was apparent Satan had finished speaking, I said, So Mary arrived safely at the home of Zachariah and Elizabeth. We celebrate this as the Second Joyful Mystery of the Rosary and is commonly referred to as The Visitation, wherein we contemplate the virtue of reaching out to help others who are in need. Can you give us some details of this three-month visit?'"

"Before I say any more, I must admit something to you."

"Well, I am not sure what it is," I responded, "but as we spoke, I could only wonder why you are now willing to spend so much time revealing the truth about Mary when you have prompted many theologians of the reformation to so vigorously lie, malign and reduce her status for the last five hundred years?"

"I did it because I knew that if I did not remove Mary's lofty status from their belief system, she would use the powerful influence of her intercession to dilute or even heal the degree of fractured Christianity I had brought about by the Reformation."

"And now?"

"You will remember before we began talking about her that I said telling the truth about Mary was one of my conditions; however, to repeat what I said earlier, I bargained with God, Who agreed that I incurred this responsibility only by just casually mentioning her unless because of something I said or did you interjected her power of intercession into our conversation."

"I remember, Satan. Actually, to be more precise, as you already mentioned it was your divulging so boastfully that you were about to persuade two young men to follow your evil inclinations down the wide road to their eternal damnation that caused me to bring Mary's intercession into play. I thought we had already established this."

"We have, but I must also confess that I had planned to speak of Mary in a manner that would be preserving her existence and admiration at Christmas, but nothing else. Now, however, I will have to keep my promise by telling the truth in a biographical dissertation."

"That was your agreement?

"Bruce, if it wasn't do you think I would be doing it?"

Not waiting for me to respond Satan began, "So after saying her goodbyes to the women she met in the caravan Mary mounted the donkey and proceeded the few miles to Ain Karim.

"Before we go any further, however, we have to go back six months to an incident that occurred in the Temple. Like Mary's Annunciation I did not observe this personally but was told of it by one of the five demons that work the area in and around Jerusalem. It seems that the angel Gabriel was sent by God to the Temple to deliver a message to Zachariah, the husband of Mary's cousin, Elizabeth. He was one of the many priests assigned to perform rituals in the Temple. One of those rituals was a ceremony that involved the priest honoring the omnipotence of God by offering the rising smoke of burning incense within the sanctuary. He had just finished and was about to leave the sanctuary and rejoin the people who were praying outside when without warning off to his side appeared a man who had a soft glow about him.

"When Zachariah saw him, he was startled and no doubt fearful. No one but priests and Levites were permitted to be in the sanctuary; however, his appearance told Zachariah that this was not an ordinary man. Then, Gabriel spoke: "Do not be afraid, Zachariah; your prayer has been heard. Your wife Elizabeth will bear you a son, and you are to call him John. He will be a joy and delight to you, and many will rejoice because of his birth, for he will be great in the sight of the Lord. He is never to take wine or other fermented drink. He will be filled with the Holy Spirit even before he is born. He will bring back many of the people of Israel to the Lord their God. And he will go on before the Lord, in the spirit and power of Elijah, to turn the hearts of parents to their children and the disobedient to the wisdom of the righteous to make ready a people prepared for the Lord." (Luke:13-17)

"Zachariah, somewhat dazed, but becoming less fearful and not sure that he might be only imagining what he saw and heard in the sanctuary nevertheless asked, "How can I be sure of this? I am an old man and my wife is well along in years." (Luke:18-20)

The person answered, "I am the archangel, Gabriel. I stand in the presence of God. I have been sent to tell you this good news. And now because you doubted my words you will not be able to speak until the day this happens, which will come true at its appointed time." (Luke:21-22)

"Meanwhile, the people were waiting for Zachariah and wondering why he stayed so long in the sanctuary. When he came out, he could not speak to them. He just stood before them trying his best to communicate with his hands. Finally, he convinced them that he could not speak because he had seen a vision in the temple. They left then asking each other why such a thing would happen to Zachariah and what this could possibly mean.

"When his time of service was completed, he returned home. He wrote down what had happened in the sanctuary. After Elizabeth read it, she kissed him. They both became sexually aroused and made love. At supper that evening Elizabeth told her husband that she felt good and warm all over. Both felt they knew that meant she could be pregnant. For five months she remained in seclusion. 'The Lord has done this for me,' she said. 'In these days he has shown his favor and taken away my disgrace among the people.'

"What did she mean by that last remark?" I asked. "And why would she remain in seclusion?"

"If you remember Nicodemus read the dissertation from Deuteronomy wherein Moses infers that if the Jews obeyed the commandments and in short kept the Mosaic Law that God would bless them with a life where all would go well. Conversely, he said that if they did otherwise, they could expect evil to befall them. At that time and for many generations after Moses the Jews believed that misfortune was punishment for a life not well lived. In short, if a woman was barren, it was because she deserved to be; therefore, many of Elizabeth's acquaintances felt that she was unable to conceive because at some time in her younger life she had transgressed the Law in such a manner that greatly displeased Jehovah."

"I suppose we can't fault them. They knew nothing about the science of reproduction; but why would she remain in seclusion for five months?"

"I can't tell you for sure, but after observing her I have to say that having her first pregnancy at fifty-two she suffered from serious and prolonged morning sickness which exhausted her. Secondly, she was fatigued to such a degree that she was fearful of a miscarriage; and in her in her seventh month Mary had assumed responsibility for the housework. Regardless, in her eighth month she made a miraculous recovery and during the eighth and ninth month spent time rejoicing with her friends."

"Returning to where we left her Mary knocked on the door and when Zachariah opened it, he stepped back in surprise as Mary embraced him saying, "Zachariah, how pleased you must be that after all these years to become a father!"

"Zachariah nodded while wondering how Mary knew, then gave her a smile in return as he waved her into the house. Mary, of course, thought it odd that Zachariah didn't speak to her, but didn't say anything about it. As Mary stood in the entranceway to the scullery and greeted her, Elizabeth, surprised, turned and walked toward her. As she did the growing baby in her womb kicked with more force than he had ever done before. Obviously, prompted by the Holy Spirit Elizabeth responded, 'Blessed are you among women, and blessed is the child you bear. But why am I so favored that the mother of my Lord should come to me? As soon as I heard your greeting the little one in my womb leapt for joy!' (Luke 1:39-45)

"She then stepped forward and taking both of Mary's hands in hers said, 'And blessed is she who believed that there would be a fulfillment of what was spoken to her from the Lord.' Mary smiled and stepped back. Then glancing at Zachariah before turning once again to Elizabeth Mary raised her eyes and hands in prayer and said:

My soul proclaims the greatness of the Lord,
And my spirit rejoices in God my Savior,
For he has looked with favor on his lowly servant.
From this day forward all generations shall call me blessed:
For the Almighty has done great things for me,
And holy is his Name.
He has been merciful to those who fear him.
In every generation.
He has shown the strength of his arm.
He has scattered the proud in their conceit.
He has cast down the mighty from their thrones,
And has lifted up the lowly.

He has filled the hungry with good things,
And the rich he has sent empty away.
He has come to the help of his servant Israel
For he remembered his promise of mercy,
The promise he made to our fathers,
to Abraham and his children forever.
(Luke 1:46-55)

"That must have set you back to hear that coming from a seventeen-year-old. Just what kind of an impression did that make on you?"

Without hesitation Satan replied, "It all but confirmed what I had feared since Gabriel's annunciation. God had patterned Mary like no woman before nor since to assume the responsibility to not only conceive, bear and birth the Messiah, but to raise him as His mother from suckling at her breast through infancy, childhood, puberty and on into manhood."

"In that respect," I asked, "What was it like for Mary and Joseph raising a boy they knew to be the Messiah? Was it like we say, 'walking on eggshells' or was it more or less like any parents raising a boy?"

"I didn't observe what is commonly referred to as The Holy Family all the time, but what I did witness or what my demons reported to me was that, except for his conversations with members of the Sanhedrin as a twelve-year-old in the Temple, Jesus kept any evidence of His Divinity suppressed. He cried and fussed as a teething youngster, He played with other boys his age; he fell down and scraped his knees and through trial and error had to learn his father's trade as a carpenter. Except for that one example in the Temple, what is commonly referred to as His hidden life was unremarkable in every respect.

"You might remember when He first proclaimed himself to be the Messiah, their Savior, in the synagogue in Nazareth, the first reply was, "What does he mean? Isn't he the Son of Joseph, the carpenter?" (Luke 4:14-30)

"Did you ever try to interfere with Joseph or Mary? You must have known that God was aware that you and your demons were watching the Child Jesus and his parents."

"I had to see what parameters I had in this regard. We spoke already about my urging King Herod to kill the child; however, we'll talk later about twice more when I tried to interfere; for now suffice it to say that both ended in colossal failures, and one of these was accompanied by a Divine warning."

Obviously not wanting to answer any more questions Satan continued, "Mary stayed with Zachariah and Elizabeth for three months doing most of the cooking, cleaning and general housework. When the time came for Elizabeth to be delivered Zachariah brought the midwife to the house.

"In accordance with the Mosaic Law on the eighth day following his birth the parents along with their relatives and close friends took the baby boy to the Temple to be circumcised where he also received his name. Those in attendance thought for sure he would be named Zachariah after his father. Elizabeth, however, said, "No, he will be called John." Since there was no one among their relatives named John they referred to Zachariah who picked up a clay tablet and scribed, His name is John. Immediately, his tongue was loosed and he began thanking those in attendance for helping them celebrate an event he and Elizabeth thought would never happen.

"Those in attendance, however, as bewildered as they were by the child's name and Zachariah's instant ability to speak again were even further mystified when Zachariah, following the child's circumcision, stepped away from them and prompted by the Holy Spirit raised his eyes and hands in prayer and chanted the following:

"Praise be to the Lord, the God of Israel,
because he has come to his people and redeemed them.
He has raised up a horn of salvation for us
in the house of his servant David

and that is salvation from our enemies
and from the hand of all who hate us—
to show mercy to our ancestors
and to remember his holy covenant,
the oath he swore to our father Abraham:
to rescue us from the hand of our enemies,
and to enable us to serve him without fear
in holiness and righteousness before him all our days.
And you, my child, will be called a prophet of the Most High;
for you will go on before the Lord to prepare the way for
him,
to give his people the knowledge of salvation
through the forgiveness of their sins,
because of the tender mercy of our God,
by which the rising sun will come to us from Heaven
to shine on those living in darkness
and in the shadow of death,
to guide our feet into the path of peace."
(Luke 1:67-80)

"John lived with his parents until the year they both passed away. He was twenty-one then and set out to live in the desert near the river Jordan. Two years later he began preaching repentance for sin and asking those who had repented and amended their life to seal their promise to Jehovah by being baptized. By the time Jesus came by to be baptized John's charismatic preaching made him the most popular person in Galilee."

"It would seem that John would be a natural target for you and yours. I presume that in accordance with your maxim 'that's what we do' you tried to stop or curtail his mission?"

"At first, we did very little. The man was a rare example of vibrant holiness. His physical appearance was mesmerizing. He stood a head taller than the average man. He had a very commanding voice that rang loud and clear no matter the size of the crowd. His massive musculature seemed to defy his diet of locusts and wild honey; but perhaps most of all John the Baptist could arouse the fear of God in a man or woman as well as or better than any of the prophets, and I heard them all. In fact after I heard him speak, I thought that except for an accident of birth he could very well have prevented the Babylonian captivity and its accompanying destruction of Solomon's temple!"

"Really!" I exclaimed. "How so?"

"Jeremiah was an excellent speaker, but his admonitions to a Jewish populace that had listened and sinfully acquiesced to me and mine went over more as a bothersome harangue; whereas after listening to John a person steeped in sin felt the Divine Hand of God was about to descend upon him in full and unlimited fury if he didn't repent and mend his ways.

"Finally, during John's time the Jews had been four hundred years without a God-appointed prophet in their midst. Many, after seeing and listening to him, believed John was the prophet for which they all yearned."

"And what was your position in this matter?"

"Frankly, even speaking as The Prince of Darkness, John was so effective that it was difficult to think otherwise.

"However, when he began publicly reprimanding Herod Antipas, the tetrarch of Galilee, and his queen, Herodias, for their unlawful marriage, I saw my opening to put a stop to a man that was otherwise invincible."

"Why did John say their marriage was unlawful?"

"It is complicated; however, as the details are little known, and as it the basis of my successful goal of doing away with John the Baptist I will explain it.

"Caesar Augustus died in 12 AD. In his will he named one of his trusted advisors, Tiberius, to succeed him. Tiberius, familiar with the difficulty of ruling the Jews, sent a messenger to Herod Antipas, tetrarch (appointed ruler) of Galilee, telling him to come to Rome for a consultation.

Years before Herod Antipas' brother, Philip, had been disinherited by his father, Herod the Great, (Bethlehem Butcher). Caesar Augustus was emperor when King Herod died. His loathing for King Herod was so great that when he found out that Herod had disinherited Philip, it gave the emperor reason to think highly of him and he invited him to come with his wife and live in Rome, which he did.

"At the command of Tiberias, Herod Antipas traveled to Rome without his wife and accepted the hospitality of his brother, Philip, and his wife, Herodias. Living with them was their very young daughter, Salome. Herodias, an exceptionally beautiful woman even in her forties, was not happy living in Rome as she was Jewish, and, therefore, was barely tolerated by the Roman wives.

"While in Rome Herod Antipas and Herodias carried on an adulterous affair. Herod Antipas showed appreciation for his brother's hospitality by departing Rome with Herodias and Salome.

"Herod's wife, the daughter of the emir of Arabia, was still living, and so both Herod and Herodias obtained civil divorces before getting married in a civil ceremony. Since their spouses were still living and they both professed Jewish allegiance their civil marriage was unlawful, and the people were not pleased with their living together. John, with his preaching, kept their adultery in the forefront and finally in order to stop the embarrassment to the court Herodias convinced Herod to have John arrested and imprisoned. However, Herod would not have him executed as Herodias wanted.

"I remembered after John baptized Jesus; he told the people that He (Jesus) must increase as I must decrease. I began working toward giving him what he wanted. With his arrest he was no longer preaching to the people, so I was halfway there.

"After he had him imprisoned Herod would frequently dismiss the guards at night and spend time talking to and listening to John. What troubled Herod was that John was everything he wanted to be but was not…"

"Everything! I exclaimed. Can you explain that further?"

"Yes. Herod Antipas was a sexual profligate. He was undisciplined, lazy and left the day-to-day duties of a ruler to his magistrate. He was what is known today as a playboy. He was given his position not because he earned it but because it was his right by inheritance. He was ill-trained to assume responsibility but enjoyed the authority. As a result of the lavish parties that he gave celebrating nothing at all He spent money above the take from taxes and was always on the verge of bankruptcy. Many such men admire and respect others whose discipline affords them strengths that are their polar opposite. To Herod such a man was John the Baptist. The only reason he had him put in prison was to keep peace with his wife.

"I tempted the captain of the guards with the idea that Herodias might reward him well if he reported Herod's clandestine visits to John; and he did just that.

"Herodias knew that as long as Herod participated in these sessions with John he would never execute him; so she looked for a way to overcome this obstacle.

"She had observed Herod staring when he wasn't leering at his stepdaughter, Salome, with lustful desire. Salome had matured over the years since returning to Galilee with her and Herod. Now sixteen, she was a nubile young woman who loved to dance.

"Shortly thereafter, at Herod's lavish birthday party, Herodias inserted a dance by Salome into the festivities. Salome's dance included lascivious gestures that caused not only him but many of his guests to become sexually aroused. She finished facing him in a perfect split with her head hanging down. She remained in this position for a few seconds before rising to kiss him sensually on the mouth. When she pulled away Herod, his inhibitions diminished by alcohol and overcome with sexual desire thanked her by offering anything she wanted up to and including half his kingdom.

"Salome, still in the naïveté of youth, backed away speechless. Her mother beckoned from behind a curtain ten feet or so to the rear of the throne. When Salome joined her Herodias whispered, 'Tell Herod you want the head of John the Baptist on a platter.' Not sure that she heard correctly Salome asked her mother to repeat what she said. 'You heard me correctly. Do what your mother tells you. The head of John the Baptist on a platter! Now go. Tell him!'

"In the meantime, Herod taking in the unbelieving stare of his guests could not believe what he had promised Salome. Convinced that she wouldn't take him seriously he sat up trying to appear as regal as possible as Salome approached. She bowed before him then raised her head and said loud enough for all to hear, "In accordance with your most generous promise, your majesty, I ask for the head of John the Baptist on a platter."

"Now it was Herod's turn to ask Salome to repeat her request. 'With all due respect,' she repeated, 'in accordance with your pledge I ask not for half your kingdom, but only that the head of the Baptist be brought to me on a platter.'

"Herod now knew two things for sure. First, the request was from Herodias, speaking to him through her daughter; and secondly, he had no choice but to comply as all the guests had heard his offer. He told the officer of the watch to decapitate the Baptist and bring him his head drained of blood on a platter.

"When the officer appeared with the head – John's dead eyes half open and his blood-smeared severed neck bone protruding on a platter, Herod called for Salome to appear before him. Instead, Herodias came forth."

"I called for Salome, woman," Herod said, in a tone that implied his recent actions had served to return him to a degree of sobriety.

"Please, Herod," she begged. "Don't do this to her."

"I didn't, Herodias. You did. Now call her out here," he ordered. "You used Salome to accomplish this reprehensible deed and I aim to see that she finishes it."

"When Salome came forth Herod ordered the officer to hand her the platter. As soon as she held it, she screamed while becoming violently ill and vomited as she released her hold on the platter. The platter hit the floor and the head, splashed with vomit rolled across the marble floor as Salome, still screaming, ran off to her quarters.

"Pick it up," Herod ordered Herodias."

"What shall I do with it?" she pleaded.

"Herod, his eyes beginning to tear replied with a voice cracking with sorrow and regret, "If you don't know that, Herodias, you shouldn't have asked Salome to get it for you." He then turned and left leaving his guests in a state of shock as they watched Herodias reach down and while turning her head and closing her eyes place the decapitated head on the platter.

"While you have been talking," I said, "Two things crossed my mind."

"And what may they be?" Satan asked.

"First of all, if God hadn't permitted John's execution you would not have succeeded in your murderous plot. Secondly, the reason you were able to succeed is that God used you to accomplish his will."

Satan, surprised, asked, "In what way?"

"In accordance with John's statement about decreasing as Jesus increased, John's following would have decreased, as listening and learning from Jesus' parables, which were accompanied by his healing miracles, they left him to follow Jesus. Little by little John's influence would have diminished and he would have been remembered as the precursor of Jesus, the Messiah, and the man who passed away having served his purpose, languishing in the obscurity of old age. Except, thanks to you, Satan, he didn't.

"Even after two thousand years John the Baptist is revered as a very holy, devoted and admired martyr; one of the most famous and stalwart of canonized saints. Unlike most others he has two calendar feast days – June 24th for his nativity and August 29th to commemorate his martyrdom. Many times we see God turning your evil deeds to His and our advantage."

Pointing to the picture on the wall I added, "St. Augustine said of Herod Antipas, 'His was an oath rashly taken and criminally kept.' I can't imagine at their deaths the terror they must have felt as Herod Antipas and Herodias standing before the judgment seat of God are charged with murdering John the Baptist!

"When Satan didn't respond I said, two years later, finding out that Jesus was a Galilean, Pontius Pilate sent him to Herod in an attempt to get out from under the pressure of the Sanhedrin. Herod, having heard of Jesus' miracles prompted Jesus to perform one for him. Jesus was perfectly silent the whole time he stood before Herod. Finally, Herod had him covered in a white sheet, called Jesus a fool and sent him back to Pilate.

"Unlike his father who was an exceptional architect and a murderer, Herod Antipas was known only for his adulterous marriage and the murder of John the Baptist. Not much of a legacy."

"Not quite," Satan responded.

"What do you mean?"

"He is also known to historians, unlike his father, for being an incompetent military general. The Arabian Emir had lost a great deal of face when Herod divorced his daughter and sent her back to him. It took him several years, but he finally raised an army large enough to attack Herod. In the melee Herod's army was roundly defeated and Rome had to rescue him. Caligula was Emperor at the time and in disgust he banished Herod to Gaul (France). From that time on Herod Antipas and Herodias vanish from the pages of history."

"After I elected not to respond, Satan said, 'Soon after John's circumcision Mary returned home again by caravan. She was now three months pregnant and just beginning to show. She believed that God had somehow explained her condition to Joseph – but God hadn't and the fact that she was gone for three months did not help Joseph believe her implausible explanation."

CHAPTER THIRTY-FOUR

"Name him Jesus, for he will save his people from their sins."

"The truth is that Joseph was torn between Mary's unlikely reason for her pregnancy and the fact that this virtuous woman whom he dearly loved could have willingly had intercourse far away from home with someone she had just met.

"I, of course, told my demon to continue prompting Joseph to end their relationship. As I mentioned earlier, I knew from his heartfelt love he would not abandon her to the stones of the Pharisees but rather tell her parents he could no longer marry her and to send her back to Ain Karim where, without threat or harm, she could bring her pregnancy to term. After an extremely vigorous period of temptation Joseph was ready to declare his decision.

That evening he went to see Mary's parents and advised them of his decision not to marry their daughter. He told them that he would put her away quietly, advising no one the reason for his decision. Both Joseph and the demon expected them to be angry. Ann, however, after whispering a short prayer just hung her head as Joachim told Joseph that as he professed himself to be a man of honor, he would have to tell Mary.

"My demon, beset with pride, invited me to watch as he wanted me to enjoy seeing Mary break down. However, when she didn't, he said almost apologetically, 'Any other woman in the village would have been in tears, agonizing over her plight – even begging Joseph or any other man to marry her to save her life by making her an honest woman. If nothing else,' he said, while raising his voice in exasperation, 'to save face and to keep from shaming her parents!'"

"But, that's not what happened," I said. "Once again you and yours have been made the fools. You continually go on about the stupidity of the human race but it seems to me that you have little justification to do so when you above all should know that when you challenge the Will of God or worse attempt to use the truly virtuous to do so, it never ends well. In fact, Satan, so much so that in most instances the end for you is worse than if you had never tried to intervene.

"Whether infuriated or just plain embarrassed, Satan, refusing to comment, replied,' Do you want to hear how Mary answered Joseph or not?'

"Of course," I said. "Please continue."

"After listening to Joseph attentively, Mary simply looked at him with care and affection. A moment later she said, 'I love you, Joseph, and God knows that you love me as well. The Lord brought us together and it is His will that we be man and wife. He has chosen you to help me raise this miraculous child. He will be a great joy to you, for this is a great privilege – a sign that God loves you very much.

"So, the doubt you have in your heart is not from God, but it will remain there until you give your heart and mind to him; until you can let go of the world and the ways of men, Joseph; until you can subjugate your will to His. I will pray this night, as I have many others, that He might soften your heart and open your mind to His holy will."

"Then, she stood, walked to her door and opened it. As Joseph walked away Mary called, 'Joseph?' "He turned around." She said, 'Shalom, Joseph. May God be with you and before the break of dawn, show you His ways.'

"As Joseph walked back to the all but completed house he had been building for Mary and himself, his feelings went from shame to disappointment to rage. Mary's response was not what he expected. She had spoken as if he hadn't told her that they were through with each other, but rather that their marriage was the will of Jehovah and there was nothing he could do to prevent it! As he entered the house her presumption raised his anger to a level he had never before experienced. 'She spoke as if I had nothing to say about it!' he exclaimed aloud as he viciously unstopped a wineskin and threw the stopper across the room. He plopped down in a chair and proceeded to consume its contents all the while screaming and hollering, 'I'll show her! She can't do this to me!' Finally in a drunken stupor Joseph relaxed his grip, as the empty wineskin, slipping from his fingers, fell silently to the floor. Joseph, the Nazarene carpenter, had passed out."

"So tell me," I said, "Did you actually witness this or was it something a demon told you?"

"If you'll remember the demon invited me to witness Mary's breakdown at hearing Joseph tell her he would not marry her. Upon hearing her unexpected response and noting my disgust the demon slinked away, but I remained on the chance that I could further stiffen Joseph's resolve. There was little I had to do, however, since as you can see his rage and determination to show her what he intended to do remained at a fever pitch.

"Despite not lying down, but rather sitting in a chair, Joseph remained totally immobile for four hours. Then he began to stir. I could tell from his outbursts and violent head turning that he was having a dream – the kind of dream humans' experience that is greatly disturbing."

"In short a nightmare," I said, "or at least a dream that imparts great fear in a person's imagination. Can you tell me about the dream?"

"Only after it was over," Satan replied, "when it was followed by a vision. If you remember I cannot read a person's mind. However, I can tell you what I heard him tell Mary.

"Finally, he stopped moaning and thrashing and became very stiff and immobile as if he were paralyzed and could not move. This, as he told Mary, happened when he felt a shudder as a deep, resonant voice shattered the otherwise deathlike silence.

"Joseph of Nazareth put away thy fear. I am Raphael, one of the seven spirits who enter and serve before the glory of the Lord. Look upon me."

"In his dream Joseph saw standing before him the most magnificent creature he had ever seen. Its body was clothed in a brilliant white robe from his neck to his ankles, and his feet were bare on the dwelling's floor. His hands, his feet and his face were like burnished bronze. His hair was blonde, laid straight back without part and held in place by a gold headband. A sash of spun gold, the width of his hand, cinctured his waist. He was tall, Joseph noted, taller than he, but his most astounding feature were two huge wings which sparkled as if soft, snow-white feathering had been sprinkled with the finest of blue sapphire dust.

"Looking down at him were two large, penetrating brown eyes from a face he did not recognize but was the fully fleshed countenance of an extremely handsome man.

"From his head shone a bright light and from the rest of his body came a lightly pulsating, golden glow. His left hand was outstretched toward him, while in his right was the sharp contrast of a plain, wooden staff.

He spoke:

"Thou art troubled and fearful, but it should not be, God has looked into thy heart, Joseph, as he did thy father, David, and chosen thee to do a mighty thing. Have no fear in taking Mary as thy wife. It is of the Holy Spirit that she has conceived this child. She is to have a Son who will be a great joy unto thee.

"God has deigned to give thee a sign – a confirmation that what I tell thee is truly the Will of God. Behold, then, I present to thee this staff as a gift from the Lord God that thou may knowest that no matter where thou art I am at all times over thee and thy holy family.

"Go now, Joseph and take Mary in holy wedlock according to the law of Moses; for even now she prepares for her wedding."

"Joseph awoke, then, and saw Raphael standing before him in a vision. After the angel motioned for him to stand Raphael presented him with the staff. The angel then raised his eyes and hands to God and said:

"Lord, behold Thy servant, Raphael, who has done as Thou hast commanded."

And he was gone.

"Joseph stood in the silence of the night and bowed his head. The swirling torrents of doubt, rage, frustration, and fear had seemed to empty into a pool of tranquil waters as he felt engulfed in a feeling of inner peace. 'My God! My God! Thank You – Thank you,' he said, as he fell to his knees.

"With both hands on the staff, he followed its length from its top to its base on the wooden floor. From its appearance, he thought, and from the way it felt, it was a plain, common walking staff. It was not unlike the man to whom it was given – a plain, ordinary man – a simple carpenter from Nazareth. But, in reality, in accordance with the will of God, neither were only what they appeared to be in accordance with the ways of men. He bowed his head once more and prayed."

"Almighty Jehovah, I kneel before you, feeling at peace in the very place where only a short time ago, being steeped in the ways of men, rage and disappointment were my only companions. But Your ways are not the ways of men. Had I been a man of faith, I would have listened as You revealed Your Will to me through Mary, whom in Your love, mercy and forbearance You have graciously allowed me to keep as my wife, despite my doubt and expressions of anger because of her perfect faith in You.

"Behold then, Your humble servant, Joseph, who asks only this, Lord: the strength and courage to bear the burdens as they come: and the wisdom to know and do Your will as You proclaim it. Amen."

"So, the only part of this revelation you saw firsthand was at the end when Raphael presents Joseph with the staff?

"Yes."

"Did Raphael know you were watching?"

"If I could see Raphael then he could see me."

"However, he didn't acknowledge you or you to him?

"Neither of us expected that we would acknowledge one another.

"As a result of our discourse, Bruce, I have told you truthfully of several occurrences of God speaking to both men and women through an angelic visitation. In each instance notice that the wording is strictly limited to the purpose decreed by the Almighty which is never to have a social conversation. Notice how Raphael speaks and even ends the task given to him. There is not one word of excess verbiage. In fact, this is a major means of ascertaining a valid supernatural vision from the hallucinations of wannabe visionaries."

"I noticed that angels never seem to present the same appearance. There is a vast difference, for instance, between Gabriel's appearance to Mary, Zachariah and the prophet, Daniel, and Raphael's appearance to Joseph. Can you comment on this?"

"First, you must remember that as spirits angels as well as I and demons have no visual appearance. However, as mankind's sight is his major means of ascertaining reality it is necessary to conjure up an appearance if God tasks an angel to communicate with one of you. Among human beings there might be some doubt when you hear a disembodied voice; but a voice coming from a visual being leaves no room for doubt.

"If you remember, Bruce, we agreed that one of the purposes of the Incarnation was to allow for increased credence in God's existence over and above the Old Testament concept of realizing Jehovah at best as a disembodied voice.

"So, getting back to your question, Bruce, the appearance of an angel is dictated by God depending on the purpose of the visit and the disposition of the recipient. The prophet Daniel, Mary of Nazareth and Zachariah were disposed to the will of God in their lives. The carpenter, Joseph, was not. He needed to be shocked – even frightened and terrorized into overcoming his resistance before he would be willing to accept the will of God.

"Seeing an angel speaking to you in the dark of night in what amounts to a full dress parade uniform while you're suffering from a hangover is enough to bring any one of you around."

"Upon visualizing that, I agreed. No doubt," I replied.

CHAPTER THIRTY-FIVE

"Mary of Nazareth is capable of getting her needed rest without his mitzvah."

"Three weeks before their wedding, Bruce, two Roman soldiers, Atticus and his much younger companion, Marcus, were sloshing their way northward on a stormy night over muddy roads on their way to Nazareth. They had planned to arrive several hours after the dinner hour but the torrential rains and accompanying deep, muddy roads slowed their horses to a protracted, time-consuming stroll. It was now just before midnight when a jagged bolt of lightning lit up the view before them followed by a sharp crack of thunder reverberating across the rain filled sky.

"'What are those?'" Marcus shouted, pulling his horse up short as lightning again flashed across the sky.

"The Gods have indeed smiled on us, Marcus. Those little white boxes you saw on the hillside are the houses of Nazarenes! Knock heavily on the door of the first house. A man will come to the door with a candle or an oil lamp. Light your torch from his fire and immediately order him and his family, in the name of Caesar Augustus, to the marketplace. Answer no questions, Marcus. If he hesitates, yank him out into the street and go into the house and raise the rest of them. When they hear your command while looking at the torchlight reflecting from your helmet, you'll get no more trouble. Then, do it nine more times."

"His entire family, Atticus? In this downpour? Women, children, in the middle of a night such as this?"

"And don't forget the babes in arms, Marcus. Everyone."

"Why? It would seem if we just had the men...."

"You are new to Israel, Marcus. In time you will learn that these people, unlike others we have conquered, bear no respect for Rome or the Emperor. The only power in their lives is their God, whom it is impossible to destroy because he has no image. There are no murals, no idols nor any statues to pull down, crush and burn. His existence is manifest only in their minds.

"And they will want to ask questions. Given the chance, they will ask questions, incessantly. Do as I say, Marcus, or you'll be standing in doorways answering questions when the sun rises."

"So we put fear in them because they perceive a threat to their families?"

Turning toward the younger man and grinning, Atticus answered, "Marcus, you're going to do just fine here in Israel!"

"Proceeding to his tenth house Marcus told himself that it wasn't as difficult as he had expected. Out of the nine doors on which he had knocked, he had to enter only two after pulling the father into the street. He had knocked hard enough so that both parents were already awake. When they saw the torch burning over their pallet in the darkness, and heard his command, they immediately awakened their children and proceeded to the marketplace in the downpour. The only questions asked were of children to their mothers who hushed and prodded them on their way.

"He raised his fist to hammer on the last door when he suddenly felt as though he were being stalked – an eerie feeling that he was not standing there alone. Slowly, he turned around, but saw and heard no one. Turning back again, he raised his fist when he was startled by a bolt of lightning as it struck and inflamed the top of a tall, dead cypress tree on the hillside to this right. Looking up he saw a searing finger of flame blaze its way down the huge trunk splitting it in two.

One-half of the bare trunk cracked at the base and began falling through the air. As it collided with the ground, he watched it bounce several times while twisting and turning crazily, crushing the new growth in its path as it toppled down the hillside. The remaining half groaned and wavered in the wind, hissing steam as the falling rain splattered its charred, glowing surface. Then its base, too, cracked and amid the noise of snapping twigs and broken branches came crashing down in his direction.

Followed by the loudest clap of thunder he had ever heard, it caused him to flinch before the sound rumbled and rolled, seemingly forever, across the length of the heavens directly above him.

Visibly shaken, Marcus cautiously raised his fist again to bang on the door, but stopped short as the feeling of the unseen presence had now grown strong enough to bode threatening. Quickly drawing his broadsword, he raised the torch over his head and looked around a second time. Again, he saw and heard no one. He placed the torch in the holder attached to the doorframe, and raising his fist once more, hesitated, then knocked gently.

As the door opened, he saw a strikingly beautiful woman with clear, dark brown eyes and long, wavy black hair standing before him. In her hand she held a lighted candle, and beneath the long, coarse, white robe Marcus could see that she was heavy with child. She looked him straight in the eye and then moved her gaze to his sword which he could feel shaking uncontrollably in his hand. Smiling, she again met his stare and asked softly, "How may I help you?"

He opened his mouth to speak – to order her out of the house – but felt the ghostly presence was now somehow between them and it frightened him. The only sound that came forth was a low, guttural, meaningless noise similar to utterances he had heard from those who were deaf and dumb.

"Perhaps we should begin by having you put up your weapon. There is no one here who wishes to harm you."

Now totally confused, he glanced down at his sword, watching the reflection from his torch dancing along the length of the blade as it continued to shake nervously in his hand. Returning his eyes to the doorway, the woman raised her eyebrows and cocked her head as if she were questioning whether he had the courage to face her without a weapon in his hand.

Raising his sword, he stabbed its point at the opening in the scabbard several times before the quivering blade found its mark.

"Now surely Rome has not stretched forth its mighty arm to knock on the door of a humble Jewess and her parents on such a night as this without a message of great importance."

"I am here...I have been ordered to...to..."

"Yes? To do what?" she asked simply.

"I am here to tell you that the Emperor Caesar Augustus commands you to go to bed and get your needed rest!" he blurted out, not believing what his ears told him he had just said.

"What is your name?" she asked, with a condescending smile.

"Mar...Marcus Flavius," he stammered.

"Well, Marcus Flavius, when next you speak to your emperor – you tell him that Mary of Nazareth appreciates his kind concern; but that she is quite capable of getting her needed rest without his mitzvah." Then smiling at him for the last time, she nodded and quietly closed the door.

Marcus stood staring at the door before glancing at the smoldering tree trunk lying asunder on the hillside. Noting that the rain had stopped, he turned and began walking toward the marketplace. As he made his way along the road that led to the bottom of the hill, he continued to shake his head in disbelief at what had just happened to him.

Approaching the huddled mass of frightened families, Marcus overheard mothers trying in vain to soothe the fears of their crying children. When he arrived in the marketplace, he could clearly hear the sound of the soothing voices and tearful faces of mothers rocking from side to side in an attempt to get the bawling infant in their arms to go back to sleep.

"Can we get on with this?" he whispered to Atticus. "I want to get away from this place as soon as possible."

Atticus glanced at the younger man and then nodded as the two soldiers stood in front of the assembled group who were staring at them in fear and wonder. Marcus took the torch from Atticus and held it aloft with his own as Atticus unfurled the vellum scroll. "What I proclaim before you is a decree from Caesar Augustus, differing only in that it has been translated into Aramaic that you may have no doubt as to its meaning. Listen, now, and understand."

"I, Caesar Augustus, Emperor of Rome, command that all who call themselves freemen, and who live within and enjoy the benevolence of the World of Rome, should be enrolled that they may be counted and their names be inscribed on the rolls for the purpose of taxation. In order that this census be completed promptly, each Imperial Governor will prescribe the manner by which it is to be accomplished within the area of his domain."

As he rolled the scroll Atticus added, "Israel is under the direct rule of Cyrenius, Governor of Syria, who has proclaimed in his wisdom that to ensure accuracy, each must be enrolled in the city of his ancestral parentage no more than thirty days following this formal proclamation of the Emperor's decree.

"Each Jew, therefore, must be enrolled in the city of the House and Family to which he belongs. You who are privileged to hear the words of the Emperor will be held responsible for proclaiming this decree to all other Nazarenes. See to it at first light and hasten to obey."

Giving them neither smile nor thanks, the two soldiers doused their torches in a puddle, mounted their steeds and departed the city. Turning to the younger soldier, Atticus remarked, "You did well, Marcus. You see how easy it is to handle these Jews when you show a little backbone?"

"Yes," Marcus replied sheepishly; then whispered to himself, "when you show a little backbone," while wagging his head, thankful that his superior had not taken a count of the families he had sent to the marketplace.

"No doubt Marcus was experiencing the protection Raphael had promised to Joseph and his family," I said.

"No doubt about it. I was there and witnessed the whole thing. Raphael is an archangel, I know well."

"Why is that or would you rather not say?"

"When someone who finds himself having to travel and asks for divine protection along the way God sends Raphael in answer to his or her prayers. In fact, if I were one of you I would have a St. Raphael medal in my car or boat and especially in my airplane.

Really!"

"Certainly. Are you familiar with the Book of Tobit?"

"Yes, I am. Raphael appears as a human being – a hired companion and guide for a young man who his father is planning to send to collect money owed him from a relative who lives at quite a distance. Raphael protects the young man, Tobiah, from not only several dangers along the way, but also a murdering demon while also serving as a marriage broker."

"I'm surprised that you are familiar with Tobit. That is one of the seven books I convinced the reformation to delete from scripture. It is missing from many Bibles."

"But not from those translated from St. Jerome's vulgate edition. It was last confirmed as valid by the Counter-Reformation at the Council of Trent in 1546."

"So it was.

CHAPTER THIRTY-SIX

The Infant Narrative – Part I

"As a result of this mandate by the emperor, Joseph would have to make the trip to Bethlehem," Satan said, "However, it was not necessary for a wife to accompany her husband. Mary, however, despite the pleading of her parents, relatives and friends insisted that Joseph be present for her baby's birth, and thus they made the journey together in the caravan. Everyone is familiar with what happened in Bethlehem: the lack of any rooms available at the inns due to the number of people who had come to the city for the census; Mary giving birth in a cave used to store hay and fodder for animals, the visit of the shepherds and finally those three men who came from the East. Suffice it to say that the eighty-mile trip on a donkey when in her ninth month of pregnancy is not something that most women could endure. It demonstrated once again the strength and resilience with which God had created Mary, His mother.

"Forty days after His birth, in accordance with the Mosaic Law," Satan continued, "Joseph and Mary went to the temple for her male birth purification and for Jesus' entry to Judaism. While there I was surprised to see a very old man, who seemed to be in a hurry, approach Joseph and Mary as they entered the interior of the temple. Joseph tipped Raphael's staff in front of Mary and glanced above him as if looking for something."

"We both know who that was."

"Yes, but evidently when there was no sign that this old man was a menace, Joseph nodded to Mary as he pulled the staff back. Then when the old man stood before Mary and asked if he could hold her baby, she looked at Joseph who nodded his approval.

"The old man then took Jesus from Mary, and supporting his neck and buttocks raised her son over his head and chanted loud enough for all to hear, 'Now, Master, according to Your word you may let your servant go in peace for my eyes have seen your salvation (this child as Savior) which you prepared in sight of all the peoples; a light for revelation to the Gentiles, and glory for your people, Israel.' (Luke 2:29-32)

"At the time neither Joseph nor Mary knew who this man was: only that he publicly announced in a place revered by all Jews as the dwelling place of God on earth that their Son, Jesus, was not the ordinary human being He appeared to be. They had become used to private revelations regarding Jesus including Mary's annunciation, Elizabeth's declaration, Joseph's dream, the shepherds in the birthing cave in Bethlehem and finally they will receive the same from the Gentiles from the East, of whom we will speak about later. But this was different. The old man attracted the attention of those in the crowded area not only for what he said, but for who he was."

"This man, Simeon," I said, "being an exceptionally holy man who spent his days praying in the temple, was well known. God had promised him that he would not die before seeing the Messiah. It had to be a shock to both Mary and Joseph when this old man approached them, but it could only be because he had been inspired by the Holy Spirit to do so. Simeon's prayer and God's promise were fulfilled and as his chant indicated he was now ready to die."

Again, without commenting, Satan continued. "As he was returning her infant he said in a voice that only Mary and Joseph could hear, 'Behold, this child is destined for the rise and fall of many in Israel; and to be a sign that will be contradicted;' and then turning specifically to Mary, added, 'You yourself a sword shall pierce so that the thoughts of many hearts may be revealed.' (Luke 2:32-35)

"With that last remark Joseph and Mary became fearful. Was someone with a weapon already in the temple looking for them? What did the old man mean by that remark? I watched as Joseph looked around but saw no one who appeared menacing, and as he relied on Raphael's promise of protection, he told Mary that if what Simeon said was true it was nothing with which they had to be concerned at present. Nevertheless, it had the effect of making them tense and uneasy.

"They were even more so when an old woman approached, Anna by name, and a widow of long standing who lived in the Temple and was revered as a very holy woman – possibly even a prophetess. She was also well known. She pointed to Mary's infant and turning to the crowd of people behind her said in a voice loud enough for all to hear, 'You who are present this day in God's temple have been blessed to behold this wonderful infant Who will launch a new era for the God fearing. In time to come He will establish a new manner of redemption not only for God's Chosen People but for the gentiles as well.' (Luke 2:36-38)

"When the people present heard both Simeon and Anna proclaim that Mary's infant was not an ordinary child, they came over to see for themselves; however, there was nothing extraordinary to see. Whether they expected to see an infant bathed in radiance or made exceptional by sitting up and speaking as he imparted a blessing, they were disappointed; for what they saw was a baby sleeping in his mother's arms. One by one, having no idea what excited Simeon and Anna, they shrugged their shoulders as they drifted back to complete their reason for being there.

"The more learned of them, however, wondered why both Simeon and Anna mentioned the gentiles in the same breath as the Jews. At that time all the gentiles were in one way or another of pagan belief – the worst of them being the Romans under whose unrelenting cruelty and devastating taxes they barely survived."

"What Simeon and Anna were announcing," I responded, "is that all men and women, Jew and gentile alike, are created by God and as such have a right to salvation if they live their lives in accordance with the precepts affirmed in the Ten Commandments."

"Correct," Satan replied, "but my position remains, Bruce, that the bulk of you, Jew and gentile alike, trade your eternal salvation for less than one hundred years of scraping the porridge bowl; that so many more stifle their consciences so they can justify taking advantage of the less fortunate – a way of life that most assuredly leads to eternal damnation; still others turn their backs on the God who made them, and at times mentally spit in His face in order to ensure they don't hear His admonishments and warnings as they tread, egotistically and self-absorbed in their sinful ways proceeding down the wide road to their inevitable, eternal destruction.

"Do not contradict me on this, Bruce. Although I am prohibited from naming individuals in Hell, I am not forbidden from quoting Jesus whom we said taught that few find the narrow road that leads to salvation. (Matthew 7:13-14) Furthermore, I have seen and even now at this moment see the vast number of you, who by the evil manner of their lives have chosen to be cast into my abyss every second of the earthly day."

"I thought about not responding but something or Someone strongly urged me not to let his remarks go unanswered. "Standing up I said, "Satan, the narrow road is difficult for many to tread because you make it so. By means of temptations you and yours are constantly placing Detour Signs and Exits that entice people to follow your beckoning to abandon the narrow and at times difficult road of virtue for the apparent delight, even at times ill-gotten fortune when choosing the wide road. I say apparent because sooner or later the emptiness of your promises is brought into the light. Adultery breeds broken marriages and forlorn children; theft, bribery, lies, perjury, dishonesty, murder and mayhem many times end in long incarcerations; and if prior to their last breath such people die without telling God they are sorry with a sincere and firm purpose of amendment, they have bartered the love and favor of God for the hate and ridicule of you and yours for an eternity of horrific agony, remorse and despair in Hell."

"Agreed," Satan replied. "However, as I have told you before it is what we do! But you have to admit that given intelligence and free will by the Almighty we cannot force human beings to do our bidding. The reason there is salvation and damnation is to reward or punish choice. A man or woman does not end up in Hell without reason. Because they live their lives going from one sinful venture to the next and in the end refuse to accept God's offer of forgiveness, they have made the choice to suffer for eternity with me and mine."

"Before your condemnation, Satan, you were asked by God to help him with His human creation; but as you stated earlier, you refused. What a different world this would be if you had not declined His request. There would be no Hell as all would be saved."

"Really, Bruce? Not likely, because knowing human nature as I do, your prediction is possibly true – but probably not."

Not waiting nor wanting me to reply, Satan said, "Now I have one last point to make before we continue. The Church holds that The Presentation in the Temple is the Fourth Joyful Mystery. I think you can see that for Mary it was sorrowful – even frightening, but hardly a source of joy. Both Simeon and Anna had linked her Son with the gentiles. The only relationship the Jews of that time had with gentiles involved the Egyptians, the Philistines, the Canaanites, the Assyrians, the Babylonians and now the Romans – all of which involved death, slavery, deportation, annihilation and war; even captivity in a pagan land for decades after the destruction of their Temple. At the time of these two prophecies, they were living under the ruthless tyranny of Rome. Moreover, Simeon had said that Mary would be subjected to the piercing of a sword! I think you will agree with me that The Presentation in the Temple for Mary and Joseph was anything but joyful."

"I can't argue with what you have said, Satan, except to say that the Presentation was joyful in that in Judaism the first-born son was dedicated to God; however, the parents were privileged to buy him back with an animal sacrifice. This was usually a lamb, but when such would present a great hardship, the poor could offer two turtle doves.

"As far as the sword is concerned it is accepted that it was symbolic for the distress and grief she felt as Mary watched her Son, who had done no wrong, being tortured and then undergoing the excruciating pain and agony of Roman crucifixion. However, in the final analysis I have to agree with you that the fright and sorrow of what happened at the time likely overrode any joy that the event produced. I say this because in addition to being the Fourth Joyful Mystery of the Rosary, the Presentation in the Temple is also asserted by the Church to be the first of Mary's Seven Sorrows."

"And so it is," Satan replied. "Now when they had completed the rituals Joseph and Mary went back to the little house they rented after the population of Bethlehem returned to normal following the census. He had found work which allowed him to provide for his family as well as to put a little aside. If they were ever going to return to Nazareth, they had to purchase a younger donkey as the one Mary had twice ridden to Jerusalem and beyond was now showing gray along with signs of fatigue and wobbly legs as they were returning from the Temple to Bethlehem which was only an eight-mile distance. Joseph knew this animal would never survive another eighty-mile trek to Nazareth.

CHAPTER THIRTY-SEVEN

The Infant Narrative – Part II

"Two days later three gentiles riding huge, bull Dromedaries and trailing five heavily loaded double humped Bactrian pack grades had arrived in Jerusalem, their fourth trading city. Their leader was also looking forward to – even expecting, to see his infant Messianic Saoshyant in the flesh.

"At the time, Bruce, there were two great empires – the Roman and the Parthian. The Parthian empire consisted of the area east of Damascus, the outlying eastern border of the Roman empire. Up until that time the Romans had tried on two different occasions to conquer the Parthians. The first attempt was under General Crassus and the second under Marc Antony. Both attempts ended in disaster as the Romans were overwhelmingly defeated having been killed at a distance by mounted archers – the Parthians primary method of warfare.

"Two of the three gentiles who arrived in Jerusalem that day were Parthians. Their religion was Zoroastrianism, the basis of which as stated in the Avesta (equivalent to their Bible), is that there is a God of virtue, the Saoshyant, whom they called Ahura Mazda, and a God of evil, whose name was Ahriman. They, of course, are at odds, each able to influence the thoughts and actions of mankind. In Zoroastrianism there was a long-held belief that Ahura Mazda at some time would become a man to better teach human beings the way of living a virtuous life.

"We will use the names for these men that are generally accepted as Melchior, Gaspar and Balthazar. Melchior was a Prince and therefore, a member of the Parthian ruling family. He was also an astronomer, a shrewd, astute trader by which he had become very wealthy and upon turning sixty retired as a Parthian general who was especially adept as a master swordsman.

"Gaspar, Melchior's ward, and recognized in Parthia as its finest archer, had been raised by Melchior. From an early age Melchior had provided him with an exceptional education by Zoroastrian priests when his widowed father, one of Melchior's commanders, was killed in battle with the Tocharians – lawless barbarians who resided in an area of Parthia known as the Khurasan.

"The third man, Balthazar, was a Black Man originally from Abyssinia (now Ethiopia in North Africa) whom Melchior had arranged to be released from a Parthian prison during his and Gaspar's stay in Seleucia (a major Parthian city at the junction of the Tigris and Euphrates rivers). Both Gaspar and Balthazar were twenty-one years old.

"Gaspar, along with a superb talent for archery in addition to his own Parthian tongue was fluent in Latin, Greek and Aramaic; and as Melchior insisted, was given a thorough grounding in the physical sciences along with mathematics, and astronomy.

"Balthazar was deadly accurate with a spear and as street smart as they come. Together, as mankind describes such a trio, they were 'a formidable force to be reckoned with.' which proved to be unfortunate for me when trading with my unscrupulous merchants or confronted by my murderous brigands during their desert crossing."

"Shocked by how casually Satan took ownership of unscrupulous traders and murderous brigands I was reminded again with whom I was conversing – that despite his pouring forth volumes of information that heretofore had been unknown Satan was doing it for his own purpose and that he must consider the enlightening of mankind to be what is presently referred to as collateral damage."

"One night while in Elymais," Satan continued, "a major city in Parthia, during his nightly observations Melchior noticed again that over a three-month period Saturn and Jupiter were closing the distance between them. If they continued to do so this, that is conjoin, according to his religious beliefs along with those of a year he had lived and studied as a young man with members of the Jewish temple in Jerusalem, he suspected that the Zoroastrian Saoshyant and the Jewish Messiah were one and the same. When a particularly bright star appeared, which he had never before observed, Melchior took it as a confirming sign. He put together a trading mission that would involve traveling by camel across more than a thousand miles of Desert with trading stops in Seleucia, Palmyra, Damascus, Jerusalem and finally in Alexandria, Egypt – an additional 350 or so miles west of Jerusalem. He and Gaspar set out a few days later on their journey."

"Your description of these men is nowhere near the depiction we are used to seeing at Christmas. Even paintings of the masters show them as old men in regal dress who are somewhat reticent while being questioned in King Herod's court. Modern day portrayals in movies and on television carry this image forward."

"It is common for human beings to equate wisdom with age," Satan replied. "However, it is not just age but also experience that engenders human wisdom; for example, Melchior had Balthazar released from prison because he knew the ways of desert thieves and how best to avoid them – a distinct advantage since Melchior knew that these marauders never left witnesses."

"So Melchior's reason for taking Balthazar along was self-serving?"

"Yes, in the beginning, but as Balthazar's knowledge and skill contributed to the safe success of their journey a close bond developed among the three men. So close that Melchior, realizing that Balthazar would eventually want to continue his life in Abyssinia, presented him with a considerable number of gold coins to re-establish himself."

"It sounds as if you are saying that the contributions of all three were necessary for the success of their crossing of the Arabian Desert, that is, from Seleucia west. I assume Melchior and Gaspar traveled in a caravan during the first part of their journey from their home to Seleucia."

"They did. When they arrived in Seleucia Melchior was told that there would not be a caravan departing for Jerusalem for thirty days. Observing the star moving relentlessly westward he didn't feel that he could wait that long, so he decided to make a solitary desert crossing – a dangerous decision due to the murdering thieves I mentioned, who, prompted by me, lie in wait for such travelers.

"While supporting himself as a thief in Seleucia Balthazar had been approached several times to join different bands of desert marauders who explained their tactics to him. Forced to live in a survival mode Balthazar had no compunction about stealing but he couldn't abide murdering people in cold blood; and try as I might I could never tempt him otherwise.

"As a matter of fact, Bruce, it was his failed attempt to steal from Melchior that got him arrested. After talking to him, Melchior refused to sign a complaint when he felt Balthazar had the knowledge he needed to make a safe, solitary crossing. As it so happened, however, they did meet up with a few brigands whom they overcame with cunning and when that failed with their weapons that killed them from a distance.

"This must have angered you. I mean seeing your evil ones handily beaten by an old man and two others that had just entered their maturity."

"Not so. As I mentioned earlier, I am incapable of love, but respect I can express in abundance for those of you, who by cooperating with the grace of God, can overcome my attempts to convince you to depart from the narrow road."

"I would complement you by saying, 'Well stated,' but you said I should not compliment you."

"Bruce, your attempt to come at me through the back door is noted."

"I didn't reply."

"It might appear that we have changed our subject from Mary to what are referred to as The Three Wise Men, Bruce; but my deviating is necessary that you might understand and appreciate what happened when they came knocking on Mary's door and how she responded. For now, keep in mind that both Simeon and Anna had linked her son favorably with the gentiles; and how incomprehensible this was to Joseph and Mary as well as to those who were in the temple and heard both Simeon and Anna proclaim this with prophetic certainty."

"Now I think I understand," I said. "I had always wondered why gentiles would travel over a thousand miles on camels across desert sands to pay homage to, as it is stated in Matthew's gospel, The Newborn King of the Jews. As we established earlier, at the time Herod, a sixty-seven-year-old man, infected with a necrotic disease, and living with his tenth wife, was the puppet King of the Jews only as long as it pleased the Roman Emperor, Caesar Augustus; and as sick as Herod was it had been many years since he had the ability to father a child."

"You mentioned that these gentiles might have been reticent when answering King Herod's questions; but I can tell you that this was not true. The reason is that King Herod, being as paranoid as he was, paid informants to mingle with the population while listening to conversations in an effort to discover ahead of time intentions or plans that were subversive or rebellious. They had told him that there were three men, obviously traders, who had arrived in Jerusalem. Two of them were very young, dressed in expensive-looking clothing not familiar to the average Judean, and asking questions about where they could find the newborn king of the Jews. The third man no one had seen since their arrival, but searching questions had discovered at which inn he could be found.

"Knowing this you might think that Herod would have had them arrested or at least brought before him to answer for their behavior. However, after hearing how they were dressed he knew the decorative coats they were wearing were caftans – and that the only people who wore them were wealthy Parthians. However, he questioned why one of them was a Black. If he were a slave or a servant he would not have been dressed as his companion."

"You're speaking, Satan, as if you were not planning to do what you do with these three men. Is that so, or are you just biding your time?"

"At that time in history I expended neither time nor effort in deserts. With the exception of thieving, murdering brigands who attack those few careless or foolish enough to travel without the safety of a caravan, they are void of significant amounts of human habitation. I much preferred to troll for souls in large cities. Not only were there more of you, but in cities there are so many more opportunities for sinful temptations with which I and mine ply our trade."

"However, these three men are no longer in the desert, but in Jerusalem, which you must admit was considered a large, major city."

"Agreed, but at that time there were several drawbacks and possible hazards I had to take into consideration. Caesar Augustus, years before, had proclaimed a Pax Romana (Period of Roman Peace) which had the full support of the Roman Senate, in which further conquest was temporarily halted while Roman rule and a method of ensuring the collection of taxes was strengthened in the conquered territories. As a result any act that might upset potential or past enemies and thereby threaten the peace of Rome would be met with swift, lethal retribution.

"The Parthians, for reasons I have mentioned, were high on this list. Because of this I prompted King Herod not to act in haste. Get to know them better. Why not send the High Priest to pay a call on the secluded man in an effort to not only discover the Parthians' true intentions; but to invite all three men to dinner at the palace? What could be more innocent, even more cordial, and also get Herod the information he wanted?"

"And did he oblige you?

"Of course. He thought he had conceived a brilliant plan.

"However, when the High Priest reported the following to Herod it engendered more confusion than enlightenment.

Melchior, the oldest of the three men, was the second-born prince of the former King of Parthia. His older brother was now King of Parthia. As the second-born prince, Melchior was given extensive military training, and now at sixty, was in fact a retired Parthian general.

That for the last twenty-two years he had been a widower as his wife, Tasha, and their two children, a twelve-year-old son and a ten-year-old daughter, along with the families of many members of his army, had been murdered by the Tocharians while they were away in the

301

west fighting the Romans. Herod was aware of the Parthian retribution against the Tocharians since it was reported as being viciously sadistic; and now suspected that Melchior, as the general who had lost his family, was responsible.

That because of current celestial manifestations, that is, that Jupiter which controls the fortunes of kings, and Saturn, which is influential in the fate of Israel had conjoined, Melchior, a gentile, was certain that the Jewish Messiah had recently been born. "The conjunction," Melchior told the High Priest, "had occurred in an area of the sky known as Pisces while is nearly void of stars."

"And why is that significant?" asked the High Priest.

'Because Ahura Mazda wanted it to be easily visible to all who were inclined or told to look,' Melchior replied. "As further confirmation," he added, "Mars is now moving to join them and I can only presume that this triune celestial maneuvering is further confirmation of the truth of what I am telling you."

That it was highly likely that the Zoroastrian Saoshyant and the Jewish Messiah were one and the same.

That Melchior had not only a remarkable knowledge of the Jewish Testament but had brought the scrolls with him that predicted the coming Messiah would be born of a virgin in Bethlehem and that He would have the ability to cure what were readily known as incurable physical maladies. That Melchior had no problem reading and pointing out these prophecies even though his scrolls were written in Hebrew.

That the two men traveling with him had just reached majority. That the Black was the son of an Abyssinian chieftain who had escaped from slavers as a youth and had been living by his wits and ability at sleight of hand in the streets of Seleucia before being caught by Melchior and arrested; after which Melchior, for reasons he chose not to reveal, refused to press charges and ordered him released from the military prison. Not only that, Melchior had him travel with them as an equal. That the other companion, who has no equal as an archer, became Melchior's ward following his father's death in battle fighting barbarians in eastern Parthia.

That the Messiah had no desire to be proclaimed a King in this world, since his teachings were for the purpose of teaching men how to live favorably with God and in peace with his fellow man; and thus, if any kingship was true or implied it was in the spiritual realm.

"In an effort to refute Melchior the High Priest told Herod he advised Melchior that if the Messiah had come among them Jehovah would have informed the High Priest before all others – and especially before any-one in the gentile world. This was so because only then could the Jewish people be properly informed within the credible authority of the Temple.

"As politely as possible, while disavowing such a necessity since it appeared nowhere in scriptural prophecy, Melchior politely denied what the High Priest said, referring to God's promise to Abraham when He stated that 'His promise of salvation would be extended to all the nations of the world...'"

After listening to this, I said, "Satan, it appears Melchior knew that he had irritated the High Priest to such an extent that he refrained from mentioning that the destruction of the temple and the cessation of ani-mal sacrifices would ensue following the murder of his Messiah."

"He didn't have to. Melchior knew that as High Priest he was aware of Daniel's prophecy as well or better than any Jew or gentile. As many did at that time, he just put it out of his mind and never thought about it. Melchior, knowing that he had said enough in a land ruled by others obviously thought it wise to do the same.

"At dinner that evening Herod had invited Ptolemaeus, his Chief Magistrate, the High Priest and a man named Zargon who was the court astrologer. Most of the conversation was between Zargon, the High Priest and Melchior who bantered back and forth in terms used only by astronomers, astrologers, and theologians. Herod permitted them to speak their piece even though much of what was said he did not under-stand. Now and then, however, Herod and Ptolemaeus would engage in conversation with Gaspar and Balthazar. Both were duly impressed with both men's answers to their questions, especially Herod, who normally had little admiration for any man who had not reached his fortieth year.

"Ptolemaeus, being a Greek, was a pagan, and a very intelligent man who tried his best to figure out why there was all this excited discussion over the birth of a baby: that is until his Jewish kingship entered into the discussion. Even though Melchior stressed that his kingship was in the spiritual realm Ptolemaeus saw the look of concern on Herod's face.

"Finally, Herod stood and raised his goblet. After staring at it for a moment he quickly downed its contents. Replacing the goblet on the table he was about to wipe his mouth with his sleeve. Then, remembering his guests took the napkin and dabbed his lips before tossing it on the table."

"I am weary of listening to talk about salvation, damnation, prophecies, celestial risings, planetary conjunctions and astrological theories," he said. "What's more I have never been comfortable discussing reward and punishment in a mythical world of the hereafter. I, Herod, King of Israel, live in the material world of the ever-present now!" he said, tapping his index finger forcibly on the table while glancing around.

"And Caesar has presented me with more than enough doubt about the future of the Herodian lineage without my having to bear attacks upon the future of my throne by way of the birth of my own people! The high priest is sure this Messiah has not been born, or perhaps even conceived as yet because Jehovah has not so advised him.

"Melchior, a Parthian prince, and his two companions, have traveled endless miles in pursuit of a glimpse of the babe whom they call Saoshyant and are just as sure has been born not ten miles from where we sit!

"All of us have lived long enough to know that no man is completely infallible whether king, high priest or prince. We have heard only one thing about this child that is clear and not contested: this being that He has been or will be born in Bethlehem.

"You have my permission, therefore, Melchior, to proceed with your two companions to the City of David and search for this wondrous child. When you find him report back to me; for as you have stated so eloquently, I, too, suspect that he has already been born. If such is true it is only right that he who presently sits on the throne of Israel should give him His due.""

Melchior nodded and said, "It is so little you ask in return for your hospitality, Your Majesty."

"Upon departing Herod's palace," Satan said, "The three men, riding their camels in single file, took the road south to Bethlehem. After a mile or so Melchior motioned for Balthazar to come forward and ride on his left side. 'What is your opinion of King Herod?' Melchior asked.

"Balthazar replied without hesitation, 'He is pompous and self-centered albeit talented in the art of survival and from what I saw of the Temple not a stranger to architecture. He is an atheist, of course, who is totally fixated on his legacy to the point where he would torture and kill his own mother if he thought her long, painful demise would ensure his bloodline would inherit his throne.'

"Turning to Gaspar who had come up on Balthazar's left; Melchior asked him if he concurred with Balthazar's opinion. 'Not only do I concur, sir, but I suspect you do also; and if so, I have to ask why you agreed to report back to Herod where he could find the child? I think we can all agree after hearing Herod's farewell that giving him His due has a hidden meaning.'

"Of course it does; and in response I simply reciprocated in kind. If you remember what I said was, 'It is so little you ask in return for your hospitality, Your Majesty.'"

"So, neither Herod nor you, Melchior, spoke your intent plainly?" Balthazar asked.

"Balthazar, In a contest between swordsmen it is called thrust and parry. Herod thrust by telling us to advise him where the child was so he could have him murdered. I simply parried not by denying his request, but rather by deflecting it."

"It seems to me," Balthazar said, "that we still have the problem of knowing where this child is; that is, how to find him."

"As a Zoroastrian, Gaspar, how would you answer Balthazar?"

Gaspar thought for a moment and then answered. "If it is the will of Ahura Mazda that we pay homage to His Incarnation then it is only just that He provides us with the means to do so."

"Did Gaspar answer your question, Balthazar?"

"I have to admit, Melchior, that in the time I have known you, your decisions have been correct; but to believe that you possess a personal relationship with your God so strong that He will give you a definite sign as an indication of His will…well, maybe. No doubt we'll know for sure before we leave Bethlehem."

"Melchior chuckled and said, 'Balthazar, before we depart this city of David, I have no doubt that Ahura Mazda will not only remove your doubt but replace it with a faith that you can live by for the rest of your life.'"

"Satan, I have two questions I'd like to ask while these three men continue on to an inn in Bethlehem. How much did Balthazar know about the child they were seeking? It appears to me that neither Melchior nor Gaspar had given him much in the way of details regarding what they believed to be the divine nature of this miraculous child."

"What you have to remember, Bruce, is that unlike the Jews who had hundreds of prophecies concerning the Messiah going back several thousand years; the Zoroastrian belief was very limited in this regard. Melchior, of course, had the advantage of having studied the Jewish prophecies, but the variety and complexity of these considering the short time they were together were beyond Balthazar's grasp.

"However, I will tell you this. A man named Nathan was a wealthy, fifty-year-old, rather portly Jew who lived in Jerusalem and was both a personal friend and longtime buyer of Melchior's spices. He just happened to be in Seleucia on his own trading mission at the same time that Melchior was. The four of them had dinner together the night before Melchior departed for Jerusalem, after which Nathan presented Melchior with a white horse in its prime to pay what he felt was a debt he owed. The horse, of course, was at Nathan's stable in Jerusalem. Soon thereafter both Melchior and Nathan left to retire for the night.

CHAPTER THIRTY-EIGHT

"If we are part of a Divine Plan, I don't think much of it."

"Gaspar and Balthazar, however, remained and after ordering another skin of wine they talked about their backgrounds. When Gaspar spoke about Melchior's quest for the newborn child, Balthazar replied, 'this astounding birth…there should be massive celebrations at such an event. It should be easy to find him, but with the crowds and the security that will be necessary, it may be difficult to see him. Have you asked Melchior about this?'

"Yes. Like you, I pictured massive crowds, but Melchior didn't think so. He told me that if celebrations were planned, then Nathan, who had departed Jerusalem a month before would be aware of them."

"He wasn't?"

"No. In fact, Nathan feels certain that we are on a futile mission. 'The idea of the Messiah is like attempting to gather fruit from a tree that is far out of reach,' he said, 'something that his descendants may experience in the far distant future; as such it is foolhardy to consider him with assured conviction for the present,' is how he put it."

"If he represents the whole of Jewish thinking, Gaspar, what do we do when we get to Jerusalem?"

"I don't know."

"Gaspar, before I met Melchior I never heard of a Messiah, an Incarnate God or Ahura Mazda. In fact, I never knew anybody who took any of the gods seriously. As for me – I believe it makes sense to believe that some Supreme Power must have created the world we live in; but beyond that the gods people acknowledge seem to me to be nothing more than a whim of somebody's imagination that took hold and became custom and tradition over the years.

"Furthermore, if we are part of a Divine Plan, I don't think much of it. Here we are a sixty-year-old prince and the two of us, barely in our twenty-second year. After departing Seleucia the prince will be out of his domain. One of the remaining two is an archer who speaks a few languages and knows some astronomy. The other is a thief! We are about to travel at night across a dangerous, vast, and desolate wasteland following the path of some kind of celestial manifestation. We have weapons, but the only one who has any experience using them in combat is the old man.

"Two of us have only a hazy idea of what we are looking for or what to expect when we get there. The third thinks he knows, but, if Nathan, a man of wealth and influence that lives in the city has no idea what he is talking about, how can he be so sure?

"Finally, you tell me we are looking for a newborn but have no idea who his parents are, exactly where he will be born, or anything specific about this child, except it will be a male born of a virgin; and you suspect he will be born in Jerusalem, or is it Bethlehem?"

"I know," Gaspar replied with a nod, "it sounds…"

"The simple truth," Balthazar interrupted, as he stood up, "is that if this were a battle plan; and you and I presented it to Melchior – as a general, he would rapidly come to the conclusion that the two of us had spent too much time in the desert sun!

"However, I have to tell you that despite what I just said there was a feeling that came over me this afternoon when the three of us laughed together: that there was, from that moment on, a strong bond which held us together and a remarkable destiny at the end of this journey which far surpasses what any of us could hope to achieve alone."

"I, too, had a similar feeling."

"When we laughed?"

"No. It was when a man who was to become my friend, after looking at the charts I prepared for making the crossing, said, 'You have never attempted a solitary desert crossing.'

"When I asked him how he knew he smiled and replied, 'Because you're still alive!'"

Laughing together, they departed the eatery.

"I smiled and said, I'm beginning to appreciate the friendship these two younger men developed. As mentioned earlier they complemented each other in a way that with Melchior's experience and leadership the three of them achieved what even two of them alone could not have accomplished."

Without commenting Satan said, "You mentioned two questions."

"Yes, you partially answered it when you mentioned the spices. What, if any other items did Melchior trade?"

"At that time there was no refrigeration. Food, especially meat, unless dried and heavily salted, spoiled quickly. Spices were popular because they made food that began to spoil palatable; and in fact, were his major commodity. The eastern border of Parthia was close enough to China and what today is India and Pakistan, that Melchior acquired spices from the latter and silks from China. He also traded in ivory, in addition to leather goods and tapestries both made in Parthia – and in aromatics, frankincense, myrrh, alabaster and semi-precious stones."

When I just nodded without commenting, Satan continued. "While Melchior was arranging for their accommodations the innkeeper's, eleven-year-old daughter joined her father at the desk. Instantly recognizing Balthazar she asked him, 'Did you find the newborn king that you and your friend were seeking?'"

Immediately her father reprimanded her, "Rebecca, it is impolite to speak to paying guests unless they first speak to you."

Raising his hand Melchior said, "No harm done, sir. May I speak to your daughter?" When the innkeeper nodded Melchior smiled and asked the girl, "You were recently in Jerusalem?"

"With my mother," she responded. "We ordered provisions to be sent to the inn, and then went shopping. While in the marketplace I heard these two men seeking the whereabouts of a newborn that they referred to as the king of the Jews."

"Yes, I'm afraid I have to accept the blame for that misnomer." Turning again to the innkeeper, Melchior said, "When approaching Jerusalem we noticed huge caravans were preparing to leave the city. I can't think of any Jewish feast days that occurred recently that would bring that many people to the city. Did I miss something?"

"Caesar Augustus's census. It brought thousands of people to Judea."

"That kind of a crowd must have pleased you."

"Yes and no," the innkeeper replied. All the inns in the city were more than full-up – two and three couples to a room, plus the ones who had to lie on the floor in the passageway. Finally, I had to turn people away. I remember one couple that was particularly heartbreaking as the woman was not only pregnant but appeared to be in the first throes of labor."

"Gaspar, who had overheard the conversation asked, 'Do you know what happened to them?'

"Yes. I have a grown son who earns his living as a farrier for the Roman legion's horses. He told the man that there was a cave nearby that was used to store fodder. 'It wasn't much,' he told them, but it will provide shelter from the elements.'

"Two days later when the crowds began thinning out my wife and I found them still in the cave with their newborn son. The husband told me that he was a carpenter and that he wanted to earn some money to purchase a younger donkey before heading home to Nazareth.

"We own two small abodes in Bethlehem that we rent. One of them was now empty so I told them they could stay there for a nominal sum until he could afford the trip home. My son said the Romans were looking for someone who could make repairs to the barracks and build an addition to the centurion's quarters.

"The centurion was so pleased with the repairs that he is paying Joseph well to enlarge his quarters."

"You said that His name is Joseph?" Melchior asked.

"Yes, Joseph. His wife's name is Mary, and they named their son Jesus."

"If we decide to visit these people, will you do us the favor of telling us how to find them?" asked Melchior.

"They're poor Jews from Nazareth, a little town in Galilee. I think three armed gentiles would get a better reception if my wife, whom they know well, were to request that they receive you."

"No doubt," Melchior replied. "In the morning I'll let you know my decision."

"As Melchior was turning to proceed to his room, the innkeeper asked, 'Excuse me for asking, sir, but he appears to be nothing more than a plain carpenter forced to make a lengthy trip at a difficult time. May I ask why three men such as yourselves would have a reason to visit them?'"

"Looks can be deceiving," Melchior answered. "If what I feel might be true that infant will be the One Whose life and teachings, if adhered to, will better the way men live. Come daylight I will know for sure.

"Good night, sir, and to you as well, young lady," Melchior added, while giving a respectful nod to the innkeeper's daughter after which the three men retired to their rooms.

"Tell me, Satan, you watched Melchior both as a child and as a youth growing into manhood. What made him the man he was?"

"Fortunately or unfortunately, depending upon how one looks at it, children born to royalty have a number of people in addition to their parents who raise them. Melchior's older brother's destiny was to rule the realm. Melchior's, being the second-born son, was to protect it. As such Melchior, after the age of twelve, spent less and less time with his parents and more time with Zoroastrian priests and military personnel. His peers were likewise sons of other Parthian nobility chosen for a combination of both mental and physical prowess.

"This provided an atmosphere of extreme competitiveness which served to sharpen their minds and develop their muscular strength; but that is not the whole of it."

"It isn't?"

"No, if it was then they would be little more than the self-serving barbarians they opposed."

"Like the Tocharians you mentioned?"

"Exactly. The ruthless, cruel, psychopaths who are devoid of empathy and so full of hate that they are incapable of love but only greed when in pursuit of power and material possessions."

"And you're proud of these fiends?"

"No, I despise them along with the rest of humanity, for they are stupidly doing to others not as they would want them to do unto them – which unrepentant means without a doubt they have willingly chosen the wide road to eternal damnation."

"However, you use them to serve your ends because it's what you do!"

"Precisely."

"So, what prevented Melchior from succumbing to the fiend way of life?"

"Ahura Mazda."

"In what way?"

"From the age of six they were taught by priests the duality of good and evil in the world – the virtuous and honorable ways of Ahura Mazda and the evil and dishonorable ways of Ahriman."

"How so?"

"In summary, Bruce, they learned the inner peace and assured conviction of putting your trust and confidence in Ahura Mazda; God if you will, because if you do this He will use you as an instrument of His will; and, since it is not possible for God to use a blunt tipped or a dull blade one's allegiance ensures that he will remain sharp and to the point in his endeavors."

"And without saying, beyond Ahriman's, that is, your grasp."

"Exactly, unless he is beguiled and ultimately succumbs to one or more of my powerful temptations."

"However, you must find this a rare occurrence since from watching Melchior I have to believe that humility is a factor in his religious training; and, as you said earlier, 'A truly humble person has no illicit and ardent desires upon which to prompt a temptation.'"

"That is true."

CHAPTER THIRTY-NINE

"Please! Do not be afraid."

"Before retiring for the night Melchior thought about the carpenter, his wife, and their newborn son. He contemplated both the Jewish scriptures as well as the Zoroastrian Avesta and didn't remember either referring to the Messiah or the Saoshyant by the name His parents had given him. Nevertheless, it appeared that both his parents' and his choice of this inn might not have been by chance; and if not, it meant that they were just given the final sign they required to complete their journey.

"Standing in the center of the room he bowed his head and prayed:

'Lord, in Your wisdom You have been so generous in this regard, that I dare not ask You to send me additional signs that what we three are intent on doing tomorrow is in fact Your will.

'What I do ask, however, is if my human frailty has caused my interpretation to be faulty then please preclude the innkeeper's wife from assisting us in this endeavor that with Your continued assistance we might seek Your Incarnate presence elsewhere.'

"At the same moment the innkeeper was telling his wife what had transpired with three guests who earlier had come to stay the night at their inn. Having heard what Melchior had said about this child she remarked, 'It sounds like this man has described a characteristic of the Messiah; except that it is hard to believe that Jehovah would allow the Messiah to come to us by way of low born parents in a cave.'"

"Who knows the ways of God?" her husband replied. "He had Moses placed in a basket and floated down a river to be found and raised by pagans in their royal palace!"

"Quite so. Tomorrow morning, I will prepare the morning meal for our guests after which I will call on Joseph and Mary and make known the men's request."

"The next morning," Satan said, "the innkeeper invited Melchior, Balthazar and Gaspar to a morning meal his wife had prepared before she left to talk to Joseph and Mary.

"Joseph looked at Mary and said, 'We have an obligation to protect Jesus from harm. I am not comfortable allowing one, let alone three gentiles to approach him.'"

"Mary answered, 'I understand your concern, Joseph, but if these men wanted to do Jesus harm would they seek our permission to do so?' Turning to Leah, the innkeeper's wife, Mary asked, 'Are these men Romans?'

"Two of the men signed our guest ledger as Parthians. The third said he was from Abyssinia."

"Can you say that their appearance supposed this to be true?" Joseph asked.

"Not only their complexion and features, but their dress in addition to the fact that they arrived on the backs of camels."

"Joseph, I can't tell you why, but I feel that these men are somehow part of God's plan. However, I'll know more when I see them."

Joseph nodded and turning to Leah asked, "Are these men armed?"

"Very much so. The older man wears a sword, the Abyssinian is armed with a spear and the third man has a bow across his chest. Also, Joseph, all three men display a sheathed dagger."

"Tell them we will see them with one stipulation," Joseph said, "They must come unarmed."

"Joseph was completing the finishing work on a cabinet for the Centurion's quarters when there was a knock on the door. He finished lightly tapping the last peg flush with the surface while thinking it might be the three men Leah had mentioned. Opening the door he stood mute as the mallet slipped from his fingers and dropped to the floor. Leah had not told him that they would be so regally attired."

"Please! Do not be afraid," the oldest of the three men pleaded with a smile. "You are Joseph," he said, with a respectful nod, "and a carpenter from Nazareth. Your wife is Mary, also from Nazareth and the Child, born but a few weeks ago here in Bethlehem, you have named, Jesus. Our appearance is strange to you because we are Gentiles and dressed in the clothes of the station we hold in our native lands."

"Ahura Mazda has graciously advised us of the Divine Nature of the Child," said one of the younger men, "and we have come to pay homage and offer our gifts."

"We have been traveling for many months," the third man said, "and at times not without great risk. May we enter?"

"Yes…yes, please do," Joseph said, retrieving the mallet. "You'll have to excuse me for appearing rude. It's just that including Leah and some shepherds we have had only simple Jewish neighbors visit since our arrival in Bethlehem."

As Joseph turned around, he saw that Mary had already entered the room. She stood intently observing the three gentiles who were rather gaudily dressed by her standards, and noted that each held what she presumed were the gifts mentioned.

"You are Mary, the Child's mother?" Melchior asked.

"I am," she answered.

"We are…"

"Yes, I know. I heard what was spoken before you entered.

"After pausing for a moment she said, 'Welcome,' smiling and extending her hands in gesture. 'This house grows bright with the joy of your presence for you would not have known what you do; or have been able to find your way here, were it not for the will of Jehovah. The Child has just finished nursing. I will bring him to you.'

"She entered the room with the Child cradled in her arm. He was awake and looking around, his head moving in the quick, exploratory motions of the very young. Seating herself on a rustic bench against the wall they watched as the young mother sat him on her lap leaning his back against her forefront.

"They immediately knelt as Melchior said, 'This day there are many who speak of you as the Messiah. They and their forefathers awaited your coming for many centuries, and yet, they know you not when you arrive. We, who have been blessed with this privilege, offer adoration and this precious oil of myrrh for your symbolic anointing as our Saoshyant.'"

"As Gentiles we offer humble worship and present these thirty-three all but flawless tears of frankincense," said Gaspar, "that as they were gathered after only many years from the flowing sap of Ahura Mazda's arboreal creation you may accomplish in your own lifetime the teaching of precepts that Jew and Gentile alike may follow to live in peace and harmony."

"I, too, kneel before you," Balthazar said, "for as I am a man who has been put upon by men, so I represent the oppressed peoples of the world. My gift is this bag of gold coins. As men have learned to love gold may they learn through your presence among us to love one another. And as the precious metal is sought after and prized because it is immune to alteration or decay, so may your teachings be for all mankind until the end of time."

"Mary smiled at each in turn as she reached out and touched his gift, then stood and handed the child to Joseph who had been standing at her side. 'Please,' she said, as she gestured for them to rise.

When they were standing before her she raised her eyes and arms to the heavens and said:

"The adoration and gifts you offer here tonight are more than the simple, generous act of three men. Rather, they are a symbolic message to all men and women from this time forth, that the teachings and redemption to come forth from the Word made Flesh are not limited to a single nation, nor to a single race, and not for only a chosen people, but for all. As such, your visit to this Child made after a long and dangerous trek will be written down that all persons throughout the world may be mindful of this truth, as each year they joyfully remember that bearing gifts in adoration you came here this day.'"

"They smiled and nodded, but before they could say anything she said, 'You may place your gifts on the table in the scullery,' as she reached for the child. 'I will find a place for them later.'"

"I have only water, meal, and a little oil to offer you. We came to Bethlehem to register for the census and spent all that we had either in making the trip, or to live after we got here. Joseph has found work but it will be several days before he finishes it and gets paid for his labor."

"Melchior, after laying his gift on the table reached out toward the infant. 'May I?'" he asked.

"Of course," she replied, offering him her Child.

Cradling the infant in one arm Melchior reached into his caftan and removed a small bag of gold coins. "Take these and go to the market-place," he said, gesturing toward Gaspar and Balthazar. "Ask for the overseer and request that he have his hirelings put together provisions for a celebratory Hebrew meal for ten people. You'll need Joseph's donkey we saw tethered out front to help you carry your purchase. When you pay the man add something generous for his service. Then hurry back. No doubt we are all getting hungry."

"For ten people?" Joseph asked. "Are there more of you coming?"

"A man who earns his family's keep with his hands and the sweat of his brow can't continue to do so on nothing but meal and oil, Joseph."

"But I…"

"Please, Joseph," Melchior interrupted. "The Almighty has not gifted me with great wealth that I might shower myself with beads, baubles, trinkets, and trifles but that I may use that treasure to alleviate need wherever He reveals it to be. All I ask is that as God wills it, you permit me to be gracious."

"I have to ask, Satan. What Mary said – it was prophetic, was it not? I mean even today, two thousand years later, we celebrate the Visit of the Magi just as Mary said we would."

"That and the fact that she prophesied earlier that 'all generations shall call me blessed.' As we said before Mary was created by God to be the mother of His Incarnate Self. Why would He create her to be less than perfect? Mary was, is and will be forevermore the Blessed Mother because she is The Mother of God. As such her power of intercession with her Son, even now and for all time is a power little acknowledged and therefore appreciated by most of the dim-witted of humanity."

"It must hurt you grievously to say that, but having no choice but to tell the truth you had no alternative."

"You cannot begin to know the rage roiling within me, especially since it was my actions in attempting to aid my demon, Humilione that has now forced me to speak the truth of Mary in depth."

CHAPTER FORTY

"You will go down in history as The Bethlehem Butcher!"

"Hearing Satan admit to even more than I had hoped for I thought it wise to return to the subject at hand, and asked, How long did they remain with the Holy Family?"

"After the meal they returned to the inn, changed into their desert clothing and when it got dark, they returned to Jerusalem."

"Why? Isn't that like returning to the lion's den? If one of King Herod's informers sees them, won't he have them brought before him to ascertain the location of the Child?"

"If you remember I said that they traveled at night dressed as desert people. You will also remember that while in Seleucia Nathan presented Melchior with a horse – to be exact it was a fine mare in her prime. You may also remember that the horse was in Nathan's stables in Jerusalem; but what I didn't tell you is that while Melchior and Nathan left the two younger men to retire for the night, Nathan offered Melchior the use of his huge, luxurious house and stables in Jerusalem. He gave Melchior a signet ring along with a note he had written for Melchior to give to Benjamin, his chief steward, as proof of his intent.

"In order to preclude Herod's informers from recognizing them Melchior told Gaspar and Balthazar to remain within the area of the house while Melchior shaved his beard and dressed in his desert clothing before conducting commercial trading in Jerusalem.

"Meanwhile, after two weeks had passed and Melchior and his two companions did not return Herod sent twelve of his Herodian guards to Bethlehem to find them. After two days they told Herod they weren't there. 'We searched the city as well as a radius around Bethlehem. We found the inn where they stayed one night, but after that it was like they vanished. I can say with utmost confidence, Your Majesty,' the captain said, 'that they are neither in Bethlehem nor anywhere around it.'"

"Inwardly, Herod seethed with anger but outwardly in front of his captain said simply, 'Very well. You are dismissed.' Then speaking to Ptolemaeus he said, 'Come – we'll go to my quarters and discuss what we must do.'

"When Ptolemaeus heard what Herod wanted to do he said, 'Your majesty I beg you not to do this thing. It will forever ruin your reputation as a great architect and builder. What you want to do is so horrendous that you will go down in history as The Bethlehem Butcher! Nothing you have done or will ever do be it ever so grand will blot this out. It will be a stigma of shame that will forever dishonor your legacy and historical remembrance.'"

"You're speaking nonsense, Ptolemaeus. These Jews breed such that in a few years the son they lost will be forgotten among sons of the new brood. I leave it to you. When you have a plan bring it to me for approval; and be quick about it. I don't want him to see the sun rise in the morning. It must begin at midnight."

"Two hours later, Ptolemaeus, carrying a scroll and accompanied by a servant carrying a silver tray with two goblets of Herod's best vintage wine, knocked lightly on the door to Herod's chambers."

"Come in, Ptolemaeus," Herod said. After the servant departed Herod swallowed half of the wine in his goblet and said, "Ptolemaeus I know this is difficult for you and you should know that the reason you hold your exalted position is that I can rely upon you to successfully accomplish hellish tasks when forced upon the crown.

"As my right hand, you, my Hellenistic friend, are the second man in the kingdom, and as such, on whom I rely, and on whom I have relied to accomplish the despicable and loathsome duties that unfortunately plague every successful monarch that has ever reigned."

"The first and foremost duty of every king is to preserve his reign – that is, his position as king, for if he loses his crown nothing else matters. His second duty is like it – to ensure that the fruit of his loins will inherit his throne upon his demise. Why? Because the usurper will see to it that anyone who has a legal right to the throne is not around to claim it."

"Ptolemaeus knew that Herod was speaking from personal experience, Bruce, since he had usurped the throne of Israel from the Jewish Hasmonean Dynasty. In an attempt to foster

legitimacy he married Mariamne, the granddaughter of the king and the only Hasmonean he permitted to survive. In addition, he converted, albeit deceptively, to Judaism; however, it was an unsuccessful endeavor. Many Jews referred to him as the Idumean (Arabian) Imposter. Years later he had Mariamne and the two sons he had by her executed after accusing her erroneously of infidelity."

"What was the real reason and why murder his two sons as well?"

"He found out that she was plotting against him to put their eldest son, Aristobolus, prematurely on the throne in an attempt to restore the Hasmonean bloodline.

"He being but a boy at the time she would be the ruler of Israel until he came of age. Of course it would also mean that she would have Herod killed so as to prevent him from any retaliation.

"Was this true?"

"Yes. And to prevent even the possibility of such in the future he had Alexander, the younger son also killed."

"Ptolemaeus knew that he could not change Herod's mind, so he just nodded and opened the scroll on the table. 'Your majesty, before we begin, we have to take into consideration the best way to approach what you, yourself, have called a loathsome thing. There are several pitfalls we have to take into consideration.'

"First, of course, is to ascertain how many male children two years and younger are in Bethlehem."

"And how do we do that?" asked Herod.

"Levites who administer the offices of the Temple have advised me of the number. It is twenty-seven."

"And this number is based on...?"

"An unimpeachable source, Your Majesty. The rabbinical circumcisions. They are a matter of record.

"Very well. What other pitfalls do we have to consider?"

"Who should kill the infants?

"The Herodian Guard! Why is that a problem?"

"It is a problem, Your Majesty, because a number of your men under arms are from Bethlehem. They have family there. Furthermore, I think Your Majesty will agree that taking infants from their mothers' arms to slaughter them would affect the self-esteem of more than a few of the men who are ordered to do it.

Before Herod could reply Ptolemaeus continued, "Your Majesty, the men in your guard are effective because they are trained warriors. I know these men. Having them butcher infants, to put it mildly, would forever affect their self-worth. It can only serve to weaken the Palace Guard. Why take this risk if we can avoid it?"

"So, what is a viable alternative? Who else would do the deed; and if we could find them, how could we trust them?"

"It is an ancient Greek belief, Your Majesty, that sufficient reward will ensure the deed."

"No doubt, but reward to whom for doing the deed?"

"Before we go any further," Satan said, "Tell me the second of Mary's seven sorrows."

"The flight into Egypt," I responded.

"And...?" Satan responded.

"And what?" I answered.

"You say that as if all they had to do was purchase tickets on a modern conveyance and lean back in air-conditioned comfort as they enjoy being effortlessly carried across the desert to Egypt."

"Well, of course not. By now, however, Joseph would have been paid by the Centurion and purchased a younger, stronger donkey."

"Like you, Bruce, most people today are ignorant about what a trip of this nature would be like for a man and his wife trying to both nurse and change a newborn in the desert heat while being jostled about on the back of a donkey. Then, there is the need for water, food and lodging and maybe worst of all the brigands waiting to waylay individuals attempting a solitary desert crossing.

"If Mary doesn't get enough nourishment her milk will dry up. Then in the desert without fire and fuel the frigid nights are all but humanly unbearable for adults and undoubtedly more so for a relative newborn.

"To make matters worse this is not a two or three day trip. They will have to travel twenty miles or so at night to reach Hebron. Then, they turn west. They will have to travel another forty-five miles just to get to the Egyptian border – and all this as I inferred across a blistering hot barren desert that turns more than a little frigid at night; and it is not until they cross the border that they are safe from Herod's malevolent intentions."

"Say in truth, Satan, what those intentions were: malevolent, yes, but sourced by the Diabolical."

"I had two chances to use evil intentioned men to kill Jesus before He was one year old. I must admit in truth that I failed both times. Herod's intentions were the first."

"And the second?"

"We are getting ahead of ourselves. We'll discuss that later. We haven't finished with King Herod's murderous fiasco.

CHAPTER FORTY-ONE

The Flight into Egypt – The Second of Mary's Seven Sorrows.

"Zared, a man who had been condemned to death for murdering five men and two women in cold blood, was dragging leg weights, while carrying several rolled parchments as he marched with armed guards on either side to a holding area in the prison. Marching in single file joined to Zared and to each other with leather collars and leg weights were five additional men chosen by Ptolemaeus because they had been sentenced and condemned to death for having murdered multiple times in cold blood.

"You are all convicted murderers," Ptolemaeus announced when they reached the holding area, "and are to be executed tomorrow morning at sunrise.

"Your king, however, in his capacity for mercy, has assigned you a task which if completed as assigned, will countermand that order, provide you with a conditional royal pardon, a horse and enough sesterces to begin your lives anew.

"Zared here will be your leader. He has the maps and your orders.

"When you are sure they all understand," he said to Zared, "call for the guards in the passageway who will escort the six of you to the rear of the prison where you will find what you need for the task. At that time the guards will remove your collars and leg weights.. Be advised, he added that your pardons are conditional. If you are ever seen within fifty miles of Jerusalem you will be arrested and held for execution as an escaped prisoner."

"Ptolemaeus, noticing the puzzled look in the eyes of several of the prisoners and having no desire to answer questions, turned and immediately left the prison. As he walked across the road to the prison stable, he thought about asking a guard to get his horse but declined. He didn't want to talk to anyone even as little as that.

"He put his left foot in the stirrup and was about to swing into the saddle when he backed off and turned away. He became nauseous and felt as if his stomach was angrily churning its way up his gullet. A second later he began violently retching against a stall.

"Melchior had been asleep for several hours when he saw a woman running toward him from a distance in an aura of bright light. As she came closer, he could see that she was both elegantly mature and beautiful, and was running toward him in her bare feet across an open field of thick, plush grass. She continued closing the distance almost effortlessly in a coasting, floating motion, her long, black hair moving sensuously from side to side. She slowed as she approached, coming to a gliding stop when near enough to speak to him. He stared in wonder and then with joy as he recognized the face of Tasha.

"You did well, Melchior, not to return to Herod, for as you surmised, he plans to kill the child and on this very night. Even now those whom he has ordered to take the lives of many to ensure the death of one are grouped in Jerusalem with blades unsheathed. Put away your anger over this hellish deed, Melchior, and remain far from the presence of Herod. Then do what is in your heart for such is the will of Ahura Mazda."

"Tasha...Tasha! Don't go!" he begged, reaching out. "The children, Tasha? What of our children?"

"As you are caring for his flesh, Melchior, so with loving care Ahura Mazda has done for ours.

"Melchior awoke, sitting with hands outstretched in a pleading gesture. Slowly lowering his arms, he looked around the room. In the dim light he could see that he was alone. It was silent. Nothing had changed from when he had gone to sleep.

"He sat on the edge of the bed with his feet on the floor convinced he had seen Tasha, or rather her spirit. He could never forget her form or the beauty of her face. She had not said God, but Ahura Mazda, a name with which they were both familiar. She had called him by name, not once but twice. And she had answered when he asked about their children.

"Tasha's spirit had been chosen as the heavenly messenger," he thought, "that he would have no doubt about what was said.

"Using avaricious ambition and unwarranted pride," he thought, "Ahriman had twisted Herod's mind to where the king would do his bidding no matter how absurd, cruel or insane it appeared to reasonable men.

"He dressed again in the desert clothing," Satan continued, "trying as she had said to control his anger as he strapped on his sword. He slipped the sheathed dagger under the sword belt and hurried along the passageways toward the stable.

"As he approached the stable, he saw someone calling out and running toward him. It was Kintry, the ten-year-old son of the Black family Nathan had purchased on the block when their master attempted to sell them individually. After a year Nathan had offered them their freedom. They accepted it with the condition that they remain in his employ at the estate. Kintry and Nathan's twelve-year-old daughter, Bethel, had developed a childhood friendship.

"Kintry? Son, what are you doing up at this hour of night?" he asked, as the young boy approached.

"It's your horse, Gabhriel!" he exclaimed, as Melchior got down on one knee. "She's gone crazy – whinnying and snorting and kicking the boards out of her stall! I was coming to get you because she's going to hurt herself!"

"She's going to be all right, son," Melchior said, as he put his arms around him. "I'll take care of her. You go back to bed now and get your rest."

"Where are you going with this?" Kintry asked, touching the sword with the tip of his finger.

"I have to go to Bethlehem. There is no time now to explain. It would be a big help if you would open the gates.

"Easy, girl," Melchior said, attaching the reins to the bridle. "Hope you don't mind, but we've got no time for a saddle," he said, as he led her from the stall to the courtyard.

"Kintry pulled the pins and pushed on the gate. It opened less than a foot and then jammed. "The night chain!" he exclaimed to himself, and then called out, "Stop, Melchior! The night chain! Melchior, the gates are locked!" Looking toward the stable he saw that Melchior had already urged the mare into a gallop. The two came thundering down on him as the rapid pounding of her hoofs on the stone pathway told him they were going to crash headlong into the immovable gates!

"Kintry slid to the ground, covering his head with his hands waiting for the pain of the inevitable collision as he heard a loud whinny amid the increasing rhythm of Gabhriel's hoofs…then silence. He peeked for a second and saw nothing, then heard a momentary thud behind him. Turning to look through the gate he listened to the decreasing pitch of her galloping hooves as he watched the two of them disappear into the night.

"He stood, then, and when both knees began shaking, he grabbed hold of the iron bars with both hands. Looking up at the top of the tall gate, he said, in a barely audible voice, 'It's got to be our secret, Melchior. Just you and me and Gabhriel, 'cause nobody else would ever believe it!'"

"Melchior rode through Bethlehem, tears coming to his eyes, as he witnessed the carnage amid the screams of horrified parents. The murderers had begun committing their unspeakable deeds on the north side of their sectors. Melchior noted they were moving south through the city, which would give Joseph the time he needed to escape the city by the South Gate.

"When he arrived at the house, he dismounted and knocked heavily on the door. 'Joseph,' he called out, 'it's Melchior!'

"Joseph opened the door then quickly closed it again as Melchior entered. 'We're leaving,' Joseph said. 'Just as soon as we get a few things packed. Melchior, Herod plans to kill the child! I had a vision in a dream. The angel said to take the child and his mother into Egypt.'

"Herod's planning is long past, Joseph. They are killing children on the next street. You have to leave now! I have a horse out front, a mare, Joseph. Take her, she's fast."

"Neither Mary nor I have ever been on a horse, Melchior, and with the infant I'm afraid that…"

"All right, you have a point. Where's the donkey?"

"She's tethered in back."

As Melchior released the knot and led the animal around to the street, Joseph said, "We need water. I'm not even sure where Egypt is or how far, but I know from the Testament it's to the southwest and that between here and there lies a vast desert."

"Melchior, why does Herod want to kill my child?" Mary asked, holding the infant close.

"His arrogance and pride have allowed Ahriman to enter and poison his mind, Mary. Herod now believes that your Son will grow up to usurp his ill-gotten throne.

"Do you have a blanket?" he asked Joseph.

"Yes, I'll get it."

"Ahriman?" Mary questioned.

"Yes, Beelzebub, as you would know him," he answered, taking the blanket from Joseph and smoothing it over the back of the donkey. "Joseph, if you want to save your son you have to put him and Mary on the back of this animal and move as fast as you can to the South Gate. The road to Egypt from Hebron lies twenty miles to the South. Just south of Hebron take the road to your right. You'll be traveling west – toward Egypt.

"I, along with Gaspar and Balthazar are going on to Alexandria. We will gather up your tools and whatever else you have here and catch up with you shortly. We'll also have food and water. Loading this animal now will only slow you down."

"What will you do now?" Mary asked, glancing down at his sword and the sheathed dagger thrust beneath his belt.

"They'll know an infant is supposed to be here," he said. I will do what I must to see that they go no further south."

"We will pray that Jehovah will keep you in His care," she said.

"Yes, and thank you, Melchior," Joseph said, "for everything."

"Melchior watched until they were beyond the stables as they followed the street leading to the South Gate. 'Meek and humble and sitting upon an ass!' he mumbled to himself, shaking his head as he remembered his Jewish scripture. (Zechariah 9:9)

CHAPTER FORTY-TWO

"'BUTCHERRRRS!' the old woman screamed when she was released."

"At the north end of the street a woman began screaming as three men dragged her and her husband from their home. 'Let's get you out of the way, girl,' he said, as he led Gabhriel around to the back of the house.

"He blew out the candle, then cracked open the door and watched as they forced the old couple down the street. The wife was struggling with a man who held a dagger to her throat.

"Jehovah," he whispered, "You sure don't make it easy for your chosen people."

"This house," he heard the man say. "A young couple with a newborn, but not from here – told my wife they were from Nazareth and they both spoke with a Galilean accent."

"Any more?" questioned the man holding his wife who continued her struggling. "No! Not on this street. In the next house is an older couple like us. In the next, an old widow and her adult son, and the one adjacent to the stables is used for storage. Look for yourself! You can see the window openings are boarded up!"

"Let them go," Zared said.

"BUTCHERRRRS!" the old woman screamed when she was released. "SONS OF CAIN!" she yelled, pointing at them as she backed up the street. "You will all burn in the Fires of Hades for this!"

"Hush, Zapporah! Hush!" her husband said, taking her hand. "Do you want them to kill us, too?"

"Pulling away, she said, 'I don't care, Gideon. I know that lovely mother and her beautiful baby!' And burying her face in her hands she broke into tears and ran up the street."

"All right, this is the last one," Zared said. "Let's get it over with and then we can get out of here. Cover the rear, Arvad. Uriah, knock on the door."

"Uriah pounded on the door and bellowed, 'Open up at once in the name of the king!'

"When there was no response Zared said, 'One more time, Uriah. If they don't come to the door, we break it down.'

"Melchior deftly raised the door latch and eased Joseph's chisel under it to hold it open, then stood with the carpenter's mallet in one hand and Joseph's awl in the other so that as the door opened, it would just clear his shoulder.

"Uriah raised his fist swinging it forward like a giant mallet. Caught by surprise when the unlatched door flew open, he lost his balance and lunged forward stumbling and falling to the floor in the darkened room.

"Dazed and confused he managed to get half off the floor when he saw an array of multi-colored stars just after a flash of white light followed by an excruciating pain on the top of his head. Then all went black and he fell unconscious to the floor. Melchior quickly pulled him aside and drove the awl through his hand and on into the planked floor with three powerful blows of the mallet."

"Uriah?" Zared called, coming closer to better see into the darkened room. "What's going on in there? Are you all right, Uriah?"

"Melchior stepped from behind the door and shoved Zared back into the street. 'There is nothing here for you,'" he said.

"I have an edict, old man, signed by Ptolemaeus, chief magistrate to the king. We have a right to be here. There is a fatal disease affecting young males in Bethlehem and all under two years of age must die to prevent its spread."

"The only fatal disease in Judea is the mind of Herod. You and the others have murdered innocent children."

"This edict is signed," he said, holding it up. "I am also authorized to kill anyone who tries to prevent this edict from being carried out."

"You have been lied to. Ptolemaeus did what he had to in order to save his position and probably his life."

"I am not alone," Zared said, pulling his dagger, hoping to frighten what appeared to be the infant's grandfather.

Melchior laughed and drew his sword. "Don't even think about it. Were we to meet under these circumstances as little as two years ago, by now all three of you would be food for jackals. As it is, one of you is unconscious, fastened to the floor inside; the other is about to learn whether or not there is life after death when he touches that horse he is admiring back there; and you're standing in the street waving parchment in my face that proclaims a lie!

"I won't repeat myself. Place your bloody dagger on the window frame and then call your murdering companion out here before he gets himself killed."

"If I'm unarmed, you'll run me through."

"If I wanted to run you through it wouldn't matter whether you were armed or not. Now call him out here. I'm going to give the three of you one chance to keep on living."

"Zared placed his dagger on the window frame and yelled, 'Arvad, come here.'"

"As Arvad came around the side of the house, he said, 'Zared, you should see the beauti...'"

"Take your dagger out slowly and place it next to your murdering companions on the window frame," Melchior said with the point of his sword against the man's chest.

"Arvad glanced at Zared who nodded. 'Do as he says. He wants to talk.'"

"And you believe him?" Arvad asked.

"Yes."

"Why?"

"Because while you were back there deafly admiring horseflesh, he fastened Uriah to the floor inside and could have killed me but didn't."

"Arvad slowly removed the dagger from his belt and placed it on the sill.

"You two have a choice. You can immediately take your friend inside along with what I suspect is in that bloody bag back to Ptolemaeus and get whatever he promised you, or you can insist on searching this house.

"If you choose the latter, you will enter it, but only to fasten each other's hand to the floor.

"Then, I will leave, but not before placing your bloody daggers next to you and then informing Zapporah that the parents of Bethlehem can find you nailed here to the floor where there is not only a mallet, but a large saw, several awls and oh yes, let us not forget the contents of that bloody, goatskin bag. They will give you a lesson in Jewish scripture – the part about, 'an eye for an eye and a tooth for a tooth.'

"Which will it be?"

"That's no choice," Zared murmured.

"Melchior, with his sword still drawn said as they broke the awl free, 'Hand it to me, blunt end first. You have horses?' he asked.

"Tied to a post just inside the North Gate," Zared replied, as they dragged Uriah, beginning to regain consciousness into the street.

"Those daggers can only get you killed if they're found on you in the city tonight," Melchior said, astride Gabhriel. "Depending upon how important it is for you to get them back you can return for them tomorrow or not."

Zared, after shoving the half-conscious Uriah into Arvad's arms, said, "Will you answer a question?"

"If I can," Melchior answered.

"Is there an infant boy in this house?"

"Like a temple," Melchior said, "it was the domicile of Ahura Mazda!" And he rode off, leaving them as dazed and confused as they were when they first met him.

CHAPTER FORTY-THREE

"Never saw a horse want to go somewhere so bad before."

"He's not in his room," Gaspar said to Balthazar as he rejoined him in the area of the stables where the camels were kept. "Are you sure he didn't say something to you about going out this evening?"

"No. The last thing he said was that he was going to get some sleep and to have the pack grades loaded and the Travelers saddled for a late-night departure. Well, here they are!"

"What is that?" Gaspar asked as he noted a noise in the horse stable.

"Sounds like scraping," Balthazar said.

"They looked at each other for an instant and then ran across the broad expanse which separated the camels and horses, past the water trough and into the stable."

"Doesn't this kid ever sleep?" Gaspar asked, as they watched Kintry cleaning out Gabhriel's stall with a rake.

"Apparently not when there's action around the stable," Balthazar replied.

"What action is there at this hour of night?"

"Gabhriel. She's gone. Where is she, Kintry?" Balthazar asked.

"Melchior took her to Bethlehem."

"When?"

"About an hour ago," Kintry said, as he continued raking the old straw and manure from the stall.

"Did he say why he was going there late at night?" Gaspar asked.

"Said he didn't have time to tell me, but we'd talk about it when he got back."

"Gaspar, with a concerned expression, glanced at Balthazar and then asked, 'Kintry, was Melchior armed? Did he have his sword with him?'"

"That and a sheathed dagger," he replied while placing the rake against the wall and grabbing a broom with which he began sweeping the remaining debris from the stall floor.

"What happened to the stall?" Balthazar asked.

"Gabhriel kicked those boards loose tonight. Just before Melchior came and got her. Never saw a horse want to go somewhere so bad before."

"Kintry," Gaspar said, "I'm going to look for him. Can I take this one?" he asked, pointing to a black gelding next to Gabhriel's stall.

"You won't need to," he said pointing to a large key hanging from a nail on a post above him. "You can use that to open the lock on the gate. That will free the night chain. Then pull the gate bolts and swing them open."

"Kintry, we can't do that until he's here. We don't even know if he's safe!"

"Yes, we do," he said, using a mallet to pound the boards back in place. "I can hear them coming up the road."

"Do you hear anything?" Gaspar asked.

"No," Balthazar said, after listening intently for a moment.

"You will by the time you get the gates open," Kintry said, taking the key off its peg and tossing it to Balthazar.

The two men shrugged and began walking down the long, stone path. When they were halfway to the gate they heard a whinny, and then another, as Melchior approached the gate.

"We're saddled, packed and ready to leave," Gaspar said, as Melchior rode through the gates. Melchior nodded, while continuing to look straight ahead as he rode Gabhriel to the stable. He dismounted and standing with the reins in his hand, sighed as he leaned his forehead against the side of the horse.

After a moment, he said, "Herod took no chances. That wretched son of Ahriman ordered the death tonight of every infant boy in Bethlehem. I feel so responsible," he said, turning to look at them, "if I had not sent you into the city asking questions none of this would have happened."

"You can't blame yourself for the act of a madman," Balthazar said. "We all did what…"

"The only consolation I have is that Joseph got the Child and His mother out of the city in time."

"He's all right? He's safe?" Gaspar asked.

"Yes. For now, anyway. The family is on its way to Egypt."

"Egypt?" Balthazar questioned. "Why Egypt?"

"The border alone is two-thirds the distance between here and Nazareth!" Gaspar exclaimed, remembering his charts. "And after they pass Hebron it's practically all desert, Melchior!"

"How are they traveling?" Balthazar asked.

"Joseph is leading them on the back of their donkey," Melchior replied.

"A small-town carpenter attempting a solitary desert crossing!" Balthazar exclaimed. "And with his wife and her newborn Child on the back of the donkey? What possessed him to try such a thing!'

"He inferred that it was the Will of God, Balthazar."

"Of course!" Gaspar exclaimed, breaking the silence. "Ahura Mazda knew they would have our help!" he exclaimed again.

"That's right," Melchior said, as he moved between them and put his arms around their shoulders. "As it is written, the Lord works in mysterious ways."

"Kintry," Melchior said, "I hate to tell you this, but we're not going to be able to have that talk as I promised. But when I return from Egypt, I'll spend at least a month here. We can then talk and do whatever you want."

"Including rest and recreate, Melchior?"

"Yes, Gaspar, that too," he said, smiling.

"I heard what you said happened in Bethlehem," Kintry said, taking the key from Balthazar. "We can't talk now, anyway. Gabhriel needs a good rubdown after that hard ride. I'll see you when you come back."

Melchior stooped and hugged the child. "You're a fine young man, Kintry," he said, "the Lord doesn't make them any better, son."

Kintry threw his arms around Melchior and said, "You stay safe, you hear? And don't worry about Gabhriel 'cause I'll take good care of her."

"I know you will, Kintry. If there's one thing I won't worry about while I'm gone it's Gabhriel!"

"As they crossed the city limit of Bethlehem Melchior said to Balthazar and Gaspar, 'Gather up Joseph's tools and anything else you see of value and load them on the last pack grade. Then we'll depart for Egypt. At the pace Joseph is moving we should overtake them shortly after they proceed west from Hebron."

"You've brought to light, Satan, something neither I nor anyone I know ever mentioned. The Holy Family could never have successfully traversed the desert between Bethlehem and the livable part of Egypt without food, water, a place to stay protected from the frigid desert night, dry clothing for Jesus plus food and water for their donkey."

"Not to mention the brigands who lay in wait for those individuals who felt forced to travel without the protection of a caravan," Satan replied.

"The account of the Visit of the Magi is told only by St. Matthew and begins and ends with twelve verses in Chapter 2. The flight into Egypt begins with verse 13 and ends with verse 23. Where did Matthew get the material for his narrative?

You will remember, Bruce, that just before his Ascension Jesus told the Apostles to go back to Jerusalem and await the Holy Spirit. For the most part they remained hidden in a large upstairs room as I said earlier because they feared being arrested by the Temple authorities and brought to Pilate for imprisonment if not death.

"A few of them wanted to return to Galilee and resume fishing but Mary convinced them to await the Holy Spirit as Jesus promised. Being locked together in a single large room, to help pass the time Mary told them stories about Jesus as he was growing up. The visit of the Wise Men and the Flight into Egypt were among them. Years later when Matthew wrote his gospel as he did with most events he included them factually without elaboration.

"It is a woman on a donkey. A man walks in front as he leads it."

"Abdul, behind a mound of elevated rocks five miles west of Hebron sat with his three sons watching the sun rise. The rocks were along the way of the caravans as they traveled to Egypt. His interest, however, was not in caravans, but rather solitary travelers who could be waylaid and robbed without the risk of dangerous resistance.

"He was not a young man anymore, and over the past five years had gone gradually blind. Thus, he was thankful that his three sons, Dismas, Amman and Kymar could provide for his needs by working the trade he had taught them.

"Do you see anything out there, Dismas?" he asked his first born, who had the best eyes of the three.

"I can just barely make out someone coming this way," he replied, "but they are still too far away to see clearly. At this distance, however, I would say there are no more than three or perhaps two and an animal."

"They must be traveling very slowly," said Kymar. "I don't see any dust."

"They are," Amman agreed. "I can see them now, and there is no dust at all."

"It is a woman riding on a donkey," Dismas said, "A man walks in front as he leads it."

"No camel?" Abdul asked. "Just a man, a woman and a donkey, Dismas? Does he wander in his step as if he were crazed?"

"No, father. He walks straight, but slowly, with the gait of a man who is very tired. And the woman holds an infant to her breast, her back shielding it from the rising sun."

"Are there any packs or bags hanging from the donkey? Is there a carrying bag strapped to this man?"

"No bags or packs. Except for the woman and her child, the donkey is clean. The man carries a small bag on a strap over his shoulder."

"Father, these people are not worth the trouble of leaving the rocks! And they carry no water! From the looks of them they'll be dead before they travel many more hours in the sun."

"I say we kill the man and the baby and then have some fun with the woman!" Amman exclaimed.

"Agreed," Kymar said. "If they have little or no coin, we can at least get something from them!"

As the two brothers prepared to mount their camels, Dismas shouted, "No!"

When his two younger brothers turned to look at him, Dismas lowered his voice, "No...don't do that."

"Why not?" Amman asked. "What are they to us?"

"Something isn't right about them," Dismas said, with a strange and unwarranted, but powerful feeling of threatening disaster. "I tell you, father, if you let them go, they will not return."

"In the desert there is something to be said for visceral feelings," Abdul said, speaking in the direction of Amman's last words. "How far away are they now?"

"Less than a quarter of a mile, father."

"Yes," agreed Kymar. "Just the right distance for chasing them around a bit before we kill him and take our pleasure with her behind the rocks."

"Let them come half again that distance. If then, there is no reason for your feelings, Dismas, let them go."

"When Dismas did not answer, Abdul asked, 'Dismas, did you hear me?'"

"Yes," he replied, turning to look at his brothers as he pointed in the distance. "There is someone coming behind them, father, at great speed on huge Travelers."

"How many?"

"Two, with a third still off in the distance. Behind him is a string of pack grades."

"How are they dressed, Dismas?"

"Like us, Father," Amman answered. "Were your eyes not scaled you could not tell us apart were we at some distance."

"Amman's eyes appear to be failing, too, father. One of them is a Black!" Kymar said.

"They are armed. One with a sword and the Black has a lance mounted to his saddle – the other a bow on his back," said Dismas.

"They are going to spoil our fun!" Amman complained, as he watched them slow down when they approached the family. "I say we ride down on them while they're busy robbing them. Then, we go after the pack grades!"

"Amman, you will never live to see thirty," Abdul said. "You have no sense of the desert. If you and Kymar had ridden down there instead of chasing this man and his wife, you would have been chased by men with weapons that kill at a distance!"

"But we have the element of surprise. They don't know we're here!"

"Strange," Dismas said, ignoring Amman.

"What is?" Abdul questioned.

"They act as if they know one another, father. They're embracing, as if it is a reunion."

"The one with the bow is standing guard as the Black is offering them water," Kymar said.

"Has he removed the bow?" Abdul asked.

"Yes," Dismas answered. "He has notched an arrow and is aiming at several ravens circling overhead."

"It went right through it!" Kymar exclaimed. "I thought at first, he had missed it! Did you see that, Amman!" he exclaimed again, as Gaspar picked the bird from the ground and wrapped it in a white cloth.

"He hit a raven on the fly?" Abdul asked.

"Yes," Dismas said. "A clean shot, father. Instant death. The bird never knew what happened. Do you still want to ride down on them, Amman?"

"The man with the pack grades has caught up with them," Dismas said, when Amman didn't answer. "He's an older man, father, and the woman is now embracing him. She and the child are going to ride with him," he said, as he watched Gaspar tether the donkey to the trailing pack grade.

"Her husband will ride with the archer," Kymar said.

"The archer is handing the dead raven to the Black, father, as the two of them talk and laugh while looking this way," Amman added.

"Do you think they know we're here?" he asked Dismas.

"We'll know soon enough, Amman," he replied, as they approached.

"When they were abeam the rocks, Balthazar veered toward them and heaved the raven's bloody remains into their midst striking Amman on the side of his head. While listening to the laughter of the Black as he rode back to the group, Dismas, after grimacing at the sight of his brother's blood-spattered face, pointed to the carcass of the dead bird oozing blood at their feet and said, 'There's your answer, Amman,'"

"Satan, so much of what you've said explains why the angel, we suspect was Raphael, told Joseph in his dream to go to Egypt. As Melchior reminded us, 'The Lord works in mysterious ways' meaning Joseph and Mary with their infant son could not have gone much further without water if Melchior, Gaspar and Balthazar had not come along."

"They would not have needed water if two of Abdul's sons had their way."

"Correct me if I am wrong, but you mentioned you had two chances to have Jesus, as a child, killed. Was Abdul and his sons your second chance?"

Satan stiffened his spine, pursed his lips, and clenched his fists before replying. "Yes", he said, just above a whisper. "Yes – yes it was and my last but not because I willed it so."

"Then what happened to cause you to quit trying?"

"You remember how Jesus appeared to me after His resurrection?"

"When He mentioned His Divine Assist?"

"Yes. Immediately following Balthazar's flinging the dead raven, Jesus appeared to me as the risen Christ – the resurrected Messiah."

"But He was still a babe in arms! I exclaimed. How could that be?"

"He wanted to remind me that with God nothing is impossible. Standing on his right side was Raphael, the archangel. He looked at me and again without saying a word let me know that neither I nor any of my demons was to use anyone to approach Jesus or his parents with evil intentions; and that this mandate would be in effect until Jesus entered His public life. Furthermore, if I violated the mandate, it would always end in failure and with each failed attempt my embarrassment would be worse than the last."

"And neither you nor yours ever did, at least as far as scripture states. There are no more satanic incidents with Jesus until your three temptations in the desert which also ended in failure."

"Yes, that happened after His Baptism which was the beginning of His public life. I knew that Jesus was one person with two natures. He received His Divine nature from God the Father and His human nature from His mother, Mary. I thought that if I could strongly appeal to His human nature, I might be able to separate the two. If so, there was a chance I could get him to succumb to at least one temptation, that being the third one. I expected to use the first two temptations to weaken his human nature and then use the allure of all the kingdoms of the world to initiate His fall."

"That was the only time I tempted Jesus directly. All the rest of my temptations involve human beings convincing them to believe directly or indirectly that they had a better idea than that given to them by God. As I said earlier this is the basis of all sin."

"Before we leave Egypt, I would like to know the answers to several more questions. The first is did Balthazar leave the group and return to Abyssinia as he intended?

"Yes.

The second question is did Mary and Joseph travel all the way to Alexandria?"

Yes, with Melchior and Gaspar. They settled there amid the huge population of diasporic Jews who had migrated there. Joseph set up an amply equipped carpentry shop attached to the house he built with material he purchased with the money he earned from the Centurion in Jerusalem and the sale of the gifts of frankincense and myrrh. They put away Balthazar's gift of gold coins for the day when they might return to Israel. That day came two-and-a-half years after their arrival when King Herod died. Once again Raphael came to Joseph in a dream and told him of Herod's death and that he should return to Israel. They made the 350 mile trip to Jerusalem within the protection of caravans.

"Upon arrival in Jerusalem, however, they discovered that Archelaus, the eldest of Herod's living sons was now ruler in Jerusalem and that he was even more of a cruel tyrant than his father. This prompted Joseph and Mary to sign on for the next caravan traveling north to Galilee. There they settled in Nazareth where they renewed friendships. Soon after Jesus twenty-fourth birthday Joseph died and Jesus inherited Joseph's shop. He remained doing carpentry for eight years until His baptism by John the Baptist."

"Finally, Satan, was Abdul's eldest son, Dismas, the same Dismas that was crucified on Jesus' right?"

"Yes. Commonly known even in the Demon World as the thief who stole Heaven, Dismas, who prevented his two brothers from attempting to accost and murder Jesus as well as Mary and Joseph asked to be remembered by Jesus when he entered His kingdom. Jesus forgave him his sins saying that upon his death Dismas would enter Paradise."

"That doesn't appear natural for a life-long thief to do and say. I should think that the reaction of the thief on his left where he taunted

Jesus by saying 'Are You not the Messiah? Save Yourself and us.' was more in line with reality." (Luke. 23:39)

"You are correct, Bruce. It wasn't reality and that which is factual but not truly reality is supernatural. As such, Dismas, who was a master thief and now near death was inspired by the Holy Spirit to seek forgiveness revealing that as long as a human being is able to draw a breath and is sincere, he or she can die repentant thereby placing themselves on the narrow road as they pass into eternity. Dismas' last act and Jesus' reply establishes this as an irrevocable fact that proves to all of God's human creation the certainty of this merciful doctrine.

"Do you have any more questions?"

"No, I replied," after marveling at Satan's perfectly worded forced to be truthful explanation – and once more awed at how powerful a help he could have been to God in dealing with mankind had he remained Lucifer and an angel of truth and light.

"I think we have explored the totality of Mary's second sorrow," I said, "except to remark that the night they departed Bethlehem must have been terrifying as they heard women begging for their child's life along with the weeping and wailing from the murderous carnage that might have become their fate as Melchior told them what was happening only one street away."

"Joseph, of course, had told Mary that Raphael was protecting them; nevertheless, Melchior's armed appearance and promise not to allow the killers to move any further south, relieved much of her anxiety."

"As it must have raised your anger, Satan. Herod's failure to kill Jesus while slaughtering more than two dozen infant boys could not have pleased you."

"I was angry, but not despondent. I still had one more very good chance to kill not only Jesus but Joseph and Mary as well.

"Abdul was a longtime ally of mine on the wide road and he had brought his three sons with him. As they lay waiting, I still had another chance."

"And, of course, thanks to Melchior, Gaspar and Balthazar that attempt also failed."

"Yes, it did, Bruce. It should now be obvious that God used these men for more than a purveyor of gifts as Matthew's gospel states. Perhaps your telling the extent of what really happened will change that.

"In the meantime, Bruce, there is only one player remaining in our account of Herod's abominable failure for whom we have to write finis. We left him in Seleucia as he retired for the night."

"Nathan?" I questioned.

"How is this near unbeliever a player?"

"He provided Melchior with a domicile in which Gaspar and especially Balthazar with his Black skin could remain hidden from Herod. He gave Melchior a fast horse that took him the eight miles from Jerusalem to Bethlehem in time to save Jesus from those seeking His life."

"So, how do we write finis to Nathan?"

"I will tell you."

CHAPTER FORTY-FIVE

"Listen then for the footsteps of the Messiah."

"Kintry opened the gates and then ran along the pathway past the stables. 'Bethel! Bethel!' he called, 'Your father is here! He's come home, Bethel! He's come home!'"

"Bethel, waving her hands and laughing with joy from atop Gabriehl exclaimed, 'Oh, I can't wait to see him, Kintry! Help me down.'"

Hurriedly wrapping Gabriehl's reins around the bronze Star of David atop one of the family tombstones, she said, "Come on! I'll race you!"

"My two angels!" Nathan exclaimed when he saw them running toward him. "How wonderful it is to see you – and such a greeting!" He bent down to catch them in his arms. "It's such a great feeling to be home again! You don't know how much I missed you." He stood, taking each of them in hand and began walking along the pathway.

"Is your mother home?" he asked, moving to the left of the path to allow men leading the camels to pass.

"No," Bethel said. "She's at the shop."

At the end of the pathway Nathan stopped when he saw Gabhriel.

"Did you meet Melchior?" he asked, his voice trailing off.

"Oh, yes," Bethel replied. "Benjamin gave him Gabhriel, just as you said to do, father."

"And he rode her!" Kintry added, with excitement. In the middle of the night, he took her to Bethlehem and back."

"Melchior went to Bethlehem in the middle of the night?" questioned Nathan.

"A terrible thing happened in Bethlehem while you were away, father," Bethel said.

Nathan turned to look at her for a moment, and then looked back at Gabhriel. "She's tethered to your grandmother's tombstone, Bethel."

"Yes Father, I did that hurriedly when Kintry told me you were at the gate.

"…and the ancient Jewish tradition, my son," he remembered his mother telling him as a young boy, "is that when a man sees the horse of a Parthian tethered to a tombstone in Israel – listen then, for the footsteps of the Messiah!'

"Wow! What was that you said about nostalgia – that it will not be denied, wasn't it?"

"Exactly, Bruce. Nathan found himself in a dilemma. His Jewish belief in the coming of the Messiah, but someday in the far distant future was shattered by remembering his mother's telling him the prediction, then the fact that he, himself, had given the horse to the Parthian, that his daughter had tethered the horse to a tombstone in Israel, and finally, that the tombstone was that of his mother who had told him of the prediction!"

"It's referred to as Divine confirmation, Satan. If God wants you to do something, to believe something, or in some way to act as an instrument of His will, He lets you know in a way that removes all doubt."

"Since you seem to be more than a little familiar with this belief can you give me an example of it occurring in your life?"

"Absolutely," I replied. "You will no doubt remember that I was unyielding toward your request to dialogue with me until you said that you had God's permission to do so on the condition that you had to tell the truth – even to being prohibited from making misleading statements or half-truths; and that the consequence for even one violation would be the end of our discussion because your physical appearance would vanish."

"Satan did not respond verbally, but only nodded before saying, "I believe we covered Mary's third sorrow when we discussed the apparent loss of Jesus as a twelve-year-old. The fourth through the seventh sorrows are centered on Jesus' passion and death. Can you tell me what they are?"

"I think so.

The fourth sorrow occurs when Mary meets Jesus, her Son, face to face seeing him dripping blood and weak from the scourging, after which He stumbles and falls while carrying the heavy crossbar strapped to his back on the way to His crucifixion.

The fifth sorrow is the crucifixion as she hears the pounding of the nails in his hands which are bound by rope to the crosspiece before raising it up and attaching it to the vertical after which men drive nails into His feet. Finally, a young Roman soldier lances His heart releasing the last of His blood mingled with water signifying that Jesus gave all He had for the love of His human creation.

Satan stopped me, then, by saying, "I, however, in contrast to Mary's tears was elated. Finally, after more than three years of Jesus' public life my temptations which elicited fear, jealousy, frustration and finally murderous rage from the leadership of His Chosen People brought about His suffering an ultimate painful, humiliating death.

"For the first time I was glad that both Herod and the sons of Abdul had failed, as there is no humiliation but only pity in the death of an infant. At last, I felt it just might be possible to have a better idea than God; for not only His human creation, but those of such He had especially selected – His Chosen People, had committed the ultimate hateful rejection of him, by   committing Deicide, which caused him to slowly gasp away His last breaths as I gloated in glee."

I decided that the best comment I could make was not to respond but to ignore Satan and continue reciting Mary's seven sorrows.

The sixth sorrow is immediately after Jesus, now dead, is taken down from the cross and placed in her arms as she sorrowfully embraces the cold, lifeless body of her Son.

The seventh sorrow takes place when, after Mary's last look at the body of her Son, was to see him lifeless lying on a slab in the tomb. The stone cover is then rolled into place while men, at the High Priest's order, secure it by pounding four foot-long spikes to ensure against his disciples stealing his body and saying that he arose from the dead as he said he would."

"I think your description is sufficient," Satan added, "and thus we need to say nothing more about the sorrow in Mary's life."

"Not wishing to delve further into these last four sorrows, myself, I agreed with Satan by replying, 'It appears we have only to discuss the wedding feast at Cana, her Virginity, the Immaculate Conception and her Assumption."

CHAPTER FORTY-SIX

"Do whatever he tells you."

"Before I reveal heretofore hidden details of the Wedding Feast at Cana I have to take into consideration several things which occurred that will help you to understand more fully just what happened there.

"Remember that as we said earlier, Jesus, unlike any other human being, is one person with two natures. From the time of his conception until He was twelve years old his human nature was dominant. As we alluded to earlier, he had to learn to sit up, to crawl, and to walk, run, eat solid food and speak his parents' language just as any other human baby. He had to learn by instruction, as well as by practice, the art of carpentry. He would have to be instructed in the Torah and other provisions of the Mosaic Law.

"At the age of twelve, as we saw earlier while spending three days in the Temple, Jesus' human nature deferred to His Divine nature. Why Jesus did this we will never know. Some theologians have surmised that He wanted to shake up the stale thinking of the Sanhedrin. Others think much of what he said was to tell the Sanhedrin who in turn would advise the people in Jerusalem that the time of the Messiah was imminent. However, we will never know what was in the mind of God.

"On the return to Nazareth his human nature again became dominant and remained so for the next twenty years."

"That being so, Satan, can you give us the chronology of Jesus? For instance, when exactly was he born?"

"I can, but in truth, much of Jesus' chronology you can figure out for yourself.

6 BC: Jesus is born in Bethlehem of Judea.

6 BC (late): Jesus is taken to Egypt by Joseph and Mary.

4 BC: Herod dies and the Holy Family returns to Nazareth.

6 AD: Jesus, now twelve, spends three days in the Temple.

18 AD: Joseph dies. Jesus is now twenty-four.

26 AD: Jesus, now thirty-two, is baptized by John the Baptist.

30 AD: Jesus is crucified and rises from the dead at age thirty-five.

"The kingpin for these dates is the death of King Herod, which as I said ancient Jewish, as well as credible Roman historians state, was translated from the Jewish year which we know as 4 BC – the year of a lunar eclipse; however, I mention this only to support what I observed firsthand.

"The apostle, John, who attended the wedding, wrote about it in his gospel. Of course, like most of John's writings he tells about it as succinctly as possible. If you wish me to tell you about it I can, but if you want the details of the full narrative, it will be necessary to begin several months before it happened. Before we do that, however, let's see how John tells it.

A reading from the holy Gospel according to John. There was a wedding in Cana in Galilee, and the mother of Jesus was there.

Jesus and his disciples were also invited to the wedding. When the wine ran short, the mother of Jesus said to him, "They have no wine."

And Jesus said to her, "Woman, how does your concern affect me? My hour has not yet come?"

His mother said to the servers, "Do whatever he tells you."

Now there were six stone water jars there for Jewish ceremonial washings, each holding twenty to thirty gallons. Jesus told them, "Fill the jars with water."

So, they filled them to the brim. Then he told them, "Draw some out now and take it to the headwaiter."

So, they took it. And when the headwaiter tasted the water that had become wine, without knowing from where it came (although the servants who had drawn the water knew), the headwaiter called the bridegroom and said to him, "Everyone serves good wine first, and then when people have drunk freely, an inferior one; but you have kept the good wine until now."

Jesus did this at the beginning of his signs in Cana in Galilee and so revealed his glory, and his disciples began to believe in him. (John 2: 1-11)

"Now, Bruce, since you asked here are the details. A year before his baptism Jesus began spending several days a week fasting while meditating in the desert. Mary knew that this behavior was a prelude to her Son leaving home to begin living the life for which he had been born.

"She was familiar with the prophecies concerning the Messiah and the miracles cited by Isaiah that would accompany his teaching the way of the New Covenant; and was sure that when Jesus commenced His public life His carpentry shop would grow silent as the oscillating rasp of his saw slicing through wood and the striking of his hammer driving home nails or pegs would no longer be a familiar part of her life.

"As a widow Mary had several close friends who had also lost their husbands. One day one of them, Esther, with whom Mary was particularly close, told her that her only son was to be married in Cana. Her friend was overjoyed because, as she told Mary, his betrothed was a girl she admired who would be a good wife to her son and with him would give her grandchildren to gladden her as she grew older. After telling her the date Esther invited Mary, her son and any of His friends to attend the wedding.

"Shortly thereafter Jesus was baptized by his cousin, John, known as the Baptist, in the river Jordan; then, after informing his mother, Jesus went off into the desert for forty days to commune with God the Father and the Holy Spirit concerning what He was going to do over the next three-and-a-half years.

"After the end of His desert retreat and handily overcoming my three temptations Jesus went about choosing five of what would eventually be his twelve Apostles: namely Simon (whose name Jesus would later change to Peter), John, Phillip, Nathaniel, and Simon's brother, Andrew. That night, at Jesus' invitation, they remained with him at his house. Mary, who had gone to Cana to help her friend with wedding preparations, was not with them. They listened as Jesus, speaking with knowledge and authority, told them that the Jewish Covenant with Abraham was about to be amended and that He, Jesus, would amend it – so much so that in time the amended covenant would be considered a New Covenant.

"Simon, shocked and scandalized, asked Jesus what gave him the authority to do this.

"Jesus answered by giving Simon the only answer he might accept, that is, he quoted scripture," 'Then will the eyes of the blind be opened and the ears of the deaf unstopped; then will the lame leap like a deer, and the mute tongue shout for joy...' (Isaiah 35:5-6).

"Simon, speechless, glanced at the others for their reaction. When, Andrew shrugged his shoulders but said nothing, Simon replied, 'Jesus I will admit that I was astonished when at your command we lowered our nets to a catch that stressed our nets, but I have to ask did you just say that you have the power to give sight to the blind, hearing to the deaf, and strength to the crippled allowing them to walk?'

"If you agree to follow me, you will see these and assuredly more," Jesus replied, as he stood and immediately retired for the night.

"The next morning Jesus prepared a morning meal for them consisting of dates, hard boiled eggs and goat's milk. When they had cleaned and cleared the scullery Jesus said, 'My mother and I have been invited to a wedding in Cana. The mother of the groom invited not only me but any friends I might want to bring. So, Jesus said smiling, you have a choice whether to spend the next few days fishing – or you can choose eating, drinking and dancing to celebrate a young couple's marital union.'

"Peter turned to look at his four companions and noted that they all nodded while Andrew said jokingly, 'Simon, I don't have to tell you that fishing hasn't been that good lately; probably because the lake needs a rest.'

"Simon replied, 'That could very well be true, Andrew. Jesus, how soon do we depart for Cana?'

"Bruce, the distance from Nazareth to Cana is about four miles – a little more than an hour to traverse on foot. Despite Simon's and Andrew's light heartedness, however, during the walk the men asked questions about the wedding in an effort to avoid having to discuss miracles of healing, the power Jesus claimed to have the previous evening.

"Shortly before they arrived, however, Mary, Jesus' mother, noticed that the waiters were not as generous with the wine. Earlier they were filling empty cups and goblets without being asked, but now guests had to call a waiter over and even then, their container was only half filled. Mary excused herself from the table at which she was talking with her friends, and asked Esther if there was a problem."

"We tried to tell him, Mary – my son, I mean, that he was ordering far too much food and not enough wine; but he wouldn't listen. The Head Waiter agreed with me, but Nathan, my son, has never been a wine lover and just didn't have the experience to know how much wine is enjoyed by just about everyone else. Most of the money we had saved for food and drink he spent on food – what was left I spent for wine. We are now in the third day of a seven-day celebration. Mary, in just a few hours we'll have no more wine. What am I going to do? If my son has to tell our guests that there is no more wine the remembrance of his embarrassment will shame my son and daughter-in-law every time one of our guests sees them together."

"Mary, feeling a sense of empathy, reached out and hugged her friend who immediately broke out in tears. 'What can I do, Mary? What can I do?'

"I'm afraid not much, Esther" Mary replied, "but perhaps I can," she added, as she noticed Jesus arriving with His friends.

"WHAT IS THIS?" Mary heard Simon shout, obviously upset, as the servant stopped pouring when his cup was less than half full.

"I am sorry, sir," the servant said, "but I am only doing what I have been ordered to do."

"After gulping down the wine in his cup, Simon turned to Jesus and said, 'Maybe to go fishing would have been the better choice.'

"When Jesus finished the paltry amount of wine in His cup, their eyes met. Mary, his mother, looked at him pleadingly and while lightly shaking her head said simply, 'They have no wine.'

"Jesus answered, 'Woman, what is that to you and to me?'

"When His mother didn't answer, Jesus took her aside and said to her defensively in a voice that was just above a whisper, 'My time has not yet come.'

"Before replying Mary envisioned the silent, darkened carpenter shop, her nephew, John, baptizing Jesus; His going into the desert for forty days and nights and finally the friends He had brought to the wedding. 'Who are these men?' she asked.

"Before Jesus could answer, Simon, who had overheard her question, replied, 'I guess you could call us his disciples.'

"Without saying any more Mary pointed in quick succession to four of the servants and motioned for them to come forward. As they stood before her wondering what Mary had in mind she pointed to Jesus, and directed them to 'Do whatever he tells you.'"

"What would you have us do?" one of them asked.

"Jesus pointed to the six purification vessels along the entrance wall. Each of them held thirty gallons. Guests would dip water from them to remove the dust from their feet and sandals before entering the main room. 'Fill each of them to the brim with water,' he said in a voice that was spoken in a manner to overcome any questions or objections they might have.

"As they were doing as Jesus told them, Simon said to his companions, 'What do you suppose he's thinking about? Look at this crowd. It is apparent that many, if not most of the guests have already arrived. What is needed here is more wine – not more purification water!'

"Philip shook his head and said, 'It appears he thinks to solve the problem by watering down what little wine they have remaining.'

"And when that is gone serve them water!" Nathaniel added.

"As the jars were being filled Jesus overheard their remarks but did not respond. When the jars were filled to overflowing Jesus turned to look at Simon for a second before raising His hands and eyes to the heavens after which he paused before handing a ladle to one of the four men while telling him, 'Dip this into one of the jars and take it to the Head Waiter,'

"The servant knowing full well the short temper of the Head Waiter hesitated and looked questioningly at Jesus as if he were wondering why Jesus and his mother would play such a cruel joke. Before he could speak, however, Jesus pointed to the jars, nodded, and while giving the servant holding the ladle a reassuring smile said in a confident but mild manner, 'Just do it!'

"The moment the servant dipped the ladle two things happened. First, the water turned wine-red giving off the bouquet of an exquisite vintage wine; and secondly, Mary returned to the company of her friends. After taking her seat as one of the four waiters, she pointed to, begins filling her cup to the brim she says, 'Well, now, what were we talking about?'

"The Head Waiter, Bruce, was sitting a short distance from the bridegroom. He was both perplexed and embarrassed as he had shortly before given the order to extend the now meager wine supply by pouring just under ½ cup to the guests. The bridegroom, with most of his original cup still on the table before him, was oblivious to the problem.

"As The Head Waiter was wondering what to do next the servant appeared at his side with the ladle of wine. 'What is this?' he asked.

"I was told to bring it to the Head Waiter," the servant replied.

"Now the Head Waiter, Bruce, thought of himself as a connoisseur of fine wines, and in fact, he was. After savoring a taste, he knew this had to be among the finest if not the finest vintage wine he had ever tasted. Turning to the bridegroom who was now headed to where people were dancing, he said in a loud voice over the music, 'Most bridegrooms serve the best wine first; and then when the guests have drunk freely serve a lesser vintage; but you have saved the best wine until now.'

"The bridegroom, having no idea what the headwaiter was talking about replied by waving both hands in the air and shouting, 'Enjoy! Enjoy!' and then began singing and dancing with his bride.

"Simon, along with his companions, looked at Jesus who simply nodded as if to give credence to what they were thinking. Then, after they accepted and tasted some of Jesus' wine, Simon said to his companions, 'Fifteen years ago I was in Jerusalem for Passover. At that time I heard a member of the Sanhedrin speak. I was told he was known as Joseph of Arimathea, a most learned and respected member. He talked about a combined prophecy from Daniel (9:24-27) and Isaiah (45:1-3) which pointed toward the Messiah appearing in the year 4073 (26 AD).'"

"That's this year," Phillip said. "Simon, do you think it's possible that Jesus could be the Messiah?"

"Take another drink from your cup, Phillip. Have you ever tasted better wine? And who do we know that could change 180 gallons of water into any wine let alone a vintage that would ordinarily be served only at the tables of the very rich?"

"We have been blessed by Jehovah," said John, the youngest member of their group. "Not only do we know Who the Messiah is, but He has asked us to follow him!"

Satan finished his narrative by saying, "And those, Bruce, are the details that were omitted in scripture concerning the wedding feast at Cana."

CHAPTER FORTY-SEVEN

"Mary underwent several lengthy and dangerous journeys."

"Satan," I responded, "after two thousand years to remember all that detail is mind boggling, but I have a few questions."

"You usually do, Satan replied.

"After Jesus told Mary it was not his time, why did he then do as she asked?"

"Other than sociopaths or a person abandoned by his mother in childhood can you think of any of your fellow human beings who would refuse a request from his mother?"

"You have a point. Furthermore, that feeling, rooted in both love and benevolent obligation, never recedes or goes away."

"Which means…?"

"Which means that feeling is still there," I replied. "The powerful intercession of Mary as the mother of Jesus, Almighty God Incarnate, is a longstanding belief among Catholics, but some Christian churches made it a point of the Reformation to abandon the relationship between Mary and Jesus. Some have proclaimed that to ask for Mary's intercession with Jesus is idolatry – that is, such a practice is akin to worshiping Mary; however, as we said earlier, when God wants to convey a message to humanity, he sends his mother. Truthful Marian apparitions, their legitimacy verified by substantiated miracles, agreed upon by believers and non-believers alike, should prove to anyone who has an open mind that Mary's status with God is exceptional."

"However, much to their disadvantage," Satan replied, "I can tell you that most of them think of Mary as a necessary role player in the birth of Jesus as a human being, but then like the core of an apple they've eaten they toss her aside as having no further use. Some even refuse to honor her as The Mother of God. They are in error, of course as they celebrate God's birth as a human being at Christmas but refuse to honor the motherhood of the woman who conceived, bore and birthed him – something which they would not deny any other biological mother."

Satan then hesitated as if he were not sure he should continue. After a rather long pause I said, "It appeared for a moment, there, that you wanted to say more."

"Bruce, you know that I stood before God and declared that I could never love his human creation. He granted me this; but God allowed me the feeling of respect. However, it isn't often that a human being engenders that emotion. I told you about Jonathan, the young member of the Sanhedrin, and now – well…these people are fond of saying that God cannot be out done in generosity, but in the case of Mary they do not believe nor practice what they preach. Mary of Nazareth gave all she had in conceiving, bearing, birthing and raising the Messiah even to accompanying Jesus on his way to the cross.

"As we discussed earlier Mary underwent several lengthy and dangerous journeys under primitive conditions – one of them to save His life. She held the Apostles together following Jesus' Ascension when some of them thought to go back to their prior life rather than wait for the Holy Spirit. She agreed to become pregnant without a husband when to do so could very easily have gotten her stoned to death.

"She never lost faith even when Joseph, her betrothed, intended to abandon her and her Child. Returning from Egypt she went back to Nazareth knowing that there were most likely some women there who would treat her with disdain because of what they thought was her sinful, extra marital pregnancy.

"Don't get me wrong, Bruce. I hate Mary even more than I hate other human beings; but as I said before, not for who she is, but for what she can accomplish through her intercession – an intercession based upon Mary being in every sense of the word the mother of Jesus Christ Incarnate, the Second Person of the Blessed Trinity: and as much as I hate her I respect her more than I do any other human being that has or will ever live."

"Why is that?" I asked.

"I cannot tell you the number of souls I had groomed for eternal damnation that shortly before taking his or her last breath, Mary, intercedes by answering the prayers of relatives and friends as she asks Jesus, her Son, a final time for the grace to have the dying man or woman ask themselves, 'What if...' and then by the grace of God they see clearly the evil they have done; and suddenly overcome with shame, sorrow and remorse they repent, and this contrition, like the Good Thief, saves them in their last minute from my fiery abyss."

"In other words, would a person rather plead a defendant's case directly to the judge or have the judge's mother do it for him."

"Not exactly, Bruce, but close enough. Perhaps a living example might help.

"When you felt that I was about to harvest two young men for my hellish abode your first thought was to ask Mary to use her power of intercession with Jesus to preclude me from doing so. Mary did and as my demon, Humilione, said '...things started off well, but then as everything fell apart, I felt like somebody entered the game with a stacked deck.'"

"That example is classic, Satan. Like a well-played chess game every move resulted in extricating Carl and Jeremy just a little further from your grasp until you admitted to Humilione, you had been defeated. I would have to assume that All Heaven rejoiced at that one."

"As well they should, Bruce, as Heaven wins so few these days."

"Satan, your defense of Mary would be commendable—even admirable—if it weren't due to the position you boxed yourself in as a condition of speaking with me. What you just said goes against every-thing you stand for. Much, if not all of the anti-Marian belief and its derived behavior is of your doing. Your desire to convince human beings to abandon God and everything He has done to ensure their salvation in favor of pursuing their destruction along the wide road of immoral, worldly and sinful behavior dictates that it could not be otherwise. As much as I admire your intelligence, I have to admit that it is offset by your despicable intent to bring God's creation of humanity to eternal damnation."

"Your insight, Bruce, is exceeded only by your ability to express it. You are correct, of course, but as we have stated before, God has not abandoned his human creation to my superior intelligence and talent for evil persuasion."

"Other than The Great Equalizer, Satan, what else, I mean specifi-cally what else, can you identify in this regard?"

"Listen, Bruce McPherson, so that you will get this right the first time, for I cannot bear to repeat it. THERE IS NOT A SINGLE PERSON – NOT EVEN ONE OF YOU THAT HAD A FERVENT DEVOTION TO MARY ALTHOUGH STRAYING FROM THE NARROW PATH FROM TIME TO TIME THAT IS IN HELL. I REPEAT, BRUCE, NOT EVEN ONE IN TWO THOUSAND YEARS: and if I were made from flesh and blood my condition would be apoplectic after revealing the truth of Mary to that extent."

"You are referring to being divinely given the grace of final repen-tance. Am I right?"

"Not solely. A life led sincerely honoring Mary as the chosen woman to be the mother of Jesus Christ, the Son of God, is by definition lived on the narrow road, and that is all I choose to say about it."

After a period of silence between us Satan said, "If we are ever go-ing to take our time travel, we must fulfill my obligation to complete our discussion of Mary.

"Three things remain," Satan replied. "Her Immaculate Conception, her Assumption and her virginity. In your junior year at Villanova your second semester religion class was dedicated to the study of the Holy Spirit and then Mary of Nazareth. During the study of Mary, you wrote a dissertation on her Immaculate Conception. It was brilliantly written and you received an A+ for a grade. It is in that folder of yours and unless you want to change something we can use it as written in order to fulfill my obligation. I will then discuss Mary's Assumption since it requires a visual presence. If you wish you can discuss Mary's virginity. Now retrieve your dissertation on the Immaculate Conception and read it to me, to see if after all these years there is anything in it you want to change."

The Immaculate Conception

THE IMMACULATE CONCEPTION OF MARY OF NAZARETH – THE MOTHER OF JESUS CHRIST WHO IS ALMIGHTY GOD IN THE FLESH

In order to appreciate Mary's Immaculate Conception, we have to first define what it is. Adam and Eve were the first human beings; both defined and reported to be the original personage created in the Image and Likeness of God. (Genesis 1:26-28) There are multiple beliefs in how mankind came into being, and it is true that we are free to believe what we want to in this regard as far as the creation or evolution of the human body is concerned; but whether God created man separately from His other creation or man's body evolved over billions of years his soul did not. The simple reason is that the human soul or life force is an immortal, spiritual entity and such entities unlike physical entities have no tangible matter capable of being acted upon and reacting to the forces of nature which is necessary for evolution to occur.

So, it is imperative then that at some point in time God raised two creatures, male and female, to His own Image and Likeness by endowing each of them with an immortal soul: and unlike the souls of all other creatures who are not human, man's soul is endowed with intelligence fortified with a free will. No other earthly creature can conjure up plans of future action; can imagine things that do not exist in reality, can think in the abstract, choose to do good or evil, utilize the mineral and vegetation of the earth to manufacture goods or by farming feed himself, employ imagination to invent and then build objects to enhance life, etc.

However, all this being true, the principal reason man can be said to be made in the Image and Likeness of God is that the soul of every human person is immortal. Like God, its creator, man's soul will live forever. Unlike God, however, Who is eternal, the human soul, from the moment of conception, has a beginning but God does not – a major distinction which differentiates the Creator from the immortal human soul He created.

Our first parents, however, in some way committed sin. Whether it was over eating a forbidden fruit or some other transgression, they misused their gift of free will to disobey a command of God; and just as their refusal to do so would have been reflected in the good we would have inherited, God willed that the consequences of their offense should be visited on every ordinary human conceived of woman in the form of a defect known as Original Sin. As God is all just, however, because we inherited this spiritual stain through no personal fault of our own, He has given us a way to erase this blemish by being baptized.

In the Old Testament, however, there is no provision for Baptism until John, a cousin of Jesus, began baptizing people in the Jordan river. By this time Jesus, by some years, is a full-grown man and elects to be baptized by John, not for the expunging of original sin which as God He doesn't have, but to enforce the credibility of John as the forerunner of the Messiah, "The voice of one crying in the wilderness: Prepare ye the way of the Lord; make straight His paths." (Isaiah 40:3)

This is exemplified by the fact that after His baptism the Holy Spirit hovered over Jesus in the form of a dove; as the voice of God the Father declared, "This is my beloved Son in Whom I am well pleased." (Matthew 3:17)

Having said all of the above we can perceive that God would want the woman whom He had chosen to be His mother, that is, to become pregnant with the Son of God not by a man but by the Holy Spirit to be without blemish – to be free from sin of any kind. Thus, God created her soul free from Original Sin at the moment she was conceived by her parents – in effect an Immaculate Conception.

Now beginning with Mary's appearance in Guadalupe, Mexico in the sixteenth century when Jesus wishes to speak directly to us, that is, to reveal a divine truth that otherwise couldn't be known He does so by a message imparted by an appearance of Mary, His mother. We can thus infer that His will was to confirm the truth of His mother's Immaculate Conception by what Mary said and/or did during the following two apparitions, the truth of which are confirmed by accompanying miracles, two of which are ongoing.

Sister Catherine Laboure (May 2, 1806 – December 31, 1876)

On July 18, 1830, Sister Catherine Laboure, a twenty-four-year-old member of the Daughters of Charity, a nursing order founded by St. Vincent de Paul, while asleep in the Parisian convent of the Order, was awakened in the middle of the night by the urgings of a young child bathed in a bright light. "Sister Laboure," the child said in a pleading voice, "Come to the chapel. The Blessed Virgin awaits you."

Familiar with the rule which forbade roaming about the convent at night Sister Laboure responded, "We shall be discovered."

The child smiled at her and replied, "Do not be uneasy. It is half past eleven. Everyone is sleeping. Come I am waiting for you."

Sister, still in her flannel nightgown, donned her slippers and followed the child to the chapel which she knew was always locked at night. Even more confusing was that the gas lights in the passageway, which she knew had been extinguished, were now all ablaze.

As she and the child approached the chapel's closed door, she was now fully awake and realized that what was happening was not a dream but reality. Just to be sure she reached out to her right and touched the wall. When they reached the chapel entrance the child still bathed in bright light touched the door. Sister heard the lock release just before it swung open of its own accord.

She was shocked by what she saw. Every lamp in the chapel was lit to its highest intensity – an illumination level that was sanctioned only once a year – for Christmas midnight Mass!

Not knowing what to do she moved toward the main altar and knelt down at the communion rail. Within a few moments, she saw a beautiful woman appear sitting in the ornate, high-backed chair reserved for the priest celebrating Mass. The child, whom Sister now knew must be an angel, stood at her side and whispered, "The Blessed Mother wishes to speak with you," and motioned for her to go to her.

The gates of the communion rail were open so she approached the woman, whom she was told was the Blessed Mother. Standing before her right side she knelt down and placed her folded hands on Mary's lap.

"God wishes to charge you with a mission," Mary began. "You will be contradicted, but do not fear; for you will have the grace to do what is necessary.

"Tell your spiritual director all that passes within you. Times are evil in France and in the world."

"The next day as she told her spiritual director what happened; she said Mary then hesitated as a painful expression crossed her face. After a long moment Mary said, 'Come to the foot of the altar. Graces will be shed on all, great and little, especially on those who ask for them. You will have the protection of God and I will always have my eyes on you. There will be much persecution. The cross will be treated with contempt. It will be hurled to the ground and blood will flow.'

"It seemed that Mary went on to tell her much more, but being so tired either she fell asleep or couldn't remember what she said. Then like a fading light, Mary was gone. Led by the child-like angel, Sister Catherine departed the chapel and returned to her place in the dormitory.

Sister Catherine's spiritual adviser, a priest, knew that some forty years before the Church had been persecuted as a result of the French Revolution. If what Sister Catherine said was true, he knew that Mary was referring to the monasteries and convents, as well as other ecclesiastical properties that had been confiscated and the monks and nuns turned out into the street. Senior members of the church hierarchy in addition to thousands of wealthy citizens, the latter, after having had their wealth appropriated by the state, were then publicly guillotined.

"In 1801, however, Napoleon Bonaparte, signed the Concordat with Pope Pius VII which restored basic rights and freedom to the Church; but twenty-nine years later (1830) much of what the Church had lost was not recovered; and even then, there were miscreants who delighted in committing malicious acts against priests and nuns as well as desecrating statues, tabernacles, the crucifix and other objects used in the Mass and other worship services within Catholic churches.

"Marian apparitions are treated with great skepticism by the Church Hierarchy. As the vast majority are fraudulent the asserted seer is looked upon with disbelief; they create extra administrative work and are generally disruptive of everyday activity in the chancery office of the local bishop. Sister Catherine in obedience to Mary told no one except her spiritual advisor (who was also her confessor) what had transpired, and in turn he kept it a secret. Sister Catherine had told him Mary said that God was charging her with a mission. The priest knew, and rightfully so, that if Sister Catherine was telling the truth she would witness another apparition in which the mission would be revealed.

Sister Catherine continued to live as a simple, prayerful, nursing nun. She couldn't forget that night in July and how she had been favored to see and listen to Mary, the Blessed Mother of God. She wished she could recall everything Mary had told her, but despite praying for it to be revealed nothing came to her.

Then a little more than four months later on Saturday, November 27th at 5:30PM, Sister Catherine along with the other nuns attended chapel for scheduled evening meditation. As she was praying she heard what sounded like the rustle of a woman's dress. Looking up she saw Mary standing on a globe of the earth above the main altar. She was surrounded by an oval frame. Within the circumference of the frame, beginning with the location of Mary's right foot and proceeding up, over, and down to just above her left foot, were inscribed, "Ô MARIE CONÇUE SANS

PÉCHÉ, PRIEZ POUR NOUS QUI AVONS RECOURS À TOI." ("O MARY CONCEIVED WITHOUT SIN, PRAY FOR US WHO HAVE RECOURSE TO THEE.")

Sister Catherine experienced awe, fear, confusion, and a sense of jubilation. None of her associates showed any sign that they were seeing what she was witnessing. After a moment the oval along with Mary began to revolve until it displayed its reverse side. Surrounded by twelve stars was the block letter "M" with a horizontal bar through the top of the letter on which a cross was mounted. Below the letter were two hearts with flames rising from the top of the hearts. The heart of Jesus on the oval's right was encircled with a crown of thorns. Mary's heart on its left was pierced with a sword confirming Simeon's prophecy in the Temple concerning the sorrows she would experience in her life.

As it finished revolving Mary again came into view; however, the palms of her hands were face up and pointing down at the globe. Both bright and dark rays were emanating from her hands. The bright rays touched and bathed the globe of the earth in light. The dark rays stopped short of touching the globe. Mary explained to her that the bright rays represented grace and help for which people had prayed. The dark rays that stopped short of the earth were those available but for which people never asked.

Mary then revealed her apparition to Sister Catherine. "What you have seen is the front and reverse of a medallion I want you to have struck and made available to all who wish to wear it around their neck signifying the wearer's love and allegiance to Jesus for his passion, death and resurrection by which he opened for them a pathway for their salvation.

"Secondly, as one who in life trod the same narrow earthly path that is often strewn with thorns and frequently takes place within a vale of tears, Jesus knows that I understand human pain, disappointment and frustration. For this reason, to wear the medallion displays a belief that as his mother, if you request my power of intercession on your behalf Jesus will look favorably upon your request if it will not impede your salvation, will not bring harm to another and is in accordance with the will of His heavenly Father."

Sister Catherine's spiritual advisor kept her under close supervision for the next two years. Having observed nothing that would seem to indicate that she was anything but honest he reported the apparition to the local bishop as church law dictates; but at Sister Catherine's request did not reveal her as the visionary.

In 1832 the Church approved the medal and it was struck and distributed in Paris. It proved to be very popular as people began reporting their prayers being answered – some of a miraculous nature; so much so that it was commonly referred to as The Miraculous Medal, a name by which it is still known even today almost two hundred years later.

In 1876, now age seventy, Sister Catherine was told by Mary to reveal to her Superiors that she was the visionary for the Miraculous Medal in which Mary revealed her Immaculate Conception and her power of intercession. She did and then died passing on to her eternal reward on the last day of 1876.

In 1933 her body was exhumed as part of the canonization process. She had been buried for fifty-seven years. The report follows:

"Today her beautiful remains still lie fresh and serene. When her body was exhumed in 1933, it was found as fresh as the day it was buried. Though she had lived seventy years and was in the grave for fifty-seven years, her eyes remained very blue and beautiful; and in death her arms and legs were as supple as if she were asleep. Her incorrupt body is encased in glass beneath the side altar at 140 Rue du Bac, Paris, beneath one of the spots where Our Lady appeared to her."

In the Chapel of the Apparition, you can gaze upon the face and the lips that for forty-six years kept a secret which has since shaken the world. The bottom line of course is that Mary, known as The Blessed Mother of Jesus Christ, Almighty God Incarnated, personally confirmed her Immaculate Conception and power of her prayerful intercession with a medallion in an approved apparition to a simple, pious nursing nun whose name is St. Catherine Laboure.

Twenty-four years after Mary's first appearance to Sister Catherine Pope Pius IX on December 8, 1854, in a Papal Bull known as Ineffabilis Deus (Indescribable God) formally promulgated the dogma of the Immaculate Conception."

CHAPTER FORTY-NINE

Bernadette Soubirous and Lourdes – Heaven's Affirmation

Four years later in 1858 Mary again made a series of apparitions to a very young and relatively uneducated fourteen-year-old peasant girl, Bernadette Soubirous, in Lourdes, France. As is common her parish priest thought this young girl was either lying for the purpose of attracting attention to herself or hallucinating and dismissed her. The town officials, many being atheists, attempted to silence her without success. Finally, after reporting the Lady's fifteenth apparition Bernadette's parish priest told her that if she appears again to ask the lady her name. "If she tells you," he said, "come and tell me what she says."

On March 25, 1858, almost four years after Pius IX had promulgated the dogma of Mary's Immaculate Conception, the Lady, as Bernadette described her, appeared to Bernadette for the sixteenth time. Remembering what her priest had told her Bernadette asked the Lady her name. The Lady replied, "Que soy era Immaculada Counceptiou." ("I am the Immaculate Conception.")

Bernadette returned to the priest's rectory and knocked. The housekeeper let her in and when Bernadette said that she came to see the priest as he told her to do, the housekeeper went to get the priest. When he saw Bernadette he asked, "I presume that you are here to tell me the Lady's name?"

"I'm not sure," Bernadette replied.

"What do you mean?" the priest asked. "Did she tell you her name or didn't she?"

"She used words I never heard before and therefore did not understand. In truth, Father, I don't know whether what she said was her name or not."

The priest becoming exasperated said, "Bernadette, just tell me what she said."

"Father, when I asked her to tell me her name, she replied, "I am the Immaculate Conception."

The priest, taken aback and in near shock, knew that this fourteen-year-old girl with less than a fourth-grade education could not be familiar with these words let alone understand their meaning. What's more she admitted so without any attempt at guile or deceit. The next morning after saying Mass he went to see the bishop.

Several years later Bernadette became a nun. She developed what was diagnosed as tuberculosis in a leg bone and died at age thirty-five. Thirty years later, as part of the canonization process, like Sister Catherine, her body was exhumed and found to be perfectly preserved (incorrupt). Today, the unembalmed body of St. Bernadette, still incorrupt, lies under glass in the main chapel of the convent of St. Gildard in Nevers, France. A constant stream of pilgrims visits her resting place.

It is evident that God wanted to elevate the stature of Mary, his mother, by having her reveal and confirm her Immaculate Conception as well as her power as our intercessory. He did this through Sister Catherine Laboure. Likewise, he confirmed this truth only a few years later through a second declaration by his mother to Bernadette Soubirous, a simple, peasant girl. He confirmed it a third time by the miracle of divinely obstructing the natural corruptive process of these two women after their deaths.

The Church Celebrates The Feast of the Immaculate Conception each year on December 8th, as a Holyday of Obligation – the Highest Ranking for a Feast Day – on a par with All Saints Day (November 1st) and Christmas (December 25th).

Respectfully submitted,
Bruce McPherson
April 30, 2003

"When I had finished reading Satan asked, 'Are you still satisfied with it? Is there something you might want to add or perhaps delete?'"

"No," I replied. "Until now, the only time I looked at it after it was returned to me with my grade was the following year during semester break. I had elected to remain at the university as the Philadelphia Archdiocese held a three-day conference at Villanova. In addition, several religious orders had scheduled three-day retreats, and I could earn some money toward my room and board by working in the student union kitchen."

"You want to elaborate on that? For instance, what use is a male college student in a kitchen?"

"I attended the University on a scholarship that covered everything except my room and board. Beginning in the second semester of my freshman year, each week I worked twenty to thirty hours in the kitchen to cover that.

"One evening after the kitchen had been secured, I spent the evening in my room toying with an addendum for my treatise on the Immaculate Conception; but I never did anything with it."

"You mean you discarded it?"

"No. I folded it in half and stuck it in the pocket on the inside of the back cover of the binder."

"I would be interested to read what you wrote."

"Interested, maybe, but you won't like it."

"We've no need to keep bantering back and forth. Unless you have a strong objection get it out and let's see what it says."

WHY WEAR THE MIRACULOUS MEDAL

If after reading Mary's revelations in which she establishes her Miraculous Medal to proclaim the truth of her Immaculate Conception as well as her potential for intercession due to her being the mother of Jesus, the Incarnate Son of God, you might wonder if there is a reason why you might want to wear the miraculous medal.

Many people incorrectly assume the medal is worn only by Catholics. While it is a very popular sacramental for Catholics, it can also be worn by anyone. Here are a few reasons for wearing the miraculous medal.

If you are privileged to be a believing, practicing Christian, it is a daily reminder of your gratitude to Jesus for his passion, death and resurrection which as Mary told Sister Catherine opened the pathway which if followed, leads to eternal salvation. Since it is used to show the connection between the Blessed Mother and an individual seeking her loving intercession, it is a good way to remind yourself to honor that special grace every day. It is also a way to remember how your religious beliefs influence the way you live your life.

Although it is a famous symbol beloved around the world, you should choose a medallion based on what holds significance for you, not what is popular. That being said, however, this symbol is recognized the world over so it is an easy way to show the world your religious conviction without ever speaking a word.

It is also a reminder to ask for help. The darkened rays coming from Mary's hands did not then and do not now reach our earthly planet. Those dark rays, Mary said, symbolize the available graces of which many people are not aware, or for which they forget or refuse to ask.

The miraculous medal, then, is a reminder that every day we need to ask for Divine assistance; especially those of us who think we don't need it. It is not until after a person places themself in the loving hands of God to be used as an instrument of His divine will that he or she realizes that before they did that they didn't know and didn't know that they didn't know the reason for their existence.

When the nun, Catherine Labouré, had her vision of the Virgin Mary, she reported that Mary told her to create these medallions because, "All who wear them will receive great graces." Notice that Mary did not restrict the use of her medallion but rather by saying "All" indicated it was for anyone who wears it with the right disposition. This belief is the leading reason why many people choose to wear the miraculous medal.

It might help to picture Jesus standing slightly behind your right side with his left hand on your shoulder, as you pray at least once each day, "IF YOU, LORD, ARE WITH ME THEN WHO CAN BE AGAINST ME?"

When Satan finished reading my addendum, he remained silent as he set the paper aside and sat there staring at the floor.

"I said you wouldn't like it."

"Did I say that I didn't like it?" Frankly," he added, now looking up at me, "it proves what I've been telling you all along; that is, with rare exception when it comes to what really matters – their eternal salvation – human beings are both stupid and stubborn.

"I don't understand."

"Bruce, if you add this addendum to your book, there will be many who will read it, maybe even think it sounds wonderful, but will not heed what it says because it means rejecting their present way of life. It means giving up their fanatical pursuit of worldly goods and pleasures that they think will bring them happiness. It means divesting themselves of a zealous, self-centered pridefulness that they feel is justified. To be more precise, Bruce, it means taking a detour from the raucous lifestyle of the wide road to enter through the narrow gate, which as Jesus said those who do so are few. (Matthew 7:13-14)

"You may be right," I replied, "but such sinful actions are primarily due to the evil enticements of you and yours. However, if I don't include it then aren't I arrogantly and unfairly preventing the few who will read it and heed Mary's offer?

"Satan, I believe the converse of what you said about partial victory applies here. Because of many people's obstinacy fervent Christians can't hope to save everybody, but if we make an effort with the grace of God we can save some – maybe even many. Either way we reverse your favorite response to now read '…forever and forever NOT mine,' as you observe those we can help slip from your grasp."

"Touché," he replied.

CHAPTER FIFTY

The Virginity of Mary, the Mother of God

"Now, let's see what you can do to prove the virginity of the woman you and others like you refer to as the Blessed Virgin Mary."

"Before I proceed, Satan, I believe it is worth noting that once again you speak about the abhorrent behavior of human beings when you and yours are responsible for leading people to live such errant, sinful lives

"Furthermore, Satan, by your own admission God created you and your demons many times more intelligent than humans. So, the intellectual difference between you and humanity is not due to any effort on your part; therefore, to refer to us as stupid or stubborn or both is a grave injustice."

"If what you say was the whole truth, Bruce, I couldn't object; but God, in the personage of Jesus, has given mankind the sacraments as well as other means of grace – one about which we just discussed, to enjoin themselves to him thereby not only allowing mankind to make up the intellectual difference but if pursued often and with reverence puts our conflict in their favor; for as God is all-just it could not be otherwise.

"However, as we've stated before, convinced that they have a better idea than God's, both men and women either cast them aside or dilute them to where they are like people hurriedly walking about in a downpour thinking that somehow they can keep dry by carrying rather than opening their umbrella."

"Although I had to admit that agreeing with Satan was not a comfortable feeling; nevertheless, I knew that since his appearance remained before me his statements were truthful. In addition, his metaphorical expressions produced mental images that precisely verified the point that he was making.

As I proceeded to my computer to begin my case for Mary's lifelong virginity I felt that I was now alone. A moment later I knew it when I heard the now familiar sound of a roaring motorcycle engine. Once again, I prayed the Memorare asking Mary to seek Jesus' help in thwarting whatever evil intentions Satan intended on pursuing.

Validating Mary's virginity was the easiest of the four remaining tasks Satan said we had to complete before our time travel back two thousand years. He inferred that going back would most easily explain what he meant by The Great Equalizer, a term he had used repeatedly but continually put off explaining. However, when he used the word dilute when speaking of the aids God had provided mankind to deal with Satan and his demons' superior intellect, I felt he could only be speaking about the Eucharist and the denial of Transubstantiation by some Christians which only heightened my anticipation for the time travel.

In the meantime, there are a number of scriptural entries which would seem to infer if not prove that Jesus had blood brothers and sisters which if true would belie His mother Mary's perpetual virginity. Let's look at a few of them.

In Mark 6:3 we read, "Isn't he a carpenter? Isn't he Mary's son and the brother of James, Joseph, Judas and Simon? Aren't his sisters here with us?"

In Mark 3:31-35 Jesus explains his family, "Then Jesus' mother and brothers arrived. Standing outside, they sent someone in to call him. A crowd was sitting around him, and they told him, 'Your mother and brothers are outside looking for you.'" Jesus paused before answering, 'Who are my brothers and my mother?' He asked. Then he looked at those seated in a circle around him and while pointing to them said,

'Here are my mother and my brothers. Whoever does God's will is my brother and sister and mother.'"

1 Chronicles 23:22 – "Eleazar died and had no sons, but daughters only, so their brothers, the sons of Kish, took them as wives." However, later translations read 'so their cousins, the sons of Kish, took them as wives.'"

So, why the confusion? It is because the ancient Hebrew and Aramaic languages did not verbally differentiate blood relations. Blood brothers, half-brothers, cousins, nephews, stepbrothers, even uncles were referred to as brothers. The word sister was used likewise.

Even today in certain cultures close friends are addressed and thought of as the brothers or the sisters; and as we see above, Jesus, himself, confirms the semantics of this practice; that is, if one is a faithful believer and practitioner of a group, he or she is thought of and addressed as a brother or a sister or even a mother!

"The problem lies, even further, in the wording between languages. Hebrew and Aramaic had been in existence and used for centuries before the birth of Jesus. Their vocabularies were primitive and limited when compared to the rich and vast precise wording available in Greek, the language in which the four evangelists wrote their gospels; and even more in modern English where there can easily be confusion and misunderstanding whether one is in the United States or Great Britain.

However, as linguistically reasonable as all this is, it is not the most confirming factor in corroborating our Blessed Mother's virginity. What is confirming can be found among Jesus' last words just before dying on the cross when He said to John, the youngest and the only unmarried of His apostles, "Woman, here is your son," and to the disciple, "Here is your mother." From that time on, this disciple took her into his home." (John 19:27)

"Now, it was a strict tradition and practice in the Judaism of Jesus' time that the oldest living son assumes the responsibility for the custody, care, and protection of his widowed mother. As Jesus was Mary's only son, and close to death, it was Jesus' obligation to find and appoint someone dependable who would be pleased to assume this responsibility. While gasping out the words spoken above Jesus chose John, the son of Zebedee, who had followed him since before the wedding feast at Cana – three-and-a-half years ago, and was the only one of His apostles to remain with him until the end. In addition, John, as we said, was unmarried as well as young enough (nineteen) that he would be expected to live long enough to see Mary through to the end of her days.

None of that would have mattered, however, if Jesus had a blood brother or blood brothers as it was understood in keeping with Jewish accepted custom and tradition that as stated above, it would be the next younger brother who would provide for Mary, the widowed mother. By appointing John to assume the obligation Jesus would have inflicted the harshest, extreme insult to a brother as well as a violation of established Jewish tradition – something that Jesus would have no reason to do.

"By this act, then, Jesus confirmed his place as her only son thereby authenticating the virginity of Mary, his mother, as well as designating Mary to be our spiritual mother and as such a powerful intercessory to Jesus, her Son, superseded only by the Mass and the Holy Eucharist in overpowering the evil influence in our lives of he who is known as The Prince of Darkness.

CHAPTER FIFTY-ONE

Once More Humilione Strikes Out in Another Attempt to Please His Master

I had now completed my second of the two dissertations concerning Mary that Satan had asked me to do. The first was a submission of a term paper written years ago and the second I had just finished writing.

While I never had any problem believing in the Assumption of Mary body and soul into Heaven, I was eagerly awaiting Satan's on-site narrative. However, he had not, as yet, returned to the cabin. I decided to use the microwave to prepare one of the frozen meals I kept in the freezer and await his return.

I had just finished cleaning up the kitchen when I heard the familiar sound of his motorcycle. To announce his presence, he revved up the engine just before shutting it down. Either that or he was expressing his anger that my prayer had once again thwarted his evil intent. I had expected him to walk right through the wall of the cabin but after knocking he entered through the front door.

Without so much as a word of greeting he blurted out, "Have you ever been in authority and have those under you completely disregard what you tell them to the extent that you felt powerless to accomplish your objective?"

"Certainly," I replied. "As a biology teacher I outline what we are in the lab to accomplish that day and the steps we have to take to get it done and about ten percent of the class thinks they have a better idea. Not only do they have to do it over but their obstinacy wastes resources which for biology do not come cheap. When he didn't respond, I asked him what happened and did he care to talk about it?"

"I had always trusted Humilione to do what I told him and had the greatest confidence that he would accomplish the deed just as I had instructed him."

"And this time he didn't?"

"From the time mankind thought to establish governing bodies to keep order and to pass laws to extract tax money from the populace politics has been a veritable easy and sure source for sin and corruption. Power to spend money from tax coffers encourages those who either attempt to use influence to have tax money come their way, or to keep from having to pay their just share of taxes. The realm of politics for breeding greed and corruption is like a Petri dish for breeding bacteria. If you don't get your desired result it means you've done something wrong.

"Why is that?" I asked.

"Because greed and dishonesty provide a fertile opportunity for me and mine to turn it upside down. People elected or appointed to a political office are to function as servants of the people; but given power most turn it over to lord it over people for personal gain. In effect they mortgage their souls to me to get elected; later they are in so deep that they are forced to sell their souls to me to get re-elected. When they die without contrition they walk off the end of the wide road into my abyss. They are given an expensive funeral and someone delivers a eulogy designed to filter the evil and exaggerate the good. When they leave the place of bereavement someone will say, 'He is now in a better place!'

"Hardly, Bruce – despite wishing it were so, the absolute truth is that he or she is now all mine. Forever and forever all mine."

"Be that as it may," I said, "you have not answered my question. What did Humilione do to stress you to this extent?"

"I had assigned him the task of pursuing a potentially corrupt political situation involving a state senator and two business executives. However, as I found out later he thought I was giving him an easy task because I had lost confidence in him over the Carl and Jeremy fiasco; so, he decided to regain my confidence by taking on a convent of devout, cloistered nuns which he knew I rate as an impossible task, that is, one that even I would not attempt."

"So, by proving to you that he could triumph over what you said was impossible you would return your confidence in him – maybe even higher than it originally was. How did it turn out?"

"As I predicted it was a total failure – a disaster! They spent a week creating incidents in an effort to induce the nuns to question their faith proven by their broken vow of silence. They caused pictures to fall off the wall; they soured their milk; they caused a pitcher of orange juice to slowly move, apparently unaided, from one end of the table to the other. They moved prayer books and rosaries from their usual place. Humilione even had one of his demon brothers remove the water from the flower vases in the chapel causing them to wilt and die before their time.

Of course, the nuns knew that the incidents could only be demonic and went about their lives in prayerful silence trusting in Jesus to put an end to them when he willed.

"In the meantime, now fearing failure Humilione and his cohorts went to the extreme of going in one night and turning the large crucifix in their chapel upside down."

"If any of the nuns had any doubts of the source of the haunting," I replied, "the crucifix incident removed all doubt."

"Not only that, Bruce, but from their beginning hundreds of years ago I've always believed that cloistered nuns are especially protected by God which is why I leave them alone."

"So, how did Humilione and his followers stand up to the expected wrath of God?"

"Humilione, puffed up with pride, along with his second in command came to tell me the next morning that they were confident that the crucifix reversal was enough to drive the nuns to abandon their faith in despair; however, when they returned to the convent they saw that not only were the nuns continuing with their daily routine in silence but that the crucifix had been returned to its upright position.

"Standing to the right of the foot of the crucifix and visible only to them, was my old nemesis, Michael the Archangel, who raised his right hand and pointed to the door.

"When Humilione hesitated a whole legion of angels began falling in behind Michael. Humilione, admitting that he had been defeated by the loving faith in God of twenty-seven nuns, ordered a retreat."

"I had no idea that such conflicts occurred in your world. How often does this happen? You said Humilione was frightened of you. Why? What could you do to him? If Humilione and his followers had resisted the Archangel's command what would have happened to them? Did Humilione then pursue the politician and two businessmen?" Is it possible he could still be successful and lessen your anger?"

"I'll answer your questions in the order you asked them.

Conflicts between angels and demons occur quite frequently. They occur almost exclusively due to the efficacy of answered prayer. In the real world, Bruce, God seldom gets directly involved in the affairs of mankind. He assigns the tasks required to answer prayer or to accomplish his will to angels whom he has endowed with the power required; and thus, are proficient in carrying out his will.

In the world of demons Humilione is responsible for the state of Michigan. He would like to be assigned to a large city like Washington, D.C., New York, San Francisco, even London, Berlin or Paris, but he knows I don't feel he is ever going to be assigned to such a place. The demons I have there now are eminently qualified, especially the demons I have assigned to Washington, D.C. and San Francisco. And lest you forget, Bruce, demons as spirits don't grow old, retire or die. No, the only way Humilione can move is downward, and he's fearful that his performance of late deems such a demotion possible if not probable."

"Do your demons ever refuse to obey an angel, and what happens if they do?"

"Not very often because they know that demons who resist the power of Heaven, that is, countermand the order of an angel, are subject to being cast into Hell and are never again permitted to roam about the earth seeking the ruin of souls.

"They spend their eternity as a jailer?"

"Bruce, I couldn't have said it better. And no, Humilione did not complete his task. I gave it to another who also failed when one of the businessmen's wives, who were sisters, discovered what was going on and put a stop to it."

"So, even if Humilione had done as you said he would have failed?"

"No, it was after Humilione began wasting his time in the convent that the wife discovered the intended bribery."

"Deo gratias," I murmured. (Thanks be to God)

"I didn't hear you," Satan said.

"Ignoring him I said, "I finished my dissertation on the Virginity of Mary."

After reading it he said, "It's not your best work but there's enough there. Now take a seat at the table and if you wish, take notes while I narrate the details of the Assumption of the Blessed Virgin Mary.

CHAPTER FIFTY-TWO

The Assumption of Mary, the Mother of God

Walking across the room and then turning around to retrace his steps Satan said, "Like most factual narratives it begins long before the actual event occurs. So, as the sequence of events unfurls be patient if I repeat some things we have already discussed. It begins with Jesus, struggling for breath, saying to Mary, his mother, 'Woman, behold your son.' Then to the only apostle who remained with him until the end, nineteen-year-old John, who was standing beside her, 'Behold your mother.' (John 19:25-27) As John wrote, Bruce, from that moment on he would take Mary into his household as if she were his own. Then Jesus uttered his last, 'It is finished.' This occurred in the spring of 30 AD."

"Following His resurrection Jesus spent forty days on earth further instructing the apostles; and at times gathering them together to speak to them about what they were going to do. As men who now spent the better part of their lives looking over their shoulder in fear of the Sanhedrin, despite their respect, even adoration of Jesus, they couldn't see how they could possibly accomplish what he expected them to do.

"Finally, Jesus told them to remain in Jerusalem where they would come to no harm and await the descent of the Holy Spirit who will teach you all things within a mantel of faith and courage that you may accomplish all that I have commanded you to do.

"Jesus' final instructions were given just before He ascended into Heaven. These words have served as marching orders for generations of Christians: 'Go therefore and make disciples of all nations, baptizing them in the name of the Father and of the Son and of the Holy Spirit, teaching them to observe all that I have commanded you. And behold, I am with you all days, even unto the consummation of the world.'" (Matthew 28:19–20).

"That happened two thousand years ago," I said, "and Satan, even with all the evil you and yours have brought down upon God's human creation – even with all the sinful degradation you and yours have prompted mankind to commit; yes, and even when there is immoral, corrupt and intrinsically disordered, sinful behavior on the part of some members of the clergy, the Church continues to serve the spiritual needs of God's human creation as Jesus, the Son of God promised it would."

"Which only goes to prove what I told you earlier; I, Satan, along with mine cannot hope for a total victory against mankind, but we can contrive to bring about a series of partial conquests resulting in massive numbers of you condemning themselves to eternal damnation."

"When I failed to respond Satan continued. 'As I mentioned earlier, Bruce, I thought Jesus was expecting more from these men than they were equipped to deliver; except for Peter, who had a brash way about him, they were a sorry lot to send out to convert the Jews, or even worse to expect that they could convince men raised in the harsh world of pagan idolatry to lay down their swords and shields and turn the other cheek.'"

"However ten days after Jesus' Ascension the room in which they were living along with Mary became radiant as a strong wind blew about the walls of the room. When it stopped a tongue of fire appeared above the head of each. It remained there, flickering for a minute or so, and then disappeared as the radiance slowly diminished. As it subsided their faces conveyed a different appearance."

"What do you mean? How so?"

"Before this occurred, an event called Pentecost, they looked very much like thousands of their brother Jews who had been beaten down and discouraged by the brutality of their Roman oppressors."

"And after Pentecost?"

"They had a steely look in their eyes. They emanated a sense of determination fortified by a courage that was now totally void of fear or trepidation."

"In short, Satan, they were filled with the Holy Spirit who as Jesus promised, would teach them all things."

"And I must admit gave them the physical, mental and spiritual means to preach, to baptize and teach all nations. I always felt that without telling me directly, Jesus used Peter on that day to tell me that their humanity was no longer the same. It was about 10:00 in the morning when Peter was moved to step out on the veranda of the building in which they were staying and began preaching to the people below. At first, they ignored him, but as he mentioned Jesus many of them stopped to listen. The Jews recognized the name of the man they had seen heal the unhealable and some had been there when Jesus raised Lazarus from the dead.

"However, as the size of the crowd grew it became apparent that many of those who stopped to listen were not Jews, but people from many different nations who spoke a myriad of languages. They were amazed that each of them heard Peter in his own language, yet when they tried to speak to each other they were not able to understand. I knew then that one of the gifts the Holy Spirit had conferred upon Mary and the apostles was the gift of tongues. Peter's talk, no doubt inspired by the Holy Spirit, was so powerfully convincing that three thousands of those who listened agreed to believe and be baptized."

"As the years have passed, Satan, the gift of tongues has been grossly distorted; no doubt due to your attempt to delude visionary wannabes into believing they have been so gifted by God. As you are bound to tell the truth I now ask you to define the gift of tongues as an authentic gift from God."

"Once again, Bruce, you are asking me to undo centuries of deception in my effort to dupe many of you who are spiritually gullible."

"You have agreed to a condition which permits me to do so."

"And so I have. The gift of tongues is the God-given ability for an individual so gifted to speak his or her native tongue and for the recipient or recipients to hear what is spoken in his or her native tongue. The converse is also true; that is, no matter what language is spoken the one so gifted hears what is spoken in his or her native tongue. Any other explanation of this Godly gift is fraudulent."

I wanted to verbally thank him for saying this, but I felt it would serve only to antagonize him so I simply nodded and waited for him to continue.

"Peter appointed James, the older brother of John to be the first bishop of Judea and the surrounding area. The apostles remained in Judea and Galilee for three-and-a-half years in an attempt to convert their fellow Jews to the truths of the New Covenant, however after the first three years they met with diminishing returns as the Sanhedrin, seeing the large number of converts from Judaism, began a series of lies and persecutions that created fear in the Jewish population. John then asked Peter for permission to take Mary to his parents' home in Capernaum to better protect her from the harshness of the Sanhedrin. The apostles, after ordaining their successors to minister to their converts began leaving Jerusalem for other lands.

"In 35 AD the Sanhedrin was looking for a way to more forcibly control the persecution of the followers of Jesus whom they had crucified. Since many of them had witnessed Jesus' miracles and some had seen him after he arose from the dead, they knew that he was no ordinary man, but that Jehovah would come to earth as a man to be among them was beyond the limits of their belief system; especially since nowhere in the Torah did it say that the Messiah would be the Son of God. 'He could have been among the greatest of the prophets,' some said, 'if only his pride had not prompted him on several occasions to proclaim himself to be God incarnate!'"

"Conversely," I replied, "Jesus never said that He was a prophet, and those who proclaim Jesus to be only such are insulting God.

"Satan did not verbally reply, but only nodded and then continued."

"In order to establish continuity, it will be necessary to once again refer to St. Paul. In 35 AD an informer of the Sanhedrin reported that he observed a man by the name of Stephen being stoned to death just outside the East Gate for preaching Christian doctrine. He also told them that the man who oversaw the killing was named Saul, a rabbinical student at the Temple.

"Shortly thereafter, at the High Priest's request, Saul appeared before the Sanhedrin. After relating how he hated the Jews who had embraced what he perceived as a rampaging, false Christian practice, they hired him to proceed to Damascus. 'Bring back to us for trial those Jews who have fled to Damascus to escape their deserved persecution after giving up the practice of Judaism for the teachings of Jesus, the blasphemer.'"

"Tell me," I said, "Was Saul one of your protégés? I mean was his fanaticism due to your input?"

"As we have previously discussed, Bruce, love and hate are the most powerful of human emotions. I know this because humanity has proven many times over that men and women will die to prove their love and kill to demonstrate their hatred. Obviously I have no reason, even if I could, to foster love, but many reasons to encourage hate. Does this answer your question?"

"I note that many of your answers are seldom a simple yes or no, but in a roundabout way I have to figure it out for myself."

"And with your level of intelligence, fortified by an excellent education, Bruce, I know you will come to the correct conclusion. Actually, by doing this, if you think about it, I am complimenting you. If I answered with a simple yes or no, I would be treating you no different than if you were an imbecile for even they understand the difference between yes and no. Agreed?"

"Somewhat at loss for a worthy reply, I answered as Satan had previously answered me: Not exactly, but close enough."

"Saul, who was now pleased to be paid for doing what he enjoyed, gathered six men to help him and proceeded on horseback to Damascus.

"The over the road distance between Jerusalem and Damascus is 220 miles – about a six-day trip unless you want to kill your horse.

"When they were approximately ten miles from the city it was midnight and Saul decided to stop for the night and enter the city in the daylight of the rising sun. However, just as Saul was preparing to dismount, the moonless sky lit up while simultaneously a bolt of lightning struck Saul off his horse and as he lay writhing and screaming on the ground a loud voice thundered, 'SAUL, SAUL WHY DO YOU PERSECUTE ME?' (Acts 9:4) Saul, continuing to shriek in pain couldn't have answered even if he wanted to, but five of his six companions thinking they were next to be struck by the threat of the unknown turned their steeds around and galloped as fast as their horses could carry them back to Jerusalem. The sixth man was older than the rest. To be honest, Bruce, his heart was not in what he considered religious fanaticism. He thought that if this new religion was not of God, it would die out of its own; on the other hand if it was the will of Jehovah, nothing man could do would stop it; but he needed the money to pay his taxes.

"Saul had now quieted down and appeared to be listening and replying to a voice the old man could not hear. When Saul could stand, however, he told the old man that he could not see and asked him if his horse was nearby. The old man told him both of their horses were feeding unharmed in a nearby grove of trees. 'Take me to Damascus,' Saul told the old man, 'and the Lord will tell us what to do.'

"Saul, who had previously thought he was doing the will of Jehovah by hunting down blasphemers, spent three days in the dark night of the soul coming to terms with the fact that he, not the Christians, was in the wrong. Truly contrite, he would wake up weeping as he thought of the men and women he had caused to suffer a slow, cruel death by being struck again and again by bone-breaking heavy stones when they refused to renounce their Christian belief.

"On the third day, a disciple named Ananias came to see him. He said he was told by God to look for Saul and to do what the Lord told him to restore Saul's sight. Saul was baptized, changing his name to Paul and was filled with the Holy Spirit much like the apostles. He was a spoken champion for Christianity to the gentiles for ten years before arriving to evangelize in Antioch, a city with a decidedly Greek influence. There, he met (45 AD) a physician by the name of Luke who had converted to Christianity. Luke then traveled with Paul and is responsible for writing much of the Book of Acts which describes the life of Paul after his conversion.

"One day Luke asked Paul about the early life of Jesus. Paul told Luke that he had never personally met Jesus, but that his mother was still alive and living with John, one of his apostles, in Ephesus, a city in Turkey. Luke, a talented writer, wanted to produce an account of Jesus; however he wanted to include a firsthand infant narrative.

"Luke traveled to Ephesus and after telling John his purpose for being there got his permission to speak to Mary. This was in 48 AD. Mary, who was born in 23 BC was now seventy-one years old, but in excellent health, both physically and mentally."

"Satan, I didn't mention this in my treatise on Mary's virginity, but if Mary had borne other children, it's reasonable to think that she would have told Luke about them and Luke would have included them in his gospel."

"How so?" Satan asked.

"Well, if Luke was so interested in the infant narrative of Jesus, it is more than likely that Mary would have mentioned his siblings.

"While what you say, Bruce, is logically so, it is not proof positive. However, I can tell you that Jesus, the Messiah, was an only child; and the fact that I remain standing before you is proof positive that what I have just said is the truth, the whole truth and nothing but the truth.

"Joseph, her husband, knew from what Raphael had told him that he was chosen by God to be the foster father of Jesus who was conceived by the Holy Spirit in the womb of Mary, his betrothed: and that he was to have the privilege of being both the provider and protector of both Jesus and his mother."

"Furthermore," I added, "the only way Joseph and Mary could have lived in close proximity, without having carnal thoughts and feelings for one another was if the Holy Spirit had endowed them with a special grace from which they lived together as brother and sister who loved one another in that way."

"Most likely," Satan replied.

"In 66 AD, Mary, who was now eighty-nine, told John that she longed to see Jerusalem once more before her death which she felt was not long in coming. John, however, in his evangelistic work had met many Christians who had immigrated to Ephesus from Jerusalem. They told of turmoil in the city due to an increasing number of rebellious Jews who felt that with enough of them they could drive the Romans from what they considered their Promised Land. The Romans, in turn, seeking revenge had used the temple to offer sacrifices to their pagan gods and posted the Roman eagle in prominent places within. What's worse, they told him that the Jews, themselves, within the city were divided into three main groups and constantly fighting, even killing each other for power and control. Violence and theft between the groups was rampant.

"Nero, the Roman Emperor, had sent Vespasian, his most competent General, to put down the rising rebellion. With him was his son, Titus, a General in his own right, who had learned much from his father. The Christians who conversed with John were familiar with Jesus' prophecy about the destruction of the Temple and the signs they should watch for signaling it was about to happen. They were convinced that they had seen some of these signs, which was the reason they left Jerusalem. 'At the rate they were leaving the city,' they told John, 'soon Jerusalem would be completely void of Christians.'

"John went to Mary and told her why it would not be in accordance with the responsibility Jesus gave him from the cross that they should enter Jerusalem: a city Jesus foretold, along with its Temple that was going to be destroyed. In addition, for John to take the mother of God into a city from which Christians were fleeing as Jesus advised them to do would be in defiance of Jesus' love which prompted His warning.

"Mary asked John if he didn't think the grace of God would protect them. John told her that he would pray on it that night and give her his answer in the morning.

"The next morning, he told Mary, 'After praying for guidance I closed my eyes in sleep and began to dream. You and I, Mary, were standing outside the walls of Jerusalem observing thousands of Roman soldiers building giant battering rams on wheels which could have no other purpose than to destroy the walls of the city. We passed by them and walked through one of the city's gates without being challenged. Once inside the gate, however, the city was nothing like what we remembered. Terror, shouting, cursing, infighting and all kinds of mayhem were all around us. Being surrounded by death and destruction we decided it would be better not to be there; and we joined up with a group who told us that they were the last of the Christians to leave the city. A few months later the Romans would allow people to enter the city but prevented any of them from leaving. Jerusalem will be under siege, Mary. The Romans plan to starve them into submission!'"

"Before John could say more, Mary replied, 'Our people, John, especially favored and chosen by God, have irretrievably broken God's covenant with our father, Abraham; not only because they disbelieved and rejected my Son, Jesus, the Son of God conceived by the Holy Spirit to be the Messiah, but because they murdered him by the disgraceful ignominious death of crucifixion. Their degree of evil is even worse than their forefathers that resulted in the destruction of Solomon's Temple as they were being led away to seventy years of captivity by the Babylonian pagans.

"God Almighty, Lord Jehovah, John, is telling us by their recent actions and the Roman response that the Mosaic Law is obsolete and therefore, no longer relevant; and that which is no longer relevant must be cleared away to make a path for what is newly relevant and that is The New Covenant.

"As confirmation God will allow the Romans to not only lay waste to Jerusalem but plunder and demolish the Temple as well, so that as Jesus foretold not one stone will remain upon another.'" (Matthew 24:1-2)

"In 67 AD Mary told John that she was feeling tired sooner than she had in the past. Soon after, she asked John to fashion a cane to help her get around. She was now ninety years of age but her appearance belied her age. Even though she did not get around as well as she did her face and hands were those of a woman much younger. It was difficult for people in Ephesus with whom she was acquainted to believe her true age.

"John now felt that Mary was approaching death and knew the Apostles would want to be with her at the end; however, they were scattered over much of the known world. At this time there were eleven of them still alive. Matthias had been chosen to take the place of Judas and twenty-three years earlier (44 AD) James, John's older brother, as we noted earlier, the first bishop of Judea, had been beheaded by Herod Antipas I (grandson of Herod the Great) in an attempt to gain favor with the Sanhedrin and Rome where the persecution of Christians was gaining favor.

"I wondered what John would do, but was not surprised when he put notifying the apostles in the hands of God."

"How so?" I asked.

"Remember, Bruce, the Apostles were personally chosen by Jesus whom they had come to know is the Son of God – for them Jehovah incarnated. Can you imagine what that was like for them? They witnessed him curing the sick, the physically incapacitated; the leprous. They saw him walk on water, feed five thousand with five small barley loaves and a couple of salted fish; control violent wind and waves with a spoken word, even raising people from the dead! Along with Mary, His mother, they were the most privileged human beings to ever walk the earth because they lived their lives face to face with Almighty God!

"So, there was a bond not only among themselves but also with Mary that only grew stronger following Pentecost; and John, privileged to care for Mary, Jesus' mother, for all those years developed a faith strong enough, as Jesus said, that could cast a mountain into the sea. (Matthew 21:21)

"That night as John said his prayers before lying down to sleep, he asked God to advise the Apostles that Mary was dying; knowing that if Jesus did this they would make the effort to come to Ephesus to be present at her bedside when she drew her last breath. He finished his prayer, then, as he always did by saying, 'Not my will but Thine be done.'"

'Satan, it seems that you are putting Mary and the Apostles in a very good light. Listening to you it almost seems as if I am listening to a saintly, holy man instead of one who is indisputably known as The Prince of Darkness – the archenemy of Almighty God, if you will."

"Bruce, I remind you that I tried to bargain with God so that I would not have to talk in depth about Mary; and for the very reason you just mentioned. I also told you that I respected her more than I respect any other human being that ever was or will ever be.

"However, despite what I am saying now, I do my best to denigrate Mary. I have succeeded in turning men and women who are otherwise practicing Jews and good Christians into propagating lies and falsehoods about her – the most prominent ones, being that her Son, Jesus, was conceived with a Roman soldier in an act of fornication; (Jewish Talmud) or that if a person has a loving admiration for her or seeks her intercession it is raising her on a level with God that amounts to adoration.

"By doing this I have succeeded in knocking out from under many of you one of the greatest aids God has given mankind to help both men and women in their quest for eternal salvation. However, my failed attempt to ensnare Carl and Jeremy due primarily if not solely to your reaching out for Mary's intercession and Jesus' acquiescence to his mother's request has forced me into the most disagreeable position of countering my denigration by paying tribute and admiration to Mary, the Mother of God!"

I responded by saying simply, "Satan, it's what we do!

"Once again he replied with a single word, 'Touché,' he said."

"Over the next six weeks the apostles arrived until all but Thomas, who was coming from India, were present. Considering the purpose of their coming together, their joy at seeing one another again was less than it might otherwise have been.

"Mary spent most of her time resting, but when she was able to sit up, she prompted the apostles to tell her about their missionary efforts. Finally, one morning even though Thomas had not yet arrived, she asked John and the other apostles who were there to come to her bedside.

"Sitting up supported by a head rest she said, 'First of all I thank you for coming. Your presence has been a great comfort. I'm so proud and thankful for how well you have taken to heart Jesus' words to preach the word and baptize men of all nations. Although no doubt in the future there will be trials the Church must face from persecution without and conspiracy within, the foundation you have laid will forever define the Church and its Divine Purpose to people the world over.

"'You have taught the way of salvation that God has ordained, and for your efforts you will receive an eternal reward in addition to being honored and forever blessed by people the world over until the end of time.'

"Mary then closed her eyes and laid back. Peter anointed her head, hands and feet with a vial of oil he had especially blessed for the occasion, commending her soul to God; after which Mary, the virgin mother of God peacefully breathed her last.

"The day following Mary's entombment Thomas arrived. He had brought aromatic spices from India with which he intended to prepare her body for burial. When told by Peter that he was too late Thomas wanted them to have the stone rolled back so he could give her the added respect he wished and felt was her due.

"The other apostles were against the idea and deferred to Peter to make the decision.

"Peter, feeling uneasy about making an immediate decision told them that he would pray on it and give them his decision the next day. The next morning Peter said, 'God answered my prayer as he always does; however, in his answer I felt that Thomas's request was not a factor in God's decision.

"What else could it be?" questioned Nathaniel.

"I don't know," replied Peter. "Perhaps when we open her tomb God will reveal why I feel this way."

When the workmen rolled back the stone the apostles stood speechless and in awe for a moment before Thomas said, "I thought you said you had entombed her. Are you sure this is the correct burial site?"

"There is no doubt about it," replied John. "After covering her body with the shroud and face covering the ten of us prayed The Lord's Prayer while the workmen rolled the stone closure into place."

Thomas looked at the workmen who had rolled back the stone. After nodding in agreement one of them said, "That's true, sir. This is the correct tomb. Although the shroud is missing her face cloth is folded neatly where her head lay."

"Now we know why I felt as I did," said Peter. "Thomas you will not be able to anoint her with your spices because God has assumed Mary, His mother, body and soul into Heaven. It is the only explanation. Your arriving when you did was part of a divine plan. Had you arrived when Mary was still alive, we would never have known about her Assumption."

"Following Mary's Assumption John continued his evangelizing efforts in Ephesus while beginning to write his gospel. Three years later, in 70 AD the tenth legion of Titus breeched the walls of Jerusalem and sacked the city killing tens of thousands of fatally resisting sick and starving Jews. Titus' men, enraged at years of having to hold the city in siege, ransacked the Temple of its golden vessels and set it on fire after which they tore down what was left and in the process completely obliterated it; thus, fulfilling Jesus' prophecy.

"In Rome today, almost two thousand years later, there still stands a massive commemorative victory arch dedicated to General Titus. It depicts men carrying a large menorah (seven-branch candelabra) along with other vessels looted from the Temple.

"As for the other apostles, with the exception of John, within the next five years they would all suffer martyrdom. John, for his preaching Christianity was exiled to the Greek island of Patmos in the Aegean Sea where he wrote the Book of Revelation from visions he received from God. He died there of natural causes at eighty-eight years of age.

After assuring himself of the universal, certain and firm consent of the church's ordinary Magisterium, Pope Pius XII solemnly defined the Assumption of Mary as a dogma of faith in the Apostolic Constitution Munificentissimus Deus (The Most Bountiful God) on November 1, 1950. It stated that, "The ever-virgin Mary, having completed the course of her earthly life, was assumed body and soul into heavenly glory."

"The feast of Mary's Assumption is celebrated each year on August 15th," I said. "Like her Immaculate Conception it is a Holy Day of Obligation."

CHAPTER FIFTY-THREE

The Destruction of the Second Temple

"In the first semester of your sophomore year, Bruce, your religion class was devoted to the study of early Church History. The class was given several options for a required term paper. Your choice was to write on the meaning of the destruction of the second Jewish Temple in 70 AD by the Romans. I think it would serve as an interesting entry for our next discussion."

"If you think so," I replied, but there were some of my classmates who thought it bordered on being anti-Semitic."

"How would they know unless you allowed them to read it?"

"Father Rogers, in order to prompt discussion, had three of us read our papers aloud. The other two centered on the history of the early Christian church; however, mine had exceptionally strong Semitic overtones."

"You must have impressed Father Rogers or he wouldn't have chosen it for discussion.

"He also made some remarks. Would you mind sharing them?"

"Once again, I was almost overwhelmed by Satan's attempt at mannered civility. It must have been very difficult for him as he stated at the beginning of our discussions how much he hated me; however, I suspect it was tempered by respect to which he also confessed.

"I saw no reason to deny his request so after removing it from the binder I read, 'Your thought processes fortified by historical accuracy are outstanding. You should know that in the classes before you few students chose this topic; and in fact, you are the sole student in your class to do so. Congratulations on a job well done.'

"He gave me an A for a grade."

"Well, why don't you read it aloud so we can see what caused all the tension?"

THE SECOND JERUSALEM TEMPLE – WHY WOULD GOD ALLOW IT TO BE DESTROYED?

All mankind should know this. Almighty God, who created man has deigned that eternal salvation is His ultimate goal for every human being. That being so, an all-just God would have to provide a way, that is, a path to follow to attain that goal and because of the finality of a person's success or failure that way must be readily available and without error. Therefore, any and all alternate paths to salvation established by mere men either deny it, alter it or revise it, and by so doing must be wrong or at best their plan is less than or other than the whole truth.

That being said, the primary purpose of the sanctuary in the Jerusalem Temple was to house the massive altar where animal life was extinguished and its entrails burned as an offering to God in reparation for the forgiveness of sins. However, because of their subordinate nature, the sacrificing of animals could never fully compensate for superior, intelligent and free willed human beings who intentionally defy God by engaging in sinful behavior.

Thus, even the sacrificing of thousands of animals for centuries again and again, day after day, never entirely repaired the rift sin caused between God and man. It wasn't until Jesus, the sinless, incarnate Son of God, taking upon himself the punishable consequences of every one of mankind's sins, was sacrificed on a cross by crucifixion that full atonement was made to God the Father for all the sins of mankind; and therefore, it is only reasonable to believe that offering God burning animal flesh was at that moment without a purpose and therefore no longer pleasing or desired by God.

We can assume then that this is the primary reason God permitted the Temple to be destroyed. In fact, Jesus predicted the destruction of the Temple almost four decades before it happened and even to the extent it would be devastated.

Jesus came out from the temple and was going away when His disciples pointed out the magnificence and beauty of the temple buildings to him. Jesus stopped and turned to face the temple and pointing his finger said to them, **"Do you not see all these things? Truly I say to you, not one stone here shall be left upon another which will not be torn down."** (Matthew 24:1-2) Any reasonable person with an open mind would know that only God could predict such a catastrophic, monumental occurrence so far in advance and have it happen just as He predicted. Note also that the disciples pointed out and were talking about the buildings which in truth Titus' tenth legion did completely lay waste.

I realize that this equates to one of the most emphatic non-politically correct statements the reader will ever see or hear; and like most such statements it is the truth that is known but will not be admitted in public discourse. If questioned about it even some members of the Christian clergy dance all around it even to the point of spouting heresy to avoid appearing anti-Semitic. Yet Jesus, who was born a Jew, left no doubt that He, as the Son of God, foretold that the Temple would be supplanted by what would be the New Covenant when he said the following, "I am the Way, the Truth and the Life. No one comes to the Father except through me." (John 14:6)

For centuries people have tried to dumb down and/or reinterpret Jesus' statement. The frustration of some has risen to such a degree that their aggravation causes them to deny that Jesus said it. However, Saint John the apostle and evangelist wrote that Jesus did say it and he was there when it was said. In other words it is not hearsay but given to us by a firsthand witness.

Note well. Jesus did not say that He is a way, as in one among many. He said emphatically that He is the way, as in the one and only. No one, regardless of personal achievement, sterling reputation or even personal holiness, can come to God the Father except through Jesus. He left no quarter to accommodate interpretation or exception. If you turn your back on Jesus because you think that you, the created, have a better idea than your Creator about the way to salvation or you act and live as if He had never been born, you will not spend your eternity with him! No man or woman said this – Jesus, the Son of God and Second Person of the Blessed Trinity did! Every person born of woman ignores, disbelieves or denies this divine statement at their own eternal peril!

In summary, prior to the death and resurrection of Jesus Christ, that is, the Messiah, the Jewish Temple served as The Abode of God on earth and a place of adoration and atonement for the Jews, the Chosen People of God. Now, however it is obvious that if we listen to Jesus' last words to His apostles "Therefore go and make disciples of all nations, baptizing them in the name of the Father and of the Son and of the Holy Spirit, teaching them to obey everything I have commanded you. And surely, I am with you always, even to the consummation of the world." From that moment on there was to be no longer just a segment of humanity that God considered to be chosen, but rather this status applied to all members (nations) of His human creation. (Matthew 28:19-20)

That being so, if the Temple continued to exist and perform animal sacrifices after Jesus died a sacrificial death whereby He atoned for all the sins of all mankind and for all time, then those who perform, condone or in any way support the sacrificial ritual of the Temple would be proclaiming that the death of Jesus Christ was useless thereby insulting, if not blaspheming Almighty God by calling him a fraud and a liar.

Thus, God permitted the Temple to be destroyed along with the genealogy records of the divinely required Levitical priesthood; so, even if a structure were to be rebuilt there would be no way of establishing legitimate priests to perform the Temple Rituals.

A reasonable man would know that Jesus is telling both Jews and gentiles that the old way, that is, the Mosaic Law, having served its purpose as a forerunner is no longer viable. The truth is that every man's salvation is now to be found in the New Covenant, that is, Christianity, wherein the Messiah amended the Mosaic Law by fulfilling it. The choice for all men, Jew and gentile alike, is to believe the truth that Jesus is the Son of God as well as the Messiah by being baptized or if not, refusing such in order to continue being mired down, slogging about in circles among the ruins of an ancient and no longer relevant past.

Submitted December 21, 2003

Bruce McPherson

"Well, Bruce, I can readily see two things – why you received an "A" and why it's possible that some of your more liberal thinking fellow students might be incensed hearing it read. Would you care to say how it played out?"

"You weren't there?"

"No, I wasn't. I got it secondhand from one of my demons as I had what I deemed a more pressing task elsewhere. As you know getting something firsthand is always the more preferable."

"I think the best way to tell you is to present it in a question-and-answer format. Benjamin Kaufman, whose mother was a devout Catholic, but whose father was Jewish was the more knowledgeable and outspoken of the students and as such he did most of the speaking:

BEN: If Jesus was God, then His prediction that there would not be one stone left upon another would have come true. The fact that the entire Western Wall of the Temple Mount, sometimes referred to as The Wailing Wall, still exists, even today, questions his claim to be divine.

MY REPLY: You are presuming that the high western wall, which you say is the location of The Wailing Wall, is the western wall of the Temple Mount. As you know there is now some question about whether it is the wall of the temple mount, or the supporting wall of the Roman's citadel known as the Fortress Antonia. However, that is not relevant to our discussion as Jesus words were reported by Matthew, who heard them firsthand. If you remember the apostles mentioned the buildings of the temple and Jesus replied in kind. Thus, the temple mount was built to support the land on which the buildings were constructed but was not itself a building.

"Furthermore, after Titus destroyed Jerusalem as well as the Temple many of the Jewish rebels under the leadership of Eleazar Ben Jair, climbed to the top of Masada, a near self-sustaining fortress built by Herod the Great on the top of a hill with near vertical sides. It took the Romans three years after Titus' decimation before the Romans, using ramps reached the top of the hill where they found that all but two women and three children had committed suicide. In his address to the rebels just before the Romans breached their defenses Eleazar said, 'Jerusalem is now demolished to the very foundations, and there is nothing left but that monument they preserved; I mean the camp of the Romans [Fortress Antonia] where they still dwell upon its ruins.' Since Eleazar and the remaining men then committed suicide, we have to believe that one or both of the surviving women conveyed this to the Romans. The point is that from Eleazar's on high observation Jerusalem was completely destroyed; and that being so then it follows that there was nothing remaining of the temple buildings."

"Was there any further discussion?" Satan asked.

"Yes, but only of a minor nature. Later at dinner in the school's cafeteria for resident students Ben Kaufman, carrying his tray, came over and sat down. 'You know I was baptized and raised as a cradle Catholic,' he said. 'My father is a Jew by birth but doesn't go to the synagogue or in any other way live as a believing Jew. In fact, he accompanies my mother to Sunday Mass. His parents, my grandparents, are getting up in age. He has inferred on occasion that when they pass on, he'll take formal instruction and be baptized.'"

"So, what was that question about?" I asked.

He laughed and then said, "Don't you remember that long silent pause after Father Rogers asked for questions? When nobody else stepped up

I knew it was up to me to save your bacon. I know more about the Jerusalem temple than almost any other Catholic."

"How so? You said your father was at best a secular Jew."

"My grandfather, Bruce. He's now ninety-one and my grandmother is eighty-nine. If they could find a sponsor they would fly off to Israel and upon their demise be buried on Israeli soil; but at their age that's not going to happen."

"So what are your true feelings about the Jerusalem Temple?"

"It was the Vatican of its day," he replied. For a thousand years, except for the hiatus between the first and second temples it served as the principal house of worship for the only members of humanity that knew of and worshipped the One True God. However, as you said with the execution – actually the martyrdom of Jesus, God Incarnate, it had served its purpose."

"How so?" I asked, "that is from your point of view."

"You know there is a group of people in Israel that are planning to build a third temple. They have drawn up architectural plans; they're making the vessels, the vestments and even weaving a new temple veil. Some even hope to reinstate animal sacrifices."

"But, Ben, despite your Grandparents' beliefs you are not in favor of this. Are you?"

"Of course not, as are most Jews around the world. Can you imagine the eruptive protests in our modern world if Israel built and operated a religious slaughterhouse?

"I don't know when it will happen, Bruce, but someday the Jews have to believe that Jesus, having fulfilled so many prophecies; and having performed so many miracles of healing which include raising people from the dead; not to mention after instituting the Holy Eucharist he raised himself from the dead within three days after being crucified must be the Messiah. No mere man could accomplish this. The old covenant, that is, waiting and preparing for the Messiah, was fulfilled when Jesus, the Messiah, arrived and established a new covenant which for all mankind is the true path to salvation and therefore, no longer by way of one that should have ended two thousand years ago.

"Finally, Bruce, Daniel was a revered, Jewish prophet of the Old Testament. In Daniel 9: 24-27 he clearly states that the temple would be destroyed after the death of the Messiah. So, those who spend their lives preparing for the coming of a Messiah whose time on earth has come and gone are calling Daniel, a prophet of God, a liar; and must someday stand before Jesus at their judgment calling him the same."

"As we finished our meal Ben invited me to play golf on the following Saturday. He shot a 71 which was one under par. My 89 meant that he beat me by a stroke a hole which he agreed was my handicap in any future games."

CHAPTER FIFTY-FOUR

Our Father Who Art in Heaven, Hallowed Be Thy Name

"As I promised," Satan said, "we will discuss the Lord's Prayer, given to the apostles by Jesus in response to their request to teach them how to pray. After which we will take our time travel to define The Great Equalizer.

"When the apostles heard Jesus begin his response to their request to teach them how to pray, they were shocked. No Jew of Jesus' time addressed God as Father. God was referred to as Jehovah or Yahweh, the latter of which was never spoken. Jehovah was thought of as the Almighty, the Creator, the One who if provoked was a God of Wrath. The God Who demanded the sacrificial life of unblemished animal life, as seen and experienced on a daily basis by the slaughter and burning of the entrails of rams, lambs, bullocks and doves in the temple.

"God was he who could call down fire and brimstone on mankind if provoked to extreme – and had done so to the people of Sodom and Gomorrah who had turned their backs on him to practice publicly, pagan rites of inordinate sexuality. Furthermore, when his Chosen People no longer respected and obeyed his Ten Commandments, he allowed the Babylonians to take them into pagan bondage following the destruction of Solomon's temple and their most precious possession – the Ark of the Covenant.

"However, Bruce, He was also their Creator, which gave him the authority to do these things as He pleased. Consequently, their relationship to God was not one of love, but rather one of obeisance based on fear. They didn't believe God loved them nor did they feel much love for him. Their relationship to God was, for the most part, that of a lowly subject hoping to avoid offending a demanding, wrathful, and vengeful Master.

"Jesus, as we now know came to change that. God loved His human creation and desired that they love him in return. His reaching out to miraculously cure them of their infirmities was prompted by this love and to prove that this was so.

"His telling Peter that he should forgive another not seven times but seventy times seven times was His way of expressing the fact that because God's love is infinite, he forgives His human creation as many times as men and women sincerely confess their sorrow for sin and vow to sin no more; and mankind is obliged to do likewise with their fellow man.

"Who art in Heaven hallowed be Thy Name. God's abode is in Heaven, the ultimate in joyful venues and mankind acknowledges his Divinity.

"Thy kingdom come; thy will be done on earth as it is in Heaven. Because it is of a spiritual nature the kingdom of God, as Jesus told Pilate, was not of this world. If the second part of this petition were adhered to by mankind the world would be the human abode of peace, love and harmony God designed it to be. If every man and woman would not only say but live this every day, 'Not my will but Thine be done,' people would not prey upon each other. Crime, wars, theft, murder, all sin, Bruce, would be non-existent."

"However, Satan, you would be powerless, for your prime purpose of existence is to convince men and women to supplant the will of God for their concupiscence inspired will of lust, murder, greed, lies and in general to prey upon their fellow man."

"Right again, Bruce, for as I have said before, 'It is what we do.' Stealing souls from God is all we of the demonic have the desire to do.

Jesus has given his human creation the grace and means to defeat us, but as he stated they can only be found by passing through the narrow gate which few of you have the will to find, and fewer still the love of God and the resultant courage to tread its path. (Matthew 7: 13-14)

"Much of all the sin and its horrendous effects are caused by me and mine; and the easiest way to steal souls from God is to convince human beings to substitute their own sinful desires for the plan that God has willed for them."

"Give us this day our daily bread. Self-explanatory. You have physical bodies which require sustenance to support life; and bread is known as the staff of life.

"And forgive us our trespasses as we forgive those who trespass against us. As I've said previously, most of you say this without thinking about what it means.

"Do you remember what I said, Bruce?"

"You said that by praying such, for better or for worse, persons bring judgment down upon themselves."

"That is correct. As I've stated many times in our discourse, 'Dying while harboring hatred in one's heart is second only to sins of the flesh the reason people choose to send themselves to Hell.' I know that it is nearly impossible for most men and women to forgive someone if they feel their hatred is justified; that is, he or she harbors hatred of a person for the evil doing they believe that person has willfully done to them, especially if the perceived evil deed involves theft or confiscation of what the person believes is legitimately and morally theirs."

"This is why you continually stoke the fires of hatred and loathing between people, nationalities and races; between differing political beliefs, between nations and even among people with different religious beliefs."

"Right again, Bruce. As I've said before and say now again, it is what we do – stealing souls from God is all we of the demonic have the desire to do.

"And lead us not into temptation but deliver us from evil. You are asking God to protect you from being tempted beyond your ability to resist and at the same time to be delivered or protected from me and mine, which is an excellent place to begin our time travel to see how God answers that part of the prayer."

"What about the doxology? You know the ending which states, 'For Thine is the Kingdom, the Power and the Glory forever.'

"Jesus never said that. The proof is that before 1611 when The King James Version had been translated into English it was not a part of scripture. The truth is that one of the translators (from Latin) found a piece of an ancient Greek manuscript and assumed it was an authentic part of scripture and added it to the translation of St. Matthew's gospel. It has remained there ever since."

CHAPTER FIFTY-FIVE

The Great Equalizer

"Before we venture forth, I should like to remind you that modern day human beings including yourself, Bruce, engage in a type of time travel almost every day."

"In what way?" I asked somewhat confused.

"You enjoy watching old westerns. Gunsmoke is a favorite of yours. These programs were made fifty and sixty years ago. The people who portrayed Marshall Dillon, Kitty, Doc Adams, Chester, Festus, etc. are all dead and buried. Yet, you see them and hear them in their own voices just as they were moving about and interacting back then. You do so as an observer. Like our time travel you have no ability to interact with them or to change the outcome."

"Amazing!" I replied. "I never thought that while watching an old movie or television program that I was time traveling.

"Having nothing more to say I asked when we would take our time travel?"

"The sun is setting," he answered. We shall depart in the morning. This step back in time will be very mentally stimulating. You will need a full night's sleep. Set your alarm for 6:00 A.M. You should feel fully rested by then. While you eat your morning meal, I will prepare you for what you will experience. Then together we will travel back two thousand years to see God's gift of The Great Equalizer."

"Until then," I responded, and feeling overly tired, went into the bedroom and shut the door.

I awoke at 5:45 A.M. and silenced the alarm. As I entered the kitchen my nose told me that he had prepared breakfast. Satan's, meal, however, consisted only of black coffee. As I drained the last drop of orange juice from my glass Satan said, "You will remember me saying that I would tell you to what additional conditions I had to agree in order to speak with you and that I would mention them as it was necessary to do so."

"Yes, of course," I replied.

"Well, then, I will begin by asking you, "What does the name, Victoria Dinetto mean to you?"

"Victoria is a twenty-eight-year-old woman with whom I am in love," I answered, while doing my best to keep from showing my surprise that Satan would bring her into our conversation. "She holds a master's degree in nursing, is the Director of Surgical Nurses at a major hospital, and holds a teaching position in the School of Nursing at Duquesne University in Pittsburgh, Pennsylvania."

"You obviously hold her in high esteem."

"As does any man who loves a woman. After receiving my Ph.D., I will ask her to marry me."

"When you do so you will give her a gift – a ring to signify your pledge of love and devotion that you will give to no other."

"Yes – an engagement ring."

"Have you purchased it?"

"Yes. It is a one-carat diamond set in platinum with three diamond baguettes on either side."

"Did you ever think of having it set with a zirconium for a lot less money? You could have given her a two carat stone and unless it was examined by a gemologist no one would know the difference."

"Satan, a traditional engagement ring, by definition, is set with a diamond. A sincere, loving person doesn't give a gift that is faux to show love and devotion if the real item is readily and financially available.

"Therefore, a ring that does not contain such is symbolic, that is, it might represent the giver's intention but is lacking in substance or essence if you prefer. I'll say it again. Any gift given as an expression of true love can never be a substitute or as it is presently expressed, a faux or knock off.

"Precisely, Bruce. Well said. Hold that thought. It will serve us well as we progress on our time travel."

After a pause I asked, "Did God really say that discussing my relationship with Victoria was a condition for your speaking with me?"

"No, of course not. I merely used your relationship with her to make a point which you defined so well and which was the condition to which I had to agree."

While cleaning up after breakfast Satan said, "Jesus had in the day before fed five thousand hungry men along with the women and children present by miraculously multiplying five barley loaves and two fish. Afterwards he had His apostles gather up the uneaten which filled twelve baskets which were then given to the poor.

"In the aftermath, however, because they had witnessed miracles of instant healing in addition to being fed by still another miracle, they wanted to make Jesus their king. Disgusted with their fixation on the temporal and material to the exclusion of the spiritual nature of his teaching he had tried to impart, Jesus fled to the northern side of the Lake of Galilee.

"That night as the apostles were rowing across the lake they were confronted with a violent storm and headwind which greatly impeded their progress. You can imagine their fear when they see coming toward them out of the darkness what appeared to be a man walking on the water. They are somewhat relieved when they hear the voice of Jesus telling them not to be afraid; followed by, 'It is I.' (John 6:20)

"Peter, looking for confirmation, tells him that if this is so, bid him to come to him by walking on the water. After successfully doing so at the behest of Jesus, Peter begins to doubt his ability to continue and starts to sink. He begs Jesus to save him which Jesus does, after which Peter exclaims, 'My Lord and my God!' When Jesus follows the now soaking wet Peter into the boat the wind subsides and they continue rowing toward the shore."

"It appears, then, by Peter's exclamation that the Apostles believe that Jesus is the promised Messiah and even more so that by his miracles can only be God Incarnate."

"They had witnessed many miracles of healing, but not being physicians they didn't fully understand the complexity that Jesus' miracles had to overcome. However, as fishermen they fully understood why no ordinary man can walk on water. In addition, at Peter's request and Jesus' invitation they witnessed Peter doing the same until he couldn't believe what he was doing, that is, lost his belief in the miraculous power Jesus had given him. His loss of faith in God caused him to slowly submerge until Jesus gave him his hand.

"I had always believed, Bruce, that Jesus' water bound miracle was to reinforce the apostles' faith and belief in him which they would need to accept what he was about to say the following day even though at the time they would not understand."

"I always wondered, Satan, if Judas was in that boat."

"Judas was a Judean. He had no experience as a fisherman. However, when faced with the decision to walk the several miles around the lake to Capernaum on the north side or ride over in a boat he chose the latter.

"Judas, however, was a lone dissenter. His sole purpose as a follower was to convince Jesus to use his miraculous power to augment those men fighting in the hills to rid the Jews of Roman rule. Judas is looking to use Jesus for temporal success and satisfaction. Like many of those who followed Jesus the spiritual message of Jesus' teaching was of little concern. Judas' concept of the Messiah was a man like King David, which is that of a mighty warrior who would restore their right to be independent of Roman rule with its oppression and taxation. Humans who are obsessed with secular or worldly aspirations are easy demonic prey. As the keeper of the purse containing donations, it was easy to convince Judas that siphoning off funds for his friends in the hills was justified."

"In other words, you convinced Judas that the reason for his thievery was proper which in turn quieted his conscience."

"Convincing mankind that in their case sin is justified is the basis of assuring them that their idea is worthy of exception. After we of the demonic accomplish that then the wide road tips downward as they travel faster and faster on their way to perdition.

"The next day Jesus and His apostles proceed to the synagogue in Capernaum where they find much of the same crowd which Jesus had fed. They are hoping to see more miracles of healing and maybe receive another free meal. Jesus offers them the gift of a meal they can have even daily for the good of their souls if they will only believe what he says."

"Before we proceed, Satan, will there be a language barrier?"

"Although all will be speaking in Aramaic you will hear them in English."

"Before I could say anything more, Satan snapped his fingers and immediately we were off to one side near the front of the synagogue. I was aghast when I saw Jesus standing before the crowd. The apostles were sitting in front of him but off to one side.

"I, like many others had seen artists' renditions of how they thought Jesus would appear. I know there are different opinions concerning the validity of the Shroud of Turin but I can tell you that Jesus' countenance and the imprint on the shroud appear more than a coincidental fit. He is half a head taller than the average man in the crowd and His voice is not only pleasing but resonates such that it can be heard distinctly by even those standing in the rear of the synagogue.

Jesus raises His hand to quiet the crowd. When they had given him their full attention, he begins by boldly stating, "I am the bread of life; whoever comes to me will never hunger, and whoever believes in me will never thirst. But I told you that although you have seen me (perform miracles), you do not believe" (when I tell you that I am Almighty God Incarnate.) (John 6:30-36)

The crowd reacts by asking each other what Jesus means by never again being hungry or thirsty. "Can this be true, they ask?"

Jesus continues. "Everything that the Father gives me will come to me, and I will not reject anyone who comes to me, because I came down from Heaven not to do my own will but the will of the One who sent me." (John 6:37-38)

Again, many in the crowd react by asking, "Why does Jesus speak of his father this way? Why does he say the father instead of my father? And what does he mean by saying that he came down from Heaven? He is a Nazarene! We know the family. His father was Joseph, a carpenter of late, and his mother's name is Mary."

Satan turns to me and whispers, "They say this because many of them have known Jesus and his parents since they returned to Nazareth from Egypt."

Ignoring both their murmuring and questions Jesus continues, "And this is the will of the One who sent me; that I should not lose anything of what he gave me, but that I should raise him up on the last day. For this is the will of my father – that everyone who sees the Son and believes in him may have eternal life, and I shall raise him on the last day." (John 6:39-40)

Now even the apostles are confused. Thomas asks Peter, "Do you have any idea what Jesus is talking about?"

"No," Peter replies. "But let's just keep listening and maybe it will become clear."

But it doesn't. If anything, it becomes even more confusing when Jesus says, "I am the living bread that came down from Heaven; whosoever eats this bread will live forever; and the bread that I will give is my flesh for the life of the world." (John 6:51)

Now it is not only the crowd that is astonished and befuddled but also the apostles who are wondering aloud what Jesus means. Jesus glances at them, but when Peter quiets them Jesus turns his attention again to the crowd. Pausing to listen to what they are saying he hears, "How can this man give us his flesh to eat?" Jesus, visibly distressed, closes his eyes and shakes his head in sorrow knowing by how they refer to him as a man that his declarations to being God coupled with his miracles failed to convince them of the truth.

Others are saying among themselves, "This is a hard saying. If he means us to take him literally, he means for us to kill him and then consume his flesh."

"How could he mean that?" asks another. "The Torah expressly forbids to Jews the drinking of blood. (Leviticus 17:10) Is not Jesus a Jew?"

"Perhaps he intends to multiply himself as he did with the five barley loaves and two fish!"

Before anyone else questions Jesus' statements he raises both hands to silence the crowd.

"Now Jesus will explain what he means," says the man who referred to Jesus' remarks as a hard saying.

Jesus continues. "Amen, amen (that is, in truth) I say to you – unless you eat the flesh of the Son of Man and drink his blood, you do not have life within you. Whoever eats my flesh and drinks my blood has eternal life, and I will raise him up on the last day. (John 6:54-55)

"For this is the bread which came down from Heaven: not as your fathers did eat manna, and are dead, but he that eats this bread shall live forever." (John 6:58) This coming from Jesus is the ultimate statement which convinces those in attendance that they don't want to hear anymore; and they begin murmuring and shaking their heads while turning their backs to him as they walk away.

Jesus says no more as the crowd disperses and leaves the synagogue. When they have all gone, however, Jesus turns to his apostles and asks, "Will you also go away?"

Peter answers for the twelve, "To whom shall we go, Lord? You have the words of eternal life."

Judas rolls his eyes and silently curses. "All this talk about eternal life, he mumbles.. What about our lives here and now? Why the incessant delays?" He is determined to somehow force Jesus to come to terms with their Roman oppressors.

After the crowd had left, and immediately following Peter's declaration, Jesus, accompanied by the Apostles, departs.

The synagogue was now eerily silent. Where only a few moments before there had been a huge crowd eager to hear what Jesus would say and do, there was now only a large, empty, quiet space. After a minute or so of silence Satan asks, "You have nothing to say, Bruce, or are you in shock?"

"Although I was familiar with Jesus' words as witnessed by St. John in the sixth chapter of his gospel," I answered, "actually hearing Jesus in his own voice respond ever more literally to each of the crowd's disbelieving protests, gives further credence to the words spoken at the Last Supper – the words of consecration that even today spoken by his priests creates for us not a symbolic representation of Jesus, but through transubstantiation our ability to join ourselves to him as Jesus intended by reception of his actual body and blood, soul and divinity. This is the supreme gift of Divine Love which you refer to as The Great Equalizer!'

"In addition, the words Jesus uses and John writes in his gospel (written in Greek) for the verb 'to eat' become more emphatic for what he is saying. Jesus begins by using the Aramaic equivalent of the Greek word phago which in addition to ingesting food can have other meanings. However, John writes that Jesus changes the force of his meaning by using the equivalent of the Greek word trogon which has only one meaning, which is to chew or masticate. (John 6:54)

"For instance, John writes that Jesus uses phago when referring to the Israelites eating manna in the desert, but trogon when referring to himself. 'This is the bread which came down from Heaven: not as your fathers did eat (phago) manna, and are dead, but he that eats (trogon) this bread shall live forever.'

"Finally, Satan, Jesus being the Son of God he can neither deceive nor be deceived. Therefore, if what he said was meant to be symbolic, he would necessarily have had to say so, as obviously believing what he said to be physically literal, all his followers except for the apostles deserted him. As John tells us Jesus did not back off or tell them he was speaking symbolically. He just watched as they turned and walked away leaving them to their belief that because what they knew was impossible in their world of men could not be possible for God whom they were either incapable of or refused to believe Jesus to be."

Satan replied, "Having said that do you have anything else to add about what you have just seen and heard?"

"Yes, I do. Jesus knew that any further statements about the Eucharist would be fruitless unless they believed him to be Jehovah incarnate. He had both told them and inferred this on several occasions, but they refused to believe him. As we said before, but bears repeating, when the Pharisees were questioning him, they asked, 'You are not yet fifty and have you seen our father, Abraham?' Jesus' answer was 'Truly, truly I say to you, before Abraham was, I AM.' (John 8:58)

"That said it all, Satan. There were several other direct statements in this regard, but none so clearly direct, except maybe his response to Caiaphas who asked Jesus if he was the Son of God to whom Jesus answered, 'Thou hast said it...'" (Matthew 26:64)

"Yes, and after each one of them as stated in John 5:18-23, and again his statement about being the Good Shepherd (John 10:27-31) they took up stones to throw at him because being stupid and stubborn they believed that Jesus had blasphemed rather than believe that only God could have performed the miracles they had witnessed with their own eyes."

"As we alluded to earlier, Satan, the Jews believed in the omnipotence of God in the abstract which included the miraculous events recorded by Moses and the prophets of old; but in their own time, despite personally witnessing his healing miracles, they shackled Jesus' power to do what they believed to be possible in their material world.

"It bears repeating that by his miracles he tried to convince them otherwise; but even then, they either could not or would not see the truth. The fact that many of them went along with the desire of the Sanhedrin to have him killed by shouting to Pilate, 'His blood be upon us and upon our children,' is proof that they considered him to be but a mere man.

"In addition, as we agreed earlier, a gift given from love is never a substitute when it is possible to give the real thing. This being so, Jesus, by speaking plainly, clearly and distinctly is telling us that as Almighty God he is presenting us with nothing less than the loving gift of his incarnate self. He never implies nor uses any language that would even hint that what he was giving us was in any way faux, a knock off or in any other way a substitute or a symbol of himself."

"Then why do you think it is so easy for me to convince so many of you otherwise?" Satan asked.

"I believe that following the Reformation the Protestant religious leaders could not believe, and rightly so, Satan, that they could, as mere men, have such power. What I mean is that it was at the Last Supper where Jesus said of the bread, 'This is my body' and of the wine, 'This is my blood" and then to 'Do this in remembrance of me' that he meant for the validly ordained in an unbroken line from the apostles to have the power to present this gift to those who wish to receive it with the right intention. I know I am repeating myself, but just to be sure The Church calls it transubstantiation and it means that at the consecration of the Mass, by the power of God, a validly ordained priest brings the body and blood soul and divinity of Jesus Christ to be physically present on the altar under the appearances of bread and wine – just as Jesus did and said to do in remembrance of him.

"As you have remarked many times, Satan, it is the gift from God that provides a means of equalizing the superior difference between you and yours and his human creation. As God is all-just presenting such a gift within the structure of a New Covenant is the primary difference between the old and the new. My personal feeling is that as the absence of such would be a glaring omission, God, because of his love for man would do no less.

"The bottom line is that Jesus, without equivocation, gave us the means, if we will to accept it, to physically couple his incarnate self to us thereby giving us the means to render you powerless to adversely affect our eternal salvation. Without that alliance, as Jesus readily admitted, your superior nature makes you and yours, whenever you will to do so, capable of sifting us as wheat." (Luke 22:31)

"You are so right, Bruce. Without a frequent worthy reception of The Great Equalizer if we do choose one of you to sift very rarely is that person not mine – all mine – forever and forever all mine.

"We will now return to your cabin where I will make my closing re-marks on The Great Equalizer before I must depart as my allotted time is nearly gone."

CHAPTER FIFTY-SIX

By Doing So, They Declined
a Gift from God

"Whereupon once again he snapped his fingers and instantly, we were again in the cabin.

"Satan poured each of us some of my late father's brandy and by doing so emptied the bottle. Upon taking a sip he placed the snifter on the end table beside him and began speaking."

"Many of you," he began, "as I mentioned previously are fond of saying that my greatest feat is convincing vast numbers of you that I do not exist and they are correct. However my second-greatest feat is very much like it; for I have succeeded in convincing the bulk of you that the duly consecrated Eucharist or Holy Communion as some call it, is only a symbol, that is, the belief that the bread and wine only represent the body and blood of Jesus Christ. By so doing I have removed the requirement of right intention and with it the available grace of the sacrament – the Great Equalizer – as you so rightly stated, Bruce, the gift from a loving God to his human creation.

"Think of it this way, Bruce; a gun with no ammunition; an automobile without an engine, a ship sitting in the desert or a movie projector without film. Potentially all four have a useful purpose, but lacking a major component they cannot serve that purpose. The same is true of unconsecrated bread and wine. They provide sustenance for the body but nothing for the soul.

"And how did this happen? Like all of mankind's' errant ventures it begins by my finding one or more of you who has no problem telling God that he has a better idea. For over fifteen hundred years I could find none of you who had this inclination and the charismatic leadership coupled with the intelligence and means to carry out my plan. The Protestant reformation along with the invention of the printing press gave me the edge I required. In less than two hundred years close to half the Christian world had told God, 'You lied to us. We don't believe you.'

"By doing so they declined to accept this ultimate gift from God, that is, his very self, by either substituting plain bread and wine (Protestantism} or by refusing to believe that through the miracle of transubstantiation they are receiving the body and blood soul and divinity of Jesus Christ, the Son of God (errant Catholics), and this heretical idea is growing still.

"Like I've said before, Bruce, the bulk of you are stupid and stubborn. If not, how could so many of you refuse this supreme gift from God that if received with the right intention ensures your salvation which is the ultimate reason for your existence? How so? Remember Jesus saying, 'For this is the bread which came down from Heaven: not as your fathers did eat manna, and are dead, but he that eats this bread shall live forever.' (John 6:58)

"My final thought on this is that this was said by Jesus Christ, the Son of God who, as a former angel, I must proclaim can neither deceive nor be deceived."

"At the expense of offending you, Satan, I will say that what you just said is the most succinct explanation of the reason for Jesus giving us the gift of himself in the Eucharist that I have ever heard. Coming from The Prince of Darkness while under restraint to tell the truth this final Eucharistic statement must have caused you great stress. However, I am pleased that you said it because the fact that you are still visible in my presence bears witness to its truth."

Satan emptied the snifter and then replied, "Another back door compliment, Bruce?"

CHAPTER FIFTY-SEVEN

"It will be our last chance to hear the truth from you."

"Before visibly departing do you have a final remark you would like to make? Perhaps a final admonition to mankind that you have no problem stating because as you have said so many times, being both stupid and stubborn, most won't believe you or take heed anyway."

"Are you sure you want me to do this? It may serve to confirm Jesus' statement that few of you find the narrow gate and the path beyond that leads to eternal life." (Matthew 7:13-14)

"I am sure – even to the extent of being absolutely certain."

"And your reason?

"It will be our last chance to hear the truth from you; however, before you begin can you precisely define what Jesus meant when he used the narrow gate and its path to illustrate a person's necessary life choice to merit eternal salvation?"

"Certainly. The narrow gate and path are in plain sight. Be baptized. Believe in the Lord Jesus Christ as the Son of God and confirm your belief by obeying the Ten Commandments, as every day you do unto others as you would have them do unto you; and finally believing everything Jesus taught as expressed in the Apostles' Creed and the Gospels found in the New Testament."

"In other words by practicing Christianity as taught by the apostles and the Church Jesus established to succeed them."

"In summary, yes."

"Anything else you might want to say before you depart?"

"Yes, there is. As I implied when we first met, Bruce, it is all but impossible for one who embraces absolute truth to be condemned. A person has to adopt living his or her life on the dubious foundation of subjective truth to spend their eternity as a permanent resident in my abode.

"Why is that?"

"Because what is termed subjective truth is an oxymoron. There is no assurance of reality in an opinion; and subjective truth is opinion because it varies not only from person to person but being inherently unstable it varies depending upon the situation. The objective truth concerning subjective truth is that its purpose is upside down because it is of my doing."

"Are you saying that subjective truth is demonic?"

"Absolutely. Make no mistake about it. You see, Bruce, objective truth is pursued to discover reality. Subjective truth is pursued to replace reality with wishful thinking. Demonic temptation and objective truth are polar opposites.

"However, as we showed earlier from observing the order in the universe and the tangible world around us it is easier to believe that there must be a prime mover, that is, that God exists than that he doesn't. We also showed why he must exist from all eternity; and that as a result of his miracles that God exists as Jesus Christ the Second Person of the Blessed Trinity who became incarnate to teach his human creation how to live; as well as to willingly suffer the appalling death of Roman crucifixion as a remedial offering to God the Father, that by contrition for his or her sins and a firm purpose of amendment, all men and women can obtain the righteousness required for salvation.

"I can also tell you as a matter of objective truth that I and mine are responsible for the temptations that convince people to adhere to subjective truth; that is, that their own opinion for them is the truth. And why do they do this? They do so, Bruce, almost exclusively, in order to ignore the reality of belief in and their subsequent obligations to God. In other words atheism, agnosticism or belief in a non-caring God allows people to live their lives on the wide road by believing they are justified when they kill or neutralize their conscience."

"It sounds to me, Satan that it's the same old adage that we stated before – men and women, after perusing the Ten Commandments just think they have a better idea."

"Exactly. The condemned are such because subjectively they form an erroneous opinion that allows them to satisfy immoral or other sinful desires by violating the laws of God. Another way to book passage on the wide road is to support getting legislation passed that overrides one or more of the Ten Commandments. These are people who believe that politics trumps religion. And since by doing so they now feel justified, being sorry for their actions is all but impossible. Death in this state of belief ensures, without exception, that they are mine, Bruce – forever and forever all of them are mine!

"The factual, objective truth that I remain visibly standing before you, attests to the truth of what I just said."

"Is that all you want to say?"

"Perhaps two more things. The definition of subjective truth is that it isn't truth at all; and any belief that is not the truth is an untruth – a lie.

Those of you who have succumbed to my temptation to embrace subjective truth in order to cover the doubt your conscience reveals feel obligated to convince others that they are right. Nothing bolsters confidence in a person's belief like convincing others to also believe. And in modern time's people who fail to convince others using words to accept subjective truth feel obligated to redefine the words."

"Can you give me an example?"

"Yes. The First Amendment of your Constitution guarantees freedom of religion. This means that people can worship as their conscience dictates, acknowledge behavior that is moral or immoral in manner and petition for legislation which ensures that morality is the basis of Law.

"If you can redefine religious freedom to mean freedom of worship you strip it of any moral implications. It now becomes like a tree that bears no fruit. It has no purpose except that it might be pleasing to the eye. If successful, morally degenerate politicians can now pass laws to persecute, suppress the freedoms or confiscate the property of the citizenry as it pleases."

"You said two things."

"Yes. Another example is the term Progressive. As Far Left, Communist, Socialist, Agnostic and Atheist secular terminology took on unfavorable connotations the leftist, socialist, Secular Press changed their belief system to being called Progressive. In reality nothing has changed, Bruce. It's just that instead of standing in the open they now hide behind a bush called Progressivism.

"I have to believe that such redefining is demonically instigated."

"Of course, Bruce. Neither you nor your readers should ever forget that IT IS WHAT WE DO!" Satan replied; "and lest you or your readers are confused define "IT" to read IMMORALITY, INIQUITY, DEPRAVITY, DISHONESTY, CORRUPTION, ADULTERY, FORNICATION, THEFT AND ANYTHING ELSE THAT VIOLATES A PERSON'S CONSCIENCE OR THE MORAL LAW OF GOD."

CHAPTER FIFTY-EIGHT

Satan's Departure

"Satan, with that self-satisfied look on your face I can see you believe that with the publication of your information you have met your objective. You are convinced that you and your demons will be back to figuratively bowling on a regulation sixty-foot-long alley and God's intention to establish a reset has been delayed for generations, if not forever."

"Bruce McPherson, you have been most accommodating during the time of our visit. Unlike most of your fellow creatures you are very astute and I might add unlike many of your kind you use the intelligence and free will God gave you to live your life in such a way as to ensure you are on the narrow road which ends in eternal salvation.

"If it were possible for me to thank you for your part in my endeavor I would. I could offer you anything in this world you desire but I won't because I know that you would not be willing to pay the price."

"Satan, one astute remark deserves another. I have never heard it better expressed than when you stated your offer to God's is like betting a pair of deuces against a royal flush; however, before you depart, I would like to say two things."

"Certainly, Bruce. Please proceed."

"Whatever God's plan was for our meeting I feel I have done my best to do His Will. However, this has been a very exhausting experience and at the expense of sounding rude, Satan, I hope never to see you again either in this world or especially, in the next.

"Secondly… I'll be blunt, Satan, as you have been so many times with me. As I mentioned twice before I believe that God has used your attempt to prevent a reset as the very reset itself."

"How so?"

"Think about it. God has used your primary strategy by turning your intention upside down. You said it yourself; that is, it can be read by millions. Everyone still breathing can, if he or she wills, learn so much more about you and your devious ways. Moreover, Satan, they now have so much more information all of which you provided with your boundless knowledge of the biblical narrative told solely as fact because as you were facing dire consequences you were compelled to tell the objective truth.

"It won't benefit everyone as there are still those who will arrogantly choose to bet their pair of deuces; but, for so many more every time they hear the ringing of a church bell, every time they hear a religious Christmas carol, attend a Baptism, a Church funeral or finally when lying on their own deathbed cannot help but ask themselves

"WHAT IF…?"

Satan then rose up to his full height and throwing his fists in the air shouted, "That isn't true!" His lie then immediately caused him to vanish leaving behind the only physical evidence that he was ever here – a copy of Scientific American, an empty brandy sniffer, a coffee cup, his handwriting and a couple of pear cores.

EPILOGUE

As a biologist I had to satisfy my curiosity. Using a fresh pair of laboratory gloves I placed the two pear cores into individual paper specimen bags and took them to Jack Marshall, a friend of mine who is the supervisor of an independent DNA Lab. Two weeks later he phoned to say that what they found was something they had never seen before. If there ever was any saliva on the pear cores it was no longer there. In fact, he said, "Both were completely void of any creature cells, human or otherwise."

He used the term sanitized and asked me where I had gotten them. I replied that it was complicated and I would have to tell him in person.

Several months later I asked him to dinner at the Altius, one of Pittsburgh's Five-Star Restaurants. As the after-dinner drinks were served I presented him with a signed copy of the book. "In here is the answer to your question about the sanitized saliva," I said. "Only it wasn't sanitized. A spiritual being has no physical makeup and therefore no cellular structure."

"You mean like an angel?" he jokingly replied.

I thought for a few seconds and then answered, "Yes and no, Jack. You'll have to read the book to see the answer in context. Out of context the answer is unbelievable!"

We all do well to follow St. John Vianney's teaching that Satan is like a chained dog. He may bark loudly and froth menacingly, or attempt to beguile us with charm and manners, but in keeping with a parallel to

Mary Hewitt's poem Satan can only hurt us if we get too close. Keep your distance and as my mother said, "Never confuse manners with virtue. Remember, an evil person no matter how charming, is not your friend."

THE END

About the Author

William McCann, a native of Pittsburgh, Pennsylvania, is a retired naval officer turned author. A leader from early on, William's life is colored by his experiences in the Navy and the steel industry. He has served in active duty, flown naval missions worldwide, and retired as a General Sales Manager after 36 years. His fascination with the world he flew over led him to become a certified big-rig driver post-retirement. A published novelist, he believes in the fusion of education and entertainment in his writings. A devout Catholic, he is also active in his parish's convert instruction and prison ministry.

Milton Keynes UK
Ingram Content Group UK Ltd.
UKHW021933281024
450365UK00017B/1071

9 798822 953000